DEBBIE MA

Under the Summer Sky

Marriage Wanted and *First Comes Marriage*

mira

Recycling programs
for this product may
not exist in your area.

ISBN-13: 978-0-7783-6807-6

Under the Summer Sky

Copyright © 2024 by Harlequin Enterprises ULC

Marriage Wanted
First published in 1993. This edition published in 2024.
Copyright © 1993 by Debbie Macomber

First Comes Marriage
First published in 1991. This edition published in 2024.
Copyright © 1991 by Debbie Macomber

This is a work of fiction. Names, characters, places and incidents are either the product of the author's imagination or are used fictitiously. Any resemblance to actual persons, living or dead, businesses, companies, events or locales is entirely coincidental.

For questions and comments about the quality of this book, please contact us at CustomerService@Harlequin.com.

TM is a trademark of Harlequin Enterprises ULC.

Mira
22 Adelaide St. West, 41st Floor
Toronto, Ontario M5H 4E3, Canada

Printed in U.S.A.

Contents

Marriage Wanted

1

Savannah Charles watched the young woman wandering around her bridal shop, checking prices and looking more discouraged by the moment. Her shoulders slumped and she bit her lip when she read the tag on the wedding gown she'd selected. She had excellent taste, Savannah noticed; the ivory silk-taffeta dress was one of her own favorites. A pattern of lace and pearls swirled up the puffed sleeves and bodice.

"Can I help you?" Savannah asked, moving toward her.

Startled, the woman turned. "I… It doesn't look like it. This dress is almost twice as much as my budget for the whole wedding. Are you Savannah?"

"Yes."

She smiled shyly. "Missy Gilbert told me about you. She said you're wonderful to work with and that you might be able to give Kurt and me some guidance. I'm Susan Davenport." She held out her hand and Savannah shook it, liking the girl immediately.

"When's your wedding?"

"In six weeks. Kurt and I are paying for it ourselves. His two younger brothers are still in college and his parents haven't got much to spare." Amusement turned up the corners of her mouth as she added, "Kurt's dad claims he's becoming poor by degrees."

Savannah smiled back. "What about your family?"

"There's only my brother and me. He's fifteen years older and, well…it isn't that he doesn't like Kurt. Because once you meet Kurt, it's impossible not to love him. He's kind and generous and interesting…."

Savannah was touched by Susan's eagerness to tell her about the man she wanted to marry.

"But Nash—my brother—doesn't believe in marriage," the young woman went on to explain. "He's an attorney and he's worked on so many divorce cases over the years that he simply doesn't believe in it anymore. It doesn't help that he's divorced himself, although that was years and years ago."

"What's your budget?" Savannah asked. She'd planned weddings that went into six figures, but she was equally adept at finding reasonable alternatives. She walked back to her desk, limping on her right foot. It ached more this afternoon than usual. It always did when the humidity was this high.

Susan told her the figure she and Kurt had managed to set aside and Savannah frowned. It wasn't much, but she could work with it. She turned around and caught Susan staring at her. Savannah was accustomed to that kind of reaction to her limp, the result of a childhood accident. She generally wore pants, which disguised the scars and disfigurement, but her limp was always noticeable, and more so when she was tired. Until they knew her better, it seemed to disconcert people. Generally she ignored their hesitation and continued, hoping that her own acceptance would put them at ease.

"Even the least expensive wedding dresses would eat up the majority of the money we've worked so hard to save."

"You could always rent the dress," Savannah suggested.

"I could?" Her pretty blue eyes lit up when Savannah mentioned the rental fee.

"How many people are you inviting?"

"Sixty-seven," Susan told her, as if the number of guests had been painfully difficult to pare down. "Kurt and I can't afford more. Mostly it's his family.... I don't think Nash will even come to the wedding." Her voice fell.

Despite never having met Susan's older brother, she already disliked him. Savannah couldn't imagine a brother refusing to attend his sister's wedding, no matter what his personal views on marriage happened to be.

"Kurt's from a large family. He has aunts and uncles and, I swear, at least a thousand cousins. We'd like to invite everyone, but we can't. The invitations alone will cost a fortune."

"Have you thought about making your own invitations?"

Susan shook her head. "I'm not very artsy."

"You don't need to be." Opening a drawer, Savannah brought out a book of calligraphy. "These are fairly simple and elegant-looking and they'll add a personal touch because they're individualized." She paused. "You'll find other ideas on the internet."

"These are beautiful. You honestly think I could do this?" She looked expectantly at Savannah.

"Without a doubt," Savannah answered with a smile.

"I wish I could talk some sense into Nash," Susan muttered, then squared her shoulders as if she was ready to take him on right that minute. "He's the only family I have. We've got aunts and uncles here and there, but no one we're close to, and Nash is being so unreasonable about this. I love Kurt and nothing's going to change the way I feel. I love his family, too. It can be lonely when you don't belong to someone. That's Nash's problem. He's forgotten what it's like to belong to someone. To be in a relationship."

Loneliness. Savannah was well acquainted with the feeling. All her life she'd felt alone. The little girl who couldn't run and play with friends. The teenage girl who never got asked to the prom. The woman who arranged the happiest days of other people's lives.

Loneliness. Savannah knew more than she wanted to about long days and longer nights.

"I'm sure your brother will change his mind," Savannah said reassuringly—even though she wasn't sure at all.

Susan laughed. "That only goes to prove you don't know my brother. Once he's set on something, it takes an Act of Congress to persuade him otherwise."

Savannah spent the next hour with Susan, deciding on the details of both the wedding and the reception. With such a limited budget it was a challenge, but they did it.

"I can't believe we can do so much with so little," Susan said once they'd finished. Her face glowed with happiness. "A nice wedding doesn't mean as much to Kurt as it does to me, but he's willing to do whatever he can to make our day special."

Through the course of their conversation, Savannah learned that Kurt had graduated from the University of Washington with an engineering degree. He'd recently been hired by a California firm and had moved to the San Francisco area, where Susan would be joining him.

After defying her brother, Susan had moved in with Kurt's family, working part-time and saving every penny she could to help with the wedding expenses.

"I can hardly wait to talk to Kurt," Susan said excitedly as she gathered her purse and the notes she'd made. "I'll get back to you as soon as he's had a chance to go over the contract." Susan paused. "Missy was right. You are wonderful." She threw both arms around Savannah in an impulsive hug. "I'll be back as soon as I can and you can take the measurements for the dress." She cast a dreamy look toward the silk-and-taffeta gown and sighed audibly. "Kurt's going to die when he sees me in that dress."

"You'll make a lovely bride."

"Thank you for everything," Susan said as she left the store.

"You're welcome." It was helping young women like Susan that Savannah enjoyed the most. The eager, happy ones who were so much in love they were willing to listen to their hearts no matter what the cost. Over the years, Savannah had worked with every kind of bride and she knew the signs. The Susans of this world were invariably a delight.

It was highly unlikely that Savannah would ever be married herself. Men were an enigma to her. Try as she might, she'd never been able to understand them. They invariably treated her differently than they did other women. Savannah assumed their attitude had to do with her damaged leg. Men either saw her as fragile, untouchable, because of it, or they viewed her as a buddy, a confidante. She supposed she should be flattered by the easy camaraderie they shared with her. They sought her advice, listened politely when she spoke, then did as they pleased.

Only a few men had seen her as a woman, a woman with dreams and desires of her own. But when it came to love, each of them had grown hesitant and afraid. Each relationship had ended awkwardly long before it had gotten close to serious.

Maybe that wasn't a fair assessment, Savannah mused sadly. Maybe it was her own attitude. She'd been terrified of ever falling in love. No matter how deeply she felt about a man, she was positive that her imperfection would come between them. It was safer to hold back, to cling to her pride than risk rejection and pain later on.

A week later, Susan came breezing through the door to Savannah's shop.

"Hello," she said, smiling broadly. "I talked to Kurt and he's as excited as I am." She withdrew a debit card from her purse. "I'd like to give you the down payment now. And I have the signed contract for you."

Savannah brought out her paperwork and Susan paid her. "My brother doesn't believe we'll be able to do it without his help, but he's wrong. We're going to have a beautiful wedding, with or without Nash, thanks to you."

This was what made Savannah's job so fulfilling. "I'll order what we need right away," she told Susan. Savannah only wished there was some way she could influence the young woman's unreasonable older brother. She knew his type—cynical, distrusting, pessimistic. A man who scoffed at love, who had no respect for marriage. How very sad. Despite her irritation with the faceless Nash, Savannah couldn't help feeling sorry for him. Whether or not he realized it, he was going to lose his sister.

There were just the two of them, so she didn't understand why Nash wouldn't support his sister in her decision. Luckily Susan had Kurt's parents. Undoubtedly this was something her brother hadn't counted on, either.

Susan left soon afterward. What remained of Savannah's day was busy. The summer months used to be her overburdened time, but that hadn't held true of late. Her services were booked equally throughout the year.

Around five-thirty, when Savannah was getting ready to close for the day, the bell chimed over her door, indicating someone had entered the shop. She looked up from her computer and found a tall, well-dressed man standing by the doorway. It had started to rain lightly; he shook off the raindrops in his hair before he stepped farther inside. She saw him glance around and scowl, as if being in such a place was repugnant to him. Even before he spoke she knew he was Susan's brother. The family resemblance was striking.

"Hello," she said.

"Hello." He slid his hands in his pockets with a contemptuous frown. Apparently he feared that even being in this place where love and romance were honored would infect him with some dread disease. It must take a good deal of energy to maintain his cynicism, Savannah thought.

"Can I help you?" she asked.

"No, thanks. I was just looking." He walked slowly through the shop. His expensive leather shoes made a tapping sound against the polished hardwood floor. She noticed that he took pains not to touch anything.

Savannah nearly laughed out loud when he passed a display of satin pillows, edged in French lace, that were meant to be carried by the ring bearer. He stepped around it, giving it a wide berth, then picked up one of her business cards from a brass holder on a small antique table.

"Are you Savannah Charles?" he asked.

"Yes," she replied evenly. "I am."

"Interesting shop you have here," he said dryly. Savannah had to admit she found him handsome in a rugged sort of way. His facial features were strong and well-defined. His mouth firm, his jaw square and stubbornly set. He walked in short, clipped steps, his impatience nearly palpable. Naturally, she might be altogether wrong and this could be someone other than Susan's brother. Savannah decided it was time to find out.

"Are you about to be married?"

"No," he said disgustedly.

"This seems like an unusual shop for you to browse through, then."

He smiled in her direction, acknowledging her shrewdness. "I believe you've been talking to my sister, Susan Davenport."

So Savannah had been right. This was Susan's hard-nosed older brother. His attitude had been a dead giveaway. "Yes, Susan's been in."

"I take it she's decided to go through with this wedding nonsense, then?" He eyed her suspiciously as if to suggest his sister might have changed her mind except for Savannah's encouragement and support.

"It would be best if you discussed Susan's plans with her."

Nash clasped his hands behind his back. "I would if we were on speaking terms."

How he knew his sister was working with her, Savannah hadn't a clue. She didn't even want to know.

"So," he said conversationally, "exactly what do you do here?"

"I'm a wedding coordinator."

"Wedding coordinator," he repeated, sounding genuinely curious. He nodded for her to continue.

"Basically I organize the wedding for the bride and her family so they're free to enjoy this all-important day."

"I see," he said. "You're the one who makes sure the flowers arrive at the church on time?"

"Something like that." His version oversimplified her role, but she didn't think he'd appreciate a detailed job description. After all, he wasn't interested in her, but in what he could learn about his sister and Kurt's plans.

He wandered about the shop some more, careful not to come into contact with any of the displays she'd so carefully arranged. He strolled past a lace-covered table with an elegant heart-shaped guest book and plumed pen as if he were walking past a nest of vipers. Savannah couldn't help being amused.

"Susan hasn't got the money for a wedding," he announced. "At least, not one fancy enough to hire a coordinator."

"Again, this is something you need to discuss with your sister."

He didn't like her answer; that much was obvious from the way his mouth thinned and the irritation she saw in his eyes. They were the same intense blue as his sister's, but that was where the resemblance ended. Susan's eyes revealed her love and enthusiasm for life. Nash's revealed his disenchantment and skepticism. She finished up the last of her paperwork, ignoring him as much as she could.

"You're a babe in the woods, aren't you?"

"I beg your pardon?" Savannah said, looking up.

"You actually believe all this…absurdity?"

"I certainly don't think of love and commitment as absurd, if that's what you mean, Mr. Davenport."

"Call me Nash."

"All right," she agreed reluctantly. In a few minutes she was going to show him the door. He hadn't bothered to disguise the purpose of his visit. He was trying to pump her for information and hadn't figured out yet that she refused to be placed in the middle between him and his sister.

"Did you ever stop to realize that over fifty percent of the couples who marry in this day and age end up divorcing?"

"I know the statistics."

He walked purposely toward her as if approaching a judge's bench, intent on proving his point. "Love is a lame excuse for marriage."

Since he was going to make it impossible for her to concentrate, she sat back on her stool and folded her arms. "What do you suggest couples do then, Mr. Davenport? Just live together?"

"Nash," he reminded her irritably. "And, yes, living together makes a lot more sense. If a man and woman are so hot for each other, I don't see any reason to muddy the relationship with legalities when a weekend in bed would simplify everything."

Savannah resisted the urge to roll her eyes. Rejecting marriage made as much sense to her as pushing a car over a cliff because the fender was dented. Instead she asked, "Is this what you want Susan and Kurt to do? Live together indefinitely? Without commitment?"

That gave him pause. Apparently it was perfectly fine for other couples to do that, but when it came to his little sister, he hesitated. "Yes," he finally said. "Until this infatuation passes."

"What about children?"

"Susan's little more than a child herself," he argued, although she was twenty-four—and in Savannah's estimation a mature twenty-four. "If she's smart, she'll avoid adding to her mistakes," he said stiffly.

"What about someone other than your sister?" she demanded, annoyed with herself for allowing him to draw her into this pointless discussion. "Are you suggesting our society should do away with family?"

"A wedding ring doesn't make a family," he returned just as heatedly.

Savannah sighed deeply. "I think it's best for us to agree to disagree," she said, feeling a bit sad. It was unrealistic to think she'd say anything that would change his mind. Susan was determined to marry Kurt, with or without his approval, but she loved her brother, too. That was what made this situation so difficult.

"Love is a lame excuse to mess up one's life," he said, clenching his fists at his sides with impotent anger. "A lame excuse."

At his third use of the word *lame*, Savannah inwardly flinched. Because she was sitting behind her desk, he didn't realize she was "lame."

"Marriage is an expensive trap that destroys a man's soul," Nash went on to say, ignoring her. "I see the results of it each and every day. Just this afternoon, I was in court for a settlement hearing that was so nasty the judge had to pull both attorneys into chambers. Do you really believe I want my little sister involved in something like that?"

"Your sister is a grown woman, Mr. Davenport. She's old enough to make her own decisions."

"Mistakes, you mean."

Savannah sensed his frustration, but arguing with him would do no good at all. "Susan's in love. You should know by now that she's determined to marry Kurt."

"In love. Excuses don't get much worse than that."

Savannah had had enough. She stood and realized for the first time how tall Nash actually was. He loomed head and shoulders over her five-foot-three-inch frame. Standing next to him she felt small and insignificant. For all their differences, Savannah could appreciate his concerns. Nash loved his sister; otherwise he wouldn't have gone to such effort to find out her plans.

"It's been interesting," Nash said, waiting for her to walk around her desk and join him. Savannah did, limping as she went. She was halfway across the room before she saw that he wasn't following her. Half turning around, she noticed that he was looking at her leg, his features marked by regret.

"I didn't mean to be rude," he said, and she couldn't doubt his sincerity. What surprised her was his sensitivity. She might have judged this man too harshly. His attitude had irritated her, but she'd also been entertained by him—and by the vigor of their argument.

"You didn't know." She finished her trek to the door, again surprised to realize he hadn't followed her. "It's well past my closing time," she said meaningfully.

"Of course." His steps were crisp and uniform as he marched across her shop, stopping abruptly when he reached her. A frown wrinkled his brow as he stared at her again.

"What's wrong?"

He laughed shortly. "I'm trying to figure something out."

"If it has to do with Susan and Kurt—"

"It doesn't," he cut in. "It has to do with you." An odd smile lifted his mouth. "I like you. You're impertinent, sassy and stubborn."

"Oh, really!" She might have been offended if she hadn't been struggling so hard not to laugh.

"Really."

"You're tactless, irritating and overpowering," she responded.

His grin was transformed into a full-blown smile. "You're right. It's a shame, though."

"A shame? What are you talking about?"

"You being a wedding coordinator. It's a waste. With your obvious organizational skills, you might've done something useful. Instead, your head's stuck in the clouds and you've let love and romance fog up your brain. But you know what?" He rubbed the side of his jaw. "There just might be hope for you."

"Hope. Funny, I was thinking the same thing about you. There just might be a slim chance of reasoning with you. You're clearly intelligent and even a little witty. But unfortunately you're misguided. Now that you're dealing with your sister's marriage, however, there's a remote possibility someone might be able to get through to you."

"What do you mean?" he asked, folding his arms over his chest and resting his weight on one foot.

"Your judgment's been confused by your clients. By their anger and bitterness and separations. We're at opposite ends of the same subject. I work with couples when they're deeply in love and convinced the relationship will last forever. You see them when they're embittered and disillusioned. But what you don't seem to realize is that you need to see the glass as half-full and not half-empty."

He frowned. "I thought we were talking about marriage."

"We are. What you said earlier is true. Fifty percent of all married couples end up divorcing—which means fifty percent of them go on to lead fulfilling, happy lives."

Nash's snort was derisive. He dropped his arms and straightened, shaking his head. "I was wrong. There's no hope for you. The fifty percent who stay together are just as miserable. Given the opportunity, they'd gladly get out of the relationship."

Nash was beginning to irritate her again. "Why is it so difficult for you to believe that there's such a thing as a happy marriage?"

"Because I've never seen one."

"You haven't looked hard enough."

"Have you ever stopped to think that your head's so muddled with hearts and flowers and happy-ever-afters that you can't and won't accept what's right in front of your eyes?"

"Like I said, it's past my closing time." Savannah jerked open the shop door. The clanging bell marked the end of their frustrating conversation. Rarely had Savannah allowed anyone to get under her skin the way she had Nash Davenport. The man was impossible. Totally unreasonable...

The woman was impossible. Totally unreasonable.

Nash couldn't understand why he continued to mull over their conversation. Twenty-four hours had passed, and he'd thought about their verbal sparring match a dozen times.

Relaxing in his leather office chair, he rolled a pen between his palms. Obviously Savannah didn't know him well; otherwise, she wouldn't have attempted to convince him of the error of his views.

His eyes fell on the phone and he sighed inwardly. Susan was being stubborn and irrational. It was plain that he was going to have to be the one to mend fences. He'd hoped she'd come to her senses, but it wasn't going to happen. He was her older brother, her closest relative, and if she refused to make the first move, he'd have to do it.

He looked up Kurt Caldwell's parents' phone number. He resented having to contact her there. Luck was with him, however, when Susan herself answered.

"It's Nash," he said. When she was little, her voice rose with excitement whenever he called. Anytime he arrived home, she'd fly into his arms, so glad to see him she couldn't hold still. He sighed again, missing the child she once was.

"Hello, Nash," Susan said stiffly. No pleasure at hearing from him was evident now.

"How are you doing?" That was the purpose of this call, after all.

"Fine. How about you?" Her words were stilted, and her stubbornness hadn't budged an inch. He would have said as much, then thought better of it.

"I'm fine, too," he answered.

The silence stretched between them.

"I understand you have a wedding coordinator now," he said, hoping to come across as vaguely interested. She might have defied him, but he would always be her big brother.

"How do you know that?"

"Word, uh, gets around." In fact, he'd learned about it from a family friend. Still, he shouldn't have said anything. And he wouldn't have if Savannah hadn't dominated his thoughts from the moment he'd met her.

"You've had someone checking into my affairs, haven't you?" Susan lowered her voice to subzero temperatures. "You can't rule my life, Nash. I'm going to marry Kurt and that's all there is to it."

"I gathered as much from Savannah Charles…."

"You've talked to Savannah?"

Nash recognized his second mistake immediately. He'd blown it now, and Susan wasn't going to forgive him.

"Stop meddling in my life, Nash." His sister's voice quavered suspiciously and seconds later the line was disconnected. The phone droned in his ear before he dejectedly replaced the receiver.

Needless to say, that conversation hadn't gone well. He'd like to blame Savannah, but it was his fault. He'd been the one to let her name slip, a stupid error on his part.

The wedding coordinator and his sister were both too stubborn and naive for their own good. If this was how Susan wanted it, then he had no choice but to abide by her wishes. Calling her had been another mistake in a long list he'd been making lately.

His assistant poked her head in his door, and he gave her his immediate attention. He had more important things to worry about than his sister and a feisty wedding coordinator who lived in a dreamworld.

★ ★ ★

"What did my brother say?" Susan demanded.

"He wanted to know about you," Savannah said absently as she arranged champagne flutes on the display table next to the five-tier wedding cake. She'd been working on the display between customers for the past hour.

"In other words, Nash was pumping you for information?"

"Yes, but you don't need to worry, I didn't tell him anything. What I did do was suggest he talk to you." She straightened, surprised that he'd followed her advice. "He cares deeply for you, Susan."

"I know." Susan gnawed on her lower lip. "I wish I hadn't hung up on him."

"Susan!"

"I... He told me he'd talked to you and it made me so mad I couldn't bear to speak to him another second."

Savannah was surprised by Nash's slip. She would've thought their conversation was the last thing he'd mention. But from the sound of it, he didn't get an opportunity to rehash it with Susan.

"If he makes a pest of himself," Susan said righteously, "let me know and I'll... I'll do something."

"Don't worry about it. I rather enjoyed talking to him." It was true, although Savannah hated to admit it. She'd worked hard to push thoughts of Nash from her mind over the past couple of days. His attitude had annoyed her, true, but she'd found him intriguing and—it bothered her to confess this— a challenge. A smile came when she realized he probably saw her the same way.

"I have to get back to work," Susan said reluctantly. "I just wanted to apologize for my brother's behavior."

"He wasn't a problem."

On her way out the door, Susan muttered something Savannah couldn't hear. The situation was sad. Brother and sister loved each other but were at an impasse.

Savannah continued to consider the situation until the bell over the door chimed about five minutes later. Smiling, she looked up, deciding she wasn't going to get this display finished until after closing time. She should've known better than to try.

"Nash." His name was a mere whisper.

"Hello again," he said dryly. "I've come to prove my point."

2

"You want to prove your point," Savannah repeated thoughtfully. Nash Davenport was the most headstrong man she'd ever encountered. He was also one of the handsomest. That did more to confuse her than to help. For reasons as yet unclear, she'd lost her objectivity. No doubt it had something to do with that pride of his and the way they'd argued. No doubt it was also because they remained diametrically opposed on the most fundamental issues of life—love and marriage.

"I've given some thought to our conversation the other day," Nash said, pacing back and forth, "and it seems to me that I'm just the person to clear up your thinking. Besides," he went on, "if I can clear up your thinking, maybe you'll have some influence on Susan."

Although it was difficult, Savannah resisted the urge to laugh.

"To demonstrate my good faith, I brought a peace offering." He held up a white sack for her inspection. "Two lattes," he explained. He set the bag on the corner of her desk and opened it, handing her one of the paper cups. The smell of hot coffee blended with steamed milk was as welcome as popcorn in a theater. "Make yourself comfortable," he said next, gesturing toward the stool, "because it might take a while."

"I don't know if this is a good idea," Savannah felt obliged to say as she carefully edged onto the stool.

"It's a great idea. Just hear me out," he said smoothly.

"Oh, all right," she returned with an ungracious nod. Savannah might have had the energy to resist him if it hadn't been so late in the day. She was tired and the meeting with Susan had frustrated her. She'd come to her upset and unhappy, and Savannah had felt helpless, not knowing how to reassure the younger woman.

Nash pried off the lid of his latte, then glanced at his watch. He walked over to her door and turned over the sign so it read Closed.

"Hey, wait a minute!"

"It's—" he looked at his watch again "—5:29 p.m. You're officially closed in one minute."

Savannah didn't bother to disagree. "I think it's only fair for you to know that whatever you have to say isn't going to change my mind," she said.

"I figured as much."

The man continued to surprise her. "How do you intend to prove your point? Parade divorced couples through my wedding shop?"

"Nothing that drastic."

"Did it occur to you that I could do the same thing and have you meet with a group of blissful newlyweds?" she asked.

He grinned. "I'm way ahead of you. I already guessed you'd enjoy introducing me to any number of loving couples who can't keep their hands off each other."

Savannah shrugged, not denying it.

"The way I figure it," he said, "we both have a strong argument to make."

"Exactly." She nodded. "But you aren't going to change my

mind and I doubt I'll change yours." She didn't know what kept some couples together against all odds or why others decided to divorce when the first little problem arose. If Nash expected her to supply the answers, she had none to offer.

"Don't be so sure we won't change each other's mind." Which only went to prove that he thought there was a chance he could influence her. "We could accomplish a great deal if we agree to be open-minded."

Savannah cocked one eyebrow and regarded him skeptically. "Can you guarantee you'll be open-minded?"

"I'm not sure," he answered, and she was impressed with his honesty. "But I'm willing to try. That's all I ask of you."

"That sounds fair."

He rubbed his palms together as though eager to get started. "If you don't object, I'd like to go first."

"Just a minute," she said, holding up her hand. "Before we do, shouldn't we set some rules?"

"Like what?"

Although it was her suggestion, Savannah didn't really have an answer. "I don't know. Just boundaries of some kind."

"I trust you not to do anything weird, and you can count on the same from me," he said. "After all—"

"Don't be so hasty," she interrupted. "If we're going to put time and effort into this, it makes sense that we have rules. And something riding on the outcome."

His blue eyes brightened. "Now there's an interesting thought." He paused and a smile bracketed his mouth. "So you want to set a wager?"

Nash seemed to be on a one-man campaign to convince her the world would be a better place without the institution of marriage. "We might as well make it interesting, don't you think?"

"I couldn't agree more. If you can prove your point and get me to agree that you have, what would you want in exchange?"

This part was easy. "For you to attend Susan and Kurt's wedding. It would mean the world to Susan."

The easy smile disappeared behind a dark frown.

"She was in this afternoon," Savannah continued, rushing the words in her eagerness to explain. "She's anxious and confused, loving you and loving Kurt and needing your approval so badly."

Nash's mouth narrowed into a thin line of irritation.

"Would it really be so much to ask?" she ventured. "I realize I'd need to rely on your complete and total honesty, but I have faith in you." She took a sip of her latte.

"So, if you convince me my thinking is wrong on this marriage issue, you want me to attend Susan's wedding." He hesitated, then nodded slowly. "Deal," he said, and his grin reappeared.

Until that moment, Savannah was convinced Nash had no idea what he intended to use for his argument. But apparently he did. "What would you want from me?" she asked. Her question broke into his musings because he jerked his head toward her as if he'd forgotten there might be something in this for him, as well. He took a deep breath and then released it. "I don't know. Do I have to decide right now?"

"No."

"It'll be something substantial—you understand that, don't you?"

Savannah managed to hold back a smile. "I wouldn't expect anything less."

"How about home-cooked dinners for a week served on your fanciest china? That wouldn't be out of line," he murmured.

She gaped at him. Her request had been generous and completely selfless. She'd offered him an excuse to attend Susan's wedding and salvage his pride, and in return he wanted her to slave in the kitchen for days on end.

"That is out of line," she told him, unwilling to agree to

anything so ridiculous. If he wanted homemade meals, he could do what the rest of the world did and cook them himself, visit relatives or get married.

Nash's expression was boyish with delight. "So you're afraid you're going to lose."

Raising her eyebrows, she said, "You haven't got a prayer, Davenport."

"Then what's the problem?" he asked, making an exaggerated gesture with both hands. "Do you agree to my terms or not?"

This discussion had wandered far from what she'd originally intended. Savannah had been hoping to smooth things over between brother and sister and at the same time prove her own point. She wasn't interested in putting her own neck on the chopping block. Any attempt to convince Nash of the error of his ways was pointless.

He finished off his latte and flung the empty container into her garbage receptacle. "Be ready tomorrow afternoon," he said, walking to the door.

Savannah scrambled awkwardly from the stool. "What for?" she called after him. She limped two steps toward him and stopped abruptly at the flash of pain that shot up her leg. She'd sat too long in the same position, something she was generally able to avoid. She wanted to rub her thigh, work the throbbing muscle, but that would reveal her pain, which she wanted to hide from Nash.

"You'll know more tomorrow afternoon," he promised, looking pleased with himself.

"How long will this take?"

"There are time restrictions? Are there any other rules we need to discuss?"

"I… We should both be reasonable about this, don't you think?"

"I was planning to be sensible, but I can't speak for you."

This conversation was deteriorating rapidly. "I'll be ready at closing time tomorrow afternoon, then," she said, holding her hand against her thigh. If he didn't leave soon, she was going to have to sit down. Disguising her pain had become a way of life, but the longer she stood, the more difficult it became.

"Something's wrong," he announced, his gaze hard and steady. "You'd argue with me if there wasn't."

Again she was impressed by his sensitivity. "Nonsense. I said I'd be ready. What more do you want?"

He left her then, in the nick of time. A low moan escaped as she sank onto her chair. Perspiration moistened her brow and she drew in several deep breaths. Rubbing her hand over the tense muscles slowly eased out the pain.

The phone was situated to the left of her desk and after giving the last of her discomfort a couple of minutes to ebb away, she reached for the receiver and dialed her parents' number. Apparently Nash had decided how to present his case. She had, too. No greater argument could be made than her parents' loving relationship. Their marriage was as solid as Fort Knox and they'd been devoted to each other for over thirty years. Nash couldn't meet her family and continue to discredit love and marriage.

Her father answered on the second ring, sounding delighted to hear from her. A rush of warm feeling washed over Savannah. Her family had been a constant source of love and encouragement to her through the years.

"Hi, Dad."

"It's always good to hear from you, sweetheart."

Savannah relaxed in her chair. "Is Mom around?"

"No, she's got a doctor's appointment to have her blood pressure checked again. Is there anything I can do for you?"

Savannah's hand tightened around the receiver. She didn't want to mislead her parents into thinking she was involved with Nash. But she needed to prove her point. "Is there any chance I could bring someone over for dinner tomorrow night?"

"Of course."

Savannah laughed lightly. "You might want to check Mom's calendar. It'd be just like you to agree to something when she's already made plans."

"I looked. The calendar's right here in the kitchen and tomorrow night's free. Now, if you were to ask about Friday, that's a different story."

Once more Savannah found herself smiling.

"Who do you want us to meet?"

"His name's Nash Davenport."

Her announcement was met with a short but noticeable silence. "You're bringing a young man home to meet your family? This is an occasion, then."

"Dad, it isn't like that." This was exactly what she'd feared would happen, that her family would misinterpret her bringing Nash home. "We've only just met...."

"It was like that with your mother and me," her father said excitedly. "We met on a Friday night and a week later I knew this was the woman I was going to love all my life, and I have."

"Dad, Nash is just a friend—not even a friend, really, just an acquaintance," Savannah said, trying to correct his mistaken impression. "I'm coordinating his sister's wedding."

"No need to explain, sweetheart. If you want to bring a young man for your mother and me to meet, we'd be thrilled, no matter what the reason."

Savannah was about to respond, but then decided that a lengthy explanation might hurt her cause rather than help it. "I'm not sure of the exact time we'll arrive."

"No problem. I'll light up the barbecue and that way you won't need to worry. Come whenever you can. We'll make an evening of it."

Oh, yes, it was going to be quite an evening, Savannah mused darkly. Two stubborn people, both convinced they were right, would each try to convert the other.

★ ★ ★

This was going to be so easy that Nash almost felt guilty. Almost... Poor Savannah. Once he'd finished with what he had to show her, she'd have no option but to accept the reality of his argument.

Nash loved this kind of debate, when he was certain beyond a shadow of a doubt that he was right. By the time he was done, Savannah would be eating her words.

Grabbing his briefcase, he hurried out of his office, anxious to forge ahead and prove his point.

"Nash, what's your hurry?"

Groaning inwardly, Nash turned to face a fellow attorney, Paul Jefferson. "I've got an appointment this evening," Nash explained. He didn't like Paul, had never liked Paul. What bothered him most was that this brownnoser was going to be chosen over him for the partnership position that was opening up within the year. Both Paul and Nash had come into the firm at the same time, and they were both good attorneys. But Paul had a way of ingratiating himself with the powers that be and parting the waters of opportunity.

"An appointment or a date?" Paul asked with that smug look of his. One of these days Nash was going to find an excuse to wipe that grin off his face.

He looked pointedly at his watch. "If you'll excuse me, Paul, I have to leave, otherwise I'll be late."

"Can't keep her waiting, now can we?" Paul said, and finding himself amusing, he laughed at his own sorry joke.

Knotting his fist at his side, Nash was happy to escape. Anger clawed at him until he was forced to stop and analyze his outrage. He'd been working with Paul for nearly ten years. He'd tolerated his humorless jokes, his conceited, self-righteous attitude and his air of superiority without displaying his annoyance. What was different now?

He considered the idea of Paul being preferred to him for the partnership. But this was nothing new. The minute he'd learned about the opening, he'd suspected Stackhouse and Serle would choose Paul. He'd accepted it as fact weeks ago.

Paul had suggested Nash was hurrying to meet a woman— which he was. Nash didn't bother to deny it. What upset him was the sarcastic way Paul had said it, as though Savannah—

His mind came to a grinding halt. Savannah.

So she was at the bottom of all this. Nash had taken offense at the edge in Paul's voice, as if his fellow attorney had implied that Savannah was, somehow, less than she should be. He knew he was being oversensitive. After all, Paul had never even met her. But still...

Nash recalled his own reaction to Savannah, his observations when he'd met her. She was small. Her dark, pixie-style hair and deep brown eyes gave her a fragile appearance, but that was deceptive. The woman obviously had a constitution of iron.

Her eyes... Once more his thoughts skidded to a halt. He'd never known a woman with eyes that were more revealing. In them he read a multitude of emotions. Pain, both physical and emotional. In them he saw a woman with courage. Nash barely knew Savannah and yet he sensed she was one of the most astonishing people he'd probably ever meet. He'd wanted to defend her, wanted to slam his colleague up against a wall and demand an apology for the slight, vague though it was. In fact, he admitted, if Paul was insulting anyone, it was more likely him than Savannah....

When he reached his car, Nash sat in the driver's seat with his key poised in front of the ignition for a moment, brooding about his colleague and the competitiveness between them.

His mood lightened considerably as he made his way through the heavy traffic to the wedding shop. He'd been looking forward to this all day.

He found a parking spot and climbed out of his car, then fed the meter. As he turned away he caught sight of Savannah in the shop window, talking to a customer. Her face was aglow with enthusiasm and even from this distance her eyes sparkled. For a reason unknown to him, his pulse accelerated as joy surged through him.

He was happy to be seeing Savannah. Any man would, knowing he was about to be proven right. But this was more than that. This happiness was rooted in the knowledge that he'd be spending time with her.

Savannah must have felt his scrutiny, because she glanced upward and their eyes met briefly before she reluctantly pulled hers away. Although she continued speaking to her customer, Nash sensed that she'd experienced the same intensity of feeling he had. It was at moments such as this that he wished he could be privy to a woman's thoughts. He would gladly have forfeited their bet to know if she was as surprised and puzzled as he felt. Nash couldn't identify the feeling precisely; all he knew was that it made him uncomfortable.

The customer was leaving just as Nash entered the shop. Savannah was sitting at her desk and intuitively he realized she needed to sit periodically because of her leg. She looked fragile and confused. When she raised her eyes to meet his, he was shocked by the strength of her smile.

"You're right on time," she said.

"You would be, too, if you were about to have home-cooked meals personally served to you for the next week."

"Don't count on it, Counselor."

"Oh, I'm counting on it," he said with a laugh. "I've already got the menu picked out. We'll start the first night with broiled New York sirloin, Caesar salad and a three-layer chocolate cake."

"You certainly love to dream," she said with an effortless laugh. "I find it amusing that you never stopped to ask if I could cook. It'll probably come as a surprise to learn that not all women are proficient in the kitchen. If by some odd quirk of fate you do happen to win this wager, you'll dine on boxed macaroni and cheese or microwave meals for seven days and like it."

Nash was stunned. She was right; he'd assumed she could cook as well as she seemed to manage everything else. Her shop was a testament to her talent, appealing to the eye in every respect. True, all those wedding gowns and satin pillows were aiding and abetting romance, but it had a homey, comfortable feel, as well. This wasn't an easy thing to admit. A wedding shop was the last place on earth Nash ever thought he'd willingly visit.

"Are you ready to admit defeat?" he asked.

"Never, but before we get started I need to make a couple of phone calls. Do you mind?"

"Not in the least." He was a patient man, and never more so than now. The longer they delayed, the better. It wasn't likely that Paul would stay late, but Nash wanted to avoid introducing Savannah to him. More important, he wanted her to himself. The thought was unwelcome. This wasn't a date and he had no romantic interest in Savannah Charles, he reminded himself.

Savannah reached for the phone and he wandered around the shop noticing small displays he'd missed on his prior visits. The first time he'd felt nervous; he didn't know what to expect from a wedding coordinator, but certainly not the practical, gutsy woman he'd found.

He trained his ears not to listen in on her conversation, but the crisp, businesslike tone of her voice was surprisingly captivating.

It was happening again—that disturbing feeling was back, deep in the pit of his stomach. He'd felt it before, several years earlier, and it had nearly ruined his life. He was in trouble. Panic shot through his blood and he felt the overwhelming urge to turn and run in the opposite direction. The last time he'd had this feeling, he'd gotten married.

"I'm ready," Savannah said, and stood.

Nash stared at her for a long moment as his brain processed what was going on.

"Nash?"

He gave himself a hard mental shake. He didn't know if he was right about what had happened here, but he didn't like it. "Do you mind riding with me?" he asked, once he'd composed himself.

"That'll be fine."

The drive back to his office building in downtown Seattle was spent in relative silence. Savannah seemed to sense his reflective mood. Another woman might have attempted to fill the space with idle chatter. Nash was grateful she didn't.

After he'd parked, he led Savannah into his building and up the elevator to the law firm's offices. She seemed impressed with the plush furnishings and the lavish view of Mount Rainier and Puget Sound from his twentieth-story window.

When she'd entered his office she'd walked directly to the window and set her purse on his polished oak credenza. "How do you manage to work with a view like this?" she asked, her voice soft with awe. She seemed mesmerized by the beauty that appeared before her.

After several years Nash had become immune to its splendor, but lately he'd begun to appreciate the solace he found there. The color of the sky reflected like a mirror on the water's surface. On a gray and hazy morning, the water was a dull shade of steel. When the sun shone, Puget Sound was a deep, iridescent greenish blue. He enjoyed watching the ferries and other commercial and pleasure craft as they intersected the waterways. In the last while, he'd often stood in the same spot as Savannah and sorted through his thoughts.

"It's all so beautiful," she said, turning back to him. Hearing her give voice to his own feelings felt oddly comforting. The sooner he presented his argument, the better. The sooner he said what had to be said and put this woman out of his mind, the better.

"You ready?" he asked, flinging opening a file cabinet and withdrawing a handful of thick folders from the top drawer.

"Ready as I'll ever be," she said, taking a chair on the other side of his desk.

Nash slapped the files down on his credenza. "Let's start with Adams versus Adams," he muttered, flipping through the pages of the top folder. "Now, this was an interesting case. Married ten years, two sons. Then Martha learned that Bill was having an affair with a coworker, so she decided to have one herself, only she chose a nineteen-year-old boy. The child-custody battle lasted two months, destroyed them financially and ended so bitterly that Bill moved out of town and hasn't been heard from since. Last I heard, Martha was clinically depressed and in and out of hospitals."

Savannah gasped. "What about their sons?" she asked. "What happened to them?"

"Eventually they went to live with a relative. From what I understand, they're both in counseling and have been for the last couple of years."

"How very sad," she whispered.

"Don't kid yourself. This is only the beginning. I'm starting with the As and working my way through the file drawer. Let me know when you've had enough." He reached for a second folder. "Anderson versus Anderson... Ah, yes, I remember this one. She attempted suicide three times, blackmailed him emotionally, used the children as weapons, wiped him out financially and then sued for divorce, claiming he was an unfit father." His back was as stiff as his voice. He tossed aside that file and picked up the next.

"Allison versus Allison," he continued crisply. "By the way, I'm changing the names to protect the guilty."

"The guilty?"

"To my way of thinking, each participant in these cases is guilty of contributing to the disasters I'm telling you about. Each made a crucial mistake."

"You're about to suggest their first error was falling in love."

"No," he returned coldly, "it all started with the wedding vows. No two people should be expected to live up to that ideal. It isn't humanly possible."

"You're wrong, Nash. People live up to those vows each and every day, in small ways and in large ones."

Nash jabbed his finger against the stack of folders. "This says otherwise. Love isn't meant to last. Couples are kidding themselves if they believe commitment lasts beyond the next morning. Life's like that, and it's time the rest of the world woke up and admitted it."

"Oh, please!" Savannah cried, standing. She walked over to the window, her back to him, clenching and unclenching her fists. Nash wondered if she was aware of it, and doubted she was.

"Be honest, Savannah. Marriage doesn't work anymore. Hasn't in years. The institution is outdated. If you want to stick your head in the sand, then fine. But when others risk getting hurt, someone needs to tell the truth." His voice rose with the heat of his argument.

Slowly she turned again and stared at him. An almost pitying look came over her.

"She must have hurt you very badly." Savannah's voice was so low, he had to strain to hear.

"Hurt me? What are you talking about?"

She shook her head as though she hadn't realized she'd spoken out loud. "Your ex-wife."

The anger that burned through Nash was like acid. "Who told you about Denise?" he demanded.

"No one," she returned quickly.

He slammed the top file shut and stuffed the stack of folders back inside the drawer with little care and less concern. "How'd you know I was married?"

"I'm sorry, Nash, I shouldn't have mentioned it."

"Who told you?" The answer was obvious but he wanted her to say it.

"Susan mentioned it...."

"How much did she tell you?"

"Just that it happened years ago." Each word revealed her reluctance to drag his sister into the conversation. "She wasn't breaking any confidences, if that's what you think. I'm sure the only reason she brought it up was to explain your—"

"I know why she brought it up."

"I apologize, Nash. I shouldn't have said anything."

"Why not? My file's in another attorney's cabinet, along with those of a thousand other fools just like me who were stupid enough to think love lasts."

Savannah continued to stare at him. "You loved her, didn't you?"

"As much as any foolish twenty-four-year-old loves anyone. Would you mind if we change the subject?"

"Susan's twenty-four."

"Exactly," he said, slapping his hand against the top of his desk. "And she's about to make the same foolish choice I did."

"But, Nash..."

"Have you heard enough, or do you need to listen to a few more cases?"

"I've heard enough."

"Good. Let's get out of here." The atmosphere in the office was stifling. It was as though each and every client he'd represented over the years was there to remind him of the pain he'd lived through himself—only he'd come away smarter than most.

"Do you want me to drive you back to the office or would you prefer I take you home?" he asked.

"No," Savannah said as they walked out of the office. He purposely adjusted his steps to match her slower gait. "If you don't mind, I'd prefer to have our, uh, wager settled this evening."

"Fine with me."

"If you don't mind, I'd like to head for my parents' home. I want you to meet them."

"Sure, why not?" he asked flippantly. His anger simmered just below the surface. Maybe this wasn't such a brilliant idea after all....

Savannah gave him the address and directions. The drive on the freeway was slowed by heavy traffic, which frustrated him even more. By the time they reached the exit, his nerves were frayed. He was about to suggest they do this another evening when she instructed him to take a left at the next light. They turned the corner, drove a block and a half down and were there.

They were walking toward the house when a tall, burly man with a thinning hairline hurried out the front door. "Savannah, sweetheart," he greeted them with a huge grin. "So this is the young man you're going to marry."

3

"Dad!" Savannah was mortified. The heat rose from her neck to her cheeks, and she knew her face had to be bright red.

Marcus Charles raised his hands. "Did I say something I shouldn't have?" But there was still a smile on his face.

"I'm Nash Davenport," Nash said, offering Marcus his hand. Considering how her father had chosen to welcome Nash, his gesture was a generous one. She chanced a look in the attorney's direction and was relieved to see he was smiling, too.

"You'll have to forgive me for speaking out of turn," her father said, "but Savannah's never brought home a young man she wants us to meet, so I assumed you're the—"

"Daddy, that's not true!"

"Name one," he said. "And while you're inventing a beau, I'll take Nash in and introduce him to your mother."

"Dad!"

"Hush now or you'll give Nash the wrong impression."

The wrong impression! If only he knew. This meeting couldn't have gotten off to a worse start, especially with Nash's present mood. She'd made a drastic mistake mentioning his marriage. It was more than obvious that he'd been badly hurt and was trying to put the memory behind him.

Nash had built a strong case against marriage. The more clients he described, the harder his voice became. The grief of his own experience echoed in his voice as he listed the nightmares of the cases he'd represented.

Nash and her father were already in the house by the time Savannah walked up the steps and into the living room. Her mother had redecorated the room in a Southwestern motif, with painted clay pots and Navajo-style rugs. A recent addition was a wooden folk art coyote with his head thrown back, howling at the moon.

Every time she entered this room, Savannah felt a twinge of sadness. Her mother loved the Southwest and her parents had visited there often. Savannah knew her parents had once looked forward to moving south. She also knew she was the reason they hadn't. As an only child, and one who'd sustained a serious injury—even if it'd happened years before—they worried about her constantly. And with no other immediate family in the Seattle area, they were uncomfortable leaving their daughter alone in the big city.

A hundred times in the past few years, Savannah had tried to convince them to pursue their dreams, but they'd continually made excuses. They never came right out and said they'd stayed in Seattle because of her. They didn't need to; in her heart she knew.

"Hi, Mom," Savannah said as she walked into the kitchen. Her mother was standing at the sink, slicing tomatoes fresh from her garden. "Can I do anything to help?"

Joyce Charles set aside the knife and turned to give her a firm hug. "Savannah, let me look at you," she said, studying her. "You're working too hard, aren't you?"

"Mom, I'm fine."

"Good. Now sit down here and have something cold to drink and tell me all about Nash."

This was worse than Savannah had first believed. She should

have explained her purpose in bringing him to meet her family at the very beginning, before introducing him. Giving them a misleading impression was bad enough, but she could only imagine what Nash was thinking.

When Savannah didn't immediately answer her question, Joyce supplied what information she already knew. "You're coordinating his sister's wedding and that's how you two met."

"Yes, but—"

"He really is handsome. What does he do?"

"He's an attorney," Savannah said. "But, Mom—"

"Just look at your dad." Laughing, Joyce motioned toward the kitchen window that looked out over the freshly mowed backyard. The barbecue was heating on the brick patio and her father was showing Nash his prize fishing flies. He'd been tying his own for years and took real pride in the craft; now that he'd retired, it was his favorite hobby.

After glancing out at them, Savannah sank into a kitchen chair. Her mother had poured her a glass of lemonade. Her father displayed his fishing flies only when the guest was someone important, someone he was hoping to impress. Savannah should have realized when she first mentioned Nash that her father had made completely the wrong assumption about this meeting.

"Mom," she said, clenching the ice-cold glass. "I think you should know Nash and I are friends. Nothing more."

"We know that, dear. Do you think he'll like my pasta salad? I added jumbo shrimp this time. I hope he's not a fussy eater."

Jumbo shrimp! So they were rolling out the red carpet. With her dad it was the fishing flies, with her mother it was pasta salad. She sighed. What had she let herself in for now?

"I'm sure he'll enjoy your salad." And if his anti-marriage argument—his evidence—was stronger than hers, he'd be eating seven more meals with a member of the Charles family.

Her. She could only hope her parents conveyed the success of their relationship to this cynical lawyer.

"Your father's barbecuing steaks."

"T-bone," Savannah guessed.

"Probably. I forget what he told me when he took them out of the freezer."

Savannah managed a smile.

"I thought we'd eat outside," her mother went on. "You don't mind, do you, dear?"

"No, Mom, that'll be great." Maybe a little sunshine would lift her spirits.

"Let's go outside, then, shall we?" her mother said, carrying the large wooden bowl with the shrimp pasta salad.

The early-evening weather was perfect. Warm, with a subtle breeze and slanting sunlight. Her mother's prize roses bloomed against the fence line. The bright red ones were Savannah's favorite. The flowering rhododendron tree spread out its pink limbs in opulent welcome. Robins chatted back and forth like long-lost friends.

Nash looked up from the fishing rod he was holding and smiled. At least he was enjoying himself. Or seemed to be, anyway. Perhaps her embarrassment was what entertained him. Somehow, Savannah vowed, she'd find a way to clarify the situation to her parents without complicating things with Nash.

A cold bottle of beer in one hand, Nash joined her, grinning as though he'd just won the lottery.

"Wipe that smug look off your face," she muttered under her breath, not wanting her parents to hear. It was unlikely they would, busy as they were with the barbecue.

"You should've said something earlier." His smile was wider than ever. "I had no idea you were so taken with me."

"Nash, please. I'm embarrassed enough as it is."

"But why?"

"Don't play dumb." She was fast losing her patience with

him. The misunderstanding delighted him and mortified her. "I'm going to have to tell them," she said, more for her own benefit than his.

"Don't. Your father might decide to barbecue hamburgers instead. It isn't every day his only daughter brings home a potential husband."

"Stop it," she whispered forcefully. "We both know how you feel about marriage."

"I wouldn't object if you wanted to live with me."

Savannah glared at him so hard, her eyes ached.

"Just joking." He took a swig of beer and held the bottle in front of his lips, his look thoughtful. "Then again, maybe I wasn't."

Savannah was so furious she had to walk away. To her dismay, Nash followed her to the back of the yard. Glancing over her shoulder, she caught sight of her parents talking.

"You're making this impossible," she told him furiously.

"How's that?" His eyes fairly sparkled.

"Don't, please don't." She didn't often plead, but she did now, struggling to keep her voice from quavering.

He frowned. "What's wrong?"

She bit her lower lip so hard, she was afraid she'd drawn blood. "My parents would like to see me settled down and married. They...they believe I'm like every other woman and—"

"You aren't?"

Savannah wondered if his question was sincere. "I'm handicapped," she said bluntly. "In my experience, men want a woman who's whole and perfect. Their egos ride on that, and I'm flawed. Defective merchandise doesn't do much for the ego."

"Savannah—"

She placed her hand against his chest. "Please don't say it. Spare me the speech. I've accepted what's wrong with me. I've accepted the fact that I'll never run or jump or marry or—"

Nash stepped back from her, his gaze pinning hers. "You're right, Savannah," he broke in. "You are handicapped and you will be until you view yourself otherwise." Having said that, he turned and walked away.

Savannah went in the opposite direction, needing a few moments to compose herself before rejoining the others. She heard her mother's laughter and turned to see her father with his arms around Joyce's waist, nuzzling her neck. From a distance they looked twenty years younger. Their love was as alive now as it had been years earlier...and demonstrating that was the purpose of this visit.

She scanned the yard, looking for Nash, wanting him to witness the happy exchange between her parents, but he was busy studying the fishing flies her father had left out for his inspection.

Her father's shout alerted Savannah that dinner was ready. Reluctantly she joined Nash and her parents at the round picnic table. She wasn't given any choice but to share the crescent-shaped bench with him.

He was close enough that she could feel the heat radiating off his body. Close enough that she yearned to be closer yet. That was what surprised her, but more profoundly it terrified her. From the first moment she'd met him, Savannah suspected there was something different about him, about her reactions to him. In the beginning she'd attributed it to their disagreement, his heated argument against marriage, the challenge he represented, the promise of satisfaction if she could change his mind.

Dinner was delicious and Nash went out of his way to compliment Joyce until her mother blushed with pleasure.

"So," her father said, glancing purposefully toward Savannah and Nash, "what are your plans?"

"For what?" Nash asked.

Savannah already knew the question almost as well as she

knew the answer. Her father was asking about her future with Nash, and she had none.

"Why don't you tell Nash how you and Mom met," Savannah asked, interrupting her father before he could respond to Nash's question.

"Oh, Savannah," her mother protested, "that was years and years ago." She glanced at her husband of thirty-seven years and her clear eyes lit up with a love so strong, it couldn't be disguised. "But it was terribly romantic."

"You want to hear this?" Marcus's question was directed to Nash.

"By all means."

In that moment, Savannah could have kissed Nash, she was so grateful. "I was in the service," her father explained. "An Airborne Ranger. A few days before I met Joyce, I received my orders and learned I was about to be stationed in Germany."

"He'd come up from California and was at Fort Lewis," her mother added.

"There's not much to tell. Two weeks before I was scheduled to leave, I met Joyce at a dance."

"Daddy, you left out the best part," Savannah complained. "It wasn't like the band was playing a number you enjoyed and you needed a partner."

Her father chuckled. "You're right about that. I'd gone to the dance with a couple of buddies. The evening hadn't been going well."

"I remember you'd been stood up," Savannah inserted, eager to get to the details of their romance.

"No, dear," her mother intervened, picking up the story, "that was me. So I was in no mood to be at any social function. The only reason I decided to go was to make sure Lenny Walton knew I hadn't sat home mooning over him, but in reality I was at the dance mooning over him."

"I wasn't particularly keen on being at this dance, either,"

Marcus added. "I thought, mistakenly, that we were going to play pool at a local hall. I've never been much of a dancer, but my buddies were. They disappeared onto the dance floor almost immediately. I was bored and wandered around the hall for a while. I kept looking at my watch, eager to be on my way."

"As you can imagine, I wasn't dancing much myself," Joyce said.

"Then it happened." Savannah pressed her palms together and leaned forward. "This is my favorite part," she told Nash.

"I saw Joyce." Her father's voice dropped slightly. "When I first caught sight of her, my heart seized. I thought I might be having a reaction to the shots we'd been given earlier in the day. I swear I'd never seen a more beautiful woman. She wore this white dress and she looked like an angel. For a moment I was convinced she was." He reached for her mother's hand.

"I saw Marcus at that precise second, as well," Joyce whispered. "My friends were chatting and their voices faded until the only sound I heard was the pounding of my own heart. I don't remember walking toward him and yet I must have, because when I looked up Marcus was standing there."

"The funny part is, I don't remember moving, either."

Savannah propped her elbows on the table, her dinner forgotten. This story never failed to move her, although she'd heard it dozens of times over the years.

"We danced," her mother continued.

"All night."

"We didn't say a word. I think we must've been afraid the other would vanish if we spoke."

"While we were on the dance floor I kept pinching myself to be sure this was real, that Joyce was real. It was like we were both in a dream. These sorts of things only happen in the movies.

"When the music stopped, I looked around and realized my buddies were gone. It didn't matter. Nothing mattered but Joyce."

"Oh, Dad, I never get tired of hearing this story."

Joyce smiled as if she, too, was eager to relive the events of that night. "As we were walking out of the hall, I kept thinking I was never going to see Marcus again. I knew he was in the army—his haircut was a dead giveaway. I was well aware that my parents didn't want me dating anyone in the military, and up until then I'd abided by their wishes."

"I was afraid I wasn't going to see her again," Savannah's father went on. "But Joyce gave me her name and phone number and then ran off to catch up with her ride home."

"I didn't sleep at all that night. I was convinced I'd imagined everything."

"I couldn't sleep, either," Marcus confessed. "Here I was with my shipping orders in my pocket—this was not the time to get involved with a woman."

"I'm glad you changed your mind," Nash said, studying Savannah.

"To tell you the truth, I don't think I had much of a choice. It was as if our relationship was preordained. By the end of the following week, I knew Joyce was the woman I'd marry. I knew I'd love her all my life, and both have held true."

"Did you leave for Germany?"

"Of course. I had no alternative. We wrote back and forth for two years and then were married three months after I was discharged. There was never another woman for me after I met Joyce."

"There was never another man for me," her mother said quietly.

Savannah tossed Nash a triumphant look and was disappointed to see that he wasn't looking her way.

"It's a romantic story." He was gracious enough to admit that much.

"Apparently some of that romance rubbed off on Savannah."

Her father's eyes were proud as he glanced at her. "This wedding business of hers is thriving."

"So it seems." Some of the enthusiasm left Nash's voice. He was apparently thinking of his sister, and Savannah's role in her wedding plans.

"Eat, before your dinner gets cold," Joyce said, waving her fork in their direction.

"How long did you say you've been married?" Nash asked, cutting off a piece of his steak.

"Thirty-seven years," her father told him.

"And it's been smooth sailing all that time?"

Savannah wanted to pound her fist on the table and insist that this cross examination was unnecessary.

Marcus laughed. "Smooth sailing? Oh, hardly. Joyce and I've had our ups and downs over the years like most couples. If there's anything special about our marriage, it's been our commitment to each other."

Savannah cleared her throat, wanting to gloat. Once more Nash ignored her.

"You've never once entertained the idea of divorce?" he asked.

This question was unfair! She hadn't had the opportunity to challenge his clients about their divorces, not that she would've wanted to. Every case had saddened and depressed her.

"As soon as a couple introduces the subject of divorce, there isn't the same willingness to concentrate on communication and problem-solving. People aren't nearly as flexible," Marcus said. "Because there's always that out, that possibility."

Joyce nodded. "If there was any one key to the success of our marriage, it's been that we've refused to consider divorce an option. That's not to say I haven't fantasized about it a time or two."

"We're only human," her father agreed with a nod. "I'll admit I've entertained the notion a time or two myself—even if I didn't do anything about it."

No! It wasn't true. Savannah didn't believe it. "But you were never serious," she felt obliged to say.

Marcus looked at her and offered her a sympathetic smile, as if he knew about their wager. "Your mother and I love each other, and neither of us could say we're sorry we stuck it out through the hard times, but yes, sweetheart, there were a few occasions when I didn't know if our marriage would survive."

Savannah dared not look at Nash. Her parents' timing was incredible. If they were going to be brutally honest, why did it have to be now? In all the years Savannah was growing up she'd never once heard the word *divorce*. In her eyes their marriage was solid, always had been and always would be.

"Of course, we never stopped talking," her mother was saying. "No matter how angry we might be with each other."

Soon after, Joyce brought out dessert—a coconut cake—and coffee.

"So, what do you think of our little girl?" Marcus asked, when he'd finished his dinner. He placed his hands on his stomach and studied Nash.

"Dad, please! You're embarrassing me."

"Why?"

"My guess is Savannah would prefer we didn't give her friend the third degree, dear," Joyce said mildly.

Savannah felt like kissing her mother's cheek. She stood, eager to disentangle herself from this conversation. "I'll help with the dishes, Mom," she said as if suggesting a trip to the mall.

Nash's mood had improved considerably after meeting Savannah's parents. Obviously, things weren't going the way she'd planned. Twice now, during dinner, it was all he could do not to laugh out loud. She'd expected them to paint a rosy picture of their idyllic lives together, one that would convince him of the error of his own views.

The project had backfired in her face. Rarely had he seen anyone look more shocked than when her parents said that divorce was something they'd each contemplated at one point or another in their marriage.

The men cleared the picnic table and the two women shooed them out of the kitchen. Nash was grateful, since he had several questions he wanted to ask Marcus about Savannah.

They wandered back outside. Nash was helping Marcus gather up his fishing gear when Savannah's father spoke.

"I didn't mean to pry earlier," he said casually, carrying his fishing rod and box of flies into the garage. A motor home was parked alongside the building. Although it was an older model, it looked as good as new.

"You don't need to worry about offending me," Nash assured him.

"I wasn't worried about you. Savannah gave me 'the look' while we were eating. I don't know how much experience you have with women, young man, but take my advice. When you see 'the look,' shut up. No matter what you're discussing, if you value your life, don't say another word."

Nash chuckled. "I'll keep that in mind."

"Savannah's got the same expression as her mother. If you continue dating her, you'll recognize it soon enough." He paused. "You are going to continue seeing my daughter, aren't you?"

"You wouldn't object?"

"Heavens, no. If you don't mind my asking, what do you think of my little girl?"

Nash didn't mince words. "She's the most stubborn woman I've ever met."

Marcus nodded and leaned his prize fishing rod against the wall. "She gets that from her mother, too." He turned around to face Nash, hands on his hips. "Does her limp bother you?" he asked point-blank.

"Yes and no." Nash wouldn't insult her father with a half-truth. "It bothers me because she's so conscious of it herself."

Marcus's chest swelled as he exhaled. "That she is."

"How'd it happen?" Curiosity got the better of him, although he'd prefer to hear the explanation from Savannah.

Her father walked to the back of the garage where a youngster's mangled bicycle was stored. "It sounds simple to say she was hit by a car. This is what was left of her bike. I've kept it all these years as a reminder of how far she's come."

"Oh, no..." Nash breathed when he viewed the mangled frame and guessed the full extent of the damage done to the child riding it. "How'd she ever survive?"

"I'm not being facetious when I say sheer nerve. Anyone with less fortitude would have willed death. She was in the hospital for months, and that was only the beginning. The doctors initially told us she'd never walk again, and for the first year we believed it.

"Even now she still has pain. Some days are worse than others. Climate seems to affect it somewhat. And her limp is more pronounced when she's tired." Marcus replaced the bicycle and turned back to Nash. "It isn't every man who recognizes Savannah's strength. You haven't asked for my advice, so forgive me for offering it."

"Please."

"My daughter's a special woman, but she's prickly when it comes to men and relationships. Somehow, she's got it in her head that no man will ever want her."

"I'm sure that's not true."

"It is true, simply because Savannah believes it is," Marcus corrected. "It'll take a rare man to overpower her defenses. I'm not saying you're that man. I'm not even saying you should try."

"You seemed to think otherwise earlier. Wasn't it you who assumed I was going to marry your daughter?"

"I said that to get a rise out of Savannah, and it worked." Marcus rubbed his jaw, eyes twinkling with delight.

"We've only just met." Nash felt he had to present some explanation, although he wasn't sure why.

"I know." He slapped Nash affectionately on the back and together they left the garage. When they returned to the house, the dinner dishes had been washed and put away.

Savannah's mother had filled several containers with leftovers and packed them in an insulated bag. She gave Savannah detailed instructions on how to warm up the leftover steak and vegetables. Attempting brain surgery sounded simpler. As it happened, Nash caught a glimpse of Marcus from the corner of his eye and nearly burst out laughing. The older man was slowly shaking his head.

"I like the coyote, Mom," Savannah said, as Nash took the food for her. She ran one hand over the stylized animal. "Are you and Dad going to Arizona this winter?"

Nash felt static electricity hit the airwaves.

"We haven't decided, but I doubt we will this year," Joyce answered.

"Why not?" Savannah asked. This was obviously an old argument. "You love it there. More and more of your friends are becoming snowbirds. It doesn't make sense for you to spend your winters here in the cold and damp when you can be with your friends, soaking up the sunshine."

"Sweetheart, we've got a long time to make that decision," Marcus reminded her. "It's barely summer."

She hugged them both goodbye, then slung her purse over her shoulder, obviously giving up on the argument with her parents.

"What was that all about?" Nash asked once they were in his car.

It was unusual to see Savannah look vulnerable, but she did now. He wasn't any expert on women. His sister was evidence of that, and so was every other female he'd ever had contact with, for that matter. It looked as though gutsy Savannah was about to burst into tears.

"It's nothing," she said, her voice so low it was almost non-existent. Her head was turned away from him and she was staring out the side window.

"Tell me," he insisted as he reached the freeway's on ramp. He increased the car's speed.

Savannah clasped her hands together. "They won't leave because of me. They seem to think I need a babysitter, that it's their duty to watch over me."

"Are you sure you're not being overly sensitive?"

"I'm sure. Mom and Dad love to travel, and now that Dad's retired they should be doing much more of it."

"They have the motor home."

"They seldom use it. Day trips, a drive to the ocean once or twice a year, and that's about it. Dad would love to explore the East Coast in the autumn, but I doubt he ever will."

"Why not?"

"They're afraid something will happen to me."

"It sounds like they're being overprotective."

"They are!" Savannah cried. "But I can't force them to go, and they won't listen to me."

He sensed that there was more to this story. "What's the real reason, Savannah?" He made his words as coaxing as he could, not wanting to pressure her into telling him something she'd later regret.

"They blame themselves for the accident," she whispered. "They were leaving for a weekend trip that day and I was to stay with a babysitter. I'd wanted to go with them and when they said I couldn't, I got upset. In order to appease me, Dad said I could ride my bicycle. Up until that time he'd always gone with me."

Nash chanced a look at her and saw that her eyes were closed and her body was rigid with tension.

"And so they punish themselves," she continued in halting tones, "thinking if they sacrifice their lives for me, it'll absolve them from their guilt. Instead it increases mine."

"Yours?"

"Do you mind if we don't discuss this anymore?" she asked, sounding physically tired and emotionally beaten.

The silence that followed was eventually broken by Savannah's sigh of defeat.

"When would you like me to start cooking your dinners?" she asked as they neared her shop.

"You're conceding?" He couldn't keep the shock out of his voice. "Just like that, without so much as an argument? You must be more tired than I realized."

His comments produced a sad smile.

"So you're willing to admit marriage is a thing of the past and has no part in this day and age?"

"Never!" She rallied a bit at that.

"That's what I thought."

"Are you ready to admit love can last a lifetime when it's nourished and respected?" she asked.

Nash frowned, his thoughts confused. "I'll grant there are exceptions to every rule and your parents are clearly that. Unfortunately, the love they share doesn't exist between most married couples.

"It'd be easy to tell you I like my macaroni and cheese extra cheesy," he went on to say, "but I have a feeling you'll change your mind in the morning and demand a rematch."

Savannah smiled and pressed the side of her head against the car window.

"You're exhausted, and if I accepted your defeat, you'd never forgive me."

"What do you suggest, then?"

"A draw." He pulled into the alley behind the shop, where Savannah had parked her car. "Let's call it square. I proved what I wanted to prove and you did the same. There's no need to go back to the beginning and start over, because neither of us is going to make any progress with the other. We're both too strong-minded for that."

"We should have recognized it sooner," Savannah said, eyes closed.

She was so attractive, so...delectable, Nash had to force himself to look away.

"It's very gentlemanly of you not to accept my defeat."

"Not really."

Her eyes slowly opened and she turned her head so she could meet his eyes. "Why not?"

"Because I'm about to incur your wrath."

"Really? How are you going to do that?"

He smiled. It'd been so long since he'd looked forward to anything this much. "Because, my dear wedding coordinator, I'm about to kiss you."

4

"You're…you're going to kiss me?" Savannah had been exhausted seconds earlier, but Nash's words were a shot of adrenaline that bolted her upright.

"I most certainly am," he said, parking his car behind hers in the dark alley. "Don't look so scared. The fact is, you might even enjoy this."

That was what terrified Savannah most. If ever there was a man whose touch she yearned for, it was Nash. If ever there was a man she longed to be held by, it was Nash.

He bent his head toward hers and what resistance she'd managed to amass died a sudden death as he pressed his chin to her temple and simply held her against him. If he'd been rough or demanding or anything but gentle, she might've had a chance at resisting him. She might've had the desire to resist him. But she didn't. A sigh rumbled through her and with heedless curiosity she lifted her hand to his face, her fingertips grazing his jaw. Her touch seemed to go through him like an electrical shock because he groaned and, as she tilted back her head, his mouth sought hers.

At the blast of unexpected sensation, Savannah buckled

against him and whimpered, all the while clinging to him. The kiss continued, gaining in intensity and fervor until Savannah felt certain her heart would pound straight through her chest.

Savannah closed her eyes, deep in a world of sensual pleasure.

"Savannah." Her name was a groan. His breathing, heavy and hard, came in bursts as he struggled to regain control. Savannah was struggling, too. She finally opened her eyes. Her fingers were in his hair; she sighed and relaxed her hold.

Nash raised his head and took her face between his hands, his eyes delving into hers. "I didn't mean for that to happen."

An apology. She should've expected it, should've been prepared for it. But she wasn't.

He seemed to be waiting for her to respond so she gave him a weak smile, and lowered her gaze, not wanting him to guess how strong her reaction had been.

He leaned his forehead against hers and chuckled softly. "You're a surprise a minute."

"What do you mean?"

He dropped a glancing kiss on the side of her face. "I wouldn't have believed you'd be so passionate. The way you kissed me…"

"In other words, you didn't expect someone like me to experience sensual pleasure?" she demanded righteously. "It might shock you to know I'm still a woman."

"What?" Nash said. "What are you talking about?"

"You heard me," she said, frantically searching for her purse and the bag of leftovers her mother had insisted she take home with her.

"Stop," he said. "Don't use insults to ruin something that was beautiful and spontaneous."

"I wasn't the one—"

She wasn't allowed to finish. Taking her by the arms, he hauled her toward him until his mouth was on hers. Her resistance disappeared in the powerful persuasion of his kisses.

He exhaled sharply when he finished. "Your leg has nothing to do with this. Nothing. Do you understand?"

"Why were you so surprised, then?" she asked, struggling to keep her indignation alive. It was almost impossible when she was in his arms.

His answer took a long time. "I don't know."

"That's what I thought." She broke away and held her purse against her like a shield. "We've agreed to disagree on the issue of love and marriage, isn't that correct?"

"Yes," he said without emotion.

"Then I don't see any reason for us to continue our debate. It's been a pleasure meeting you, Mr. Davenport. Goodbye." Having said that, she jerked open the car door and nearly toppled backward. She caught herself in the nick of time before she could tumble headfirst into the alley.

"Savannah, for heaven's sake, will you—"

"Please, just leave me alone," she said, furious with herself for making such a dramatic exit and with him for reasons as yet unclear.

Because he made her feel, she guessed sometime later, when she was home and safe. He made her feel as if she was whole and without flaws. As if she was an attractive, desirable woman. Savannah blamed Nash for pretending she could be something she wasn't and the anger simmered in her blood long after she'd readied for bed.

Neatly folding her quilt at the foot of her bed, Savannah stood, seething, taking deep breaths to keep the tears at bay.

In the morning, after she'd downed her first cup of coffee, Savannah felt better. She was determined to put the incident and the man out of her mind. There was no reason for them to see each other again, no reason for them to continue with this farce. Not that Nash would want to see her, especially after the idiotic way she'd behaved, scrambling out of his car as if escaping a murderer.

As was so often the case of late, Savannah was wrong. Nash was waiting on the sidewalk in front of her shop, carrying a white bag, when she arrived for work.

"Another peace offering?" she asked, when she unlocked the front door and opened it for him.

"Something like that." He handed her a latte, then walked across the showroom and sat on the corner of her desk, dangling one leg, as though he had every right to make himself comfortable in her place of business.

Savannah hadn't recovered from seeing him again so soon; she wasn't prepared for another confrontation. "What can I do for you?" she asked stiffly, setting the latte aside. She sat down and leaned back in the swivel chair, hoping she looked relaxed, knowing she didn't.

"I've come to answer your question," he said, leg swinging as he pried loose the lid on his cup. He was so blasé about everything, as if the intensity of their kisses was a common thing for him. As if she was one in a long line of conquests. "You wanted to know what was different last night and I'm here to tell you."

This was the last thing Savannah expected. She glanced pointedly at her watch. "Is this going to take long? I've got an appointment in ten minutes."

"I'll be out of here before your client arrives."

"Good." She crossed her arms, trying to hold on to her patience. Their kisses embarrassed her now. She was determined to push the whole incident out of her mind and forget him. It'd been crazy to make a wager with him. Fun, true, but sheer folly nonetheless. The best she could do was forget she'd ever met the man. Nash, however, seemed unwilling to let that happen.

"Well?" she pressed when he didn't immediately speak.

"A woman doesn't generally go to my head the way you did," he said. "When I make love to a woman I'm the one in control."

"We weren't making love," she said heatedly, heat flushing her cheeks with instant color. Her fingers bit into the soft flesh of her arms as she fought to keep the embarrassment to herself.

"What do you call it, then?"

"Kissing."

"Yes, but it would've developed into something a whole lot more complicated if we hadn't been in my car. The last time I made love in the backseat of a car, I was—"

"This may come as a surprise to you, but I have no interest in hearing about your sexual exploits," she interjected.

"Fine," he snapped.

"Besides, we were nowhere near making love."

Nash's responding snort sent ripples of outrage through Savannah. "You overestimate your appeal, Mr. Davenport."

He laughed outright this time. "Somehow or other, I thought you'd say as much. I was hoping you'd be a bit more honest, but then, I've found truth an unusual trait in most women."

The bell above her door chimed just then, and her appointment strolled into the shop. Savannah was so grateful to have this uncomfortable conversation interrupted, she almost hugged her client.

"I'd love to continue this debate," she lied, "but as you can see, I have a customer."

"Perhaps another time," Nash suggested.

She hesitated. "Perhaps."

He snickered disdainfully as he stood and sipped from the take-out cup. "As I said, women seem to have a hard time dealing with the truth."

Savannah pretended not to hear him as she walked toward her customer, a welcoming smile on her face. "Good morning, Melinda. I'm so glad to see you."

Nash said nothing as he sauntered past her and out the door. Not until he was out of sight did Savannah relax her guard. He claimed she went to his head. What he didn't know was that his effect on her was startlingly similar. Then again, perhaps he did know....

The woman irritated him. No, Nash decided as he hit the sidewalk, his stride clipped and fast, she more than irritated him. Savannah Charles incensed him. He didn't understand this oppressive need he felt to talk to her, to explain, to hear her thoughts. He'd awakened wishing things hadn't ended so abruptly between them, wishing he'd known what to say to convince her of his sincerity. Morning had felt like a second chance.

In retrospect, he suspected he was looking for help himself in working through the powerful emotions that had evolved during their embrace. Instead, Savannah claimed he'd miscalculated her reaction. The heck he had.

He should've realized she was as confused as he was about their explosive response to each other.

Nash arrived at his office half an hour later than usual. As he walked past his assistant's desk, she handed him several telephone messages. He was due in court in twenty minutes, and wouldn't have time to return any calls until early afternoon. Shuffling through the slips, he stopped at the third one.

Susan.

His sister had called him, apparently on her cell. Without further thought he set his briefcase aside and reached for the phone, punching out the number listed.

"Susan, it's Nash," he said when she answered. If he hadn't been so eager to talk to her, he might have mulled over the reason for her call. Something must have happened; otherwise she wouldn't have swallowed her pride to contact him.

"Hello, Nash."

He waited a moment in vain for her to continue. "You called me?"

"Yes," she said abruptly. "I wanted to apologize for hanging up on you the other day. It was rude and unnecessary. Kurt and I had a…discussion about it and he said I owed you an apology."

"Kurt's got a good head on his shoulders," he said, thinking his sister would laugh and the tension between them would ease. It didn't.

"I thought about what he had to say and Kurt's right. I'm sorry for the way I reacted."

"I'm sorry, too," Nash admitted. "I shouldn't have checked up on you behind your back." If she could be so generous with her forgiveness, then so could he. After all, Susan was his little sister. He had her best interests at heart, although she wouldn't fully appreciate his concern until later in life, when she was responsible for children of her own. He wasn't Susan's father, but he was her closest relative. Although she was twenty-four, he felt she still needed his guidance and direction.

"I was thinking we might have lunch together some afternoon," she ventured, and the quaver in her voice revealed how uneasy she was making the suggestion.

Nash had missed their lunches together. "Sounds like a great idea to me. How about Thursday?"

"Same place as always?"

There was a Mexican restaurant that was their favorite, on a steep side street not far from the King County courthouse. They'd made a point of meeting there for lunch at least once a month for the past several years. The waitresses knew them well enough to greet them by name.

"All right. See you Thursday at noon."

"Great."

Grinning, Nash replaced the receiver.

He looked forward to this luncheon date with his sister the way a kid anticipates the arrival of the Easter bunny. They'd both said and done things they regretted. Nash hadn't changed his mind about his sister marrying Kurt Caldwell. Kurt was decent, intelligent, hardworking and sincere, but they were both too young for marriage. Too uninformed about it. Judging by Susan's reaction, she wasn't likely to heed his advice. He hated to think of her making the same mistakes he had, but there didn't seem to be any help for it. He might as well mend the bridges of communication before they became irreparable.

"Is something wrong?" Susan asked Savannah as they went over the details for the wedding. It bothered her how careful Susan and Kurt had to be with their money, but she admired the couple's discipline. Each decision had been painstaking.

"I'm sorry." Savannah's mind clearly wasn't on the subject at hand. It had taken a sharp turn in another direction the moment Susan had shown up for their appointment. She reminded Savannah so much of her brother. Susan and Nash had the same eye and hair color, but they were alike in other ways, as well. The way Susan smiled and her easy laugh were Nash's trademarks.

Savannah had worked hard to force all thoughts of Nash from her mind. Naively, she felt she'd succeeded, until Susan had come into the shop.

Savannah didn't know what it was about this hardheaded cynic that attracted her so strongly. She resented the fact that he was the one to ignite the spark of her sensual nature. There was no future for them. Not when their views on love and marriage were so diametrically opposed.

"Savannah," Susan asked, "are you feeling okay?"

"Of course. I'm sorry, my thoughts seem to be a thousand miles away."

"I noticed," Susan said with a laugh.

Her mood certainly seemed to have improved since their previous meeting, Savannah noticed, wishing she could say the same. Nash hadn't contacted her since their last disastrous confrontation a few days earlier. Not that she'd expected he would.

Susan had entered the small dressing room and stepped into the wedding gown. She came out, lifting her hair at the back so Savannah could fasten the long row of pearl buttons.

"I'm having lunch with Nash on Thursday," Susan announced unexpectedly.

"I'm glad you two have patched up your differences."

Susan's shoulders moved in a reflective sigh. "We haven't exactly—at least, not yet. I called him to apologize for hanging up on him. He must have been eager to talk to me because his assistant told me he was due in court and I shouldn't expect to hear from him until that afternoon. He phoned back no more than five minutes later."

"He loves you very much." Savannah's fingers expertly fastened the pearl buttons. Nash had proved he was capable of caring deeply for another human being, yet he staunchly denied the healing power of love, wouldn't allow it into his own life.

Perhaps you're doing the same thing.

The thought came at her like the burning flash from a laser gun, too fast to avoid, and too painful to ignore. Savannah shook her head to chase away the doubts. It was ridiculous. She'd purposely chosen a career that was steeped in romance. To suggest she was blocking love from her own life was ludicrous. Yet the accusation repeated itself over and over....

"Savannah?"

"I'm finished," she said quickly. Startled, she stepped back.

Susan dropped her arms and shook her hair free before slowly turning around to face Savannah. "Well?" she asked breathlessly. "What do you think?"

Although she was still preoccupied with a series of haunting doubts, Savannah couldn't help admiring how beautiful Nash's sister looked in the bridal gown. "Oh, Susan, you're lovely."

The young woman viewed herself in the mirror, staring at her reflection for several minutes as if she wasn't sure she could believe what she was seeing.

"I'm going to ask Nash to attend the wedding when we have lunch," she said. Then, biting her lip, she added, "I'm praying he'll agree to that much."

"He should." Savannah didn't want to build up Susan's expectations. She honestly couldn't predict what Nash would say; she only knew what she thought he should do.

"He seemed pleased to hear from me," Susan went on to say.

"I'm sure he was." They stood beside each other in front of the mirror. Neither seemed inclined to move. Savannah couldn't speak for Susan, but for her part, the mirror made the reality of her situation all too clear. Her tailored pants might not reveal her scarred and twisted leg, but she remained constantly aware of it, a not-so-gentle reminder of her deficiency.

"Let me know what Nash says," Savannah said impulsively just before Susan left the shop.

"I will." Susan's eyes shone with a childlike enthusiasm as she turned and walked away.

Savannah sat at her desk and wrote down the pertinent facts about the wedding gown she was ordering for Susan, but as she moved the pen across the paper, her thoughts weren't on dress measurements. Instead they flew straight to Nash. If nothing else, he'd given her cause to think over her life and face up to a few uncomfortable truths. That wasn't a bad day's work for a skeptical divorce attorney. It was unfortunate he'd never realize the impact he'd had on her.

Nash was waiting in the booth at quarter after twelve on Thursday, anxiously glancing at his watch every fifteen seconds, convinced Susan wasn't going to show, when she strolled into the restaurant. A smile lit her face when she saw him. It was almost as if they'd never disagreed, and she was a kid again coming to her big brother for advice.

"I'm sorry I'm late," she said, slipping into the vinyl seat across from him. "I'm starved." She reached for a salted chip, weighing it down with spicy salsa.

"It's good to see you," Nash ventured, taking the first step toward reconciliation. He'd missed Susan and he said so.

"I've missed you, too. It doesn't feel right for us to fight, does it?"

"Not at all."

"You're the only real family I have."

"I feel the same way. We've both made mistakes and we should learn from them." He didn't cast blame. There was no point.

The waitress brought their menus. Nash didn't recognize the young woman, which made him consider just how long it was since he'd had lunch with Susan. Frowning, he realized she'd been the one to approach him about a reconciliation, when as the older, more mature adult, he should've been working toward that end himself.

"I brought you something," Susan said, setting her handbag on the table. She rooted through it until she found what she was looking for. Taking the envelope from her purse, she handed it to him.

Nash accepted the envelope, peeled it open and pulled out a handcrafted wedding invitation, written on antique-white parchment paper in gold letters. He didn't realize his sister knew calligraphy. Although it was obviously handmade, the effort was competent and appealing to the eye.

"I wrote it myself," Susan said eagerly. "Savannah suggested Kurt and I would save money by making our own wedding invitations. It's much more personal this way, don't you think?"

"Very nice."

"The gold ink on the parchment paper was Kurt's idea. Savannah gave me a book on calligraphy and I've been practicing every afternoon."

He wondered how many more times his sister would find an

excuse to drag the wedding coordinator's name into their conversation. Each time Susan mentioned Savannah it brought up unwelcome memories of their few short times together. Memories Nash would rather forget.

"Do you like it?" Susan asked eagerly. She seemed to be waiting for something more.

"You did a beautiful job," he said.

"I'm really glad you think so."

Susan was grinning under the warmth of his praise.

The waitress returned and they placed their order, although neither of them had looked at the menu. "We're certainly creatures of habit, aren't we?" his sister teased.

"So," he said, relaxing in the booth, "how are the wedding plans going?"

"Very well, thanks to Savannah." She folded her hands on top of the table, flexing her long fingers against each other, studying him, waiting.

Nash read over the invitation a second time and saw that it had been personally written to him. So this was the purpose of her phone call, the purpose of this lunch. She was asking him if he'd attend her wedding, despite his feelings about it.

"I don't expect you to change your mind about me marrying Kurt," Susan said anxiously, rushing the words together in her eagerness to have them said. "But it would mean the world to me if you'd attend the ceremony. There won't be a lot of people there. Just a few friends and Kurt's immediate family. That's all we can afford. Savannah's been wonderful, showing us how to get the most out of our limited budget. Will you come to my wedding, Nash?"

Nash knew when he was involved in a losing battle. Susan would marry Kurt with or without his approval. His kid sister was determined to do this her way. He'd done his best to talk some sense into her, but to no avail. He'd made the mistake of threatening her, and she'd called his bluff. The past weeks had been miserable for them both.

"I'll come."

"Oh, Nash, thank you." Tears brimmed and spilled over her lashes. She grabbed her paper napkin, holding it beneath each eye in turn. "I can't begin to tell you how much this means to me."

"I know." He felt like crying himself, but for none of the same reasons. He didn't want to see his sister hurt and that was inevitable once she was married. "I still don't approve of your marrying so young, but I can't stop you."

"Nash, you keep forgetting, I'm an adult, over twenty-one. You make me sound like a little kid."

He sighed expressively. That was the way he saw her, as his kid sister. It was difficult to think of her married, with a family of her own, when it only seemed a few years back that she was in diapers.

"You'll love Kurt once you get to know him better," she said excitedly, wiping the moisture from her cheeks. "Look at what you've done to me," she muttered. Her mascara streaked her face in inky rows.

His hand reached for hers and he squeezed her fingers. "We'll get through this yet, kid," he joked.

Nash suspected, in the days that followed, that it was natural to feel good about making his sister so happy. All he'd agreed to do was attend the ceremony. He hadn't figured out what was going to keep him in his seat when the minister asked anyone who opposed the union to speak now or forever hold their peace. Attending the ceremony itself, regardless of his personal feelings toward marriage, was the least he could do for causing the rift between them.

The card from Savannah that arrived at his office took him by surprise. He stared at the return address on the envelope for a moment before turning it over and opening it with eager fingers. Her message was straightforward: "Thank you." Her elegant signature appeared below.

Nash gazed at the card for several minutes before slapping it down on his desk. The woman was driving him crazy.

He left the office almost immediately, shocking his assistant, who rushed after him, needing to know what she was supposed to do about his next appointment. Nash suggested she entertain him with some law journals and coffee. He promised to be back in half an hour.

Luckily he found a parking spot on the street. Climbing out of his car, he walked purposely toward the bridal shop. Savannah was sitting at her desk intent on her task. When she glanced up and saw him, she froze.

"I got your card," he said stiffly.

"I… It made Susan so happy to know you'd attend her wedding. I wanted to thank you," she said, her eyes following his every move.

He marched to her desk, not understanding even now what force had driven him to her. "How many guests is she inviting?"

"I…believe the number's around sixty."

"Change that," he instructed harshly. "We're going to be inviting three hundred or more. I'll have the list to you in the morning."

"Susan and Kurt can't afford—"

"They won't be paying for it. I will. I want the best for my sister, understand? We'll have a sit-down dinner, a dance with a ten-piece orchestra, real flowers and a designer wedding dress. We'll order invitations because there'll be too many for Susan to make herself. Have you got that?" He motioned toward her pen, thinking she should write it all down.

Savannah looked as if she hadn't heard him. "Does Susan know about all this?"

"Not yet."

"Don't you think you should clear it with her first?"

"It might be too soon, because a good deal of this hinges on one thing."

Savannah frowned. "What's that?"

"If you'll agree to attend the wedding as my date."

5

"Your date?" Savannah repeated as she leapt to her feet. No easy task when one leg was as unsteady as hers. She didn't often forget that, but she did now in her incredulity. "That's emotional blackmail," she cried, before slumping back in her chair.

"You're right, it is," Nash agreed, leaning forward and pressing his hands against the edge of her oak desk. His face was scant inches from her own, and his eyes cut straight through her defenses. "It's what you expect of me, isn't it?" he demanded. "Since I'm so despicable."

"I never said that!"

"Maybe not, but you thought it."

"No, I didn't!" she snapped, then decided she probably had. She'd been shaken by his kiss, and then he'd apologized as if he'd never meant it to happen. And, perhaps worse, maybe he wished it hadn't.

A slow, leisurely smile replaced Nash's dark scowl. "That's what I thought," he said as he raised his hand and brushed a strand of hair from her forehead. His fingertips lingered at her face. "I wish I knew what's happening to us."

"Nothing's happening," Savannah insisted, but her voice

lacked conviction even to her own ears. She was fighting the powerful attraction she felt for him for all she was worth, which at the moment wasn't much. "You aren't really going to black-mail me, are you?"

He gently traced the outline of her face, pausing at her chin and tilting it upward. "Do you agree to attend the wedding with me?"

"Yes, only—"

"Then you should know I had no intention of following through with my threat. Susan can have the wedding of her dreams."

Savannah stood, awkwardly placing her weight on her injured leg. "I'm sure there are far more suitable dates for you," she said crisply.

"I want you."

He made this so difficult. "Why me?" she asked. By his own admission, there were any number of other women who'd jump at the chance to date him. Why had he insisted on singling her out? It made no sense.

Nash frowned as if he wasn't sure himself, which lent cre-dence to Savannah's doubts. "I don't know. As for this wedding, it seemed to me I could be wrong. It doesn't happen often, but I have been known to make an error in judgment now and again." He gave her a quick, self-deprecating grin. "Susan's my only sister—the only family I've got. I don't want there to be any regrets between us. Your card helped, too, and the way I see it, if I'm going to sit through a wedding, I'm not going to suffer alone. I want you there with me."

"Then I suggest you ask someone who'd appreciate the in-vitation," she said defiantly, straightening her shoulders.

"I want to be with you," he insisted softly, his eyes reveal-ing his confusion. "Darned if I know why. You're stubborn, defensive and argumentative."

"One would think you'd rather...oh, wrestle a rattlesnake than go out with me."

"One would think," he agreed, smiling boyishly, "but if that's the case, why do I find myself listening for the sound of your voice? Why do I look forward to spending time with you?"

"I...wouldn't know." Except that she found herself in the same situation. Nash was never far from her thoughts; she hadn't been free of him from the moment they'd met.

His eyes, dark and serious, wandered over her face. Before she could protest, he lowered his head and nuzzled her ear. "Why can't I get you out of my mind?"

"I can't answer that, either." He was going to kiss her again, in broad daylight, where they could be interrupted by anyone walking into the shop. Yet Savannah couldn't bring herself to break away, couldn't offer so much as a token resistance.

A heartbeat later, his mouth met hers. Despite her own hesitation, she kissed him back. Nash groaned, drawing her more securely into his embrace.

"Savannah," he whispered as he broke off the kiss. "I can hardly believe this, but it's even better than before."

Savannah said nothing, although she agreed. She was trembling, and prayed Nash hadn't noticed, but that was too much to ask. He slid his fingers into her hair and brought her face close to his. "You're terrified, aren't you?" he asked, his cheek touching hers.

"Don't be ridiculous," she muttered. She felt his smile against her flushed skin and realized she hadn't fooled him any more than she had herself. "I don't know what I am."

"I don't know, either. Somehow I wonder if I ever will. I don't suppose you'd make this process a lot easier and consider just having an affair with me?"

Savannah stiffened, not knowing if he meant what he was saying. "Absolutely not."

"That's what I thought," he said with a lengthy sigh. "It's going to be the whole nine yards with you, isn't it?"

"I have no idea what you mean," she insisted.

"Perhaps not." Pulling away, he checked his watch and seemed surprised at the time. "I've got to get back to the office. I'll give Susan a call this afternoon and the three of us can get together and make the necessary arrangements."

Savannah nodded. "We're going to have to move quickly. Planning a wedding takes time."

"I know."

She smiled shyly, wanting him to know how pleased she was by his change of heart. "This is very sweet of you, Nash."

He gestured weakly with his hands, as if he wasn't sure he was doing the right thing. "I still think she's too young to be married. I can't help thinking she'll regret this someday."

"Marriage doesn't come with guarantees at any age," Savannah felt obliged to tell him. "But then, neither does life. Susan and Kurt have an advantage you seem to be overlooking."

"What's that?"

"They're in love."

"Love." Nash snickered loudly. "Generally it doesn't last more than two or three weeks."

"Sometimes that's true, but not this time," Savannah said. "However, I've worked with hundreds of couples over the years and I get a real sense about the people who come to me. I can usually tell if their marriages will last or not."

"What about Kurt and Susan?"

"I believe they'll have a long, happy life together."

Nash rubbed the side of his face, his eyes intense. He obviously didn't believe that.

"Their love is strong," she said, trying to bolster her argument.

Nash raised his eyebrows. "Spoken like a true romantic."

"I'm hoping the skeptic in you will listen."

"I'm trying."

Savannah could see the truth in that. He was trying, for Susan's sake and perhaps hers. He'd come a long way from where he was when they'd first met. But he had a lot farther to go.

Nash had no idea weddings could be so demanding, so expensive or so time-consuming. The one advantage of all this commotion and bother was all the hours he was able to spend with Savannah. As the weeks progressed, Nash came to know Savannah Charles, the businesswoman, as well as he did the lovely, talented woman who'd attracted him from the beginning. He had to admit she knew her stuff. He doubted anyone else could have arranged so large and lavish a wedding on such short notice. It was only because she had long-standing relationships with those involved—the florists, photographers, printers, hotel managers and so on—that Nash was able to give Susan an elaborate wedding.

As the days passed, Nash lost count of how often he asked Savannah out to dinner, a movie, a baseball game. She found a plausible excuse each and every time. A less determined man would have grown discouraged and given up.

But no more, he mused, looking out his office window. As far as she was concerned, he held the trump card in the palm of his hand. Savannah had consented to attend Susan's wedding with him, and there was no way he was letting her out of the agreement.

He sat at his desk thinking about this final meeting scheduled for later that afternoon. He'd been looking forward to it all week. Susan's wedding was taking place Saturday evening, and Savannah had flat run out of excuses.

Nash arrived at the shop before his sister. He was grateful for these few moments alone with Savannah.

"Hello, Nash." Her face lit up with a ready smile when he walked into the shop. She was more relaxed with him now.

She stood behind a silver punch bowl, decorating the perimeter with a strand of silk gardenias.

Her knack for making something ordinary strikingly beautiful was a rare gift. In some ways she'd done that with his life these past few weeks, giving him something to anticipate when he got out of bed every morning. She'd challenged him, goaded him, irritated and bemused him. It took quite a woman to have such a powerful effect.

"Susan's going to be a few minutes late," Nash told her. "I was hoping she'd changed her mind and decided to call off the whole thing." He'd hoped nothing of the sort, but enjoyed getting a reaction out of Savannah.

"Give it up. Susan's going to be a beautiful bride."

"Who's going to be working the wedding?" he asked, advancing toward her.

"I am, of course. Together with Nancy. You met her last week."

He nodded, remembering the pleasant, competent young woman who'd come to one of their meetings. Savannah often contracted her to help out at larger events.

"Since Nancy's going to be there, you can attend as my date and leave the work to her."

"Nash, will you please listen to reason? I can't be your date.... I know it's short notice but there are plenty of women who'd enjoy—"

"We have an agreement," he reminded her.

"I realize that, but—"

"I won't take no for an answer, Savannah, not this time."

She stiffened. Nash had witnessed this particular reaction on numerous occasions. Whenever he asked her out, her pride exploded into full bloom. Nash was well acquainted with how deeply entrenched that pride was.

"Nash, please."

He reached for her hand and raised it to his lips. His mouth grazed her fingertips. "Not this time," he repeated. "I'll pick you up just before we meet to have the pictures taken."

"Nash…"

"Be ready, Savannah, because I swear I'll drag you there in your nightgown if I have to."

Savannah was in no mood for company, nor was she keen on talking to her mother when Joyce phoned that same evening. She'd done everything she could to persuade Nash to change his plans. But he insisted she be his date for Susan's wedding. Indeed, he'd blackmailed her into agreeing to it.

"I haven't heard from you in ages," her mother said.

"I've been busy with the last-minute details of Susan Davenport's wedding."

"She's Nash's sister, isn't she?"

Her mother knew the answer to that. She was looking for an excuse to bring Nash into the conversation, which she'd done countless times since meeting him. If Savannah had to do that wager over again, she'd handle it differently. Her entire day had been spent contemplating various regrets. She wanted to start over, be more patient, finish what she'd begun, control her tongue, get out of this ridiculous "date" with Nash.

But she couldn't.

"Your father's talking about taking a trip to the ocean for a week or two."

"That sounds like an excellent idea." Savannah had been waiting all summer for them to get away.

"I'm not sure we should go…."

"For heaven's sake, why not?"

"Oh, well, I hate to leave my garden, especially now. And there've been a few break-ins in the neighborhood the last few weeks. I'd be too worried about the house to enjoy myself." The excuses were so familiar, and Savannah wanted to scream with frustration. But her mother had left out the real reason for her uncertainty. She didn't want to leave Savannah. Naturally, her parents had never come right out and said that, but it was their underlying reason for staying close to the Seattle area.

Savannah had frequently tried to discuss this with them. However, both her parents just looked at her blankly as if they didn't understand her concerns. Or they changed the subject. They didn't realize what poor liars they were.

"Have you seen much of Nash lately?" Her mother's voice rose expectantly.

"We've been working together on the wedding, so we've actually been seeing a lot of each other."

"I meant socially, dear. Has he taken you out? He's such a nice young man. Both your father and I think so."

"Mother," Savannah said, hating this, "I haven't been dating Nash."

Her mother's sigh of disappointment cut through Savannah. "I see."

"We're friends, nothing more. I've told you that."

"Of course. Be sure and let me know how the wedding goes, will you?"

Seeing that Nash had spared little expense, it would be gorgeous. "I'll give you a call early next week and tell you all about it."

"You promise?"

"Yes, Mom, I promise."

Savannah replaced the receiver with a heavy heart. The load of guilt she carried was enough to buckle her knees. How could one accident have such a negative impact on so many people for so long? It wasn't fair that her parents should continue to suffer for what had happened to her. Yet they blamed themselves, and that guilt was slowly destroying the best years of their lives.

Nash arrived at Savannah's house to pick her up late Saturday afternoon. He looked tall and distinguished in his black tuxedo and so handsome that for an awkward moment, Savannah had trouble taking her eyes off him.

"What's wrong?" he said, running his finger along the inside of his starched collar. "I feel like a concert pianist."

Savannah couldn't keep from smiling. "I was just thinking how distinguished you look."

His hand went to his temple. "I'm going gray?"

She laughed. "No."

"*Distinguished* is the word a woman uses when a man's entering middle age and losing his hair."

"If you don't get us to this wedding, we're going to miss it, and then you really will lose your hair." She placed her arm in his and carefully set one foot in front of the other. She rarely wore dress shoes. It was chancy, but she didn't want to ruin the effect of her full-length dress with flats. Nash couldn't possibly know the time and effort she'd gone to for this one date, which would likely be their first and last. She'd ordered the dress from New York, a soft, pale pink gown with a pearl-studded yoke. The long, sheer sleeves had layered pearl cuffs. She wore complementary pearl earrings and a single-strand necklace.

It wasn't often in her life that Savannah felt beautiful, but she did now. She'd worked hard, wanting to make this evening special for Susan—and knowing it would be her only date with Nash. She suspected there was a bit of Cinderella in every woman, the need to believe in fairy tales and happy endings, in true love conquering against impossible odds. For this one night, Savannah longed to forget she was crippled. For this one night, she wanted to pretend she was beautiful. A princess.

Nash helped her across the yard and held open the door for her. She was inside the car, seat belt buckled, when he joined her. His hands gripped the steering wheel, but when he didn't start the car, she turned to him.

"Is something wrong?"

He smiled at her, but she saw the strain in his eyes and didn't understand it. "It's just that you're so beautiful, I can hardly keep my hands off you."

"Oh, Nash," she whispered, fighting tears. "Thank you."

"For what?"

She shook her head, knowing she'd never be able to explain.

The church was lovely. Savannah had rarely seen a sanctuary decorated more beautifully. The altar was surrounded with huge bouquets of pink and white roses, and their scent drifted through the room. The end of each pew was decorated with a small bouquet of white rosebuds and gardenias with pink and silver bows. The effect was charming.

Seated in the front row, Savannah closed her eyes as the organ music swelled. She stood, and from the rustle of movement behind her, she knew the church was filled to capacity.

Savannah turned to see Nash escort his sister slowly down the center aisle, their steps in tune to the music. They were followed by the bridesmaids and groomsmen, most of them recruited late, every one of them delighted to share in Susan and Kurt's happiness.

Savannah had attended a thousand or more weddings in her years as a coordinator. Yet it was always the same. The moment the music crescendoed, her eyes brimmed with tears at the beauty and emotion of it all.

This wedding was special because the bride was Nash's sister. Savannah had felt a part of it from the beginning, when Susan had approached her, desperate for assistance. Now it was all coming together and Susan was about to marry Kurt, the man she truly loved.

Nash was uncomfortable with love, and a little jealous, too, although she doubted he recognized that. Susan, the little sister he adored, would soon be married and would move to California with her husband.

When they reached the steps leading to the altar, Susan kissed

Nash's cheek before placing her hand on Kurt's arm. Nash hesitated as if he wasn't ready to surrender his sister. Just when Savannah was beginning to get worried, he turned and entered the pew, standing next to her. Either by accident or design, his hand reached for hers. His grip was tight, his face strained with emotion.

Savannah was astonished to see that his eyes were bright with tears. She could easily be mistaken, though, since her own were blurred. A moment later, she was convinced she was wrong.

The pastor made a few introductory comments about the sanctity of marriage. Holding his Bible open, he stepped forward. "I'd like each couple who's come to celebrate the union of Susan and Kurt to join hands," he instructed.

Nash took both of Savannah's hands so that she was forced to turn sideways. His eyes delved into hers, and her heart seemed to stagger to a slow, uneven beat at what she read in them. Nash was an expert at disguising his feelings, yes, but also at holding on to his anger and the pain of his long-dead marriage, at keeping that bitterness alive. As he stared down at her, his eyes became bright and clear and filled with an emotion so strong, it transcended anything she'd ever seen.

Savannah was barely aware of what was going on around them. Sounds faded; even the soloist who was singing seemed to be floating away. Savannah's peripheral vision became clouded, as if she'd stepped into a dreamworld. Her sole focus was Nash.

With her hands joined to Nash's, their eyes linked, she heard the pastor say, "Those of you wishing to renew your vows, repeat after me."

Nash's fingers squeezed hers as the pastor intoned the words. "I promise before God and all gathered here this day to take you as my wife. I promise to love and cherish you, to leave my heart and my life open to you."

To Savannah's amazement, Nash repeated the vow in a husky whisper. She could hear others around them doing the same.

Once again tears filled her eyes. How easy it would be to pretend he was devoting his life to hers.

"I'll treasure you as a gift from God, to encourage you to be all He meant you to be," Savannah found herself repeating a few minutes later. "I promise to share your dreams, to appreciate your talents, to respect you. I pledge myself to you, to learn from and value our differences." As she spoke, Savannah's heart beat strong and steady and sure. Excitement rose up in her as she realized that what she'd said was true. These were the very things she yearned to do for Nash. She longed for him to trust her enough to allow her into his life, to help him bury the hurts of the past. They were different, as different as any couple could be. That didn't make their relationship impossible. It added flavor, texture and challenge to their attraction. Life together would never be dull for them.

"I promise to give you the very best of myself, to be faithful to you, to be your friend and your partner," Nash whispered next, his voice gaining strength. Sincerity rang through his words.

"I offer you my heart and my love," Savannah repeated, her own heart ready to burst with unrestrained joy.

"You are my friend," Nash returned, "my lover, my wife."

It was as if they, too, were part of the ceremony, as if they, too, were pledging their love and their lives to each other.

Through the minister's words, Savannah offered Nash all that she had to give. It wasn't until they'd finished and Kurt was told to kiss his bride that Savannah remembered this wasn't real. She'd stepped into a dreamworld, the fantasy she'd created out of her own futile need for love. Nash had only been following the minister's lead. Mortified, she lowered her eyes and tugged her trembling fingers free from Nash's.

He, too, apparently harbored regrets. His hands clasped the pew in front of them until his knuckles paled. He formed a fist with his right hand. Savannah dared not look up at him, certain he'd recognize her thoughts and fearing she'd know his. She couldn't have borne the disappointment. For the next several hours they'd be forced to share each other's company, through the dinner and the dance that followed the ceremony. Savannah wasn't sure how she was going to manage it now, after she'd humiliated herself.

Thankfully she was spared having to face Nash immediately after the ceremony was over. He became a part of the reception line that welcomed friends and relatives. Savannah was busy herself, working with the woman she'd hired to help coordinate the wedding and reception. Together they took down the pew bows, which would serve as floral centerpieces for the dinner.

"I don't think I've ever seen a more beautiful ceremony," Nancy Mastell told Savannah, working furiously. "You'd think I'd be immune to this after all the weddings we attend."

"It…was beautiful," Savannah agreed. Her stomach was in knots, and her heart told her how foolish she'd been; nevertheless, she couldn't make herself regret what had happened. She'd learned something about herself, something she'd denied far too long. She needed love in her life. For years she'd cut herself off from opportunity, content to live off the happiness of others. She'd moved from one day to the next, carrying her pain and disappointment, never truly happy, never fulfilled. Pretending.

This was why Nash threatened her. She couldn't pretend with him. Instinctively he knew. For reasons she'd probably never understand, he saw straight through her.

"Let me get those," Nancy said. "You're a wedding guest."

"I can help." But Nancy insisted otherwise.

When Savannah returned to the vestibule, she found Nash waiting for her. They drove in silence to the high-end hotel, where Nash had rented an elegant banquet room for the evening.

Savannah prayed he'd say something to cut the terrible tension. She could think of nothing herself. A long list of possible topics presented itself, but she couldn't come up with a single one that didn't sound silly or trite.

Heaven help her, she didn't know how they'd be able to spend the rest of the evening in each other's company.

Dinner proved to be less of a problem than Savannah expected. They were seated at a table with two delightful older gentlemen whom Nash introduced as John Stackhouse and Arnold Serle, the senior partners of the law firm that employed him. John was a widower, she gathered, and Arnold's wife was in England with her sister.

"Mighty nice wedding," Mr. Stackhouse told Nash.

"Thank you. I wish I could take credit, but it's the fruit of Savannah's efforts you're seeing."

"Beautiful wedding," Mr. Serle added. "I can't remember when I've enjoyed one more."

Savannah was waiting for a sarcastic remark from Nash, but one never came. She didn't dare hope that he'd changed his opinion, and guessed it had to do with the men who were seated with them.

Savannah spread the linen napkin across her lap. When she looked up, she discovered Arnold Serle watching her. She wondered if her mascara had run or if there was something wrong with her makeup. Her doubts must have shown in her eyes, because he grinned and winked at her.

Savannah blushed. A sixty-five-year-old corporate attorney was actually flirting with her. It took her a surprisingly short time to recover enough to wink back at him.

Arnold burst into loud chuckles, attracting the attention of Nash and John Stackhouse, who glanced disapprovingly at his partner. "Something troubling you, Arnold?"

"Just that I wish I were thirty years younger. Savannah here's prettier than a picture."

"You been at the bottle again?" his friend asked. "He becomes quite a flirt when he has," the other man explained. "Especially when his wife's out of town."

Arnold's cheeks puffed with outrage. "I most certainly do not."

Their salads were delivered and Savannah noted, from the corner of her eye, that Nash was studying her closely. Taking her chances, she turned and met his gaze. To her astonishment, he smiled and reached for her hand under the table.

"Arnold's right," he whispered. "Every other woman here fades compared to you." He paused. "With the exception of Susan, of course."

Savannah smiled.

The orchestra was tuning their instruments in the distance and she focused her attention on the group of musicians, feeling a surge of regret and frustration. "I need to tell you something," she said.

"What?"

"I'm sorry, I can't dance. But please don't let that stop you."

"I'm not much of a dancer myself. Don't worry about it."

"Anything wrong?" Arnold asked.

"No, no," Nash was quick to answer. "Savannah just had a question."

"I see."

"That reminds me," John began. "There's something we've been meaning to discuss with you, Nash. It's about the position for senior partner opening up at the firm," he said.

"Can't we leave business out of this evening?" Arnold asked, before Nash could respond. Arnold frowned. "It's difficult enough choosing another partner without worrying about it day and night."

Nash didn't need to say a word for Savannah to know how much he wanted the position. She felt it in him, the way his body tensed, the eager way his head inclined. But after Arnold's protest, John hadn't continued the discussion.

The dinner dishes were cleared from the table by the expert staff. The music started, a wistful number that reminded Savannah of sweet wine and red roses. Susan, in her flowing silk gown, danced with Kurt as their guests looked on, smiling.

The following number Kurt danced with his mother and Nash with Susan. His assurances that he wasn't much of a dancer proved to be false. He was skilled and graceful.

Savannah must have looked more wistful than she realized because when the next number was announced, Arnold Serle reached for her hand. "This dance is mine."

Savannah was almost too flabbergasted to speak. "I…can't. I'm sorry, but I can't."

"Nonsense." With that, the smiling older man all but pulled her from her chair.

6

Savannah was close to tears. She couldn't dance and now she was being forced onto the ballroom-style floor by a sweet older man who didn't realize she had a limp. He hadn't even noticed it. Humiliation burned her cheeks. The wonderful romantic fantasy she was living was about to blow up in her face. Then, when she least expected to be rescued, Nash was at her side, his hand at her elbow.

"I believe this dance is mine, Mr. Serle," he said, whisking Savannah away from the table.

Relief rushed through her, until she saw that he was escorting her onto the dance floor himself. "Nash, I can't," she said in a heated whisper. "Please don't ruin this day for me."

"Do you trust me?"

"Yes, but you don't seem to understand…."

Understand or not, he led her confidently onto the crowded floor, turned and gathered her in his arms. "All I want you to do is relax. I'll do the work."

"Nash!"

"Relax, will you?"

"No… Please take me back to the table."

Instead he grasped her hands and raised them, tucking them

around his neck. Savannah turned her face away from him. Their bodies fit snugly against each other and Nash felt warm and substantial. His thigh moved against hers, his chest grazed her breasts and a slow excitement began to build within her. After holding her breath, she released it in a long, trembling sigh.

"It feels good, doesn't it?"

"Yes." Lying would be pointless.

"We're going to make this as simple and easy as possible. All you have to do is hold on to me." He held her close, his hands clasped at the base of her spine. "This isn't so bad now, is it?"

"I'll never forgive you for this, Nash Davenport." Savannah was afraid to breathe again for fear she'd stumble, for fear she'd embarrass them both. She'd never been on a dance floor in her life and try as she might, she couldn't make herself relax the way he wanted. This was foreign territory to her, the girl who'd never been asked to a school dance. The girl who'd watched and envied her friends from afar. The girl who'd only waltzed in her dreams with imaginary partners. And not one of them had been anything like Nash.

"Maybe this will help," Nash whispered. He bent his head and kissed the side of her neck with his warm, moist mouth.

"Nash!" She squirmed against him.

"I've wanted to do that all night," he whispered. Goose bumps shivered up her arms as his tongue made lazy circles along one ear. Her legs felt as if they'd collapse, and she involuntarily pressed her weight against him.

"Please stop that!" she said from between clenched teeth.

"Not on your life. You're doing great." He made all the moves and, holding her the way he was, took the weight off her injured leg so she could slide with him.

"I'll embarrass us both any minute," she muttered.

"Just close your eyes and enjoy the music."

Since they were in the middle of the floor, Savannah had

no choice but to follow his instructions. Her chance to escape gracefully had long since passed.

The music was slow and easy, and when she lowered her lashes, she could pretend. This was the night, she'd decided earlier, to play the role of princess. Only she'd never expected her Cinderella fantasy to make it all the way to the ballroom floor.

"You're a natural," he whispered. "Why have you waited so long?"

She was barely moving, which was all she could manage. This was her first experience, and although she was loath to admit it, Nash was right; she was doing well. This must be a dream, a wonderful romantic dream. If so, she prayed it'd be a very long time before she woke.

As she relaxed, Nash's arms moved to a more comfortable position. She lowered her own arm just a little, and her fingers toyed with the short hair at his neck. It was a small but intimate gesture, to run her fingers through his hair, and she wondered at her courage. It might be just another facet of her fantasy, but it seemed the action of a lover or a wife.

Wife.

In the church, when they'd repeated the vows, Nash had called her his friend, his lover, his wife. But it wasn't real. But for now, she was in his arms and they were dancing cheek to cheek, as naturally as if they'd been partners for years. For now, she would make it real, because she so badly wanted to believe it.

"Who said you couldn't dance?" he asked her after a while.

"Shh." She didn't want to talk. These moments were much too precious to waste on conversation. This time was meant to be savored and enjoyed.

The song ended, and when the next one started almost without pause, the beat was fast. Her small bubble of happiness burst. Her disappointment must have been obvious because Nash chuckled. "Come on," he said. "If we can waltz, we can do this."

"Nash… I could do the slow dance because you were holding me, but this is impossible."

Nash, however, wasn't listening. He was dancing. Without her. His arms jerked back and forth, and his feet seemed to be following the same haphazard course. He laughed and threw back his head. "Go for it, Savannah!" He shouted to be heard above the music. "Don't just stand there. Dance!"

She was going to need to move—off the dance floor. She was about to turn away when Nash clasped her around the waist, holding her with both hands. "You can't quit now."

"Oh, yes, I can. Just watch me."

"All you need to do is move a little to the rhythm. You don't need to leap across the dance floor."

There was no talking to him, so she threw her arms in the air in abject frustration.

"That's it," he shouted enthusiastically.

"Excuse me, excuse me," Arnold Serle's voice said from behind her. "Nash, would you mind if I danced with Savannah now?" he shouted.

Nash looked at Savannah and grinned, as cheerful as a six-year-old pulling a prank on his first-grade teacher. "Savannah would love to. Isn't that right?" With that, he danced his way off the floor.

"Ready to rock 'n' roll?" Arnold asked.

Savannah didn't mean to laugh, but she couldn't stop herself. "I'm not very good at this."

"Shall we?" he said, holding out his palm to her.

Reluctantly she placed her hand in his. She didn't want to offend Nash's boss, but she didn't want to embarrass herself, either. Taking Nash's advice, she moved her arms, just a little at first, swaying back and forth, convinced she looked like a chicken attempting flight. Others around her were wiggling and twisting in every which direction. Savannah's movements, or lack of them, weren't likely to be noticed.

To her utter amazement, Mr. Serle began to twist vigorously. His dancing was reminiscent of 1960s teen movies she'd seen on TV. With each jerking motion he sank closer to the floor, until he was practically kneeling. After a moment he stopped moving. He hunkered there, one arm stretched forward, one elbow back.

"Mr. Serle, are you all right?"

"Would you mind helping me up? My back seems to have gone out on me."

Savannah looked frantically around for Nash, but he was nowhere to be seen. She was silently calling him several colorful names for getting her into this predicament. With no other alternative, she bent forward, grabbed the older man's elbow and pulled him into an upright position.

"Thanks," he said, with a bright smile. "I got carried away there and forgot I'm practically an old man. Sure felt good. My heart hasn't beaten this fast in years."

"Maybe we should sit down," she suggested, praying he'd agree.

"Not on your life, young lady. I'm only getting started."

Nash made his way back to the table, smiling to himself. He hadn't meant to embarrass Savannah. His original intent had been to rescue her. Taking her onto the dance floor was pure impulse. All night he'd been looking for an excuse to hold her, and he wasn't about to throw away what might be his only chance.

Beautiful didn't begin to describe Savannah. When he'd first met her, he'd thought of her as cute. He'd dated women far more attractive than she was. On looks alone, she wasn't the type that stood out in a crowd. Nor did she have a voluptuous body. She was small, short and proportioned accordingly. If he was looking for long shapely legs and an ample bust, he wouldn't find either in Savannah. She wasn't a beauty, and yet she was the most beautiful woman he'd ever known.

That didn't make a lot of sense. He decided it was because he'd never met anyone quite like Savannah Charles. He didn't fully understand why she appealed to him so strongly. True, she had a compassionate heart, determination and courage— all qualities he admired.

"Is Arnold out there making a world-class fool of himself?" John Stackhouse asked, when Nash joined the elder of the two senior partners at their table.

"He's dancing with Savannah."

John Stackhouse was by far the most dignified and reserved of the two. Both were members of the executive committee, which had the final say on the appointment of the next senior partner. Stackhouse was often the most disapproving of the pair. Over the years, Nash had been at odds with him on more than one occasion. Their views on certain issues invariably clashed. Although he wasn't particularly fond of the older man, Nash respected him, and considered him fair-minded.

John Stackhouse sipped from his wineglass. "Actually, I'm pleased we have this opportunity to talk," he said to Nash, arching an eyebrow. "A wedding's not the place to bring up business, as Arnold correctly pointed out, but I believe now might be a good time for us to talk about the senior partnership."

Nash's breath froze in his lungs, and he nodded. "I'd appreciate that."

"You've been with the firm a number of years now, and worked hard. We've won some valuable cases because of you, and that's in your favor."

"Glad to hear that." So Paul Jefferson didn't have it sewn up the way he'd assumed.

"I don't generally offer advice…"

This was true enough. Stackhouse kept his opinions to himself until asked, and it boded well that he was willing to make a few suggestions to Nash. Although he badly wanted the position, Nash still didn't think he had a chance against Paul. "I'd appreciate any advice you care to give me."

"Arnold and a couple of the other members of the executive committee were discussing names. Yours was raised almost immediately."

Nash moved forward, perching on the end of his chair. "What's the consensus?"

"Off the record."

"Off the record," Nash assured him.

"You're liked and respected, but there's a problem, a big one as far as the firm's concerned. The fact is, I'm the one who brought it up, but the others claimed to have noticed it, as well."

"Yes?" Nash's mind zoomed over the list of potential areas of trouble.

"You've been divorced for years now."

"Yes."

"This evening's the first time I've seen you put that failure behind you. I've watched you chew on your bitterness like an old bone, digging it up and showing it off like a prized possession when it suited you. You've developed a cutting, sarcastic edge. That's fine in the courtroom, but a detriment in your professional life as well as your private life. Especially if you're interested in this senior partnership."

"I'm interested," Nash was quick to tell him, too quick perhaps because Stackhouse smiled. That happened so rarely it was worth noting.

"I'm glad to hear you say that."

"Is there anything I could do to help my chances?" This conversation was unprecedented, something Nash had never believed possible.

The attorney hesitated and glanced toward the dance floor, frowning. "How serious are you about this young woman?"

Of all the things Nash had thought he might hear, this was the one he least expected. "Ah…" Nash was rarely at a loss for words, but right now he had no idea how to answer. "I don't know. Why do you ask?"

"I realize it's presumptuous of me, and I do hope you'll forgive me, but it might sway matters if you were to marry again."

"Marry?" he repeated, as if the word was unfamiliar to him.

"It would show the committee that you've put the past behind you," John continued, "and that you're trying to build a more positive future."

"I…see."

"Naturally, there are no guarantees and I certainly wouldn't suggest you consider marriage if you weren't already thinking along those lines. I wouldn't have said anything, but I noticed the way you were dancing with the young lady and it seemed to me you care deeply for her."

"She's special."

The other man nodded. "Indeed she is. Would you mind terribly if I danced with her myself? I see no reason for Arnold to have all the fun." Not waiting for Nash to respond, he stood and made his way across the dance floor to Savannah and his friend.

Nash watched as John Stackhouse tapped his fellow attorney on the shoulder and cut in. Savannah smiled as the second man claimed her.

Marry!

Nash rubbed his face. A few months earlier, the suggestion would have infuriated him. But a few months earlier, he hadn't met Savannah.

Nor had he stood in a church, held hands with an incredible woman and repeated vows. Vows meant for his sister and the man she loved. Not him. Not Savannah. Yet these vows had come straight from his heart to hers. He hadn't intended it to be that way. Not in the beginning. All he'd wanted to do was show Savannah how far he'd come. Repeating a few words seemed a small thing at the time.

But it wasn't as simple as all that. Because everything had

changed from that moment forward. He'd spoken in a haze, not fully comprehending the effect it was having on him. All he understood was that he was tired. Tired of being alone. Tired of pretending he didn't need anyone else. Tired of playing a game in which he would always be the loser. Those vows he'd recited with Savannah had described the kind of marriage she believed in so strongly. It was an ideal, an uncommon thing, but for the first time in years he was willing to admit it was possible. A man and a woman could share this loving, mutually respectful partnership. Savannah had made it real to him the moment she'd repeated the vows herself.

Marry Savannah.

He waited for the revulsion to hit him the way it usually did when someone mentioned the word *marriage*. Nothing happened. Of course, that was perfectly logical. He'd spent time in a wedding shop, making a multitude of decisions that revolved around Susan's wedding. He'd become immune to the negative jolt the word always struck in him.

But he expected some adverse reaction. A twinge, a shiver of doubt. Something.

It didn't come.

Marriage. He repeated it slowly in his mind. No, he'd never consider anything so drastic. Not for the sole reason of making senior partner. He'd worked hard. It was a natural progression; if he didn't get the appointment now, he would later.

Marriage to Savannah. If there was ever a time the wine was talking, it was now.

Savannah had never experienced a night she'd enjoyed more. She'd danced and drunk champagne, then danced again. Every time she'd turned around, there was someone waiting to dance with her or fill her glass.

"Oh, Nash, I had the most incredible night of my life," she

said, leaning against the headrest in his car and closing her eyes. It was a mistake, because the world went on a crazy spin.

"That good, was it?"

"Yes, oh, yes. I hate to see it end."

"Then why should it? Where would you like to go?"

"You'll take me anywhere?"

"Name it."

"The beach. I want to go to the beach." She was making a fool of herself, but she didn't care. She wanted to throw out her arms and sing. Where was a mountaintop when she needed one?

"Your wish is my command," Nash said to her.

She slipped her hand around his upper arm and hugged him, resting her head on his shoulder. "That's how I feel about tonight. It's magical. I could ask for anything and somehow it would be given to me."

"I believe it would."

Excited now that her fantasy had become so real, she lowered the car window and let out a wild whoop of joy.

Nash laughed. "What was that for?"

"I'm so happy! I never dreamed I could dance like that. Did you see me? Did you see all the men who asked me?" She brought her hand to her chest. "Me. I always thought I couldn't dance, and I did, and I owe it all to you."

"I knew you could do it."

"But how…"

"You can walk, can't you?"

"Yes, but I assumed it was impossible to dance." The champagne had affected her, but she welcomed the light-headedness it produced. "Oh, did you see Mr. Stackhouse? I thought I'd burst out laughing. I'm convinced he's never done the twist in his life." The memory made her giggle.

"I couldn't believe my eyes," Nash said and she heard the amusement in his voice. "Neither could Arnold Serle. Arnold said they've been friends for thirty-five years and he's never seen

John do anything like it, claimed he was just trying to outdo him. That's when he leapt onto the dance floor, too, and the three of you started a conga line."

"There's magic to this night, isn't there?"

"There must be," he agreed.

Her leg should be aching, and would be soon, but she hadn't felt even a twinge. Perhaps later, when adrenaline wasn't pumping through her body and she was back on planet Earth, she'd experience the familiar discomfort. But it hadn't happened yet.

"Your beach," Nash announced, edging into the parking space at Alki Beach in West Seattle. A wide expanse of sandy shore stretched before them. Seattle's lights glittered in the distance like decorations on a gaily lit Christmas tree. Gentle waves lapped the driftwood-strewn sand, and the scents of salt and seaweed hung in the air. "Make all your wishes this easy to fulfill, will you?"

"I'll do my best," she promised. Her list was short, especially for a woman who, on this one night, was a princess in disguise.

"Any other easy requests?" Nash asked. He moved closer and draped his arm across her shoulders.

"A full moon would be nice."

"Will a crescent-shaped one do, instead?"

"It'll have to."

"Perhaps I could find a way to take your mind off the moon," Nash suggested, his voice low and oddly breathless.

"Oh?" *Oh, please let him kiss me,* Savannah pleaded. The night would be perfect if only Nash were to take her in his arms and kiss her....

"Do you know what I'm thinking?" he asked.

She closed her eyes and nodded. "Kiss me, Nash. Please kiss me."

His mouth came down on hers and she thought she was ready for his sensual invasion, since she'd yearned for it so badly. But nothing could have prepared her for the greed they felt for each other. She linked her arms around his neck and gave herself to his touch.

"Why is it," Nash groaned, long minutes later as he breathed kisses across her cheeks, "that we seem to be forever kissing in a car?"

"I...don't know."

His lips toyed with hers. "You're making this difficult."

"I am." Her effect on him made Savannah giddy. It made her feel strong, and for a woman who'd felt weak most of her life, this was a potent aphrodisiac.

"You're so beautiful," Nash whispered, just before he kissed her again.

"Tonight I'm invincible," she murmured. Privately she wondered if Cinderella had spent time like this with her prince before rushing off and leaving him with a single glass slipper. She wondered if her counterpart had the opportunity to experience such unexpected pleasure.

Nash kissed her again and again, until a host of dizzying sensations accosted her from all sides. She broke away and buried her face in his chest in a desperate effort to clear her head.

"Savannah." Taking her by the shoulders, he eased back. "Look at me."

Blindly she obeyed him, running her tongue over lips that were swollen from the urgency of their kisses. "Touch me," she pleaded, gazing at the desire in his eyes, the desire that was a reflection of her own.

Nash went still, his breathing labored. "I can't.... We're on a public beach." He closed his eyes. "That does it," he said forcefully, pulling away from her. "We're going to do this right. We're not teenagers anymore. I want to make love to you, Savannah, and I'm not willing to risk being interrupted by a policeman who'll arrest me for taking indecent liberties." He reached for the ignition and started the car. She saw how badly his hand shook.

"Where are we going?"

"My house."

"Nash…"

"Don't argue with me."

"Kiss me first," she said, not understanding his angry impatience. They had all night. She wouldn't stop being a princess for hours yet.

"I have every intention of kissing you. A lot."

"That sounds nice," she whispered, and with a soft sigh pressed her head against his shoulder.

After several minutes of silence, she said, "I'm not always beautiful." She felt she should remind him of that.

"I hate to argue with you, especially now," he said, planting one last kiss on the corner of her mouth, "but I disagree."

"I'm really not," she insisted, although she thought it was very kind of him to disagree.

"I want you more than I've ever wanted any other woman in my life."

"You do?" It was so nice of him to say such things, but it wasn't necessary. Unexpected tears filled her eyes. "No one's ever said things like that to me before."

"Stupid fools." They stopped at a red light and Nash reached for her and kissed her as if he longed to make up for a lifetime of rejection. Savannah brought her arms around his neck and sighed when he finally broke off the kiss.

"You're not drunk, are you?" Nash demanded, turning a corner sharply. He shot a wary glance at her, as if this was a recent suspicion.

"No." She was, just a little, but not enough to affect her judgment. "I know exactly what I'm doing."

"Right, but do you know what I intend on doing?"

"Yes, you're taking me home so we can make love in your bed. You'd prefer that to being arrested for doing it publicly."

"Smart girl."

"I'm not a girl!"

"Sorry, slip of the tongue. Trust me, I know exactly how much of a woman you are."

"No, you don't. You haven't got a clue, Nash Davenport, but that's all right because no one else does, either." Herself included, but she didn't say that.

Nash pulled into his driveway and was apparently going faster than he realized, because when he hit his brakes the car jerked to an abrupt stop. "The way I've been driving, it's a miracle I didn't get a ticket," he mumbled as he leapt out of the car. He opened her door, and Savannah smiled lazily and lifted her arms to him.

"I don't know if I can walk," she said with a tired sigh. "I can dance, though, if anyone cares to ask."

He scooped her effortlessly into his arms and carried her to his front porch. Savannah was curious to see his home, curious to learn everything she could about him. She wanted to remember every second of this incredible night.

It was a bit awkward getting the key in the lock and holding her at the same time, but Nash managed. He threw open the door and walked into the dark room. He hesitated, kicked the door closed and traipsed across the living room, not bothering to turn on the lights.

"Stop," she insisted.

"For what? Savannah, you're driving me crazy."

Languishing in his arms, she arched back her head and kissed his cheek. "What a romantic thing to say."

"Did you want something?" he asked impatiently.

"Oh, yes, I want to see your home. A person can find out a great deal about someone just by seeing the kind of furniture he buys. Little things, too, like his dishes. And books and music and art." She gave a tiny shrug. "I've been curious about you from the start."

"You want to know the pattern of my china?"

"Well, yes..."

"Can it wait until tomorrow? There are other things I'd rather be doing...."

Nash moved expertly down the darkened hallway to his room. Gently he placed her on the mattress and knelt over her. She smiled up at him. "Oh, Nash, you have a four-poster bed. But...tomorrow's too late."

"For what?"

"Us. This—being together—will only work for one night. Then the princess disappears and I go back to being a pumpkin." She frowned. "Or do I mean scullery maid?" She giggled, deciding her fracturing of the fairy tale didn't matter.

Nash froze and his eyes met hers, before he groaned and fell backward onto the bed. "You are drunk, aren't you?"

"No," she insisted. "Just happy. Now kiss me and quit asking so many questions." She was reaching for him when it happened. The pain shot like fire through her leg and, groaning, she fell onto her side.

7

Nash recognized the effort Savannah made to hide her agony. It must have been excruciating; it was certainly too intense to disguise. Lying on her back, she squeezed her eyes tightly shut, gritted her teeth and then attempted to manage the pain with deep-breathing exercises.

"Savannah," he whispered, not wanting to break her concentration and at the same time desperately needing to do something, anything, to ease her discomfort. "Let me help," he pleaded.

She shook her head. "It'll pass in a few minutes."

Even in the moonlight, Nash could see how pale she'd become. He jumped off the bed and was pacing like a wild beast, feeling the searing grip of her pain himself. It twisted at his stomach, creating a mental torment unlike anything he'd ever experienced.

"Let me massage your leg," he insisted, and when she didn't protest he lifted the skirt of her full-length gown and ran his hands up and down her thigh. Her skin was hot to the touch and when he placed his chilled hands on her, she groaned anew.

"It'll pass." He repeated her own words, praying he was right. His heart was pounding double-time in his anxiety. He couldn't bear to see Savannah endure this unbearable pain, and stand by and do nothing.

Her whole leg was terribly scarred and his heart ached at the agony she'd endured over the years. Her muscles were tense and knotted but gradually began to relax as he gently worked her flesh with both hands, easing them up and down her thigh and calf. He saw the marks of several surgeries; the scars were testament to her suffering and her bravery.

"There are pills in my purse," she whispered, her voice barely discernible.

Nash quickly surveyed the room, jerking his head from left to right, wondering where she'd put it. He found the small clutch purse on the carpet. Grasping it, he emptied the contents on top of the bed. The brown plastic bottle filled with a prescription for pain medication rolled into view.

Hurrying into his bathroom, he ran her a glass of water, then dumped a handful of the thick chalky tablets into the palm of his hand. "Here," he said.

Levering herself up on one elbow, Savannah took three of the pills. Her hands were trembling, he noted, and he could hardly resist taking her in his arms. Once she'd swallowed the pills, she closed her eyes and laid her head on the pillow.

"Take me home, please."

"In a few minutes. Let's give those pills a chance to work first."

She was sobbing openly now. Nash lay down next to her and gathered her in his arms.

"I'm sorry," she sobbed.

"For what?"

"For ruining everything."

"You didn't ruin anything." He brushed his lips over the crown of her head.

"I...didn't want you to see my leg." Her tears came in earnest now and she buried her face in his shoulder.

"Why?"

"It's ugly."

"You're beautiful."

"For one night…"

"You're wrong, Savannah. You're beautiful every minute of every day." He cradled her head against him, whispering softly in her ear. Gradually he felt her tension diminish, and he knew by the even sound of her breathing that she was drifting off to sleep.

Nash held her for several minutes, wondering what he should do. She'd asked that he take her home, but waking her seemed cruel, especially now that the terrible agony had passed. She needed her sleep, and movement might bring back the pain.

What it came down to, he admitted reluctantly, was one simple fact. He wanted Savannah with him and was unwilling to relinquish her.

Kissing her temple, he eased himself from her arms and crawled off the bed. He got a blanket from the top shelf in his closet and covered her with it, careful to tuck it about her shoulders.

Looking down on her, Nash shoved his hands in his pockets and stared for several minutes.

He wandered into the living room, slumped into his recliner and sat in the dark while the night shadows moved against the walls.

He'd been selfish and inconsiderate, but above all he'd been irresponsible. Bringing Savannah to his home had been the most recent in a long list of errors in judgment.

He was drunk, but not on champagne. His intoxication was strictly due to Savannah. The idealist. The romantic. Attending his sister's wedding hadn't helped matters any. Susan had been a beautiful bride and if there was ever a time he could believe in the power of love and the strength of vows, it was at her wedding.

It'd started early in the evening when he'd exchanged vows with Savannah as if *they* were the ones being married. It was a moment out of time—dangerous and unreal.

He'd attempted to understand what had happened, offered a litany of excuses, but he wasn't sure he'd ever find one that would satisfy him. He wished there was someone or something he could blame, but that wasn't likely. The best he could hope for was to forget the whole episode and pray Savannah did the same.

Savannah. She was so beautiful. He'd never enjoyed dancing with a woman like he did with her. Smiling to himself, he recalled the way he'd been caught up in the magic of her joy. Being with her, sharing this night with her, was like being drawn into a fairy tale, impossible to resist even if he'd tried. And he hadn't.

Before he knew it, they were parked at Alki Beach, kissing like there was no tomorrow. He'd never desired a woman more.

Wrong. There'd been a time, years earlier, when he'd been equally enthralled with a woman. In retrospect it was easy to excuse his naïveté. He'd been young and impressionable. And because of that, he'd fallen hopelessly in love.

Love. He didn't even like the sound of the word. He'd found love to be both painful and dangerous.

Nash didn't love Savannah. He refused to allow himself to wallow in that destructive emotion a second time. He was attracted to her, but love was out of the question. Denise had taught him everything he needed to know about that.

He hadn't thought of her, except in passing, in years. Briefly he wondered if she was happy, and doubted his ex-wife would ever find what she was searching for. Her unfaithfulness continued to haunt him even now, years after their divorce. For too long he'd turned a blind eye to her faults, all in the glorious name of love.

He'd made other mistakes, too. First and foremost he'd married the wrong woman. His father had tried to tell him, but Nash had refused to listen, discrediting his advice, confident his father's qualms about Nash's choice in women were part and parcel of being too old to understand true love. Time had proved otherwise.

Looking back, Nash realized he'd shared only one thing with Denise. Incredible sex. He'd mistaken her physical demands for love. Within a few weeks of meeting, they were living together and their sexual relationship had become addictive.

It was ironic that she'd been the one to bring up the subject of marriage. Until then she'd insisted she was a "free spirit." Not until much later did he understand this sudden need she had for commitment. With his father seriously ill, there was the possibility of a large inheritance.

They'd been happy in the beginning. Or at least Nash had attempted to convince himself of that, and perhaps they were, but their happiness was short-lived.

He'd first suspected something was wrong when he arrived home late one evening after a grueling day in court and caught the scent of a man's cologne. He'd asked Denise and she'd told him he was imagining things. Because he wanted to believe her, because the thought of her being unfaithful was so completely foreign, he'd accepted her word. He had no reason to doubt her.

His second clue came less than a month later when a woman he didn't know met him outside his apartment. She was petite and fragile in her full-length coat, her hands deep in the pockets, her eyes downcast. She hated to trouble him, she said, but could Nash please keep his wife away from her husband. She'd recently learned she was pregnant with their second child and wanted to keep the marriage together if she could.

Nash had been stunned. He'd tried to ask questions, but she'd turned and fled. He didn't say anything to Denise, not that night and not for a long time afterward. But that was when he started to notice the little things that should've been obvious.

Nash hated himself for being so weak. He should have demanded the truth then and there, should have kicked her out of his home. Instead he did nothing. Denial was comfortable for a week and then two, while he wrestled with his doubts.

Savannah's scarred leg was a testament to her bravery, her endless struggle to face life each and every day. His scarred emotions were a testament to his cowardice, to knowing that his wife was cheating on him and accepting it rather than confronting her with the truth.

His wife had been *cheating* on him. What an ineffectual word that was for what he felt. It sounded so…trivial. So insignificant. But the sense of betrayal was sharper than any blade, more painful than any incision. It had slashed his ego, punctured his heart and forever changed the way he viewed love and life.

Nash had loved Denise; he must have, otherwise she wouldn't have had the power to hurt him so deeply. That love had burned within him, slowly twisting itself into a bitter desire to get even.

The divorce had been ugly. Nash attempted to use legal means to retaliate for what Denise had done to him emotionally. Unfortunately there was no compensation for what he'd endured. He'd learned this countless times since from other clients. He'd wanted to embarrass and humiliate her the way she had him, but in the end they'd both lost.

Following their divorce, Denise had married again almost immediately. Her new husband was a man she'd met three weeks earlier. Nash kept tabs on her for some time afterward and was downright gleeful when he learned she was divorcing again less than a year later.

For a long while Nash was convinced he hated Denise. In some ways he did; his need for revenge had been immature. But as the years passed, he was able to put their short marriage in perspective, and he was grateful for the lessons she'd taught him. Paramount was the complete unreliability of love and marriage.

Denise had initiated him into this kind of thinking, and the hundreds of divorce cases he'd handled since then had reinforced it.

Then he'd met Savannah. In the beginning, she'd irritated him no end. With her head in the clouds, subsisting on the thin air of romance, she'd met each of his arguments as if she alone was responsible for defending the institution of marriage. As if she alone was responsible for changing his views.

Savannah irritated him—that was true enough—but she'd worn down his defenses until he was doing more than listening to her; he was beginning to believe again. It took some deep soul-searching to admit that.

He must believe, otherwise she wouldn't be sleeping in his bed. Otherwise they wouldn't have come within a heartbeat of making love.

What a drastic mistake that would have been, Nash realized a second time. He didn't know when common sense had abandoned him, but it had. Perhaps he'd started breathing that impossibly thin air Savannah had existed on all these years. Apparently it had tricked him as it had her.

Nash should have known better than to bring Savannah into his home. He couldn't sleep with her and expect their relationship to remain the same. Everything would change. Savannah wasn't the type of woman to engage in casual affairs and that was all Nash had to offer. A few hours in bed would have been immensely pleasurable, but eventually disastrous to them both.

Savannah woke when dawn light crept through a nearby window. Opening her eyes, she needed a moment to orient herself. She was in a strange bed. Alone. It didn't take long to remember the events of the night before. She was in Nash's home.

Sitting up required an effort. The contents of her purse were strewn across the bed and, gathering them together as quickly as possible, she went in search of her shoes.

Nash was nowhere to be seen. If her luck held, she could call a cab and be out of his home before he realized she'd gone.

Her folly weighed heavily on her. She'd never felt more embarrassed in her life.

She moved stealthily from the bedroom into the living room. Pausing, she saw Nash asleep in his recliner. Her breath caught in her throat as she whispered a silent prayer of thanksgiving that he was asleep.

Fearing the slightest sound would wake him, she decided to sneak out the back door, find a phone elsewhere and call for a cab. Her cell phone was at home; there hadn't been room for it in the tiny beaded purse she'd brought with her yesterday.

Her hand was on the lock to the back door, a clean escape within her reach, when Nash spoke from behind her.

"I thought you wanted to check out my china pattern."

Savannah closed her eyes in frustration. "You were sleeping," she said without turning around.

"I'm awake now."

Her face was so hot, it was painful. Dropping her hands, she did her best to smile before slowly pivoting around.

"How were you planning on getting home?" he asked.

"A taxi."

"Did you bring your cell?"

He knew perfectly well she hadn't. "No, I was going to locate a phone somewhere and call a cab."

"I see." He began to make a pot of coffee as if this morning was no different from any other. "Why did you find it so important to leave now?" he asked in what she was sure were deceptively calm tones.

"You were sleeping...."

"And you didn't want to disturb me."

"Something like that."

"We didn't make love, so there's no need to behave like an outraged virgin."

"I'm well aware of what we did and didn't do," Savannah said stiffly. He was offended that she was sneaking out of his home. That much was apparent.

Nash was an experienced lover, but she doubted he'd ever dealt with a situation similar to what had happened to them. Most women probably found pleasure in his touch, not excruciating pain. Most women sighed with enjoyment; they didn't *sob* in agony. Most women lived the life of a princess on a day-to-day basis, while her opportunity came once in a lifetime.

"How's your leg feel?"

"It's fine."

"You shouldn't have danced—"

"Nothing on this earth would have stopped me," she told him, her voice surprisingly strong. "The pain's something I live with every day. It's the price I paid for enjoying myself. I had a wonderful time last night, Nash. Don't take that away from me."

He hesitated, then said, "Sit down and have a cup of coffee. We'll talk and then I'll drive you home." He poured two cups and set them on the round kitchen table. "Cream and sugar?"

She shook her head.

He sat casually in one of the chairs.

"I… I'm not much of a conversationalist in the morning," she said.

"No problem. We can wait until afternoon if you'd rather."

She didn't and he knew that. All she wanted was to escape. Reluctantly she pulled out the chair opposite his and sat down. The coffee was too hot to drink, but just the right temperature to warm her hands. She cradled the cup between her palms and focused her attention on it. "I want you to know how sorry I am for—"

He interrupted her. "If you're apologizing for last night, don't bother."

"All right, I won't."

"Good."

Savannah took her first tentative sip of coffee. "Well," she said, looking up but avoiding his eyes, "what would you suggest we talk about?"

"What happened."

"Nothing happened," she said.

"It almost did."

"I know that better than you think, Nash. So why are we acting like strangers this morning? Susan's wedding was beautiful. Dancing with you and the two gentlemen from your office was wonderful. For one incredible night I played the glamorous role of a princess. Unfortunately, it ended just a little too soon."

"It ended exactly where it should have. Our making love would have been a mistake."

Savannah was trying to put everything in perspective, but his statement felt like a slap in the face. It shouldn't have hurt so much, but it did. Unwanted tears sprang to her eyes.

"You don't agree?"

"Does it matter?" she asked, refusing to let him know how deeply he'd hurt her.

"I suppose not."

"It doesn't," she said more forcefully. She was having a difficult time holding back the tears. They threatened to spill down her face any second. "I'd like to go home now," she said.

"It wouldn't have worked, you know."

"Of course I know that," she flared.

She felt more than saw Nash's hesitation. "Are you all right?" he asked.

"I've never been better," she snapped. "But I want to go home. Sitting around here in this dress is ridiculous. Now either you drive me or I'm calling a cab."

"I'll drive you."

The ride back to her place was a nightmare for Savannah. Nash made a couple of attempts at conversation, but she was in no mood to talk and certainly in no mood to analyze the events of the night before. She'd been humiliated enough and didn't want to make things worse.

The minute Nash pulled into her driveway, Savannah opened the car door, eager to make her escape. His hand at her elbow stopped her.

Savannah groaned inwardly and froze. But Nash didn't seem to have anything to say.

"Susan's wedding was very nice. Thank you," he finally told her.

She nodded, keeping her back to him and her head lowered.

"I enjoyed our time together."

"I...did, too." Even though that time was over now. It was daylight, and the magic of last night was gone.

"I'll give you a call later in the week."

She nodded, although she didn't believe it. This was probably a line he used often. Just another way of saying goodbye, she figured.

"What about Thursday?" he asked unexpectedly, after he'd helped her out of the car.

"What about it?"

"I'd like to take you out.... A picnic or something."

He couldn't have surprised her more. Slowly she raised her head, studying him, confident she'd misunderstood.

He met her gaze steadily. "What's wrong?"

"Are you asking me out on a date?"

"Yes," he said, taking her house keys from her lifeless hand and unlocking her front door. "Is that a problem?"

"I... I don't know."

"Would you prefer it if we went dancing instead?" he asked, his mouth lifting in a half smile.

Despite their terrible beginning that morning, Savannah smiled. "It'd be nice, but I don't think so."

"I'll see what I can arrange. I'll pick you up around six at the shop. Okay?"

Savannah was too shocked to do anything but nod.

"Good." With that he leaned forward and brushed his lips over hers. It wasn't much as kisses went, but the warmth of his touch went through her like a bolt of lightning.

Savannah stood on her porch, watching him walk away. He was at his car before he turned back. "You were a beautiful princess," he said.

Nash wasn't sure what had prompted the invitation for a picnic for Thursday. It wasn't something he'd given any thought to suggesting. In fact, he felt as surprised as Savannah looked when he'd asked her.

A date. That was simple enough. It wasn't as if he hadn't gone out on dates before, but it had been a long while since he'd formally asked a woman out. He was making more of this than necessary, he decided.

By Wednesday he would have welcomed an excuse to get out of it. Especially after John Stackhouse called him into his office. The minute he received the summons, Nash guessed this was somehow linked to Savannah.

"You wanted to see me?" Nash asked, stepping inside the senior partner's office later that afternoon.

"I hope I'm not calling you away from something important?"

"Not at all," Nash assured him. It might have been his imagination, but Stackhouse's attitude seemed unusually friendly. Although they were always polite to each other, he wasn't John's favorite, not the way Paul Jefferson was. But then, Paul wasn't prone to disagree with anyone who could advance his career.

"I have a divorce I want you to handle," his boss said casually.

These cases were often assigned to him. He'd built his reputation on them. Lately, though, they hadn't held his interest and he was hoping to diversify.

"This man is a friend of mine by the name of Don Griffin. It's a sad case, very sad." John paused, shaking his head.

"Don Griffin," Nash repeated. The name was familiar, but he couldn't place it.

"You might have heard of him. Don owns a chain of seafood restaurants throughout the Pacific Northwest."

"I think I read something about him not long ago."

"You might have," John agreed. "He's mentioned in the paper every now and then. But getting back to the divorce… Don and Janice have been married a lot of years. They have two college-age children and then Janice learned a few years back that she was pregnant. You can imagine their shock."

Nash nodded sympathetically.

"Unfortunately the child has Down syndrome. This came as a second blow, and Don took it hard. So did Janice."

Nash couldn't blame the couple for that. "They're divorcing?"

"Yes." John's expression was filled with regret. "I don't know all the details, but apparently Janice was devoting all her time and attention to little Amy and, well, in a moment of weakness, Don got involved with another woman. Janice found out and filed for divorce."

"I see. And is this what Don wants?"

The senior partner's face tightened with disappointment. "Apparently so. I'm asking you, as a personal favor, to handle this case, representing Don. My late wife and I were good friends with both Don and Janice."

"I'll help in any way I can," Nash said, but without real enthusiasm. Another divorce case, more lives ripped apart. He'd anesthetize his feelings as best he could and struggle to work out the necessary details, but only because John had asked him.

"I'll make an appointment to have Don come in for the initial consultation Friday morning, if that's agreeable?" Once more he made it a question, as if he expected Nash to decline.

This was the first personal favor Stackhouse had ever asked of him.

"I'll be happy to take the case," Nash said again. So he'd been wrong; this had nothing to do with Savannah.

"Good." John reached for his phone. "I'll let Don know I got him the best divorce attorney in town."

"Thank you." Compliments were few and far between from the eldest of the senior partners. Nash suspected he should feel encouraged that the older man trusted him with a family friend.

On his way out of the office, Nash ran into Arnold Serle. "Nash," the other man said, his face lighting up. "I haven't seen you all week."

"I've been in court."

"So I heard. I just wanted you to know how much I enjoyed your sister's wedding."

"We enjoyed having you." So he wasn't going to escape hearing about Savannah after all.

"How's Savannah?" Arnold asked eagerly.

"Very well. I'll tell her you asked about her."

"Please do. My niece is thinking about getting married. I'd like to steer her to Savannah's shop. If your sister's wedding is evidence of the kind of work Savannah does, I'd like to hire her myself." He chuckled then. "I sincerely hope you appreciate what a special woman she is."

"I do."

"Pleased to hear it," Arnold said, grinning broadly.

By Thursday evening, Nash had run through the full range of emotions. Knowing he'd be seeing Savannah later was both a curse and a blessing. He looked forward to being with her and at the same time dreaded it.

He got there right at six. Savannah was sitting at her desk, apparently working on her computer; she didn't hear him enter the shop because she didn't look up. She was probably entertaining second thoughts of her own.

"Savannah." He said her name lightly, not wanting to frighten her.

She jerked her head up, surprise written on her face. But it wasn't the shock in her eyes that unnerved him, it was the tears.

"It's Thursday," he reminded her. "We have a date."

Nash wondered if she'd forgotten.

"Are you going to tell me what's upset you so much?" he asked.

"No," she said with a warm smile, the welcome in her eyes belying her distress. "I'm glad to see you, Nash. I could do with a friend just now."

8

Savannah hadn't forgotten about her date with Nash. She'd thought of little else in the preceding days, wondering if she should put any credence in his asking. One thing she knew about Nash Davenport—he wasn't the type to suggest something he didn't want.

"I had the deli pack us dinner," he told her. "I hope you're hungry."

"I am," she said, wiping the last tears from her face. Nash was studying her with undisguised curiosity and she was grateful he didn't press her for details. She wouldn't have known how to explain, wouldn't have found the words to tell him about the sadness and guilt she felt.

"Where are we going?" she asked, locking the shop. If ever there was a time she needed to get away, to abandon her woes and have fun, it was now.

"Lake Sammamish."

The large lake east of Lake Washington was a well-known and well-loved picnic area. Savannah had been there several times over the years, mostly in the autumn, when she went to admire the spectacular display of fall color. She enjoyed walking along the shore and feeding the ducks.

"I brought a change of clothes," she said. "It'll only take me a minute to get out of this suit."

"Don't rush. We aren't in any hurry."

Savannah moved into the dressing room and replaced her business outfit with jeans and a large sweatshirt with Einstein's image. She'd purchased it earlier in the week with this outing in mind. When she returned, she discovered Nash examining a silk wedding dress adorned with a pearl yoke. She smiled to herself, remembering the first time he'd entered her shop and the way he'd avoided getting close to anything that hinted of romance. He'd come a long way in the past few months, further than he realized, much further than she'd expected.

"This gown arrived from New York this afternoon. It's lovely, isn't it?"

She thought he'd shrug and back away, embarrassed that she'd commented on his noticing something as symbolic of love as a wedding dress.

"It's beautiful. Did one of your clients order it?"

"No. It's from a designer I've worked with in the past and I fell in love with it myself. I do that every once in a while— order a dress that appeals to me personally. Generally they sell, and if they don't, there's always the possibility of renting it out."

"Not this one," he said in a voice so low, she had to strain to hear him. He seemed mesmerized by the dress.

"Why not?" she asked.

"This is the type of wedding gown…" He hesitated.

"Yes?" she prompted.

"When a man sees the woman he loves wearing this dress, he'll cherish the memory forever."

Savannah couldn't believe what she was hearing. This was Nash? The man who'd ranted and raved that love was a wasted emotion? The man who claimed marriage was for the deluded?

"That's so romantic," Savannah murmured. "If you don't object, I'd like to advertise it that way."

Nash's eyes widened and he shook his head. "You want to use that in an ad?"

"If you don't mind. I won't mention your name, unless you want me to."

"No! I mean… Can we just drop this?"

"Of course. I'm sorry, I didn't mean to embarrass you."

"You didn't," he said, when it was clear that she had. "I seem to have done this to myself." He made a point of looking at his watch. "Are you ready?"

Savannah nodded. This could prove to be an interesting picnic.…

They drove to Lake Sammamish in Nash's car and he seemed extra talkative. "Arnold Serle asked about you the other day," he told her as he wove in and out of traffic.

"He's a darling," Savannah said, savoring the memories of the two older men who'd worked so hard to bolster her self-confidence, vying for her the way they had. "Mr. Stackhouse, too," she added.

"You certainly made an impression on them."

Although the night had ended in disaster, she would always treasure it. Dancing with John and Arnold. Dancing with Nash…

"What's the smile about?" Nash asked, momentarily taking his eyes off the road.

"It's nothing."

"The tears were nothing, too?"

The tears. She'd almost forgotten she'd been crying when he arrived. "I was talking to my parents this afternoon," she said as the misery returned. "It's always the same. They talk about traveling, but they never seem to leave Seattle. Instead of really enjoying life, they smother me with their sympathy and their sacrifices, as if that could bring back the full use of my leg." She was speaking fast and furiously, and not until she'd finished did she realize how close she was to weeping again.

Nash's hand touched hers for a moment. "You're a mature adult, living independently of them," he said. "You have for years."

"Which I've explained so many times, I get angry just thinking about it. Apparently they feel that if something were to happen, no one would be here to take care of me."

"What about other relatives?"

"There aren't any in the Seattle area. I try to reassure them that I'm fine, that no disasters are about to strike and even if one did, I have plenty of friends to call on, but they just won't leave."

"Was that what upset you this afternoon?" he asked.

Savannah dropped her gaze to her hands, now clenched tightly in her lap. "They've decided to stay in Seattle this winter. Good friends of theirs asked if they'd travel with them, leaving the second week of September and touring the South before spending the winter in Arizona. My dad's always wanted to visit New Orleans and Atlanta. They said they'll go another year," Savannah muttered, "but I know they won't. They know it, too."

"Your parents love you. I understand their concern."

"How can you say that?" she demanded angrily. "They're doing this because they feel guilty about my accident. Now I'm the one who's carrying that load. When will it ever end?"

"I don't know," he said quietly.

"I just wish they loved me enough to trust me to take care of myself. I've been doing exactly that for a long time now."

Nodding, he exited the freeway and took the road leading into Lake Sammamish State Park. He drove around until he found a picnic table close to the parking lot. The gesture was a thoughtful one; he didn't want her to have a long way to walk.

It might not be very subtle, but Savannah didn't care. She was determined to enjoy their outing. She needed this. She knew it was dangerous to allow herself this luxury. She was well aware that Nash could be out of her life with little notice. That was something she'd always taken into account in other relationships, but her guard had slipped with Nash.

He helped her out of the car and carried the wicker basket to the bright blue picnic table. The early evening was filled with a symphony of pleasant sounds. Birds chirped in a nearby tree, their song mingling with the laughter of children.

"I'm starved," Nash said, peering inside the basket. He raised his head and waggled his eyebrows. "My, oh, my, what goodies."

Savannah spread a tablecloth across one end of the table and Nash handed her a large loaf of French bread, followed by a bottle of red wine.

"That's for show," he said, grinning broadly. "This is for dinner." He took out a bucket of fried chicken and a six-pack of soda.

"I thought you said the deli packed this."

"They did. I made a list of what I wanted and they packed it in the basket for me."

"You're beginning to sound like a tricky defense attorney," she said, enjoying this easy banter between them. It helped take her mind off her parents and their uncomfortable conversation that afternoon.

They sat across from each other and with a chicken leg in front of her mouth, Savannah looked out over the blue-green water. The day was perfect. Not too warm and not too cool. The sun was shining and a gentle breeze rippled off the lake. A lifeguard stood sentinel over a group of preschool children splashing in the water between bursts of laughter. Farther out, a group of teens dived off a large platform. Another group circled the lake in two-seater pedal boats, their wake disrupting the serenity of the water.

"You're looking thoughtful," Nash commented.

Savannah blushed, a little embarrassed to be caught so enraptured with the scene before her. "When I was a teenager I used to dream a boy would ask me to pedal one of the boats with him."

"Did anyone?"

"No…." A sadness attached itself to her heart, dredging up the memories of a difficult youth. "I can't pedal."

"Why not? You danced, didn't you?"

"Yes, but that's different."

"How?"

"Don't you remember what happened after the dance?"

"We could rent a pedal boat and I'll do the work," he said. "You just sit back and enjoy the ride."

She lowered her gaze, not wanting him to see how badly she longed to do what he'd suggested.

"Come on," he wheedled. "It'll be fun."

"We'd go around in circles," she countered. She wasn't willing to try. "It won't work if we don't each do our share of the pedaling. I appreciate what you're doing, but I simply can't hold up my part."

"You won't know that until you try," he said. "Remember, you didn't want to dance, either." His reminder was a gentle one and it hit its mark.

"We might end up looking like idiots."

"So? It's happened before. To me, anyway." He stood and offered her his hand. "You game or not?"

She stared up at him, and indecision kept her rooted to the table. "I don't know if it's a good idea."

"Come on, Savannah, prove to me that you can do this. But more importantly, prove it to yourself. I'm not going to let you overdo it, I promise."

His confidence was contagious. "If you're implying that you could've kept me off the dance floor, think again. I danced every dance."

"Don't remind me. The only way I could dance with you was to cut in on someone else. At least this way I'll have you to myself."

Savannah placed her hand firmly in his, caught up in his smile.

"If anyone else comes seeking the pleasure of your company this time," he said, "they'll have to swim."

Savannah's mood had been painfully introspective when Nash arrived. Now, for the first time in what seemed like days, she experienced the overwhelming urge to laugh. Hugging Nash was a spontaneous reaction to the lightheartedness she felt with him.

He stiffened when her arms went around him, but recovered quickly, gripping her about her waist, picking her up and twirling her around until she had to beg him to stop. Breathless, she gazed at him, and said, "You make me want to sing."

"You make me want to—"

"What?" she asked.

"Sing," he muttered, relaxing his hold enough for her feet to touch the ground.

Savannah could have sworn his ears turned red. "I make you want to do what?" she pressed.

"Never mind, Savannah," he answered. "It's better that you don't know. And please, just this once, is it too much to ask that you don't argue with me?"

"Fine," she said, pretending to be gravely disappointed. She mocked him with a deep sigh.

They walked down to the water's edge, where Nash paid for the rental of a small pedal boat. He helped her board and then joined her, the boat rocking precariously as he shifted his weight.

Savannah held tightly to her seat. She remained skeptical of this idea, convinced they were going to look like a pair of idiots once they left the shore. She didn't mind being laughed at, but she didn't want him laughed at because of her.

"I...don't think we should do this," she whispered, struck by an attack of cowardice.

"I'm not letting you out of this now. We haven't even tried."

"I'll embarrass you."

"Let me worry about that."

"Nash, please."

He refused to listen to her and began working the pedals, making sure the pace he set wasn't too much for her. Water rustled behind them and Savannah jerked around to see the paddle wheel churning up the water. Before she realized it, they were speeding along.

"We're moving," she shouted. "We're actually moving."

It seemed that everyone on the shore had turned to watch them. In sheer delight, Savannah waved her arms. "We're actually moving."

"I think they've got the general idea," Nash teased.

"I could just kiss you," Savannah said, resisting the urge to throw her arms around his neck and do exactly that.

"You'll need to wait a few minutes." His hand reached for hers and he entwined their fingers.

"Let's go fast," she urged, cautiously pumping her feet. "I want to see how fast we can go."

"Savannah...no."

"Yes, please, just for a little bit."

He groaned and then complied. The blades of the paddle behind them churned the water into a frothy texture as they shot ahead. Nash was doing most of the work. Her efforts were puny compared to his, but it didn't seem to matter. This was more fun than she'd dared to dream. As much fun as dancing.

Savannah laughed boisterously. "I never knew," she said, squeezing his upper arm with both hands and pressing her head against his shoulder. "I never thought I could do this."

"There's a whole world out there just waiting to be explored."

"I want to skydive next," Savannah said gleefully.

"Skydive?"

"All right, roller-skate. I wanted to so badly when I was growing up. I used to skate before the accident, you know. I was pretty good, too."

"I'm sure you were."

"All my life I've felt hindered because of my leg and suddenly all these possibilities are opening up to me." She went from one emotional extreme to the other. First joy and laughter and now tears and sadness. "Meeting you was the best thing that's ever happened to me," she said, and sniffled. "I could cry, I'm so happy."

Nash stiffened and Savannah wondered if she'd offended him. His reaction would have been imperceptible if they hadn't been sitting side by side.

Nash was pedaling harder now; her own feet were set in motion by his efforts. "Where are we going?" she asked, noting that he seemed to be steering the craft toward shore. She didn't want to stop, not when they were just getting started. This was her one fear, that she'd embarrass him, and apparently she had.

"See that weeping willow over on the far side of the bank?" he asked, motioning down the shoreline. She did, noting the branches draped over the water like a sanctuary. It appeared to be on private property.

"Yes."

"We're headed there."

"Why?" she asked, thinking of any number of plausible reasons. Perhaps he knew the people who lived there and wanted to stop and say hello.

"Because that weeping willow offers a little more privacy than out here on the lake. And I intend to take you up on your offer, because frankly, I'm not going to be able to wait much longer."

Offer, she mused. What offer?

Nash seemed to enjoy her dilemma and raised her hand to his mouth, kissing the inside of her palm. "I seem to remember you saying you wanted to kiss me. So I'm giving you the opportunity."

"Now?"

"In a moment." He steered the boat under the drooping limbs of the tree. The dense growth cut off the sunlight and cooled the late-afternoon air.

Nash stopped and the boat settled, motionless, in the water. He turned to her and his gaze slid across her face.

"Has anyone ever told you how beautiful you are?"

Besides him and her parents? And they had to praise her, didn't they? No one. Not ever. "No."

"Is the rest of the world blind?"

His words were followed by silence. A silence that spanned years for Savannah. No man had looked past her flaw and seen the desirable woman she longed to be. No man but Nash.

His mouth came down on hers, shattering the silence with his hungry need, shattering the discipline she'd held herself under all these years. She wrapped herself in his embrace and returned the kiss with the potency of her own need.

Nash moaned and kissed her hard, and she responded with every ounce of her being. She kissed him as if she'd been waiting all her life for this moment, this man. In ways too numerous to count, she had been.

She moaned softly, thinking nothing seemed enough. Nash made her greedy. She wanted more. More of life. More of laughter. More of him.

Dragging his mouth from hers, he trailed a row of moist kisses down her neck. "If we were anyplace but here, do you know what we'd be doing now?"

"I… I think so." How odd her voice sounded.

"We'd be in bed making love."

"I…"

"What?" he prompted. "Were you about to tell me you can't? Because I'll be more than happy to prove otherwise." He directed her mouth back to his.... Then, slowly, reluctantly, as though remembering this was a public place and they could be interrupted at any time, he ended the kiss.

Savannah had more difficulty than Nash in returning to sanity. She needed the solid reality of him close to her. When he eased himself from her arms, his eyes searched out hers.

"If you say that shouldn't have happened, I swear I'll do something crazy," she whispered.

"I don't think I could make myself say it."

"Good," she breathed.

Nash pressed his forehead to hers. "I wish I knew what it is you do to me." She sensed that it troubled him that she could break through that facade of his. She was beginning to understand this man. She was physically handicapped, but Nash was crippled, too. He didn't want love, but he couldn't keep himself from needing it, from caring about her, and that worried him. It worried her, too.

"You don't like what I do to you." That much was obvious, but she wanted to hear him admit it.

Nash gave a short laugh. "That's the problem, I like it too much. There's never been anyone who affects me this way. Not since Denise."

"Your ex-wife?"

"Yes." He regretted mentioning her name, Savannah guessed, because he made a point of changing the subject immediately afterward.

"We should go back to the pier."

"Not yet," Savannah pleaded. "Not so soon. We just got started."

"I don't want you to strain your leg. You aren't accustomed to this much exercise."

"I won't, I promise. Just a little while longer." This was so much fun, she didn't want it to ever end. It wasn't every day that she could turn a dream into reality. It wasn't every day a man kissed her as if she were his cherished love.

Love. Love. Love. The word repeated itself in her mind. She was falling in love with Nash. It had begun weeks earlier, the first time he'd kissed her, and had been growing little by little. Love was a dangerous emotion when it came to Nash. He wouldn't be an easy man to care about.

He steered them away from the tree and into the sunlight. Savannah squinted against the glare, but it didn't seem to affect Nash. He pedaled now as if he was escaping something. The fun was gone.

"I'm ready to go back," Savannah said after several minutes of silence.

"Good." He didn't bother to disguise his relief.

The mood had changed so abruptly that Savannah had trouble taking it all in. Nash couldn't seem to get back to shore fast enough. He helped her out of the boat and placed his arm, grudgingly it seemed, around her waist to steady her. Once he was confident she had her balance, he released her.

"I think we should leave," he said when they returned to the picnic table.

"Sure," she agreed, disappointed and sad. She folded up the tablecloth and handed it to him. He carried the basket to the car and loaded it in the trunk.

Savannah knew what was coming; she'd been through it before. Whenever a man feared he was becoming—or might become—emotionally attached to her, she could count on the same speech. Generally it began with what an exceptional woman she was, talented, gifted, fun, that sort of thing. The conclusion, however, was always the same. Someday a special man would come into her life. She'd never expected her relationship with Nash to get even that far. She'd never expected to see him after Susan's wedding. This outing was an unforeseen bonus.

They were on the freeway, driving toward Seattle, before Savannah found the courage to speak. It would help if she broached the subject first.

"Thank you, Nash, for a lovely picnic."

He said nothing, which was just as well.

"I know what you're thinking," she said, clasping her hands tightly together.

"I doubt that."

She smiled to herself. "I've seen this happen with other men, so you don't need to worry about it."

"Worry about what?"

"You're attracted to me and that frightens you—probably more than the other men I've dated because a woman you once loved has deeply hurt you."

"I said I don't want to talk about Denise."

"I'm not going to ask about her, if that's what concerns you," she said quickly, wanting to relieve him about that. "I'm going to talk about us. You may not realize it now, but I'm saving you the trouble of searching for the right words."

He jerked his head away from traffic and scowled at her. "I beg your pardon?"

"You heard me right. You see, it's all familiar to me, so you needn't worry about it. This isn't the first time."

"It isn't?" The question was heavy with sarcasm.

"I've already explained it's happened before."

"Go on. I'd be interested in hearing this." The hard muscles of his face relaxed and the beginnings of a smile came into play.

"You like me."

"That should be fairly obvious," he commented.

"I like you, too."

"That's a comfort." The sarcastic edge was back, but it wasn't as biting.

"In fact, you're starting to like me a little too much."

"I'm not sure what that means, but go on."

"We nearly made love once."

"Twice," he corrected. "We were closer than you think a few minutes ago."

"Under a tree in a pedal boat?" she asked with a laugh.

"Trust me, honey, where there's a will, there's a way."

Savannah blushed and looked pointedly away. "Let's not get sidetracked."

"Good idea."

He was flustering her, distracting her train of thought. "It becomes a bit uncomfortable whenever a man finds me attractive."

"Why's that?"

"Because...well, because they have to deal with my problem, and most people are more comfortable ignoring it. If you deny that there's anything different, it might go away."

"Have I done that?" This question was more serious than the others.

"No," she admitted. "You've been accepting of my...defect. I'm just not sure—"

"I've never viewed you as defective," he interrupted.

It seemed important to him that she acknowledge that, so she did. "I'm grateful to have met you, Nash, grateful for the fun we've had."

"This is beginning to sound like a brush-off."

"It is," she murmured. "Like I said, I'm saving you the trouble of coming up with an excuse for not seeing me again. This is the better-to-be-honest-now-instead-of-cruel-later scenario."

"Saving me the trouble," he exploded, and then burst into gales of laughter. "So that's what this is all about."

"Yes. You can't tell me that isn't what you were thinking. I know the signs, Nash. Things got a bit intense between us and now you're getting cold feet. It happened the night of Susan's wedding, too. We didn't make love and you were grateful, remember?"

He didn't agree or disagree.

"Just now…at the lake, we kissed, and you could feel it happening a second time, and that's dangerous. You couldn't get away from me fast enough."

"That's not entirely true."

"Your mood certainly changed."

"Okay, I'll concede that, but not for the reasons you're assuming. My mood changed because I started thinking about something and frankly it threw me for a loop."

"Thinking about what?" she pressed.

"A solution."

"To what?"

"Hold on, Savannah, because I don't know how you're going to react. Probably about the same way I did."

"Go on," she urged.

"It seems to me…"

"Yes?" she said when he didn't immediately finish.

"It seems to me that we might want to think about getting married."

9

"Married," Savannah repeated in a husky whisper.

Nash knew he'd shocked her, but no more than he had himself. The notion of marriage went against the grain. Something was either very wrong—or very right. He hadn't decided yet.

"I don't understand." Savannah shook her head, making a vague gesture with her hands.

"Unfortunately, I don't know if I'll do a decent job of explaining it," Nash said.

"Try." Her hands were at her throat now, fingering the collar of her sweatshirt.

"This could work, Savannah, with a little effort on both our parts."

"Marriage? You hate the very word.... I've never met anyone with a more jaded attitude toward love and romance. Is this some kind of joke?"

"Trust me. I was just as shocked at the idea as you are, but the more I thought about it, the more sense it made. I wish it was a joke." Nash's choice of words must have been poor because Savannah recoiled from him. "It would be a marriage of convenience," he added, hoping that might reassure her—or at least not scare her off.

"What?" she cried. "In other words, you intend to take what I consider sacred and make a mockery of it."

It was difficult not to be defensive when Savannah was acting so unreasonable. "If you'll listen, you might see there are advantages for both of us."

"Take me back to my shop," she said in a icy voice.

"I'm going there now, but I was hoping we could talk first."

She said nothing, which didn't bode well. Nash wanted to explain, ease her mind, ease his own, but he wasn't sure he could. He'd spoken prematurely without giving the matter sufficient consideration. It was after they'd kissed under the weeping willow that the idea had occurred to him. It had shocked him so completely that for a time he could barely function. He'd needed to escape and now that they were on their way back into Seattle, he realized he needed to talk this over with her.

"I know this comes as a surprise," he said, looking for a way to broach the subject once again. He exited from the freeway and was within a mile of Savannah's shop.

Savannah looked steadfastly out the window, as if the houses they were passing mesmerized her.

"Say something," Nash demanded. He drove into the alley where her car was parked and turned off the engine. He kept his hands tightly on the steering wheel.

"You wouldn't want to hear what I'm thinking," Savannah told him through clenched teeth.

"Maybe not," he agreed. "But would you listen to what I have to say?"

She crossed her arms and glared at him. "I don't know if I can and keep a straight face."

"Try," he said, just as she had earlier.

"All right, go on, explain." She closed her eyes.

"When I came to pick you up this afternoon, you were upset."

She shrugged, unwilling to acknowledge even that much. It

wasn't an encouraging sign. He'd been premature in mentioning marriage. He wasn't sure why he'd considered it so urgent that he couldn't take the night to sleep on it first. Perhaps he was afraid he'd change his mind. Perhaps this was what he'd always wanted, and he needed to salvage his pride with the marriage-of-convenience proposal. Either way, it didn't matter; he'd already shown his hand.

"You love your parents and want them to go after their dream, isn't that right?"

"Would you simply make your point?"

"Fine, I will," he said, his argument gaining momentum. "I'm offering you the perfect solution. You marry me."

"In other words, you're suggesting we mislead my parents into believing this is a love match?"

"I hadn't thought of it in those terms, but, yes, I guess we would be misleading them. If that makes you uncomfortable, tell them the truth. Keep your maiden name if you want. That wouldn't bother me at all. The point is, if you were married, your father and mother would feel free to move south for the winters the way they've always wanted."

"What's in this for you?" she demanded. "Don't try to tell me you're doing it out of the goodness of your heart, either. I know better."

"You're right, there're advantages to me, too."

She snickered softly. "Somehow I thought there would be."

"That's the beauty of my idea," he said, trying to keep his irritation in check. Savannah was treating this like a joke while he was dead serious. A man didn't mention the word *marriage* lightly. Nash had been through this before, but this time marriage would be on his terms.

"Go on," Savannah snapped.

"As I said, there are certain advantages in this marriage for me, as well. The night of Susan's wedding, John Stackhouse pulled me aside and told me that I was being considered for the position of senior partner."

"But it would help if you were married."

Savannah wasn't slow-witted, that was for sure. "Something like that," he admitted. "It seems the other senior partners are afraid that my bitterness about my own divorce has spilled over into other areas of my life."

"Imagine that."

Nash tried to hide his annoyance. Savannah was making this extremely difficult.

"There're no guarantees for either of us, of course. If you agree to the terms of this marriage, that doesn't mean your parents will pack up and head south. If we did go ahead with it, there's nothing to say I'll be made senior partner. There's an element of risk for us both. You might get what you want and I might not. Or vice versa."

"Ah, now I understand," Savannah said in a slow, singsong voice. "That's where the convenience part comes into play. You want an out."

"That has nothing to do with it," Nash flared.

"Do you think I'm stupid, Nash? Of course it does. No one wants a cripple for a wife," she said furiously, "and if you can put an escape clause in the marriage contract, all the better."

"That's ridiculous! It has nothing to do with this."

"Would you have proposed marriage to any other woman this way, suggesting a short-term relationship for the sake of convenience? Heaven forbid that you might feel some genuine affection for me!"

It took Nash a moment to compose himself. He'd acted on impulse, which was not only uncharacteristic but a huge mistake, one that had only led to greater confusion. "Maybe this wasn't such a bright idea after all," he began. "I should've ironed out the details before talking to you about it. If you want to find fault with me for that, then I'll accept it with a heartfelt apology, but this business about me using you because I consider you less of a woman—you couldn't be more wrong. Your suggestion insults us both."

"Why do I have a hard time believing that?" Savannah asked. She sounded suspiciously close to tears, which grieved him more than her anger had.

"All I'm looking for here is a way of being fair to us both," Nash argued. "Despite what you think, I didn't mean to insult you."

"I'm sure you didn't. You're probably thinking people will admire you. Imagine Nash Davenport taking pity on that—"

"Savannah, stop." He pressed his lips tightly together. She was making a mockery of his proposal, a mockery of herself.

"Are you saying I'm wrong?"

His self-control was stretched to the limit. "Don't even suggest that," he said.

"I have to go," Savannah whispered. She turned from him, her fingers closing around the door handle. "It'd be best if we didn't see each other again."

Nash knew that the minute she left his car it would be over between them. He couldn't allow that to happen, couldn't let her leave, not without righting the wrong. He needed to do something, anything, to convince her he was sincere.

"Not yet," Nash said, taking her by the shoulder.

"Let go of me."

"Not without this." He locked his arms around her waist and pulled her against him.

She didn't resist, not for a second. Her own arms crept around his neck, and then they were kissing again, with the same passion as before.

He didn't know how long they were in each other's arms—or what brought him back to sanity. Possibly a noise from the street, or Savannah herself. He jerked his head up and buried his face in her shoulder, which was heaving with the strength of her reaction. Her fingers were buried in his hair.

"I find it amazing," she whispered brokenly, "that you're looking for a marriage in name only."

He wasn't sure if she was being humorous or not, but he wasn't taking any chances. "We might need to revise that part of the agreement."

"There won't be any agreement, Nash."

He was afraid of that. "Would you kindly listen to reason, Savannah? I wasn't trying to insult you... I thought you'd like the idea."

"Think again." She was breathing deeply, clearly fighting to regain her composure.

"Are you willing to listen to reason?" he asked again, hoping he'd reached her, if on no other level than the physical.

"I've had to deal with a certain amount of cruelty in my life," she said in a low voice. "Children are often brutal with their taunts and their name-calling. It was something I became accustomed to as a child. It hurt. Sticks and stones may break your bones, but words cut far deeper."

"Savannah, stop." That she'd compare his proposal to the ridicule she'd endured as a child was too painful to hear.

She stiffened, her back straight. "I don't want to see you again."

The words hit him hard. "Why not?"

She opened the car door and stepped awkwardly into the alley. Her leg seemed to be bothering her and with some effort she shifted her weight. "I don't trust myself with you... and I don't trust you with me. I've got to take care of myself."

"I want to help you, not hurt you," he insisted.

She hung her head and Nash suspected she did so to hide the fact that she was crying. "Goodbye, Nash. Please don't try to see me again.... Don't make this any more difficult than it already is."

★ ★ ★

Two weeks later, Nash's sister, Susan, strolled into Savannah's shop. Savannah felt a sense of awe at the happiness that shone from the young woman's eyes.

"What are you doing here?" she asked. "You're supposed to be on your honeymoon."

"We've been back for several days."

Following the wedding, Savannah rarely saw her clients. Whenever someone made the effort to stop in, it was a special treat. More so with Susan because Savannah had been so actively involved in the wedding. Actively involved with Nash, if she was willing to be honest, which at the moment she wasn't.

"You look—" Savannah searched for the right word "—serene." The two women hugged and Savannah held her friend tightly as unexpected tears moistened her eyes. She didn't allow them to fall, not wanting Susan to see how emotional she'd become. "I've missed you," she said. She had, but more than that, she'd missed Nash.

"Nash said the same thing. You both knew before I was married that I'd be moving to California with Kurt. Now you're acting like it's a big shock. By the way, Kurt sends his love."

Savannah eased from Susan's embrace. "What are you doing back in Seattle so soon? Kurt's with you, isn't he?"

"Why I'm here is a long story. As to your second question, Kurt couldn't come. With the wedding and the honeymoon, he couldn't get away. It's the first time we've been apart since the wedding and I miss him dreadfully." A wistful look came over her.

"What brings you to Seattle?"

Susan hesitated just a fraction of a second. "Nash."

So her big brother had sent her. This was exactly what she should have expected from Nash. The man wasn't fair—he'd use any means at his disposal to achieve his purpose.

"He doesn't know I'm here," Susan said as if reading Savannah's thoughts. "He'd be furious if he ever found out. I phoned him when Kurt and I got home from our honeymoon and he said he was having several pieces of furniture shipped to us. Things that belonged to our parents. I was a little surprised, since we're living in a small apartment and don't have much space. Nash knows that. Kurt talked to him, too, and afterward we agreed something was wrong. The best way to handle the situation was for me to visit."

"I see." Savannah made busywork around her desk, turning off her computer, straightening papers, rearranging pens in their holder. "How is Nash?"

"Miserable. I don't know why and he's doing an admirable job of pretending otherwise. He's spending a lot of time at the office. Apparently he's tied up with an important case."

"Divorce?" Savannah asked unnecessarily. That was his specialty—driving a wedge deeper and deeper between two people who'd once loved each other, increasing misery and heartache. Each divorce he handled lent credence to his pessimistic views. That wasn't going to change, and she was a fool if she believed otherwise.

"You might have read about this case. It's the one with Don Griffin, the man who owns all those great seafood restaurants. It's really sad."

Savannah did remember reading something about it. Apparently Mr. Griffin had an affair with a much younger woman. It was a story as old as time. She hadn't realized Nash was involved, but should have. He was Seattle's top divorce attorney, and naturally a man as wealthy and influential as Don Griffin would hire the very best.

"I know the case," Savannah admitted.

"Nash's been working late every night." Susan paused and waited for Savannah to comment.

"He enjoys his work."

"He used to, but I'm not so sure anymore. Something's really bothering him."

Their conversation was making Savannah uncomfortable. "I'm sorry to hear that."

"It's more than what's going on at the law firm, though. Kurt and I both think it has something to do with you, but when I asked him, Nash nearly bit my head off. He wouldn't even talk about you."

Savannah smiled to herself. "Neither will I. Sometimes it's better to leave well enough alone. We both appreciate your love and support, but what's going on between Nash and me is our own business. Leave it at that, please."

"All right." Susan wasn't happy about it, Savannah could tell, but the last thing she and Nash wanted or needed was Susan and Kurt meddling in their lives. Susan looked regretfully at the time. "I have to get back. The movers are coming this afternoon. I'm not taking much—we simply don't have room for it. And with the stuff Nash is shipping… I don't know why he insisted on sending us the rocking horse. Dad built it for him when he was a little kid and it was understood that Nash would hand it down to his own children. It's been in the basement for years. I don't know why he sent it to me. Kurt and I aren't planning to start a family for a couple of years. Men just don't make sense sometimes."

"You're only discovering that now?" Savannah teased.

Susan laughed. "I should know better after living with my brother all those years."

They hugged and Susan left shortly afterward.

The day was exceptionally slow, and with time on her hands, Savannah sat at her desk and drew a design for a flower arrangement. Intent on her task, she worked for several minutes before she saw that it wasn't a flower arrangement that was taking shape, but a child's rocking horse.

★ ★ ★

"What do you mean Janice turned down our settlement proposal?" Don Griffin shouted. He propelled his large frame from the chair across from Nash's desk and started pacing. His movements were abrupt and disjointed. "It was a fair offer, more than fair. You said so yourself."

"That's how these things work, Mr. Griffin. As I explained earlier, if you'll recall, it was unlikely that your wife and her attorney would accept our first offer. It's just the way the game's played. Your wife's attorney wouldn't be earning his fee if he didn't raise some objections."

"How much longer is this going to drag on?" his client demanded. "I want this over with quickly. Give Janice what she wants. If she insists on taking control of the restaurants, fine, she can have them. She can have the house, the cars, our investments, too, for all I care."

"I can't allow you to do that."

"Why not?" He slammed his hand down on the desk.

"You've hired me to represent you in a court of law, to look after your interests. If you make a decision now based on emotion, you'll regret it later. These matters take time."

"I haven't got time," the tall, stocky man said. Don Griffin was in his fifties, and beginning to show his age.

"Is there a reason we need to rush?" Nash hated surprises. If Don's ex-girlfriend was pregnant, he didn't want to find out about it in the courtroom.

"Yes!" the other man shouted. "There's a very good reason. I hate this constant fighting, hate having my reputation raked over the coals in the press. Twenty-seven years of marriage— and after one indiscretion, Janice makes me look like a serial murderer. The restaurant's receipts actually dropped ten percent after that story was leaked."

Nash didn't know who was responsible for that, but he could make an educated guess. Janice Griffin's attorney, Tony Pound, stirred up controversy whenever possible, especially if it helped his case.

Nash made a note of the lost revenue and decided that when he phoned Tony later this afternoon, he'd tell him Janice's compensation might not be as big as she'd hoped—not if the business failed due to negative publicity.

"If it goes on like this," Don continued, "we may be filing for bankruptcy next."

"I'll make sure Mr. Pound learns this."

"Good, and while you're at it," Don said, waving his finger at Nash, "do what you can about me seeing my daughter. Janice can't keep me away from Amy, and this bull about me being a negative influence on our daughter is exactly that—bull."

"I'll arrange visitation rights for you as soon as I can."

"See if I can have her this weekend. I'm going to the beach and Amy's always loved the beach."

"I'll see what I can do. Is there anything else?"

His client paced, rubbing his hands together. "Have you seen my wife and daughter recently?" he asked.

"No. That would be highly unusual. Is there a reason you're asking?"

"I... I was just wondering how they looked, that's all. If they're well."

It was there in his eyes, Nash saw, the way it always was. The pain, the loneliness, the sense of loss so strong it brought powerful men and women to their knees. Nash thought of these moments when clients realized they were about to lose what they'd once considered their anchor. The chains were broken. With the anchors gone, it became a struggle to keep from drifting. Storms rose up, and that was when Nash learned the truth about his clients. Some weathered these tempests and came out stronger and more confident. Others struggled to stay afloat and eventually drowned.

Sadly, he didn't know which kind of person Don Griffin would prove to be.

★ ★ ★

The urgency in her father's voice frightened Savannah. His phone call came during her busiest time of day. It took her a moment to decipher what he was saying.

"Mom's in the hospital?" Savannah repeated. Her blood ran cold at the thought.

"Yes." Her father, who was always so calm and collected, was near panic. "She collapsed at home.... I didn't know what to do so I called an aid car and they've brought her to the hospital. The doctors are with her now."

"I'll be there in five minutes," Savannah promised. Fortunately, Nancy had come in to help her, so she didn't have to close the shop.

She'd always hated the smell of hospitals, she thought as she rushed into the emergency entrance of Northend Memorial. It was a smell that resurrected memories she'd pushed to the back of her mind.

Savannah found her father in the emergency waiting room, his shoulders hunched, his eyes empty. "Daddy," she whispered, "what happened?"

"I...don't know. We were working in the yard when your mother called out to me. By the time I turned around she'd passed out. I was afraid for a moment that she was dead. I nearly panicked."

Savannah sat in the seat beside him and reached for his hand.

"I forgot about you not liking hospitals," her father said apologetically.

"It's all right. I wouldn't want to be anyplace else but here with you."

"I'm scared, sweetheart, really scared."

"I know." Savannah was, too. "Have you talked to the doctors yet?"

He shook his head. "How long will it take? She's been in there for over an hour."

"Anytime now, I'm sure." At the moment, Savannah wasn't sure of anything, least of all how her father would cope without her mother if it turned out that something was seriously wrong....

"Mr. Charles." The doctor approached them, his face revealing concern.

Automatically Savannah and her father got to their feet, bracing themselves for whatever he might say.

"Your wife's suffered a stroke."

In the past few weeks, Nash had made a habit of staying late at the office. He no longer liked spending time at the house. It'd been nearly a month since Savannah had been inside his home and he swore that whenever he walked inside, he caught a whiff of her perfume. He knew it was ridiculous, but he'd taken to placing air fresheners at strategic points.

His bed was also a problem. Savannah had left her imprint there, as well. When he woke in the morning, he could sense her presence. He could almost hear her breathing, feel her breath, her mouth scant inches from his own. It bothered him that a woman could have this powerful an effect on him.

She'd meant what she said about ending the relationship. Not that he'd expected to hear from her again. He hoped he would, but that was entirely different from expecting her to call.

More times than he cared to count, he'd resisted the urge to contact her. He'd considered sending flowers with a humorous note, something to break the ice, to salvage his pride and hers, then decided against it.

She'd made herself clear and he had no option but to abide by her wishes. She didn't want to see him again. So she wouldn't. The next move, if there was one, would have to be hers.

As for that absurd proposal of marriage... Seldom had he regretted anything more. It embarrassed him to think about it, so he avoided doing so whenever possible.

Someone knocked softly on his office door. He checked his watch, surprised to discover he wasn't alone at 10:00 p.m.

"Come in."

The door opened and Savannah stood there. She was pale, her features ashen, her eyes red-rimmed as if she'd recently been crying.

"Savannah," he said, hurrying around his desk. "What's wrong?" He didn't reach for her, much as he wanted to, not knowing if she'd welcome his touch.

"I've come," she said in a voice that was devoid of emotion, "to tell you I've reconsidered. I'll accept your offer of a marriage of convenience.... That is, if it's still open."

10

"You're sure about this?" Generally Nash wasn't one to look a gift horse in the mouth, but this time was the exception. Something had happened to cause Savannah to change her mind, something drastic. Nash was convinced of that.

"I wouldn't be here if I wasn't sure." Nervously she reached inside her purse and took out a well-creased slip of paper. "I've made up a list of issues we need to discuss first…if you're willing."

"All right." He gestured toward the guest chair and sat down himself. "But first tell me what happened."

"My mother," she began, and paused as her lower lip began to tremble. She needed a moment to compose herself enough to continue speaking. "Mom's in the hospital…. She had a stroke."

"I'm sorry to hear that."

Savannah nodded. "Her prognosis for a complete recovery is excellent, but it frightened me terribly—Dad, too."

"I understand."

"Mom's stroke helped me realize I might not have my parents much longer. I refuse to allow them to sacrifice their dreams because of me."

"I see."

She unfolded the piece of paper in her hands. "Are you ready to discuss the details?"

"By all means." He reached for his gold pen and a fresh legal pad.

"There will be no…lovemaking. You mentioned earlier that you preferred this to be a marriage of convenience, and I'm in full agreement."

That had been a hasty suggestion, certainly not one he'd carefully thought out. In light of their strong physical attraction, Nash didn't believe this stipulation would hold up for more than a few days, a week at the most. The minute he kissed her, or took her in his arms, the chemistry they shared would return.

"You're sure about this?" he asked.

"Positive."

Suggesting they wouldn't be able to keep their hands off each other would inevitably trigger a heated argument. Savannah would accuse him of being arrogant. Nash decided to agree with her for the present and let time prove him right.

"Do you agree?" Her eyes challenged him to defy her.

Nash rolled the pen between his palms and relaxed in his leather chair, not wanting to give her any reason to suspect that he had reservations or what they were. "If a marriage in name only is what you want, then naturally I'll agree to those terms."

"Good." She nodded, much too enthusiastically to suit him.

"Unless we mutually agree otherwise at some point," he added.

Savannah's eyes darted back to his. "I wouldn't count on that if I were you. I'm agreeing to this marriage for one reason and one reason only. I want to be sure you understand that."

"In other words, you don't plan to trick me into falling in love with you." He heard the edge in his own voice and regretted it. Savannah had sacrificed her pride the minute she'd walked through his door; goading wasn't necessary.

"This isn't a game to me, Nash," she said, her voice sharp.

"I'm serious. If you aren't, maybe we should call it quits right now."

"I was the one who suggested this," he reminded her, not bothering to mention that it had been a spur-of-the-moment idea he'd deplored ever since. He stared at Savannah, noting the changes in her. He'd always viewed her as delicate, feminine. But there was a hardness to her now, a self-protective shell. She didn't trust him not to hurt her. Didn't trust him not to destroy her once-unshakable faith in love and marriage.

"I'll draw up the papers to read that this will be a marriage of convenience unless we mutually agree otherwise. Does that wording satisfy you?"

"All right, as long we understand each other." Her gaze fell to her list. "The second item I have here has to do with our living arrangements. I'll move in with you for a brief period of time."

"How brief?" This didn't sound any more encouraging than her first stipulation.

"Until my mother's well enough to travel south. That's the reason I'm willing to go through with this, after all. But to be as fair as possible, I'll stay with you until a senior partner's named."

"I'd appreciate that." The announcement would come within the month, Nash was certain, although it was taking much longer than he'd assumed. He'd like nothing better than to pull a fast one on Paul. The pompous ass would likely leave the firm. Nash smiled just thinking about it.

"After that there won't be any need for us to continue this farce. I'll move back to my home and we can have the marriage, such as it is, dissolved. Of course, I'll make no claims on you financially and expect the same."

"Of course," Nash agreed. Yet this talk of divorce so soon after marriage grated on him. It wouldn't look good to John Stackhouse and Arnold Serle if he was only married for a few weeks. And a quick divorce—any divorce—was the last thing he wanted. "For propriety's sake, I'd like to suggest we stay married a year," he said.

"A year," she repeated, making it sound as long as a lifetime. She sighed. "Fine. I'll accept that, provided we both adhere to all the other conditions."

"Anything else?" he asked, after making a second notation on the legal pad.

"Yes, as a matter of fact, I have a few more points."

Nash groaned inwardly, but presented a calm exterior.

"While I'm living with you, I insist we sleep in separate bedrooms. The less we have to do with each other, the better. You live your life the same as always and I'll live mine."

Nash wrote this down, as well, but made a point of hesitating, making sure she was aware of his uneasiness about this latest dictate. This would be the ideal setup if he was looking for a roommate, but Nash was seeking a deeper commitment.

"Since you mention propriety..." Savannah began.

"Yes?" he prompted when she didn't immediately continue.

"Although our marriage will be one of convenience, I feel strongly that we should practice a certain code of ethics." The words were rushed, as if she thought he'd disagree. "I expect you to stop dating other women," she said, speaking more slowly now. "If I were to discover that you'd been seeing someone else, I would consider that immediate grounds for divorce."

"The same would hold true for you," he returned calmly. It made him wonder what kind of man she thought he was. "If I found out you were interested in another man, then I'd see no reason to continue our agreement."

"That isn't likely to happen," she blurted out defensively.

"Any more than it is with me."

She clamped her mouth shut and Nash guessed she didn't believe him. Where had she gotten the impression that he was a playboy? It was true that after his divorce he'd occasionally dated, but there'd never been anyone he was serious about—

until Savannah. "We'll need to be convincing," she said next, her voice quavering slightly, "otherwise my parents, especially my father, will see through this whole thing in an instant. They aren't going to be easily fooled, and it's important we persuade them we're getting married because we're in love."

"I can be convincing." He'd gained his reputation swaying twelve-member juries; an elderly couple who wanted to believe he was in love with their daughter would be a piece of cake.

"I'll do my best to be the same," Savannah assured him, relaxing slightly. She neatly folded the sheet of paper, running her fingers along the crease. "Was there anything you wanted to add?"

Without time to think over their agreement, Nash was at a disadvantage. "I might later."

"I...was hoping we could come to terms quickly so I can tell my parents right away."

"We'll tell them together," Nash said. "Otherwise they'll find it odd. What do you want to do about the actual wedding ceremony?"

She looked away, then lowered her gaze. "I wasn't sure you'd agree so I hadn't given it much thought. I guess I should have, since I arrange weddings for a living."

"Don't look so chagrined. This isn't a normal, run-of-the-mill marriage."

"Exactly," she was quick to concur. "I'd like a small gathering. My parents and a few good friends—no more than ten or so. What about you?"

"About that number." He'd make sure Serle and Stackhouse received invitations.

"I'll arrange for the ceremony, then, followed by dinner. Is that agreeable?"

He shrugged, not really caring. Small and private appealed to him far more than the lavish gathering Susan had had. At least Savannah wasn't going to subject him to that, although he felt mildly guilty about cheating her out of a fancy wedding.

"How long do you think you'll need to come up with any further stipulations?" she asked.

"Not long," he promised, but he had one thought that he mentioned before he could censure it. "I'd like us to make a habit of eating dinner together."

"Dinner?" Savannah sounded incredulous.

His sole condition did seem surprising. But he felt that if they were going to the trouble of getting married, they shouldn't remain strangers. "We need to spend some time together, don't you think?"

"I don't see why that's necessary."

"It will be if we're going to create the facade of being married. We'll need to know what's going on in each other's lives."

Her nod was reluctant. "I see your point."

"We can share the housework, so you don't need to worry about me sticking you with the cooking and the cleanup afterward. I want to be fair about this."

"That seems equitable."

"I don't intend to take advantage of you, Savannah." It was important she believe that, although it was obvious she didn't. Even married to Savannah, he didn't hold out much hope of becoming a senior partner. Not when Paul Jefferson was ingratiating himself with anyone and everyone who could advance his career. But if there was the slightest possibility that he might beat out Paul, Nash was willing to risk it. His dislike for the man increased daily, especially since Paul resented that Nash had been given the Don Griffin case and had made his feelings obvious.

"What day should I arrange the wedding for?" Savannah asked, flipping through the pages of a small pocket calendar.

"In a week, if at all possible." He could tell by the way her eyes widened that she expected more time. "Is that too soon?"

"Not really.... A week shouldn't be a problem, although people are going to ask questions."

"So? Does that bother you?"

"Not exactly."

"Good." Nash had little success in hiding a smile.

"In that case, I think you should write up the agreement right away," she said. "You can add whatever provisions you want and if I disagree, I'll cross them out."

"Okay. When would you like to tell your parents?"

"As soon as possible. Tomorrow evening?"

Nash stood and replaced his pen in the marble holder. "Is your mother still in the hospital?"

Savannah nodded. "Dad spends almost every minute with her. The nurses told me they tried to send him home the first night, but he refused and ended up sleeping on a cot beside her."

"He's taken this hard, hasn't he?"

Savannah nodded. "He's worried sick.... That's the main reason I decided to accept your proposal. Mom loves the sunshine and I can't think of any place she'd enjoy recuperating more than in Arizona with her friends."

"In that case, we'll do everything we can to be sure that happens."

"Oh, Savannah." Her mother's eyes glistened with the sheen of tears as she sat up in her hospital bed early the next evening. "You're going to be married."

Nash slid his arm around Savannah's waist with familiar ease and smiled down on her. "I know my timing couldn't be worse," he murmured, "but I hope you'll forgive me."

"There's nothing to forgive. We're thrilled, aren't we, Marcus?" Her mother smiled blissfully. Nash was eating up the attention, nuzzling Savannah's neck, planting kisses on her cheek when he was sure her parents would notice. These open displays of affection were unlike him and were fast beginning to irritate Savannah.

"This does seem rather sudden, though, doesn't it?" her father asked. He might have embarrassed her by acting as if Nash was practically her fiancé that first evening, but he was astute about people, and Savannah knew that convincing him would be much more difficult than persuading her mother. Nash must have realized it, too, because he was playing the role as if he expected to earn an award for his performance as the besotted lover.

"Savannah and I've been dating off and on all summer." He brought her close to his side and dropped a quick kiss on the side of her neck. The moment they were alone, she'd tell him to keep his kisses to himself. Every time he touched his lips to her skin, a shiver of awareness raced up her spine. Nash knew it; otherwise he wouldn't take every opportunity to make her so uncomfortable.

"Are you in love?" her father asked her directly.

"Marcus, what a thing to ask," her mother said with a flustered laugh. "Savannah and Nash have come to us wanting to share their wonderful news. This isn't any time to ask a lot of silly questions."

"Would I marry Nash if I didn't love him?" Savannah asked, hoping that would be enough to reassure her father.

"We'd like to have the wedding as soon as possible," Nash added, looking down at her adoringly.

"There's a rush?" her father asked.

His attitude surprised Savannah. She was prepared for a bit of skepticism, but not this interrogation. Once he was convinced Savannah loved Nash—and vice versa—she didn't figure there would be any problems.

"I want Savannah with me," Nash answered. "It took me a long time to decide to marry again and now that I have, each day without her feels like an eternity." He reached for her hand

and raised it to his lips, then placed a series of soft kisses on her knuckles. He was overdoing it, making fools of them both, and Savannah fumed.

"You feel the same way about Nash?"

"Yes, Daddy," she returned smoothly.

"I've waited all my life for a woman like Savannah."

Savannah couldn't help it; she stepped on Nash's foot and he yelped, then glared at her accusingly.

"I'm sorry, darling, did I hurt you?" she asked sweetly.

"No, I'm fine." His eyes questioned her, but she ignored the silent entreaty.

Her father stood at the head of the bed, which was angled up so that her mother was in a sitting position. They were holding hands.

"Do you object to Savannah marrying Nash?" her father questioned.

Her mother's sigh was filled with relief and joy. "Savannah's far too old to require our approval, and you know it. She can do as she pleases. I don't understand why you're behaving as if this is some…some tragedy when our little girl is so happy. Isn't this what we've prayed for all these years?"

"I know it's come at you out of the blue, Daddy," Savannah whispered, the words sticking in her throat, "but you know me well enough to know I'd never marry a man I didn't love with all my heart."

"The sooner Savannah's in my life, the sooner I can be complete," Nash added with a dramatic sigh.

Although he was clearly making an effort to sound sincere, it was all Savannah could do not to elbow him in the ribs. Anyone who knew Nash would recognize that he was lying, and doing a poor job of it. Presumably he was more effective in front of a jury.

"I should be out of the hospital by Friday," her mother said excitedly. "That'll give me a couple of days to rest at home before the wedding."

"If you need a few extra days to rest, we don't mind waiting. It's important that you be there, isn't that right, darling?"

Savannah felt him nudging her and quickly nodded. "Of course. Having you both there is more important than anything."

Her father shook his head. "I don't understand why you insist on having the wedding so soon. You've only known each other for a few months."

"We know each other better than you think," Nash said. The insinuation that they were lovers was clear. Savannah bit her tongue to keep from claiming otherwise. If Nash was trying to embarrass her, he'd surpassed his wildest expectations. Her face burned, and she couldn't meet her parents' eyes.

"I don't think we need to question Savannah and Nash any longer," her mother said. "They know their own minds. You have my blessing."

"Daddy?" Savannah whispered, holding her breath.

He didn't say anything, then nodded.

"There are a thousand things to do before Wednesday," Savannah said abruptly, bending over to kiss her mother's pale cheek. "If you don't mind, Nash and I'll leave now."

"Of course," her father said.

"Thank you so much for the wonderful news, sweetheart." Her mother was tiring; their departure came at the opportune moment.

Savannah couldn't wait until they were well outside the hospital room before turning on Nash. "How dare you," she flared, hands clenched at her sides. The man had no sense of decency. She'd told him how important it was to be convincing, but Nash cheerfully went about making fools of them both. His behavior angered her so much she could hardly speak.

"What did I do?" he demanded, wearing a confused, injured

look that was meant to evoke sympathy. It wouldn't work—not this time.

"You implied…you—you let my parents believe we were lovers," she sputtered. And that was just for starters.

"So?" Nash asked. "Good grief, Savannah, you're thirty years old. They know you're not a virgin."

She punched the elevator button viciously. The rush of tears was a mingling of outrage and indignation, and she blinked furiously in an effort to keep them from spilling.

Nash exhaled softly and rubbed the back of his neck. "You are a virgin, aren't you?"

"Do you mind if we don't discuss such private matters in a public place?" she ground out. The elevator arrived just then, and Savannah eagerly stepped on.

There were a couple of other people who stared at her. Her limp sometimes made her the center of attention, but right now she suspected it was her tears that prompted their curiosity.

She managed to keep quiet until they reached the parking lot. "As for that stupid declaration of being so crazy about me you couldn't wait another minute to make me yours—I wanted to throw up."

"Why? You should be praising me instead of getting all bent out of shape."

"Praising you? For what?"

"Convincing your father we're in love."

"Oh, please," Savannah whispered, gazing upward. The sun had begun to set, spreading shades of gold and pink across the sky. It was all so beautiful, when she felt so ugly. Nash was saying the things every woman longs to hear—beautiful words. Only, his were empty. Perhaps that was what troubled her so much, the fact that he didn't mean what he was saying when she wanted it to be true.

"You're not making any sense." His patience was clearly gone as he unlocked the passenger door, then slammed it shut. "Let's have this out right here and now."

"Fine!" she shouted.

"I was doing everything I could think of to convince your parents we're madly in love. Correct me if I'm wrong, but wasn't that the objective?"

"You didn't need to lay it on so thick, did you?"

"What do you mean?"

"Did you have to hold on to me like you couldn't bear to be separated from me for a single second? The kissing has got to stop. I won't have you fawning all over me like...like a lovesick calf."

"Fine. I won't lay another hand on you as long as we're together. Not unless you ask."

"You make that sound like a distinct possibility and trust me, it's not."

He laughed shrewdly, but didn't reply. The look he gave her just then spoke volumes. Savannah found herself getting even angrier.

"You could practice being a bit more subtle, couldn't you?" she went on. "If anyone should know the power of subtlety, it's you. I thought you were this top-notch attorney. Don't you know anything about human nature?"

"I know a little." He went strangely quiet for a moment. "You don't think we fooled your father?"

"No, Nash, I don't," she said, calmer now. "The only people we seem capable of fooling are ourselves. I'm afraid this simply isn't going to work."

"You want out already?" he demanded, sounding shocked and surprised. "Our engagement isn't even three hours old and already you're breaking it."

"We don't have any choice," she insisted. "Anyone with sense is going to see through this charade in a heartbeat. If we can't handle announcing the news to my parents, how do you expect to get through the wedding ceremony?"

"We'll manage."

"How can you be so sure of that?"

"We did before, didn't we?" he asked softly. "At Susan's wedding."

He would bring that up. The man didn't fight fair. Her behavior at the wedding ceremony had been a slip of judgment and now he was waving it in front of her like a red flag, challenging her to a repeat performance. "But that wasn't real...we weren't the center of attention."

"Like I said, we'll manage very well—just wait and see."

Nash walked around to the front of his car and leaned against the hood, crossing his arms. "Your parents are okay with it, so I suggest we continue as planned. Are you game?"

Savannah nodded, feeling she had no other choice. She suspected she could convince her father that she was in love with Nash; she wasn't sure he'd believe Nash was in love with her.

Nash was busy at his desk, reviewing the latest settlement offer from Don Griffin, when his secretary buzzed him and announced that a Mr. Marcus Charles was there to see him without an appointment.

"Send him in," Nash instructed. He closed the file, set it aside and stood.

Savannah's dad was a gentle, reflective man who reminded him a little of his own father. "Come in, please," Nash said pleasantly. "This is a surprise."

"I should have phoned."

"We all behave impulsively at one time or another," Nash said, hoping Savannah's father would catch his meaning. He'd tried hard to make it sound as if their wedding plans were impulsive, which was more or less the truth. He'd tried to convince her family that he was crazy in love with her and, according to Savannah, he'd overplayed his hand. Perhaps she was right.

"Do you mind if I sit down?"

"Of course not," Nash said immediately, dismayed by his own lack of manners. Apparently he was more shaken by this unforeseen visit than he'd realized. "Is there anything I can get you? Coffee, tea, a cold drink?"

"No, thanks." He claimed the chair across from Nash's and crossed his legs. "It looks like Joyce will be released from the hospital a day early."

Nash was relieved. "That's wonderful news."

"The news from you and Savannah rivaled that. The doctor seems to think it's what helped Joyce recover so quickly."

"I'm pleased to hear that."

"It's going to take several months before she's fully recovered, but that's to be expected."

Nash nodded, not thinking any comment was necessary. He was rarely nervous, but he felt that way now.

Marcus was silent for a moment. "So you want to marry Savannah."

"Yes, sir." This much was true and his sincerity must have rung clear in his response because it seemed to him that Savannah's father relaxed.

"My daughter's accident damaged her confidence, her self-image, at least in emotional situations." He paused. "Do you know what I mean?"

"Yes," he said honestly.

Marcus stood and walked over to the window. "I'm not going to ask if you love Savannah," he said abruptly. "For a number of reasons that doesn't matter to me as much as it did earlier. If you don't love her, you will soon enough.

"You came to me the other night seeking my blessing and I'm giving it to you." He turned and held out his hand.

The two men exchanged handshakes. When they'd finished, Marcus Charles reached inside his suit jacket, withdrew a business-size envelope and set it on Nash's desk.

"What's that?"

Marcus smiled. "Savannah's mother and I thought long and hard about what we should give you as a wedding present, then decided the best gift would be time alone. Inside is a map to a remote cabin in the San Juan Islands that we've rented for you. We're giving you one week of uninterrupted peace."

11

"What did you expect me to do?" Nash demanded as they drove off the Washington State ferry. "Refuse your parents' wedding gift?" This marriage was definitely getting off to a rocky start. They'd been husband and wife less than twelve hours and already they were squabbling.

"A remote cabin...alone together," she groaned. "I've never heard of anything more ridiculous."

"Most newlyweds would be thrilled with the idea," he said.

"We're not most newlyweds."

"I don't need you to remind me of that," Nash snapped. "You try to do someone a favor..."

"Are you insinuating that marrying me was a favor?" Savannah was huddled close to the door. "That you were doing it out of kindness?"

Nash prayed for patience. So this was what their marriage was going to be like—this constant barrage of insults, nit-picking, faultfinding.

"No, Savannah, I don't consider marrying you a favor and I didn't do it out of kindness. You're my wife and—"

"In name only," she said in icy tones.

"Does that mean we're enemies now?"

"Of course not."

"Then why have we been at each other's throats from the moment we left the wedding dinner? I'm sorry your family insisted on giving us a honeymoon. I'm well aware that you'd rather spend time with anyone but me. I was hoping we'd make the best of this."

She didn't respond, for which he was grateful. The silence was a welcome contrast to the constant bickering.

"It was a beautiful wedding," she said softly, unexpectedly.

"Yes, it was." Savannah was beautiful in her ivory silk suit with a short chiffon veil decorated with pearls. Nash had barely been able to take his eyes off her. It was a struggle to remember this wasn't a real, till-death-do-us-part marriage.

"I've been acting defensive," she added apologetically. "I'm sorry, Nash, for everything. It isn't your fault we're stuck together like this."

"Well, it was my idea, after all. And our marriage could be a good thing in lots of ways."

"You're right," she said, but she didn't sound convinced. "We might find we enjoy each other's company."

Nash was offended by the comment. He'd enjoyed being with Savannah from the beginning, enjoyed goading her, challenging her views on marriage. He'd found himself seeking her out, looking for excuses to be with her, until she'd insisted she didn't want to see him again. He'd abided by her wishes, but he'd missed her, far more than he cared to admit.

"I saw Mr. Serle and Mr. Stackhouse talking to you after the ceremony."

Nash grinned, feeling a sense of satisfaction. Both of the senior partners had been delighted to see Nash marry Savannah. She'd managed to completely captivate those two. Arnold Serle had been acutely disappointed that they'd decided against a wedding dance. He'd been counting on another spin around the floor with Savannah.

"Did they say anything about the senior partnership?" Savannah asked.

He was annoyed that she already seemed eager to get out of their arrangement. "No, but then, a wedding isn't exactly the place to be discussing business." He didn't mention that it was at his sister's reception that John Stackhouse had originally introduced the subject.

"I see." She sounded disappointed, and Nash's hands tightened on the steering wheel. Luckily the drive was a beautiful one through lush green Lopez Island. Although Nash had lived in Washington all his life, he'd never ventured into the San Juan Islands. When they drove off the ferry he was surprised by the quiet coves and breathtaking coastline. In an effort to fill their time, he'd arranged for him and Savannah to take a cruise and explore the northernmost boundary islands of Susia and Patos, which were the closest to the Canadian border. He'd wanted their honeymoon to be a memorable experience; he'd planned a shopping excursion to Friday Harbor for another day. He'd read about the quaint shops, excellent restaurants and a whale museum. Women liked those sorts of things. It seemed now that his efforts were for naught. Savannah had no intention of enjoying these days together.

"Have your parents said anything about traveling south?"

"Not yet," she said, her voice disheartened.

"They might not, you know." In other words, she could find herself living with him for the next few years, like it or not. The thought didn't appeal to him any more than it did her, especially if she continued with this attitude.

"How much farther is it to the cabin?" she asked stiffly. Nash wasn't sure. He didn't have GPS but he had a detailed map and instructions. However, since he'd never been on Lopez Island, he wasn't any expert. "Soon, I suspect."

"Good."

"You're tired?"

"A little."

It'd been a full day. First the wedding, then the dinner followed by the drive to the ferry and the ride across Puget Sound. Darkness would fall within the hour and Nash had hoped they'd be at the cabin before then.

He reached the turnoff in the road and took a winding, narrow highway for several miles. Savannah was suspiciously silent, clutching her wedding bouquet. He was surprised she'd chosen to bring it with her.

He found the dirt road that led to the cabin and slowly drove down it, grateful he'd rented a four-wheel-drive vehicle. The route was filled with ruts, which didn't lend him much confidence about this remote cabin. If this was any indication of what the house would be like, they'd be lucky to have electricity and running water.

He was wrong and knew it the minute he drove into the clearing. This was no cabin, but a luxurious house, built with a Victorian flair, even to the turret and wraparound porch.

"Oh, my...it's lovely," Savannah whispered.

The house was a sight to behold all on its own, but the view of the water was majestic.

"I'll get the luggage," Nash said, hopping out of the Jeep. He thought better of it, hurried around to Savannah's side and helped her down.

With his hands around her waist, he lifted her onto the ground. He longed to hold her against him, to swing her into his arms and carry her over the threshold like any new husband, but he didn't dare. Savannah would assume he was making a mockery of this traditional wedding custom. That was how she seemed to be dealing with everything lately, distrusting him and his motives. She made marriage feel like an insult. If this attitude lasted much longer, they'd have the shortest marriage on record.

"I'll get the luggage," he said again, unnecessarily. At least if his hands were full, he wouldn't be tempted to reach for Savannah.

"I'll open the door," she said, and for the first time she sounded enthusiastic. She hurried ahead of him and he noticed that she favored her injured leg more than usual. Sitting for any length of time must make movement more difficult. She rarely spoke about her leg—about the accident, her long rehabilitation or the pain she still suffered. He wished he knew how to broach the subject, but every attempt had been met with bristly pride, as if she believed that sharing this imperfect part of herself would make her too vulnerable.

She had the door open when he joined her. Stepping inside the house was like stepping into the nineteenth century. The warmth and beauty of this house seemed to greet them with welcoming arms.

The living room was decorated with a mix of antiques, and huge windows created a room that glowed in the setting sun.

"Oh, Nash," Savannah said, "I don't think I've ever seen anything more beautiful."

"Me, neither."

"Dad must have seen an ad for this house, maybe on a vacation website. He knows how much I love anything Victorian, especially houses."

Nash stashed that away in his storehouse of information about Savannah. When it was time to celebrate her birthday or Christmas, he'd know what to buy her.

"I'll put these in the bedrooms," he said. He didn't like the idea of them sleeping separately, but he didn't have any choice. He'd agreed to do so until she changed her mind, and from the look of things that could be a decade from now—if ever.

The master bedroom was equally attractive, with a huge four-poster mahogany bed. French lace curtains hung from the windows and the walls were papered in pale yellow. He set down Savannah's suitcase and headed for the second bedroom, which would be his. It was originally intended as a children's room, he realized. Instead of spending his wedding night with the woman he'd just married, he was destined to stare at row after row of tin soldiers. So much for romance!

Savannah woke early the next morning. The sunlight spilling in from the window was filtered through the lace curtains until a spidery pattern reflected against the floor. She yawned and sat up in bed. Surprisingly, she'd fallen asleep right away without the sadness or tears she'd expected.

"You're a married woman," she said aloud, thinking she might believe it if she heard herself say it. Her wedding and all that led up to it was still unreal to her. Afterward she'd been awful to Nash.

It took her a long time to understand why she'd behaved in such an uncharacteristic manner. Just before she went to bed, she'd realized what was going on. She was lashing out at him, blaming him for making a farce of what she considered holy. Only, he wasn't to blame; they were in this together. Marriage was advantageous to them both.

She heard him rummaging around in the kitchen. The aroma of coffee urged her out of bed. She threw on her robe and shoved her feet into slippers.

"'Morning," she said when she joined him. He'd obviously been up for hours. His jacket hung on a peg by the back door with a pair of rubber boots on the mat. His hair was wet, and he held a mug of steaming coffee and leaned against the kitchen counter.

"'Morning," he said, grinning broadly.

"You've been exploring." It hurt a little that he'd gone outside without her, but she couldn't really fault him. She hadn't been decent company in the past week or so. And walking along the beach with her wouldn't be much fun, since her gait was slow and awkward.

"I took a walk along the beach. I found you something." He reached behind him and presented her with a perfectly formed sand dollar.

Savannah's hand closed around her prize.

"I'm not sure, but I think I saw a pod of whales. It's a little difficult to tell from this distance."

Savannah made busywork about the kitchen, pouring herself a cup of coffee and checking the refrigerator for milk, all the while struggling to hold back her disappointment. She would've loved to see a pod of whales, even from a distance.

"What would you like for breakfast?" she asked, hoping to get their day off to a better start.

"Bacon, eggs, toast and a kiss."

Savannah froze.

"You heard me right. Come on, Savannah, loosen up. We're supposed to be madly in love, remember? This isn't going to work if you act the part of the outraged virgin."

What he said was true, but that didn't make it any easier. She turned away from him and fought down a confused mixture of anger and pain. She wanted to blame him, and knew she couldn't. She longed to stamp her foot, as she had when she was a little girl, and cry out, "Stop! No more." No more discord. No more silliness. But it wouldn't do any good. She was married but resigned to a life of loneliness. These were supposed to be the happiest days of her life and here she was struggling not to weep.

Nash had moved behind her and placed his hands on her shoulders. "Do you find me so repugnant?" he whispered close to her ear.

His warm breath was moist. She shut her eyes and shook her head.

"Then why won't you let me kiss you?"

She shrugged, but was profoundly aware of the answer. If Nash kissed her, she'd remember how much she enjoyed his touch. It'd been like that from the beginning. He knew it. She knew it. Now he intended to use that against her.

He brought his mouth down to her neck and shivers of awareness moved up and down her spine. Needing something to hold on to, Savannah reached for the kitchen counter.

"One kiss," he coaxed. "Just one."

"Y-you promise?"

"Of course. Anything you say."

She made a small, involuntary movement to turn around. His hands on her shoulders aided the process. She quivered when his mouth met hers and a familiar heat began to warm her. As always, their need for each other was so hot and intense, it frightened her.

Slowly, he lifted his mouth from hers. "Do you want me to stop?" he asked in a husky whisper.

Savannah made an unintelligible sound.

"That's what I thought," he said, claiming her mouth again.

She locked her arms around his neck. Soon the kissing wasn't enough....

Savannah felt as though her body was on fire. She'd been empty and lonely for so long. No man had ever kissed her like this. No man had ever wanted her so badly.

"You don't want me to stop, do you?" he begged. "Don't tell me you want me to stop."

Incapable of a decision, she made a second unintelligible sound.

"If we continue like this, we're going to end up making love on the kitchen floor," Nash whispered.

"I don't know what I want," she whimpered.

"Yes, you do. Savannah. If it gets much hotter, we're both going to explode. Let me make love to you."

She started to protest, but he stopped her, dragging his mouth back to hers. Only she could satisfy him, his kisses seemed to be saying. Savannah didn't know if he was telling her this or if she was hearing it in her mind. It didn't matter; she got the message.

"No," she said with a whimper. She couldn't give him her body. If they made love, he'd own her completely, and she couldn't allow that to happen. Someday he was going to walk away from her. Someday he was going to announce that it was over and she was supposed to go on her merry way without him. She was supposed to pretend it didn't matter.

"You don't mean that," Nash pleaded. "You can't tell me you don't want me." The words were issued in a heated whisper. "Don't do this, Savannah."

She buried her face in his shoulder. "Please...don't. You promised. You said you'd stop...whenever I asked."

He released her then, slowly, her body dragging against his as her feet slid back to the floor. She stepped away from him, anxious to break the contact, desperately needing room to breathe. She pressed her hand to the neckline of her gown and drew in several deep breaths.

Nash's eyes were squeezed shut as he struggled to bring himself under control. When he opened them, Savannah swore they were filled with fire.

Without a word to her, he reached for his jacket, opened the door and walked out.

She was trembling so hard, she had to pull out a chair and sit down. She didn't know how long she was there before she felt strong enough to stand, walk back into the bedroom and dress.

It was a mistake to let him kiss her; she'd known it even as she agreed, known it would be like this between them. Gnawing on her lower lip, she argued with herself. She and Nash had created an impossible situation, drawn up a list of rules and regulations and then insisted on testing each one to the limits of their endurance.

She'd just placed their coffee cups in the dishwasher when the back door opened and Nash appeared. She studied him. He looked calm and outwardly serene, but she wasn't fooled. She could see the angry glint in his eyes.

"If you're looking for an apology, you can forget it," he said. "I'm...not."

"Good."

Now didn't seem the time to mention that he hadn't helped matters any by suggesting the kiss. Both of them knew what would happen when they started flirting with the physical aspect of their relationship.

Nash poured himself a cup of coffee. "Let's sit down and talk this over."

"I...don't know what there is to say," she said, preferring to avoid the issue completely. "It was a very human thing to happen. You're an attractive, healthy man with...needs."

"And you're a red-blooded woman. You have *needs*, too. But admitting that takes real honesty, doesn't it?"

Savannah found the remark insulting, but then, Nash didn't seem inclined to be generous with her. Since she didn't have an argument to give him, she let it pass.

"I did some thinking while I walked off my frustration."

"Oh?" She was curious about what he'd decided, but didn't want to press him.

"The way I see it, I'm setting myself up for constant frustration if we have any more bouts like this last one. If you want to come out of this marriage as pristine as the freshly fallen snow, then far be it from me to hit my head against a brick wall."

"I'm not sure I understand."

"You don't need to. You have your wish, Savannah. I won't touch you again, not until you ask me, and the way I feel right now, you're going to have to do a whole lot more than ask. You're going to have to beg."

Nash hadn't known it was possible for two human beings to live the way he and Savannah had spent the past two weeks. The so-called honeymoon had been bad enough, but back in civilization, living in his house, the situation had gone from unbearable to even worse. The electricity between them could light up a small city. Yet they continued to ignore their mutual attraction.

They lived as brother and sister. They slept in separate rooms, inquired about each other's day, sat at the dinner table every night and made polite conversation.

In two weeks Nash hadn't so much as held her hand. He dared not for fear he'd get burned. Not by her rejection, but by their need for each other.

Part of the problem was the fact that Savannah was a virgin. She didn't know what she was missing, but she had a fairly good idea, and that added a certain amount of intrigue. He sincerely hoped she was miserable, at least as miserable as he was.

"Mr. Griffin is here to see you," his assistant announced.

Nash stood to greet his client. Don Griffin had lost weight in the past month. Nash had, too, come to think of it. He didn't have much of an appetite and was working out at the gym most nights after dinner.

"Did you hear from Janice's attorney?" Don demanded.

"Not yet."

"Does he normally take this long to return phone calls?" Agitated, Don started to pace.

"He does when he wants us to sweat," he said.

"Raise Janice's monthly allotment by five hundred dollars."

Nash sighed inwardly. This was a difficult case and not for the usual reasons. "Sit down, Mr. Griffin," he said. "Please."

Don complied and sat down. He bounced his fingers against each other and studied Nash as he leaned back in his chair.

"Janice hasn't requested any extra money," Nash said.

"She might need it. Amy, too. There are a hundred unexpected expenses that crop up. I don't want her having to scrimp. It's important to me that my wife and daughter live comfortably."

"You've been more than generous."

"Just do as I say. I'm not paying you to argue with me."

"No, you're paying me for advice and I'm about to give you some, so kindly listen. It doesn't come cheap."

Don snorted loudly. "No kidding. I just got your last bill."

Nash smiled. His clients were often shocked when they learned how expensive divorce could be. Not only financially, but emotionally. Nash had seen it happen more times than he cared to think about. Once his clients realized how costly a divorce could be, they were already embroiled in bitterness and it was impossible to undo the damage.

"Do you know what you're doing, giving Janice extra money?" he asked.

"Sure I do. I'm attempting to take care of my wife and daughter."

"You're already doing that. Offering them more money is more about easing your conscience. You want to absolve your guilt because you had an affair."

"It wasn't an affair," Don shouted. "It was a one-night thing, a momentary lapse that I've regretted every moment since. Janice would never have found out about it if it hadn't been for— never mind, that doesn't matter now. She found out about it and immediately called an attorney."

"My point is, she learned about your indiscretion and now you want to buy peace of mind. Unfortunately, it doesn't work like that."

"All I'm trying to do is get this divorce over with."

Tony Pound, Janice's attorney, wasn't a fool. He knew exactly what he was doing, dragging the proceedings out as long as possible to prolong the guilt and the agony. To Nash's way of thinking, his client had been punished enough.

"This is one mistake you aren't going to be paying monetarily for the rest of your life," Nash assured him. "And I plan to make sure of it. That's why John Stackhouse asked me to take your case. You've lost your wife, your home, your daughter. You've paid enough. Now go back to your apartment and relax. I'll contact you when I hear from Mr. Pound."

Don Griffin nodded reluctantly. "I don't know how much more of this I can take."

"It shouldn't be much longer," Nash assured him.

He rose slowly from the chair. "You'll be in touch soon?"

Nash said he would. Don left the office and Nash sat down to review his file for the hundredth time. He was missing something, he realized. That cold-blooded instinct for the kill.

He wasn't enjoying this, wasn't even close to experiencing the satisfaction he usually gained from bringing his opponents to their knees. Somewhere along the line he'd changed. He'd sensed things were different shortly after he'd met Savannah. Now there was no hiding his feelings. He'd lost it. Only, he wasn't sure what he'd found in exchange.

"Have you got a moment?" John Stackhouse stuck his head in Nash's office.

"Sure. What can I do for you?"

The senior partner was smiling from ear to ear. "Would you mind coming down to the meeting room?"

Nash's pulse accelerated wildly. The executive committee had been meeting with the other senior partners that afternoon to make their recommendation for new senior partner.

"I got the position?" Nash asked hesitantly.

"I think that would be a fair assessment," the older man said, slapping Nash on the shoulder. "It wasn't a hard decision, Nash. You're a fine attorney and an asset to this firm."

A half hour later, Nash rushed out of the office and drove directly to Savannah's shop. As luck would have it, she was busy with a customer. He tried to be patient, tried to pretend he was some stranger who'd casually strolled in.

Savannah looked at him with wide, questioning eyes and he delighted in unnerving her by blowing her a kiss.

"When did you say the wedding was?" she asked the smartly dressed businesswoman who was leafing through a book of invitations.

"In December."

"You have plenty of time, but it's a good idea to set your budget now. I'll be happy to assist you in any way I can."

"I appreciate that," Nash heard the woman say.

He wandered over to her desk and sorted through her mail. Without being obvious, Savannah walked over to where he was sitting, took the envelopes from him and gently slapped his hands. "Behave yourself," she said under her breath.

"I have a few extra expenses coming up," he said in a low whisper. "I hope you're doing well. I might need a loan."

"What expenses?" she asked in the same low voice.

"New business cards, stationery and the like."

"New stationery?" she repeated more loudly.

The customer turned around. "I'm sorry," Savannah said apologetically. "I was commenting on something my husband said."

The woman smiled graciously. "I thought you two must be married. I saw the way you looked at each other when he walked in the door."

Neither Nash nor Savannah responded.

Savannah started to walk away, when Nash caught her hand. It was the first time he'd purposely touched her since the morning after their wedding. Apparently it caught her by surprise, because she turned abruptly, her gaze seeking out his.

"I'm the new senior partner."

Savannah's eyes lit up with undisguised delight. "Nash, oh, Nash." She covered her mouth with both hands and blinked back tears. "Congratulations."

"If you don't mind, I'll come back another time with my fiancé," Savannah's customer said.

"I'm sorry," Savannah said, limping toward the woman.

"Don't apologize. Celebrate with your husband. You both

deserve it." When she reached the front door, she turned the sign to "Closed," winked at Nash and walked out of the store.

"When did you find out?" Savannah asked, rubbing her index finger beneath her eye.

"About half an hour ago. I thought we'd go out to dinner and celebrate."

"I...don't know what to say. I'm so happy for you."

"I'm happy, too." It was difficult not to take her in his arms. He stood and walked away from her rather than break his self-imposed restriction.

"Where are you going?" Savannah asked, sounding perplexed.

"I need to keep my distance from you."

"Why?"

"Because I want to hold you so much, my arms ache."

Savannah broke into a smile. "I was just thinking the same thing," she said, opening her arms to him.

12

Nash checked his watch for the time, set aside the paper and hurried into the kitchen. It was his night to cook and he'd experimented with a new recipe. If anyone had told him he'd be hanging around a kitchen, fretting over elaborate recipes, he would've stoutly denied such a thing could even happen.

Marriage had done this to him, and to his surprise Nash wasn't complaining. He enjoyed their arrangement, especially now that they were on much friendlier terms. The tension had lessened considerably following the evening they'd celebrated his appointment as senior partner. It felt as if the barriers were gradually being lowered.

He was bent over the oven door when he heard Savannah come into the house. She'd called him at the office to let him know she'd be late, which had become almost a nightly occurrence.

"I'm home," she said, entering the kitchen. She looked pale and worn-out. He'd never have guessed September would be such a busy month for weddings. Savannah had overbooked herself and spread her time and energy much too thin. He'd resisted the urge to lecture her, although it'd been difficult.

"Your timing couldn't be better," he said, taking the sausage, cabbage and cheese casserole out of the oven and setting it on the counter. The scent of spicy meat filled the kitchen.

"That smells delicious," Savannah said, and Nash beamed proudly. He'd discovered, somewhat to his surprise, that he enjoyed cooking. Over the years he'd learned a culinary trick or two, creating a small repertoire of dinners. Nothing, however, that required an actual recipe. Now he found himself reading cookbooks on a regular basis.

"I've got the table set if you're ready to eat," he told her.

"You must've known I was starving."

"Did you skip lunch again today?" he asked, using oven mitts to carry the glass casserole dish to the table. Once again he had to stop himself from chastising her. Their peace was too fragile to test. "Sit down and I'll bring you a plate."

It looked as if Savannah was in danger of falling asleep as he joined her at the table.

"Nash," she said after the first taste, "this is wonderful!"

"I'm glad you approve."

"Keep this up and you can do all the cooking," she teased, smiling over at him.

Nash set his fork aside and folded his hands. He couldn't keep silent any longer. "You're working too hard."

She lowered her gaze and nodded. "I know. I scheduled the majority of these weddings soon after our own. I... I thought it would be a good idea if I spent as much time at the shop as possible."

In other words, less time with him. "I hope you've changed your mind."

"I have." Her hand closed around her water glass. "I assumed our...arrangement would be awkward, but it hasn't been, not since the beginning."

"I've enjoyed spending time with you." It frustrated him, living as they did, like polite strangers, but that, too, had changed in the past couple of weeks. Their relationship had become that of good friends. Their progress was slow but steady, which gave Nash hope that eventually Savannah would be comfortable enough with him to make love. He realized his attitude was shortsighted. Breaching that barrier had been a challenge from the first, but he hadn't thought beyond it. He didn't want to think about it now.

When they finished eating, Savannah carried their plates to the sink. They had an agreement about cleanup, one of many. When one of them did the cooking, the other washed the dishes.

"Sit down," Nash ordered, "before you collapse."

"This will only take a couple of minutes," she insisted, opening the dishwasher.

Nash took her by the hands and led her into the living room. Pushing her down on the sofa, he said, "I want you to relax."

"If I do that, I'll fall asleep, and I need to go back to the shop later to finish up a few things."

"Don't even think about it, Savannah." Those were fighting words, but he counted on her being too tired to argue with him. "You're exhausted. I'm your husband, and I may not be a very good one, but I refuse to allow you to work yourself this hard."

She closed her eyes and leaned her head against the sofa cushion. She gave him a small smile. "You are a good husband, Nash. Thoughtful and considerate."

"Right." He hoped she wasn't expecting an argument. As it was, he should be awarded some kind of medal.

He reached for her legs and placed them on his lap. "Just relax," he urged again when she opened her eyes, silently questioning him. He removed her shoes and massaged her tired feet. She sighed with pleasure and wiggled her toes.

"I haven't been to my place in a week," she said, and Nash found that an odd comment until he thought about it. She was admitting how comfortable she'd gotten living with him. It was a sign, a small one, that she was willing to advance their relationship. Nash didn't intend to waste it.

"I've moved nearly all my clothes here," she continued in sleepy tones.

"That's very good, don't you think?" he asked, not expecting her to reply.

"Hmm."

He continued to rub her feet and ankles, marveling at the delicate bone structure. He let his hands venture upward over her calves. She sighed and nestled farther down in the sofa. Gaining confidence, Nash risked going higher, where her skin was silky warm and smooth. He wasn't sure how this was affecting Savannah, but it was having a strong effect on him. His breathing went shallow and his heart started to thunder in his ears. He'd promised himself that he wouldn't ask her to make love again. She'd have to come to him. He wanted her to beg—but if anyone was going to do any begging, it was him.

"It's very relaxing," Savannah murmured with a sigh.

Funny, it wasn't relaxing for him....

"Nash." His name was released on a harshly indrawn breath.

His hands froze. His heart went still and his breath caught. "Yes?" He struggled to sound expressionless, although that was nearly impossible. The less she recognized how critical his need was for her, the better.

"I think I should stop, don't you?" Where he dredged up the strength to suggest that was beyond him.

"It feels good."

"That's the problem. It feels so good."

"For you, too?"

Sometimes he forgot what an innocent she was. "For me, too."

Her head was propped against the back of the sofa, her eyes closed. Her mouth was slightly parted and she moistened her lips with the tip of her tongue. Nash groaned inwardly and forced himself to look away.

"Maybe we should kiss," she whispered.

Nash wasn't interested in a repeat performance of what had taken place earlier, but at the same time he wasn't about to turn down her offer. She wasn't begging, but this was close enough.

He shifted his weight and brought her into his arms.

Perspiration broke out on his forehead and he held his breath while he reined in his desire. "If we start kissing, we might not be able to stop."

"I know."

"You know that?" Something was wrong with him. He should be carrying her into the bedroom and not asking questions until afterward. A long time afterward.

"We can follow through with our agreement, can't we?" she asked. Her eyes fluttered open.

"What agreement?" His mind could only hold one thing at the moment, and that was his painful physical need for her.

"We'll separate once my parents decide to travel," she said, and it sounded more like a reassurance. "In the meantime, I'm not going to be trapped in a loveless marriage. As per the contract, we can initiate divorce proceedings when the year's up."

"Fine," he said, willing to agree to any terms. "Whatever you want."

"Do you think it would be a mistake to make love?" she asked.

"No." He sounded as if he'd choked on something. "That seems like a good idea to me," he said a couple of seconds later. He got off the sofa, reached down and scooped her into his arms.

She gave a small cry of surprise when he lifted her up and marched down the darkened hallway. He walked into his bedroom and placed her on his bed.

He was afraid of going too fast—and of not going fast enough. Afraid of not lasting long enough, of cheating her out of what lovemaking should be for her first time. His fears managed to make him feel indecisive.

"Is something wrong?" she asked, staring up at him, her eyes wide and questioning.

Unable to answer, he shook his head.

She smiled then, softly, femininely, and stretched her arms up, bringing him down next to her. He noticed that her breathing was as quick and shallow as his own. Carefully he peeled open the front of her shirt and eased it from her shoulders. Her bra and everything else soon followed....

They fell asleep afterward, their arms and legs intertwined, their bodies joined in the most elemental of ways. Nash had never known such peace, never experienced such serenity, and it lulled him into a deep sleep.

It was after midnight when he woke. The lights were still on in the living room and the kitchen. Carefully, so as not to wake Savannah, he crawled out of the bed and reached for his robe. Shuffling barefoot out of the bedroom, he yawned.

He felt good. Like he could run a marathon or swim a mile in world-record time. He finished the dinner dishes and was turning off the kitchen light when he looked up and saw Savannah standing inside the living room. Her hair was tousled, yet he'd never seen her look more beautiful. She'd donned her blouse, which covered precious little of her body.

"I woke up and you were gone," she said in a small voice.

"I was coming back to bed."

"Good." She led him back, not that he required any coaxing. The room was dark, but streaks of moonlight floated against the wall as they made their way to the bed.

Nash held back the covers and Savannah climbed in. He followed, gathering her in his arms, cradling her head against his shoulder.

He waited for her to speak, wondering what she was thinking, afraid to ask. With utter contentment he kissed her hair. She squirmed against him, nestling in as close as possible, and breathed out a long, womanly sigh.

Although he was an experienced lover, Nash had never heard a woman sigh the way Savannah did just then. It seemed to come from deep inside her, speaking of pleasure and the surprise of mutual satisfaction.

"Thank you," he whispered.

"No," she said. "Thank you." And then she snuggled up to him again, as if she needed this closeness as much as he did. As if she craved these peaceful moments, too.

He waited a few more minutes, wanting to be sure she hadn't drifted off to sleep. "We should talk."

"I know," she whispered. "I thought about that, too."

"And?"

"I planned on discussing things with you, reassessing the issues, that sort of thing."

"Why didn't you?" He couldn't help being curious.

He felt her lips move in a smile. "When the time came, all I wanted was you."

His chest rose with an abundance of fierce male pride. "I wanted you, too."

Serenity surrounded him and he sank into its warmth.

"Should we talk now?" Savannah asked after a while.

The last thing Nash wanted right this minute was a lengthy conversation about their marriage. Words would destroy the tranquillity, and these moments were too precious to waste.

"This doesn't have to change anything, if you don't want it to," he murmured, rubbing his chin over her head, loving the silky feel of her hair.

Savannah went still, and he wondered if he'd said something wrong. "You're content with our arrangement the way it is?" she asked.

"For now I am. We don't have to make any decisions tonight, do we?"

"No," she agreed readily.

"Then relax and go back to sleep." His eyes drifted shut as he savored this closeness.

"Nash."

"Hmm?"

"It was nothing like I expected," she told him.

"Better, I hope."

"Oh, yes." And then she kissed him.

Don and Janice Griffin's meeting before Judge Wilcox was scheduled for two in the afternoon. Nash was well prepared for this final stage of the divorce proceedings.

Don Griffin arrived at his office an hour early and—in what was fast becoming a habit—started pacing the room.

"I'm ready anytime you are," his client said.

"If we leave now, we'll end up sitting outside in the hallway," Nash told him.

"I don't care. I want this over with as quickly and cleanly as possible, understand?"

"That message came through loud and clear," Nash assured him. "Settle down and relax, will you?"

Don thrust both hands into his hair. "Relax? Are you crazy, man? You might've gone through this a thousand times, but it's almost thirty years of my life we're throwing out the window. The stress is getting to me."

"What's this I hear about putting a divorce special on your restaurants' menu?" Nash asked in an effort to take the older man's mind off the coming proceedings. "Anyone who comes into any of your restaurants the day his divorce is final eats for free."

"That's right, and I'd rather you didn't say anything derogatory about it. I've met a number of men just like me. Some of 'em married twenty, thirty years and all of a sudden it's gone. Poof. Suddenly they're lost and alone and don't know what to do with the rest of their lives."

"I'm not going to say anything negative. I think it's a generous thing you're doing."

Don Griffin eyed him as if he wasn't sure he should believe that.

When they arrived at the courtroom, Mr. Griffin and Nash took their seats behind one table. Janice Griffin and Tony Pound sat behind the other. Nash noticed the way Don stole a look at his almost ex-wife. Next, he caught a glimpse of Janice looking at Don. It wasn't anything he hadn't seen countless times before. One last look, so to speak, before the ties were severed. A farewell. An acceptance that it was soon to be over—the end was within sight. This marriage was about to breathe its last breath.

Judge Wilcox entered the room and everyone stood. In a crisp, businesslike manner, he asked a series of questions of each party. Janice responded, her voice shaking. Don answered, sounding like a condemned man. They sat back down and the final decree was about to be pronounced when Nash vaulted out of his seat.

For a moment he didn't know what had forced him into action. "If you'll pardon me, Your Honor," he said, with his back to his client, "I'd like to say a few words."

He could hear Tony begin to object. Nash didn't give him the opportunity.

"My client doesn't want this divorce, and neither does his wife."

A string of hot words erupted behind him as Tony Pound flew out of his chair. The judge's gavel pounded several times, the noise deafening.

"Your Honor, if you'll indulge me for just a moment."

No one was more surprised than Nash when he was given permission. "Proceed."

"My client has been married for almost thirty years. He made a mistake, Your Honor. Now, he'll be the first to admit it was a foolish, stupid mistake. But he's human and so is his wife. They've both paid dearly for this blunder and it seems to me they've paid enough."

He turned to face Janice Griffin, who was shredding a tissue in her hand. "You've made mistakes in your life, too, haven't you, Mrs. Griffin?"

Janice lowered her gaze and nodded.

"You can't cross-examine my client," Pound yelled.

Nash ignored him, and thankfully so did Judge Wilcox.

"My client has loved his wife and family for nearly thirty years. He still loves her. I saw the way he looked at Mrs. Griffin when she walked into the courtroom. I also saw the way she looked at him. These two people care deeply for each other. They've been driven apart by their pain and their pride. Thirty years is a very long time out of a person's life, and I don't believe anyone should be in a rush to sign it away."

"Your Honor, I find this outburst extremely unprofessional," Tony Pound protested.

Nash didn't dare turn around.

"Don Griffin has suffered enough for his indiscretion. Mrs. Griffin has been through enough agony, too. It's time to think about rebuilding lives instead of destroying them."

There wasn't a sound in the courtroom. Having had his say, Nash returned to his seat.

Judge Wilcox held his gavel with both hands. "Is what Mr. Davenport said true, Mr. Griffin? Do you love your wife?"

Don Griffin rose slowly to his feet. "A thousand times more than I thought possible."

"Mrs. Griffin?"

She, too, stood, her eyes watering, her lips trembling. "Yes, Your Honor."

The judge glared at them both and set down the gavel. "Then

I suggest you try to reconcile your differences and stop wasting the court's time."

Nash gathered together the papers he'd removed from his briefcase and slipped them back inside. Don Griffin walked behind him and was met halfway by his wife. From his peripheral vision, Nash watched as Janice Griffin, sobbing, walked into her husband's arms. They held on to each other, weeping and laughing and kissing all at once.

Not bad for an afternoon's work, Nash decided.

He picked up his briefcase and walked out of the courtroom. He hadn't taken two steps when Tony Pound joined him.

"That was quite a little drama you put on just now."

"I couldn't see two people who were obviously in love end their marriage," Nash said. They marched side by side through the halls of justice.

"It's true, then," Tony commented.

"What is?"

"That you've lost your edge, that killer instinct you're famous for. I have to admit I'm glad to see it. People said it'd happen when they learned you were married, but no one expected it to be this soon. Whoever took you on as a husband must be one heck of a woman."

Nash smiled to himself. "She is."

"It doesn't look like I'll be seeing you in court all that often."

"Probably not. I'm not taking on any new divorce cases."

"Dad, what an unexpected surprise," Savannah said, delighted that her father had decided to drop in at her store. He didn't visit often and his timing was perfect. She was about to take a break, sit down and rest her leg. "How's Mom?"

"Much better," he said, pulling out a chair as Savannah poured him a cup of coffee.

"Good."

"That's what I've come to talk to you about."

Savannah poured herself a cup and joined him. Her mother had made impressive progress in the past six weeks. Savannah called and visited often, and several times Nash had accompanied her. Joyce was growing stronger each day. She was often forgetful and that frustrated her, but otherwise she was recuperating nicely.

"I thought it'd be a good idea if I talked to you first," her father said.

"About what?"

"Your mother and I traveling."

It was the welcome news she'd been waiting to hear. At the same time it was the dreaded announcement that would end the happiest days of her life.

"I think you should travel. I always have."

"I was hoping to take your mother south. We might even look for a place to buy."

"Arizona," she suggested, raising the cup to her lips. "Mom's always loved the Southwest."

"The sunshine will do her good," her father agreed.

Savannah didn't know how she'd be able to pull this off, when she felt like she was dying on the inside. Over the years she'd become proficient at disguising her pain. Pain made others uncomfortable, so she'd learned to live with it.

"You wouldn't object to our going?" Her father didn't often sound hesitant but he did now.

"Of course I don't! I want you to travel and enjoy your retirement years. I've got Nash now, so there's no need to worry about me. None whatsoever."

"You're sure?"

"Dad! Go and enjoy yourselves," Savannah said and managed to laugh.

Three hours later, she sat in the middle of Nash's living room, staring aimlessly into space. All that was left now was the waiting—that, and telling him….

Nash got home shortly after six. His eyes were triumphant as he marched into the house. "Savannah," he said, apparently delighted to see her. "You didn't work late tonight."

"No," she responded simply.

He lifted her off the sofa as if she weighed nothing and twirled her around. "I had the most incredible day."

"Me, too."

"Good. We'll celebrate." Tucking his arm beneath her knees, he started for the bedroom. He stopped abruptly when he saw her suitcase sitting at the end of the hallway. His eyes were filled with questions as they met hers.

"Are you going somewhere?"

She nodded. "My parents have decided to take an extended trip south."

"So?"

"So, according to the terms of our marriage agreement, I'm moving back into my own home."

13

"You're moving out just like that?" Nash asked, lowering her feet to the ground. He stepped away from her as if he needed to put some distance between them. His eyes narrowed and he studied her, his expression shocked.

Savannah hadn't expected him to look at her like that. This was what they'd decided in the beginning, it was what he said he wanted after the first time they'd made love. She'd asked, wanting to be clear on exactly what her role in his life was to be, and Nash had said that making love changed nothing.

"This shouldn't come as a surprise," she said, struggling to keep her voice as even as possible.

"Is it what you want?" He thrust his hands deep inside his pockets and glared at her icily.

"Well?" he demanded when she didn't immediately answer.

"It doesn't matter what I think. I'm keeping my end of the bargain. What do you want me to do?"

Nash gave a nonchalant shrug of his shoulders. "I'm not going to hold you prisoner here against your wishes, if that's what you're asking."

That wasn't what she was asking. She wanted some indication that he loved her and wanted her living with him. Some indication that he intended to throw out their stupid prenuptial agreement and make this marriage real. Apparently Nash wasn't interested.

"When are your parents leaving?"

"Friday morning, at dawn."

"So soon?"

She nodded. "Dad wanted to wait until Mom was strong enough to travel comfortably...and evidently she is now."

"I see." Nash wandered into the kitchen. "So you're planning to move out right away?"

"I...thought I'd take some clothes over to my house this evening."

"You certainly seem to be in a rush."

"Not really. I've managed to bring quite a few of my personal things here. I...imagine you'll want me out as quickly as possible." The smallest sign that he loved her would be enough to convince her to stay. A simple statement of need. A word. A look. Anything.

Nash offered nothing.

He opened the refrigerator and took out a cold soda, popping it open.

"I started dinner while I was waiting for you," she said. "The casserole's in the oven."

Nash took a long swallow of his soda. "I appreciate the effort, but I don't seem to have much of an appetite."

Savannah didn't, either. Calmly she walked over and turned off the oven. She stood with her back to Nash and bit her lip.

What a romantic fool she was, hoping the impossible would happen. She'd known when she agreed to marry him that it would be like this. He was going to break her heart. She'd tried to protect herself from exactly this, but it hadn't worked.

These past few weeks had been the happiest of her life and nothing he said now would take them away from her. He loved her, she knew he did, as much as it was possible for Nash to love anyone. He'd never said the words, but he didn't need to. She felt them when she slept in his arms. She experienced them each time they made love.

Her heart constricted with fresh pain. She didn't want to leave Nash, but she couldn't stay, not unless he specifically asked, and it was clear he had no intention of doing so.

She heard him leave the room, which was just as well since she was having a hard time not breaking into tears.

She was angry then. Unfortunately there wasn't a door to slam or anything handy to throw. Having a temper tantrum was exactly what she felt like doing.

Dinner was a waste. She might as well throw the whole thing in the garbage. Opening the oven door, she reached inside and grabbed the casserole dish.

Intense, unexpected pain shot through her fingers as she touched the dish.

She cried out and jerked her hand away. Stumbling toward the sink, she held her fingers under cold running water.

"Savannah?" Nash rushed into the kitchen. "What happened?"

"I'm all right," she said, fighting back tears by taking deep breaths. If she was lucky, her fingers wouldn't blister, but she seemed to be out of luck lately.

"What happened?" Nash demanded again.

"Nothing." She shook her head, not wanting to answer him because that required concentration and effort, and all she could think of at the moment was pain. Physical pain. Emotional agony. The two were intermingled until she didn't know where one stopped and the other started.

"Let me look at what you've done," he said, moving close to her.

"No," Savannah said, jerking her arm away from him. "It's nothing."

"Let me be the judge of that."

"Leave me alone," she cried, sobbing openly now, her shoulders heaving. "Just leave me alone. I can take care of myself."

"I'm your husband."

She whirled on him, unintentionally splashing him with cold water. "How can you say that when you can hardly wait to be rid of me?"

"What are you talking about?" he shouted. "I wasn't the one who packed my bags and casually announced I was leaving. If you want to throw out questions, then you might start by asking yourself what kind of wife you are!"

Savannah rubbed her uninjured hand beneath her nose. "You claimed you didn't want a wife."

"I didn't until I married you." Nash opened the freezer portion of the refrigerator and brought out a tub of ice cubes. "Sit down," he said in tones that brooked no argument. She complied. He set the tub on the table and gently placed her burned fingers inside it. "The first couple of minutes will be uncomfortable, but after that you won't feel much," he explained calmly.

Savannah continued to sob.

"What did you do?" he asked.

"I was taking out the baking dish."

Nash frowned. "Did the oven mitt slip?"

"I forgot to use one," she admitted.

He took a moment to digest this information before kneeling down at her feet. His eyes probed hers and she lowered her gaze. Tucking his finger beneath her chin, he leveled her eyes to his.

"Why?"

"Isn't it obvious? I...was upset."

"About what?"

She shrugged, not wanting to tell him the truth. "These things happen and..."

"Why?" he repeated softly.

"Because you're an idiot," she flared.

"I know you're upset about me not wanting dinner, but—"

"Dinner?" she cried, incredulous. "You think this is because you didn't want dinner? How can any man be so dense?" She vaulted to her feet, her burned fingers forgotten. "You were just going to let me walk out of here."

"Wrong."

"Wrong? And how did you plan to stop me?"

"I figured I'd move in with you."

She blinked. "I beg your pardon?"

"You heard me. The agreement, as originally written, states that you'll move out of my premises after your parents decide to travel and you—"

"I know what that stupid piece of paper says," Savannah said, frowning.

"If you don't want to live with me, then it makes perfect sense for me to—"

"I do want to live with you, you idiot," she broke in. "I was hoping you'd do something—anything—to convince me to stay."

Nash was quiet for a few seconds. "Let me see if I have this straight. You were going to move out, although you didn't want to. Is that right?"

She nodded.

"Why?"

"Because I wanted you to ask me to stay."

"Ah, I understand now. You do one thing, hoping I'll respond by asking you to do the opposite."

She shrugged, realizing how silly it sounded in the cold light of reason. "I…guess so."

"Let this be a lesson to you, Savannah Davenport," Nash said, taking her in his arms. "If you want something, all you need to do is ask for it. If you'd simply sought my opinion, you'd have learned an important fact."

"Oh?"

"I'm willing to move heaven and earth to make sure we're together for the rest of our natural lives."

"You are?"

"In case you haven't figured it out yet, I'm in love with you." A surprised look must have come over her because he added, "You honestly didn't know?"

"I...prayed you were, but I didn't dare hope you'd admit it. I've been in love with you for so long I can't remember when I didn't love you."

He kissed her gently, his mouth coaxing and warm. "Promise you won't ever stop loving me. I need you so badly. It wasn't until you were in my life that I saw how jaded I'd become. Taking on so many divorce cases didn't help my attitude any. I've made a decision that's due to your influence on me. When I graduated from law school, I specialized in tax and tax laws. I'm going back to that."

"Oh, Nash, I'm so pleased."

He kissed her with a hunger that left her weak and clinging.

"I can ask for anything?" she murmured between kisses.

"Anything."

"Throw away that stupid agreement."

He smiled boyishly and pressed his forehead against hers. "I already have.... The first night, after we made love."

"You might have told me!"

"I intended to when the time was right."

"And when did you calculate that to be?" she asked, having difficulty maintaining her feigned outrage.

"Soon. Very soon."

She smiled and closed her eyes. "But not soon enough."

"I had high hopes for us from the first. I opened my mouth and stuck my foot in it at the beginning by suggesting that ludicrous marriage-of-convenience idea. Marriage, the second time around, is a lot more frightening because you've already made one mistake."

"Our marriage isn't a mistake," she assured him. "I won't let it be."

"I felt that if I had control of the situation, I might be able to control my feelings for you, but after Susan's wedding I knew that was going to be impossible."

"Why didn't you follow your own advice and ask how I felt?" she said, thinking of all the weeks they'd wasted.

"We haven't been on the best of terms, have we?" he murmured.

Savannah was embarrassed now by what a shrew she'd been. She slid her arms around his neck and kissed him soundly in an effort to make up for those first weeks.

"You said I can ask for anything I want?" she said against his lips.

"Hmm…anything," he agreed.

"I'd like a baby."

Nash's eyes flew open with undisguised eagerness. "How soon?"

"Well… I was thinking we could start on the project tonight."

A slow, lazy smile came into place. "That's a very good idea. Very good indeed."

Three years later…

"I can't believe the changes in Nash," Susan commented to Savannah. She and Kurt had flown up from California to spend the Christmas holiday with them this year. The two women were working in the kitchen.

"He's such a good father to Jacob," Savannah said, blinking back tears. She cried so easily when she was pregnant, and she was entering her second trimester with this baby. If the ultrasound was accurate, they were going to have a little girl.

"Nash is doing so well and so are you. But don't you miss working at the shop?"

"No, I've got a wonderful manager and you can imagine how busy a fourteen-month-old keeps me. I've thought about going back part-time and then decided not to, not yet at any rate. What about you? Will you continue teaching?" Savannah softly patted Susan's slightly distended stomach.

"No, but I'll probably work on a substitute basis to keep up my credentials so when our family's complete, I can return without a lot of hassle."

"That's smart."

"She's my sister, isn't she?" Nash said, walking into the kitchen, cradling his son in his arms. Jacob babbled happily, waving his rattle in every direction. He'd been a contented baby from the first. Their joy.

Kurt's arms surrounded his wife and he flattened his hands over her stomach. "We've decided to have our two close together, the same way you and Savannah planned your family."

Savannah and Nash exchanged smiles. "Planned?" she teased her husband.

"The operative word there is *two*," Nash said, eyeing her suspiciously.

"Sweetheart, we've been over this a hundred times. I really would like four."

"Four!" Nash cried. "The last time we talked you said three."

"I've changed my mind. Four is a nice even number."

"Four children is out of the question," Nash said with a disgruntled look, then seemed to notice Kurt and Susan staring at him. "We'll talk about this later, all right? But we will talk."

"Of course we will," Savannah promised, unable to hold back a smile.

"She's going to do it," Nash grumbled to his sister and brother-in-law. "Somehow, before I've figured out how she's managed it, we'll be a family of six."

"You'll love it, Nash, I promise." The oven timer rang and Savannah glanced at the clock. "Oh, dear, I've got to get busy. Mr. Serle and Mr. Stackhouse will be here any minute."

"This is something else she didn't tell me before we were married," Nash said, his eyes shining with love. "She charms the most unexpected people...."

"They love Jacob," Savannah reminded him.

"True," Nash said wryly. "I've never seen two old men more taken with a toddler."

"And I've never seen a man more taken with his wife," Susan added. "I could almost be jealous, but there's no need." She turned to her husband and put her arms around his neck. "Still, it doesn't do any harm to keep him on his toes."

"No, it doesn't," Savannah agreed. And they all laughed.

★ ★ ★ ★ ★

First Comes Marriage

1

"You must be Zachary Thomas," Janine said breathlessly as she whirled into the office. "Sorry I'm late, but I got hung up in traffic on Fourth Avenue. I didn't realize they'd torn up the whole street." Still a little winded, she unfastened her coat, tossed it over the back of the visitor's chair and threw herself down, facing the large executive desk.

The man on the other side blinked twice as though he didn't know quite what to think.

"I'm Janine Hartman." She drew in a deep breath. "Gramps said if he wasn't back from his appointment, I should introduce myself."

"Yes," Zachary said after a moment of strained silence. "But he didn't tell me you'd be wearing—"

"Oh, the bandanna dress," Janine said, smoothing one hand over her lap. The dress had been constructed of red and blue bandannas; it featured a knee-length zigzag hemline and closely hugged her hips. "It was a gift. And since I'm meeting the girl who made it later, I thought I should wear it."

"And the necklace?"

Janine toyed with the colored Christmas-tree lights strung

between large beads on a bootlace that dangled from her neck. "It's a bit outrageous, isn't it? That was a gift, too. I think it's kind of cute, don't you? Pamela is so clever."

"Pamela?"

"A teenager from the Friendship Club."

"I…see," Zach said.

"I do volunteer work there and the two of us hit it off as soon as we met. Pam's mother doesn't live in the area and she's at that awkward age and needs a friend. For some reason she took a liking to me, which was fine because I think she's wonderful."

"I see," he said again.

Janine doubted he did.

"The necklace is *different* I'll grant you," Zach was saying—which wasn't admitting to much. His dark eyes narrowed as he studied it.

Now that she'd met Zachary Thomas, Janine could understand why her grandfather was so impressed with him—if appearances were anything to judge by. In his well-tailored suit, he was the very picture of a high-powered executive, crisp, formal and in control. He was younger than she'd assumed, possibly in his early thirties, but it was difficult to tell. His facial features were attractive enough, but he wasn't strikingly handsome. Still, she found herself fascinated by the strength of character she saw in the uneven planes of his face. His dark hair was cut military short. His jaw was strong, his cheekbones high and his mouth full. That was the way she'd describe him physically, but there was apparently much more to this man than met the eye. At least, her grandfather was convinced of it.

Several months earlier Anton Hartman had merged his well-established business-supply firm with the fast-expanding company owned by Zachary Thomas. Together the two men had quickly dominated the market.

For weeks now, Gramps had wanted Janine to meet Zachary. His name had popped up in every conversation, no matter what they were discussing. To say her grandfather thought highly of his partner was an understatement.

"Gramps has spoken...well of you," she said next.

A hint of a smile—just the merest suggestion—touched his mouth, giving her the impression that he didn't smile often. "Your grandfather has one of the keenest business minds in the country."

"He's incredible, isn't he?"

Zachary's nod betrayed no hesitation.

There was a polite knock on the door and a tall middle-aged woman wearing a navy-blue pin-striped suit stepped into the room. "Mr. Hartman phoned," she announced primly. "He's been delayed and asked that you meet him at the restaurant."

Zach's lean dark face tightened briefly before he cast Janine an uneasy glance. "Did he say when he was going to get there?"

"I'm sorry, Mr. Thomas, but he didn't."

Janine looked at her watch. She was supposed to meet Pam at three. If they were delayed much longer, she'd be late.

She scowled at Zach's apparent reluctance to entertain her in Gramp's absence. "Maybe it would be best if we rescheduled for another day," she offered brightly. She wasn't any happier about the prospect of waiting in a restaurant, just the two of them, than he was. "Gramps is held up, I'm meeting Pam, and you're obviously a busy man."

An uncomfortable silence followed her remark. "Is it your habit not to show up when your grandfather's expecting you?" he asked sharply.

Janine bristled. "Of course not." She swallowed the words to defend herself. Her suggestion hadn't been unreasonable and he had no right to insinuate that she was inconsiderate and rude.

"Then I feel we should meet your grandfather at the restaurant as he requested," he finished stiffly.

"By all means," she said, forcing a smile. She stood and reached for her coat, watching Zach from the corner of her eye. He didn't like her. That realization had a peculiar effect on Janine. She felt disappointed and a little sad. Zach hadn't said much, and actually there hadn't been time for a real conversation, but she'd sensed his attitude almost from the first. He thought of her as spoiled and frivolous, probably because he knew she didn't hold a responsible job and loved to travel. Part of her longed to explain that there were good reasons she'd chosen the lifestyle she had. But from the looks he was sending her, it would be a waste of breath.

Besides, it was more important to maintain the peace, however strained, for Gramps's sake. She'd have enjoyed getting to know Zach, perhaps even becoming friends, but that didn't seem likely.

That morning, before Gramps had left the house, he'd been as excited as a little boy about their luncheon date. He'd come down the stairs whistling when he'd joined her for breakfast, his blue eyes sparkling. When she'd refused the use of the limousine, he'd spent the next fifteen minutes giving her detailed directions, as though she'd never driven in downtown Seattle.

Almost as an afterthought, he'd mentioned that he had a morning meeting with an important client. If he hadn't returned by the time she arrived, she was to go directly to Zach's office, introduce herself and wait for him there.

Shrugging into a raincoat, Zachary moved toward the door. "Are you ready?"

She nodded, burying her hands in her pockets.

Thankfully the restaurant her grandfather had chosen was close by. Without further discussion, they began to walk the few short blocks, although Janine had trouble matching her stride with Zach's much longer one.

Struggling to keep up with him, Janine studied Zachary Thomas, trying to determine exactly what disturbed her about the man. His height was a good example. He wasn't tall—under six feet, she guessed—and since she was almost five-eight there wasn't more than a few inches' difference between them. Why, then, did he make her feel much shorter?

He must have sensed her scrutiny because he turned and glared at her. Janine gave him a feeble smile, and felt the color rise in her cheeks. Zach's dismissive glance did nothing to boost her ego. She wasn't vain, but Janine knew she was attractive. Over the years, plenty of men had told her so, including Brian, the man who'd broken her heart. But she could have warts on her nose for all the notice Zachary Thomas gave her.

If he found the bandanna dress disconcerting, he was probably put off by her hairstyle as well. She wore it short, neatly trimmed in the back with extra-long bangs slanted across her forehead. For years Janine had kept her hair shoulder-length, parted in the middle. One afternoon a few weeks earlier, for no particular reason, she'd decided to have it cut. She was in the mood for something radical and the style she now sported seemed more appropriate to the pages of a fashion magazine. Pam had been crazy about the change, insisting she looked "phenomenal." Janine wasn't convinced. Her one comfort was that, given time, her hair would grow back.

Janine suspected Zach had characterized her as flamboyant, if not downright flashy. She, in turn, would describe him as austere and disciplined, perhaps solitary. Her grandfather saw all that, she knew, and a good deal more.

"Mr. Hartman is waiting for you," the maître d' informed them when they entered the plush waterfront restaurant. He led them across the thick carpet to a high semicircular booth upholstered in blue velvet.

"Janine, Zach." Anton Hartman smiled broadly as they approached. The years had been kind to her grandfather. His bearing was still straight and confident, although his hair had grown completely white. His deep blue eyes, only a little faded, were filled with warmth and wisdom. "I apologize for the inconvenience."

"It wasn't any problem," Zach answered for both of them before Janine could respond—as if he'd expected her to complain!

Ignoring him, Janine removed her coat and kissed her grandfather's leathery cheek.

"Janine," he began, then gasped. "Where did you get that... dress?"

"Do you like it?" She threw out her arms and whirled around once to give him the full effect. "I know it's a bit unconventional, but I didn't think you'd mind."

Gramps's gaze flickered to Zach, then back to her. "On anyone else it would be scandalous, but on you, my dear, it's a work of art."

"Honestly, Gramps," she said, laughing softly. "You never could lie very well." She slid into the booth next to her grandfather, forcing him into the center, between her and Zach. Gramps looked a bit disgruntled, but after her turbulent first encounter with Zach, she preferred to keep her distance. For that matter, he didn't seem all that eager to be close to her, either.

She glanced at him and noted, almost smugly, that he was already studying the menu. No doubt he found ordinary conversation a waste of time. Janine picked up her own menu. She was famished. At breakfast she'd only had time for coffee and a single piece of toast, and she had every intention of making up for it now.

When the waiter came to take their order, Janine asked for the seafood entrée and soup *and* salad. She'd decide about dessert later, she said. Once he'd left, Gramps leaned toward Zach. "Janine never has to worry about her weight." He made this sound as if it was a subject of profound and personal interest to them both. "Her grandmother was the same way. How my Anna could eat, and she never gained an ounce. Janine's just like her."

"Gramps," Janine whispered under her breath. "I'm sure Zach couldn't care less how much I weigh."

"Nonsense," Gramps said, gently patting her hand. "I hope you two had the chance to introduce yourselves."

"Oh, yes," Janine returned automatically.

"Your granddaughter is everything you claimed," Zachary said, but the inflection in his voice implied something completely different to Janine than it did to her grandfather. She guessed that to Anton, he seemed courteous and complimentary. But he was telling Janine he'd found her to be the spoiled darling he'd long suspected. He didn't openly dislike her, but he wasn't too impressed with her, either.

Unfortunately, that was probably due to more than just the dress and the lightbulb necklace.

Janine watched for her grandfather's reaction to Zach's words and she knew she was right when his gaze warmed and he nodded, obviously pleased by his partner's assessment. Zachary Thomas was clever, Janine had to grant him that much.

"How did the meeting with Anderson go?" Zach asked.

For a moment her grandfather stared at him blankly. "Oh, Anderson... Fine, fine. Everything went just as I'd hoped." Then he cleared his throat and carefully spread the linen napkin across his lap. "As you both know," he said, "I've been wanting the two of you to meet for some time now. Janine is the joy of my life. She's kept me young and brought me much happiness over the years. I fear that, without her, I would have turned into a bitter old man."

His look was so full of tenderness that Janine had to lower her eyes and swallow back a rush of tears. Gramps had been her salvation, too. He'd taken her in after the sudden deaths of her parents, raised her with a gentle hand and loved her enough to allow her to be herself. It must've been difficult for him to have a six-year-old girl unexpectedly thrust into his life, but he'd never complained.

"My only son died far too young," Anton said slowly, painfully.

"I'm sorry," Zachary murmured.

The genuine compassion Janine heard in his voice surprised her. And it definitely pleased her. Zach's respect and affection for her grandfather won her immediate approval—even if the man didn't seem likely to ever feel anything so positive toward *her*.

"For many years I mourned the loss of my son and his wife," Anton continued, his voice gaining strength. "I've worked all my life, built an empire that stretches across these fifty states, and in the process have become a wealthy man."

Janine studied her grandfather closely. He was rarely this serious. He wasn't one to list his accomplishments, and she wondered at his strange mood.

"When Zach brought his business into the area, I saw in him a rare gift, one that comes along seldom in this life. It's said that there are men who make things happen, those who watch things happen and those who wonder what happened. Zachary is a man who makes things happen. In many ways, the two of us are alike. That's one of the primary reasons I decided to approach him with a proposal to merge our companies."

"I'm honored that you should think so, sir."

"Sir," Anton repeated softly and chuckled. He raised his hand, motioning for the waiter. "You haven't called me that in six months, and there's no reason to start again now."

The waiter returned with a bottle of expensive champagne. Soon glasses were poured and set before them.

"Now," Anton continued, "as I said earlier, I have the two people I love most in this world together with me for the first time, and I don't mind telling you, it feels good." He raised his glass. "To happiness."

"Happiness," Janine echoed, sipping her champagne.

Her eyes met Zach's above the crystal flute and she saw a glint of admiration. If she were dining on it, she'd starve—to quote a favorite expression of her grandfather's—but it was just enough for her to know that he'd think more kindly of her because of her love for Anton.

Her grandfather chuckled and whispered something in his native tongue, a German dialect from the old country. Over the years she'd picked up a smattering of the language, but when she'd repeated a few phrases to a college German professor, he'd barely recognized the words. Gramps paused and his smile lingered on Janine, then went to Zach. Whatever Gramps was muttering appeared to please him. His blue eyes fairly twinkled with delight.

"And now," he said, setting his glass aside, "I have an important announcement to make."

He turned to Janine and his face softened with affection. "I feel as though I've been an impossible burden to you, child, what with running this company." He shook his head. "Never in all my dreams did I expect to accumulate so much in a single lifetime. I've stayed in the business far longer than I should. It's time for me to retire and do a little traveling."

"It's past time," Janine said. For years, she'd been urging her grandfather to lessen his heavy work schedule. He'd often spoken of revisiting his birthplace and the surrounding countries. He talked at length of cousins and friends he'd left behind in the small German settlement. It was located in what was now part of Russia.

"This is where Zachary comes into the picture," Anton explained. "I know myself all too well. Full retirement would be impossible for me. If I stopped working, I'd shrivel up and die. That's just the way I am," he said simply.

Neither Janine nor Zachary disputed his words.

"I'll never be able to keep my fingers out of the business, yet I want to enjoy my travels. I couldn't do that if I was fretting about what was going on at the office." He paused as if he expected one of them to contradict him. "I believe I've come upon a solution. As of this afternoon, Zachary, I'm handing the reins to you. You will assume my position as chairman of the board. I realize this is sooner than we discussed, but the time is right and I hope you'll agree."

"But, Anton—"

"Gramps—"

Anton held up his hand. "I've thought about this long and hard," he said confidently. "I find Zach's honesty unquestionable, his loyalty certain and his intelligence keen. He's shrewd, perceptive and insightful. I can think of no better man, and there's no better time."

Janine noticed that Zach seemed uncomfortable with the praise. "Thank you," was all he said.

"A share of this company will belong to you someday, Janine," Anton said next. "Do you have any objections to this appointment?"

She opened her mouth, but nothing came out. Of course she approved. What else could she do? "Whatever you decide is fine with me."

Anton turned his attention to the other man. "Zachary, do you accept?"

Although their acquaintance had been brief, Janine knew instinctively that it took a lot to fluster this man. But her grandfather had managed to do so.

Zachary continued to stare at him as though he couldn't quite believe what he was hearing. But when he spoke, his voice was well modulated, revealing little emotion. "I'm honored."

"For the next few months, we'll be working closely together, much as we have in the past, but with a difference. No longer will I be showing you the ropes. I'll be handing them to you."

The first course of their lunch arrived, and after that, the conversation flowed smoothly. Her grandfather made sure of it. He was jubilant and entertaining, witty and charming. It would have been impossible not to be affected by his good humor.

When they'd finished the meal, Zachary looked at his watch. "I'm sorry to leave so soon, but I have an appointment."

Janine took a last sip of her coffee. "I should be leaving, too." She reached for her purse and coat, then slid out of the booth, waiting for her grandfather to join her.

"If neither of you objects, I'm going to linger over my coffee," Anton said, nodding toward his steaming cup.

"Of course." Janine leaned over to kiss him goodbye.

Zachary walked out to the street with her. Before he left, he shook her hand. "It's been a pleasure, Ms. Hartman."

"You're sure?" she teased, unable to stop herself.

"Yes." His eyes held hers and he smiled. She walked away feeling oddly excited about their meeting. Zach wasn't an easy person to know, but she suspected he was everything her grandfather claimed and more.

Gramps's mood remained cheerful when he got home later that evening. Janine was in the library sipping herbal tea with her feet tucked under her as she watched the local news.

Sitting in the wingback leather chair next to her, Gramps crossed his legs and chose one of his Havana cigars. Janine shook her head affectionately as he lit it; she loved her grandfather dearly and wished he'd stop smoking, though she no longer bothered to express that wish. He was the kind of man who did exactly as he chose, got exactly what he wanted. He was obviously pleased with the way their luncheon had gone, and she wondered briefly if Zach had said anything about her afterward. Somehow she doubted it.

"Well," he said after a moment, "What do you think of Zachary Thomas?" He blew a steady stream of smoke at the ceiling while he awaited her answer.

All afternoon, Janine had prepared herself for his question. Several complicated answers had presented themselves, clever replies that would sidestep her true feelings, but she used none of them now. Her grandfather expected the truth, and it was her duty to give it to him.

"I'm not sure. He's a very...reserved man, isn't he?"

Anton chuckled. "Yes, he is, but I've never known you to walk away from a challenge. The boy's a little rough around the edges, but on the inside, he's pure gold."

Janine hadn't thought of Zach in those terms—a challenge. Frankly, she doubted there'd be much reason for her to have any future contact with him. Gramps and Zach would be working closely together, but she had almost nothing to do with the business.

"I've earned his trust, but it took time," Gramps was saying now.

"I'm glad you've decided to retire," she said absently, half listening to the weather report.

"Zachary will change," her grandfather added.

He had her full attention now. "Gramps," she said patiently, holding in a laugh. "Why should he? He's achieved considerable financial success. Everything's looking good for him. What possible reason could there be for him to change?"

Anton stood and poured himself a liberal dose of brandy, swirling it slowly in the bottom of the snifter. "You're going to change him," he said after a thoughtful moment.

"Me?" Janine laughed outright. "*I'm* going to change Zachary Thomas?" she repeated in wide-eyed disbelief. That would be the day!

"Before you argue with me, and I can see that's what you're dying to do, I have a story I want to tell you. A rather sad one as it happens."

Janine picked up the remote control and snapped off the television. She'd often listened to her grandfather's parables. "So tell me."

"It's about a boy, born on the wrong side of the tracks to an alcoholic father and a weak mother. He never had much of a chance in life. His father was abusive enough for the state to remove the lad and his younger sister. He was barely eight and subjected to a long series of foster homes, but he refused to be separated from his sister. He'd promised her he'd always take care of her.

"Once, there wasn't any alternative and the two were sent to separate homes. Beside himself with worry for his sister, the young boy ran away. The authorities were in a panic, but three days later, he turned up two hundred miles away at the home where they'd placed Beth Ann."

"He probably felt responsible for her."

"Yes. Which made matters much worse when she drowned in a swimming accident. He was twelve at the time."

"Oh, no." A pain squeezed Janine's heart at the agony the boy had suffered.

"He blamed himself, of course," Anton said softly.

"The poor kid."

"This lad never seemed to belong to anyone after that," Gramps said, staring into his brandy. "He never quite fit in, but that wasn't entirely his fault." He paused to take another puff of his cigar. "His mother died a month after his sister. They were the only ones who'd ever truly loved him. He lost contact with his father, which was probably for the best. So his family was gone and no one seemed to want this troubled, hurting boy."

"Did he turn into a juvenile delinquent?" It made sense to Janine that he would; she'd dealt with a number of troubled teenagers through her volunteer work and was familiar with the tragic patterns that so often evolved in cases like this.

"No, I can't say he did." Gramps dismissed her question with a shake of his head, more interested in continuing his tale than getting sidetracked by her questions. "He drifted through adolescence without an anchor and without ever being allowed to enjoy those formative years."

"Gramps—"

He raised his hand to stop her. "When he was eighteen, he joined the military. He did well, which isn't surprising, considering his intelligence and the fact that he had little regard for his own well-being. There was no one to mourn if he died. Because of his courage, he advanced quickly, volunteering for the riskiest assignments. He traveled all over the world to some of the most dangerous political hot spots. His duties were often top secret. There's no telling how far he might have gone had he chosen to remain in the armed services, but for some reason, he resigned. No one understood why. I suspect he wanted to start his life over. This was when he opened a business-supply company. Within a year, he had my attention. His methods were aggressive and creative. I couldn't help admiring the way he handled himself and the company. Within five years, he'd become one of my most serious rivals. I saw a strength in him that age had stolen from me. We met. We talked. As a result of these talks we joined forces."

"Obviously you're telling me about Zachary's life."

Anton grinned and slowly sipped his brandy. "You noticed his remoteness quickly. I thought knowing all this would help you. Zach's never had the security that a caring home and family provide. He's never really experienced love, except what he shared with his sister, Beth Ann. His life has been a long progression of painful experiences. By sheer force of will, he's managed to overcome every obstacle placed in his path. I realize Zachary Thomas isn't going to win any Mr. Personality contests, but by heaven, he's earned my respect."

Janine had rarely heard such emotion in her grandfather's voice. "Zach told you all this?"

Anton's laughter echoed through the room. "You're joking, aren't you? Zach has never spoken of his past to me. I doubt that he has to anyone."

"You had him investigated?"

Gramps puffed on his cigar before answering. "It was necessary, although I'd guessed early on that his life hadn't been a bed of roses."

"It's all very sad, isn't it?"

"You're going to be very good for him, my dear."

Janine blinked. "Me?"

"Yes, you. You're going to teach him to laugh and enjoy life. But most important, you're going to teach him about love."

She hesitated, uncertain of her grandfather's meaning. "I don't think I understand. I realize Zach and I will probably see each other now and then since he's assuming your responsibilities with the company, but I don't see how I could have any great impact on his life."

Gramps smiled, a slow lazy smile that curved the corners of his mouth. "That's where you're wrong, my dear. You're going to play a very big role in Zach's life, and he in yours."

Janine was still confused. "Perhaps I missed something this afternoon. I thought you made Zach the chairman of the board."

"I did." A lazy swirl of smoke circled his head.

"I don't understand where I come into the picture."

"I don't suppose you do," he said softly. "You see, Janine, I've chosen Zachary to be your husband."

2

For a stunned moment, Janine said nothing. "You're teasing, aren't you, Gramps?"

"No," he said, lighting a second cigar. He paused to stare at the glowing tip, his eyes filled with mischief—and with something else, less easily defined. "I'm serious."

"But…" Janine's thoughts were so jumbled she couldn't make sense of them herself, let alone convey her feelings to her grandfather.

"I've been giving the matter serious consideration for some time now. Zach's perfect for you and you're the ideal complement to him. You're going to have beautiful blond-haired children."

"But…" Janine discovered she was absolutely speechless. One minute she was listening to a touching story, and the next her grandfather was telling her about the husband he'd arranged for her—and even the color of her children's hair.

"Once you think about it," Gramps said confidently, "I'm sure you'll agree with me. Zach is a fine young man, and he'll make you an excellent husband."

"You… Zach talked…agreed?" The words stumbled over the end of her tongue.

"Do you mean have I suggested this arrangement to Zach?" Gramps asked. "Heavens, no. At least not yet." He chuckled as if he found the thought amusing. "Zach wouldn't appreciate my blatant interference in his personal affairs. With him, I'll need to be far more subtle. To be honest, I considered making this marriage part of my handing over the chairmanship, but after thinking it through, I changed my mind. Zach would never have agreed. There are other ways, I decided, better ways. But I don't want you to worry about it. That's between Zach and me."

"I…see." At this point, Janine wasn't sure *what* she saw, other than one determined old man caught between two worlds. In certain respects, the old ways continued to dominate his thinking, but his success in America allowed him to appreciate more modern outlooks.

Gramps inhaled deeply on his cigar, his blue eyes twinkling. "Now, I realize you probably find the idea of an arranged marriage slightly unorthodox, but you'll get used to it. I've made a fine choice for you, and I know you're smart enough to recognize that."

"Gramps, I don't think you fully understand what you're suggesting," she said, trying to gather her scattered wits, hoping she could explain the ridiculousness of this whole scheme without offending him.

"But I do, my child."

"In this country and in this age," she continued slowly, "men and women choose their own mates. We fall in love and then marry."

Gramps frowned. "Sadly, that doesn't work," he muttered.

"What do you mean, it doesn't work?" she cried, losing her patience. "It's been like this for years and years!"

"Look at the divorce rate. I read in the paper recently that almost fifty percent of all marriages in this country fail. In the old country, there was no divorce. Parents decided whom a son or daughter would marry, and their decision was accepted without question. First comes marriage, and then comes love."

"Gramps," Janine said softly, wanting to reason this out with him. Her grandfather was a logical man; surely, if she explained it properly, he'd understand. "Things are done differently now. First comes love, then comes marriage."

"What do you young people know about love?"

"A good deal, as it happens," she returned, lying smoothly. Her first venture into love had ended with a broken heart and a shattered ego, but she'd told Gramps little if anything about Brian.

"Pfft!" he spat. "What could you possibly know of love?"

"I realize," she said, thinking fast, "that your father arranged your marriage to Grandma, but that was years ago, and in America such customs don't exist. You and I live *here* now, in the land of the free. The land of opportunity."

Gramps gazed down into his brandy for a long moment, lost in thought. Janine doubted he'd even heard her.

"I'll never forget the first time I saw my Anna," he said in a faraway voice. "She was sixteen and her hair was long and blond and fell in braids to her waist. My father spoke to her father and while they were talking, Anna and I sat at opposite ends of the room, too shy to look at each other. I wondered if she thought I was handsome. To me, she was the most beautiful girl in the world. Even now, after all these years, I can remember how my heart beat with excitement when I saw her. I knew—"

"But, Gramps, that was nearly sixty years ago! Marriages aren't decided by families anymore. A man and a woman discover each other without a father introducing them. Maybe the old ways were better back then, but it's simply not like that now." Gramps continued to stare into his glass, lost in a world long since enveloped by the passage of time.

"The next day, Anna's parents visited our farm and again our two fathers spoke. I tried to pretend I wasn't concerned, determined to accept whatever our families decided. But when I saw our fathers shake hands and slap each other on the back, I knew Anna would soon be mine."

"You loved her before you were married, didn't you?" Janine asked softly, hoping to prove her point.

"No," he returned flatly, without hesitation. "How could I love her when I'd only seen her twice before the wedding? We hadn't said more than a handful of words to each other. Love wasn't necessary for us to find happiness. Love came later, after we arrived in America."

"Wasn't it unusual for a marriage to be arranged even then? It wasn't *that* long ago." There had to be some point for her to contend, Janine mused.

"Perhaps it was unusual in other parts of the world, but not in Vibiskgrad. We were a small farming community. Our world had been ravaged by war and hate. We clung to each other, holding on to our own traditions and rituals. Soon our lives became impossible and we were forced to flee our homes."

"As I said before, I can understand how an arranged marriage—back then—might be the best for everyone involved. But I can't see it working in this day and age. I'm sorry to disappoint you, Gramps, but I'm not willing to accept Zachary Thomas as my husband, and I'm sure he'd be equally unwilling to marry me."

Briefly Gramps's face tensed with a rare display of disappointment and indignation, then quickly relaxed. Janine had seldom questioned his authority and had never openly defied him.

"I suppose this is a shock to you, isn't it?" he said.

If it astonished *her*, she couldn't wait to hear what Zachary Thomas thought! They'd only met once, but he hadn't disguised his opinion of her. He wouldn't take kindly to Gramps's plan of an arranged marriage—especially to a woman he viewed as spoiled and overindulged.

"All I'm asking is that you consider this, Janine," Gramps

said. "Promise me you'll at least do that. Don't reject marriage to Zach simply because you think it's old-fashioned."

"Oh, Gramps..." Janine hated to refuse him anything. "It isn't just me. What about Zach? What about *his* plans? What if he—"

Gramps dismissed her questions with an abrupt shrug. "How often do I ask something of you?" he persisted.

Now he was going to use guilt. "Not often," she agreed, frowning at him for using unfair tactics.

"Then consider Zach for your husband!" His eyes brightened. "The two of you will have such beautiful children. A grandfather knows these things."

"I promise I'll think about it." But it wouldn't do any good! However, discretion was a virtue Janine was nurturing, and there'd never been a better time to employ it than now.

Gramps didn't mention Zach Thomas or even hint at the subject of her marrying his business partner again until the following evening. They'd just sat down to dinner, prepared to sample Mrs. McCormick's delicious fare, when Gramps looked anxiously at Janine. "So?" he asked breathlessly.

From the moment he'd walked into the house that afternoon, Gramps's mood had been light and humorous. Grinning, he handed her the platter of thinly sliced marinated and grilled flank steak. It happened to be one of Janine's favorite meals. "So?" he repeated, smiling at her. "What did you decide?"

Janine helped herself to a crisp dinner roll, buttering it slowly as her thoughts chased each other in frantic circles. "Nothing."

His smile collapsed into a frown. "You promised me you'd consider marrying Zach. I gave you more time than Anna's father gave her."

"You have to know now?"

"Now!"

"But, Gramps, a simple yes or no isn't an appropriate response to something as complex as this. You're asking me to decide on a lifelong commitment in less than twenty-four hours." She was stalling for time, and Gramps had probably guessed as much. Frankly, she didn't know what to tell him. She couldn't, wouldn't, marry Zach—even if he was willing to marry her— but she hated disappointing her grandfather.

"What's so difficult? Either you marry him or not!"

"I don't understand why you've decided to match me up with Zach Thomas," she cried. "What's wrong with Peter?" She'd been dating the other man casually for the last few months. Her heart was too bruised after what had happened with Brian for her to date anyone seriously.

"You're in love with that whitewashed weakling?"

Janine signed loudly, regretting the fact that she'd introduced Peter into their conversation. "He's very nice."

"So is chocolate mousse!" Gramps muttered. "Peter Dona-hue would make you a terrible husband. I'm shocked you'd even think about marrying him."

"I hadn't actually thought about him in those terms," she said. Peter was witty and fun, but Gramps was right; they weren't suited as husband and wife.

"I thank the good Lord you've been given some sense."

Janine took a deep breath and finally asked a question that had been nagging at her all afternoon. "Did—did you arrange my father's marriage?"

Gramps lowered his eyes, but not before he could disguise the pain there. "No. He fell in love with Patrice while he was in college. I knew the match wasn't a good one, but Anna re-minded me that this was America and young people fell in love by themselves. She convinced me they didn't need a father's guiding hand the way we did in the old country."

"Do you think he would've listened if you'd wanted to ar-range a marriage?"

Her grandfather hesitated, and his hand tightened on his

water glass. "I don't know, but I'd like to believe he would have."

"Instead he married my mother."

Neither spoke for a long moment. Janine remembered little of her parents, only bits and pieces of memory, mostly unconnected. What she did recall were terrible fights and accusations, a house filled with strife. She could remember hiding under her bed when the shouting started, pressing her hands to her ears. It was her father who used to find her, who comforted her. Always her father. Her memory included almost nothing of her mother. Even pictures didn't jar her recollection, although Janine had spent hour upon hour looking at photographs, hoping to remember *something*. But the woman who'd given birth to her had remained a stranger to her in life and in death.

"You're the only consolation I have from Steven's marriage," Anton said hoarsely. "At least I had you after Steven and Patrice died."

"Oh, Gramps. I love you so much and I hate to disappoint you, but I can't marry Zach and I can't see him agreeing to marry me."

Her grandfather was silent after that, apparently mulling over her words as he finished his dinner. "I suppose I seem like a feeble old man, still trying to live the old ways."

"Gramps, no, I don't think that at all."

He planted his elbows squarely on the table and linked his fingers, gazing at her. His brow was puckered in a contemplative frown. "Perhaps it would help if you told me what you want in a husband."

She hesitated, then glanced away, avoiding eye contact. Once she'd been so certain of what she wanted. "To be perfectly honest, I'm not sure. Romance, I suppose."

"Romance." Gramps rolled the word off his tongue as though he was tasting an expensive wine.

"Yes," she said with a nod of her head, gaining confidence.

"And what exactly is romance?"

"Well…" Now that she'd been called upon to define it, Janine couldn't quite put that magical feeling into words. "It's… it's an awareness that comes from the heart."

"The heart," her grandfather repeated, smacking his palm against his chest.

"Romance is the knowledge that a man would rather die than live his life without me," she said, warming to the subject.

"You want him to die?"

"No, just to be willing."

Gramps frowned. "I don't think I understand."

"Romance is forbidden trysts on lonely Scottish moors," she added, thinking of an historical romance she'd read as a teenager.

"There aren't any moors in the Seattle area."

"Don't distract me," she said, smiling, her thoughts gaining momentum. "Romance is desperate passion."

He snorted. "That sounds more like hormones to me."

"Gramps, please!"

"How can I understand when all you say is ridiculous things? You want romance. First you claim it's a feeling in the heart, then you say it's some kind of passion."

"It's more than that. It's walking hand in hand along the beach at twilight and gazing into each other's eyes. It's speaking of love without ever having to say the words." She paused, feeling a little foolish at getting so carried away. "I don't know if I can adequately describe it."

"That's because you haven't experienced it."

"Maybe not," she agreed reluctantly. "But I will someday."

"With Zach," he said with complete assurance and a wide grin.

Janine didn't bother to argue. Gramps was being obstinate and arguing with him was pointless. The only recourse she had was time itself. Soon enough he'd realize that neither she nor Zach was going to fall in with his scheme. Then, and only then, would he drop the subject.

A week passed and Gramps hadn't said another word about arranging a marriage between her and Zachary Thomas. It was a cold windy March evening and the rain was coming down in torrents. Janine loved nights like this and was curled up in her favorite chair with a mystery novel when the doorbell chimed. Gramps had gone out for the evening and she wasn't expecting anyone.

She turned on the porch light and looked out the peephole to discover Zach standing there, a briefcase in his hand. His shoulders were hunched against the pelting rain.

"Zach," she said in surprise, throwing open the door.

"Hello, Janine," he said politely, stepping inside. "Is your grandfather here?"

"No." She held the book against her chest, her heart pounding hard. "He went out."

Zach frowned, clearly confused. "He asked me to stop by. There were some business matters he wanted to discuss. Did he say when he'd be home?"

"No, but I'm sure if he asked you over, it'll be soon. Would you care to wait for him?"

"Please."

She took his raincoat, then led him into the library where she'd been reading. A fire was burning, and its warmth hugged the room. The three-story house, situated in Seattle's Mt. Baker district, was a typical turn-of-the-century home with high ceilings and spacious rooms. The third floor had once housed several servants. Charles was their only live-in help now, and his quarters had always been an apartment over the carriage house. He worked exclusively for Gramps, driving the limousine. Mrs. McCormick arrived early in the mornings and was responsible for housekeeping and meal preparation.

"Can I get you something to drink?" she asked, once he was comfortably seated.

"Coffee, if you have it."

"I made a fresh pot about twenty minutes ago."

Janine brought him a cup from the kitchen, then sat across from Zach, wondering what, if anything, she should say about Gramps and his idea of an arranged marriage.

She doubted that Gramps had broached the subject yet. Otherwise he wouldn't be sitting there so calmly sipping coffee. He'd be outraged and infuriated, and studying him now, she concluded that he wasn't even slightly ruffled. It was on the tip of her tongue to warn him about what was coming, but she decided against it. Better that he learn the same way she had.

Lacing her fingers together, she smiled, feeling awkward and a little gauche. "It's nice to see you again."

"You, too. I'll admit I'm a bit disappointed, though."

"You are?"

"On the drive over, I was trying to guess what you'd be wearing this time. A dress made from bread sacks? A blouse constructed out of men's socks?"

She muttered under her breath, annoyed by his teasing. He had the uncanny ability to make her feel fifteen all over again. So much for any possibility that they'd ever be compatible. And Gramps seemed to think he knew them both so well.

"I'll admit that an Irish cable-knit sweater and jeans are a pleasant surprise," he said.

A flicker of admiration sparked in his dark eyes, something that had been missing the first time they met.

In that instant, Janine knew.

She went stock-still, almost dizzy with the realization. Not only had Gramps approached Zach, but they'd apparently reached some sort of agreement. Otherwise Zach would never have been this friendly, this openly appreciative. Nor would he arrive unannounced when Gramps had specifically stated that he'd be gone for the evening.

They were obviously plotting against her. Well, she had no intention of putting up with it. None. If Zach and Gramps thought they could lure her into marriage, they had a real shock coming.

Squaring her shoulders, she slid to the edge of her chair. "So you gave in to the pressure," she said, shooting him a scalding look. Unable to stay seated, she jumped to her feet and started pacing, rubbing her palms together as she cornered her thoughts. "Gramps got to you, didn't he?"

"I beg your pardon?" Zach stared up at her, his eyes curious.

"And you agreed?" She threw up her hands and groaned, "I don't believe it, I simply don't believe it. I thought better of you than this."

"What don't you believe?"

"Of all the men I've met over the years, I would've sworn you were the type who'd refuse to be bought. I'm disappointed in you, Zach."

He remained calm and unperturbed, which infuriated her more than anything he could have said or done.

"I haven't got the slightest idea what you're talking about," was all he said.

"Oh, sure, play the innocent," she snapped. She was so incensed that she continued to pace. Standing still was impossible.

In response, Zach merely glanced at his watch and drank his coffee. "Does your grandfather know you suffer from these bouts of hysteria?"

"Funny, Zach, very funny."

He exhaled an exaggerated sigh. "All right, I'll take the bait. What makes you think I've been bought? And what exactly am I getting in exchange?"

"Technically you're not getting anything, and I want that

understood this very minute, because *I* refuse to be sold." Arms akimbo, she turned to glare down at him with the full force of her disdain. "What did he offer you? The entire company? Lots of money?"

Zach shrugged. "He's offered me nothing."

"Nothing," she repeated slowly, feeling unreasonably insulted. "He was just going to *give* me away." That was enough to deflate the billowing sails of her pride. Stunned, she sat down again. "I thought the bride's family was supposed to supply some kind of dowry. Gramps didn't even offer you money?"

"Dowry?" Zach repeated the word as if he'd never heard it before.

"Gramps's family received a cow and ten chickens from my grandmother's family," she said, as if that explained everything. "But apparently I'm not even worth a single hen."

Zach set his coffee aside and sat straight in his chair. "I think we'd better begin this conversation again. I'm afraid I lost you back there when you said something about cracking under pressure. Perhaps you should enlighten me about what I'm supposed to have done."

Janine just glared at him.

"Humor me."

"All right, if you insist. It's obvious that Gramps talked to you about the marriage."

"Marriage," he echoed in a shocked voice. His face went blank. "To whom?"

"Me, of course."

Zach flung himself out of the chair, bolting to his feet. "To you?"

"Don't look so horrified! My ego's taken about all it can for one evening. I'm not exactly the Wicked Witch of the West, you know. Some men would be more than happy to marry me." Not Brian, and certainly not Peter, but she felt it was important that Zach think she was sought after.

"Marriage between us is...would be impossible. It's completely out of the question. I don't ever plan to marry—I have no use for a wife or family."

"Tell that to Gramps."

"I have every intention of doing so." His face tightened and Janine guessed her grandfather was due for an earful when he got home. "What makes that crazy old man think he can order people's lives like this?" he asked angrily.

"His own marriage was arranged for him. Trust me, Zach, I argued until I was exhausted, but Gramps hasn't given up his old-country beliefs and he thinks the two of us—now this is really ridiculous—are perfect for each other."

"If you weren't serious, I'd find this highly amusing."

Janine noticed that he seemed rather pale. "I appear to have jumped to the wrong conclusion earlier. I apologize for that but, well, I thought... I assumed Gramps had spoken to you already and you'd agreed."

"Was that when you started mumbling about a cow and a few chickens?"

She nodded and her long bangs fell over her eyes. Absently she pushed them aside. "For a moment there, I thought Gramps was offering me to you gratis. I know it's silly, but I felt insulted by that."

For the first time since they'd entered into this conversation, Zach's face softened and he granted her a faint smile. "Your grandfather loves you, no question."

"I know." Feeling self-conscious, she threaded her fingers through her hair. "I've used every argument I could come up with. I explained the importance of romance and told him how vital it is for men and women to fall in love with the person of their choice. However, he refused to accept any of it."

"He wouldn't listen to you?"

"He listened," she replied, feeling defeated, "but he disputed everything I said. Gramps says the modern version of love and marriage is a complete failure. With the divorce rate what it is, I'm afraid I don't have much of an argument."

"That's true enough," Zach said, looking frustrated.

"I told him men and women fall in love and then decide to get married, but Gramps insists it's better if marriage comes first."

Zach rubbed a hand over his face. "Now that I think about it, your grandfather's been introducing you into every conversation, telling me how wonderful you are."

Janine gasped softly. "He's done the same to me about you. He started weeks before we even met."

Pressing his lips together, Zach nodded. "A lot of things are beginning to make sense."

"What should we do?" Janine wondered aloud. "It's perfectly obvious that we'll have to agree on a plan of action. I hate to disappoint Gramps, but I'm not willing to be married off like…like…" Words failed her.

"Especially to me."

Although his low words were devoid of emotion, Janine recognized the pain behind his statement. Knowing what she did about his past, the fact that he'd experienced only brief patches of love in his life and little or no approval tugged at her heart.

"I didn't mean it to sound like that," she insisted. "My grandfather wouldn't have chosen you if he didn't think you were pretty special. He prides himself on his ability to judge character, and he's always been impressed with you."

"Let's not kid ourselves, Janine," Zach returned, his voice hardening. "You're an uptown girl. We're totally unsuited."

"I agree with you there, but not for the reasons you assume. From the minute I stepped into your office, you made it clear that you thought of me as some kind of snob. I'm not, but I refuse to waste my breath arguing with you."

"Fine."

"Instead of hurling insults at each other," she suggested, crossing her arms in a show of indignation, "why don't we come up with a plan to deal with Gramps's preposterous idea?"

"That isn't necessary," he countered. "I want no part of it."

"And you think I do?"

Zach said nothing.

Janine expelled her breath loudly. "It seems to me the solution is for one of us to marry someone else. That would quickly put an end to this whole thing."

"I already told you I have no intention of marrying," he said emphatically. "You're the one who insinuated you had plenty of men hanging around just waiting for you to say 'I do.'"

"None that I'd consider marrying, for heaven's sake," she grumbled. "Besides, I'm not currently in love with anyone."

Zach laughed, if the sound that came from his throat could be called a laugh. "Then find a man who's current. If you fall in and out of love that easily, surely there's got to be at least one prospect on the horizon."

"There isn't. *You're* going to have to come up with someone! Why don't you go out there and sweep some sweet young thing off her feet," she muttered sarcastically.

"I'm not willing to sacrifice my life so you can get off scot-free." His words were low and furious.

"But it's perfectly all right for *me* to sabotage mine? That makes a lot of sense."

"Okay," he said after a tense moment. He paused, shaking his head. "That idea's obviously not going to work. I guess we'll have to come up with something better."

"Okay, then." Janine gestured toward him. "It's your turn."

He glared at her, seeming to dislike her even more. In all honesty, Janine wasn't too pleased with the way she was behaving, either. She'd been sarcastic and needlessly rude, but then, Zach had driven her to it. He could be the most unpleasant man.

Still, Janine was about to say something conciliatory when the sound of the front door opening distracted her. Her gaze flew to Zach and he nodded, reassuring her that he'd handle the situation.

They'd returned to their chairs and were seated by the time Gramps appeared in the library doorway.

"Zach, I'm sorry for the delay. I'm glad to see Janine entertained you." Her grandfather smiled brightly as if to tell her he approved and hoped she'd taken advantage of this hour alone with Zach.

"We did manage to have a stimulating conversation," Zach said, his eyes briefly meeting Janine's.

"Good. Good."

Zach stood and reached for his briefcase. "There were some figures you wanted to go over with me?"

"Yes." Looking satisfied with himself, Gramps led the way out of the room. Zach followed him, with a glance back at Janine that said he'd get in touch with her later.

Later turned out to be almost a week. She was puttering around outside, trimming back the rosebushes and deciding where to plant the geraniums this year, when Mrs. McCormick came to tell her she was wanted on the phone.

"Hello," Janine said cheerfully.

"We need to talk," Zach said without preamble.

"Why?" she demanded. If he was going to keep her hanging for six anxious days, then she wasn't going to give the impression that she was thrilled to hear from him.

"Your grandfather laid his cards on the table this afternoon. I thought you might be interested in hearing what he's offering me to take you off his hands."

3

"All right," Janine said, bracing herself. "What's he offering you? Huge bonuses?"

"No," Zach said quickly.

"Cash? I want to know exactly how much."

"He didn't offer me money."

Janine frowned. "What then?"

"I think we should meet and talk about it."

If her grandfather had openly approached Zach with the arranged-marriage idea, Janine knew darn well that Gramps would've made it worth Zach's while. Despite his claims to the contrary, it wouldn't have surprised Janine to discover that the newly appointed chairman of the board of Hartman-Thomas Business Supply had taken the bait.

"You want us to meet?" she repeated in a faltering voice.

"There's a restaurant on University Way—Italian 642. Have you heard of it?"

"No, but I'll find it."

"Meet me there at seven." Zach paused, then added, "And listen, it might not be a good idea to tell your grandfather that we're getting together. He might misunderstand."

"I won't say anything," she promised.

Zach hesitated once more. "We have a lot to discuss."

Janine's heartbeat accelerated, and she felt the perspiration break out on her forehead. "Zach," she began, "you haven't changed your mind, have you? I mean, you're not actually considering this ridiculous idea of his? You can't… We agreed, remember?" She swiped at her forehead with the back of her free hand as she waited for him to answer.

"There's nothing to worry about," he finally said.

Replacing the receiver, Janine had the sudden horrible sensation of being completely at her grandfather's mercy. He was an unshakably stubborn man who almost always got what he wanted. Faced with a mountain, Anton Hartman either climbed it, tunneled through it or forged a path around it; failing such active alternatives, he settled down in the foothills and waited for the mountain to dissolve. He claimed he won a majority of his battles by simply displaying patience. Janine called it not knowing when to pack up and go home.

She knew her grandfather's methods, but then so did Zach. She hoped Anton's candidate for her husband would at least be able to withstand a few bribes, however tempting. Apparently he did, because he'd told her she had nothing to worry about. On the other hand, he sounded downright eager to discuss the subject with her.

"He *says* he never wants to get married," she muttered aloud in an effort to reassure herself. Indeed, Zachary Thomas was the last man who'd be humming "The Wedding March"— especially when someone else was directing the band.

Janine was waiting in the library, coat draped over her arm, when her grandfather got home at six-thirty. He kissed her dutifully on the cheek and reached for the evening paper, scanning the headlines as he settled into his big leather chair.

"Zach called," she said without thinking. She hadn't intended to mention that to Gramps.

Anton nodded. "I thought he might. You meeting him for dinner?"

"Dinner? Zach and me?" she squeaked. "No, of course not! Why would you even think I'd agree to a dinner date with... him?" Darn, she'd nearly forgotten her promise to keep their meeting a secret. She detested lying to her grandfather, but there was no help for it.

"But you are dining out?"

"Yes." She couldn't very well deny that, dressed as she was and carrying her coat.

"Then you're seeing Peter Donahue again?"

"No. Not exactly," Janine said uncomfortably, "I'm meeting a...friend."

"I see." The corners of Gramps's mouth quirked into a knowing smile.

Janine could feel the telltale heat saturating her face. She was a terrible liar and always had been. Gramps knew as surely as if she'd spelled it out that she was meeting Zach. And when she told Zach she'd let it slip, he'd be furious with her, and rightly so.

"What did Zach want?"

"What makes you think he wanted anything?" Janine asked fervently. Her heart was thundering as she edged toward the door. The sooner she escaped, the better.

"You just said Zach phoned."

"Oh. Yes, he did, earlier, but it wasn't important. Something about...something." Brilliant! She rushed out of the house before Gramps could question her further. What a fool she was. She'd blurted out the very thing she'd wanted to keep secret.

By the time Janine located the Italian restaurant in the University district and found a parking place, she was ten minutes late.

Zach was sitting in a booth in the farthest corner of the room.

He frowned when he saw her and glanced at his watch, just so she'd know she'd kept him waiting.

Ignoring his disgruntled look, Janine slid onto the polished wooden bench, removed her coat and casually announced, "Gramps knows."

Zach's frown deepened. "What are you talking about?"

"He knows I'm having dinner with you," she explained. "The minute he walked in the door, I told him you'd called— I just wasn't thinking—and when he asked why, I told him it had to do with *something*. I'm sure you'll be able to make up an excuse when he asks you later."

"I thought we agreed not to say anything about our meeting."

"I know," she said, feeling guiltier than ever. "But Gramps asked if I was going out with Peter and he just looked so smug when I told him I wasn't." At Zach's sudden movement, she burst out, "Well, what was I supposed to do?"

He grunted, which wasn't much of an answer.

"If I wasn't going out with Peter, I'd have to come up with another man on the spot, and although I'm clever, I don't think *that* fast." She was breathless with frustration when she'd finished.

"Who's Peter?"

"This guy I've been seeing off and on for the past few months."

"And you're in love with him?"

"No, I'm not." Doubtless Zach would suggest she simply marry Peter and put an end to all of this annoyance.

Zach reached abruptly for the menu. "Let's order, and while we're eating we can go over what we need to discuss."

"All right," Janine said, grateful to leave the topic of her blunder. Besides, seven was later than she normally dined, and she was famished.

The waitress appeared then, and even as she filled Janine's

water glass, her appreciative gaze never strayed from Zach. Once more Janine was struck by the knowledge that although he wasn't handsome in the traditional sense, he seemed to generate a good deal of female interest.

"I'll have the clam spaghetti," Janine said loudly, eyeing the attractive waitress, who seemed to be forgetting why she was there. The woman was obviously far more interested in studying Zach than in taking their order.

"I'll have the same," Zach said, smiling briefly at the waitress as he handed her his menu. "Now, what were you saying?" he asked, returning his attention to Janine.

"As I recall, you were the one who insisted we meet. Just tell me what my grandfather said and be done with it." No doubt the offer had been generous; otherwise Zach wouldn't have suggested this dinner.

Zach's hand closed around the water glass. "Anton called me into his office to ask me a series of leading questions."

"Such as?"

Zach shrugged. "What I thought of you and—"

"How'd you answer him?"

Zach took a deep breath. "I said I found you attractive, energetic, witty, a bit eccentric—"

"A bandanna dress and a string of Christmas-tree lights doesn't make me eccentric," Janine said, her voice rising despite herself.

"If the Christmas-tree lights are draped around your neck it does."

They were attracting attention, and after a few curious stares, Zach leaned closer and said, "If you're going to argue with everything I say, we'll be here all night."

"I'm sure our waitress would enjoy that," Janine snapped, then immediately regretted it. She sounded downright *jealous*— which, of course, was ridiculous.

"What are you talking about?"

"Never mind."

"Shall we return to the conversation between your grand-father and me?"

"Please," she said, properly chastised.

"Anton spent quite a long time telling me about your volunteer work at the Friendship Club and your various other community activities."

"And I'll bet his report was so glowing, I rank right up there with Joan of Arc and Florence Nightingale."

Zach grinned. "Something like that, but then he added that although you were constantly busy, he felt your life lacked contentment and purpose."

Janine could see it coming, as clearly as if she were standing on a track and a freight train was heading toward her. "Let me guess. He probably said I needed something meaningful in my life—like a husband and children."

"Exactly." Zach nodded, his grin barely restrained. "In his opinion, marriage is the only thing that will fulfill you as a woman."

Janine groaned and sagged against the back of her seat. It was worse than she thought. And to her chagrin, Zach actually seemed amused.

"You wouldn't look so smug if he said marriage was the only thing that would fulfill you as a *man*," she muttered. "Honestly, Zach, do I look like I'm wasting away from lack of purpose?" She gestured dramatically with her hands. "I'm happy, I'm busy...in fact I'm completely delighted with my life." It wasn't until she'd finished that she realized she was clenching her teeth.

"Don't take it so personally."

Janine rolled her eyes, wondering what his reaction would be if he was on the receiving end of this discussion.

"In case you didn't know it, Anton's a terrible chauvinist," he remarked, still smiling. "An old-fashioned word, perhaps, for an old-fashioned man."

"That's true, but he *is* my grandfather," she said. "And he's so charming, it's easy to forgive him."

Zach picked up his wineglass and gazed at it thoughtfully. "What I can't figure out is why he's so keen on marrying you off now. Why not last year? Or next year?"

"Heavens, I don't know. I suppose he thinks it's time. My biological clock's ticking away and the noise is probably keeping him awake at night. By age twenty-four, most of the women from the old country had four or five children."

"He certainly seems intent on the idea of seeing you married soon."

"Tell me about it!" Janine cried. "I'd bet cold cash that when he brought up the subject he said you were the only suitable man he'd found for me."

"Anton also said you have a generous heart, and that he feared some fast-talker would show up one day and you'd fall for him."

"Really?" she asked weakly. Her heart stopped, then jolted to life again. Anton's scenario sounded exactly like her disastrous romance with Brian. She sighed deeply. "So then he told you he wants me to marry someone he respects, someone he loves like a son. A man of discretion and wisdom and honor. A man he trusts enough to merge companies with."

Zach arched his brows. "You know your grandfather well."

"I can just imagine what came next," Janine added scathingly and her stomach tensed at her grandfather's insidious cleverness. Zach wasn't someone who could be bought, at least not with offers of money or prestige. Instead, Gramps had used a far more subtle form of inducement. He'd addressed Zach's pride, complimented his achievements, flattered him. To hear Gramps tell it, Zachary Thomas was the only man alive capable of taking on the task of becoming Janine's husband.

"What did you tell him?" she asked, her voice low.

"I told him no way."

Janine blinked back surprise mingled with a fair amount of

indignation. "Just like that? Couldn't you at least have mulled it over?" Zach was staring at her as though he thought someone should rush over and take her temperature. "Forget I said that," she mumbled, fussing with her napkin in order to avoid meeting his eyes.

"I didn't want to encourage him."

"That was wise." Janine picked up her water glass and downed half the contents.

"To your grandfather's credit, he seemed to accept my answer."

"Don't count on it," Janine warned.

"Don't worry, I know him, too. He isn't going to give up easily. That's the reason I suggested you and I meet to talk about this. If we keep in touch, we can anticipate Anton's strategy."

"Good idea."

Their salads arrived and Janine frowned when the waitress tossed Zach another suggestive glance. "So," she began in a conversational tone once the woman had left, "Gramps was smart enough not to offer you a large incentive if you went along with his scheme."

"I didn't say that."

She stabbed viciously at her salad. "I hadn't expected him to stoop that low. Exactly what tactics did he use?"

"He said something about family members having use of the limousine."

Janine's fork made a clanging sound as it hit the side of her salad bowl. "He offered you the limousine if you married me? That's all?"

"Not even that," Zach explained, not bothering to disguise his amusement, "only the *use* of it."

"Why…why, that's insulting." She crammed some salad into her mouth and chewed the crisp lettuce as though it were leather.

"I considered it a step above the cow and ten chickens you suggested the first time we discussed this."

"Where he came from, a cow and ten chickens were worth a lot more than you seem to realize," Janine exclaimed, and immediately regretted raising her voice, because half the patrons in the restaurant turned to stare. She smiled blandly at those around her, then slouched forward over her salad.

She reached for a bread stick, broke it in half and glared at it. "The use of the limo," she repeated, indignant.

"Don't look so upset." He grinned. "I might have accepted."

Zach was deriving far too much pleasure from this to suit her. "Your attitude isn't helping any," she said, frowning righteously.

"I apologize."

But he didn't act the least bit apologetic. When she'd first met Zach, Janine had assumed he was a man who rarely smiled, yet in the short time they'd spent together today, he'd practically been laughing outright.

The waitress brought their entrées, but when Janine took her first bite, she realized that even the pretense of eating was more than she could manage. She felt too wretched. Tears sprang to her eyes, which embarrassed her even more, although she struggled to hide them.

"What's wrong?" Zach surprised her by asking.

Eyes averted, Janine shook her head, while she attempted to swallow. "Gramps believes I'm a poor judge of character," she finally said. And she was. Brian had proved it to her, but Gramps didn't know about Brian. "I feel like a failure."

"He didn't mean any of it," Zach said gently.

"But couldn't he have come up with something a little more flattering?"

"He needed an excuse to marry you off, otherwise his suggestion would have sounded crazy." Zach hesitated. "You know, the more we discuss this, the more ludicrous the whole thing seems." He chuckled softly and leaned forward to set his elbows on the table. "Who would've believed he'd come up with the idea of the two of us marrying?"

"Thank you very much," Janine muttered. He sat there shredding her ego and apparently found the process just short of hilarious.

"Don't let it get to you. You're not interested in me as a husband, anyway."

"You're right about that—you're the last person I'd ever consider marrying," she lashed out, then regretted her reaction when she saw his face tighten.

"That's what I thought." He attacked his spaghetti as though the clams were scampering around his plate.

The tension between them mounted. When the waitress arrived to remove their plates, Janine had barely touched her meal. Zach hadn't eaten much, either.

After paying for their dinner, Zach walked her to her car, offering no further comment. As far as Janine was concerned, their meeting hadn't been at all productive. She felt certain that Zach was everything Gramps claimed—incisive, intelligent, intuitive. But that was at the office. As a potential husband and wife, they were completely ill-suited.

"Do you still want me to keep in touch?" she asked when she'd unlocked her car door. They stood awkwardly together in the street, and Janine realized they hardly knew what to say to each other.

"I suppose we should, since neither of us is interested in falling in with this plan of his," Zach said. "We need to set our differences aside and work together, otherwise we might unknowingly play into his hands."

"I won't be swayed and you won't, either." Janine found the thought oddly disappointing.

"If and when I do marry," Zach informed her, "which I sincerely doubt, I'll choose my own bride."

It went without saying that Janine was nothing like the woman he'd want to spend his life with.

"If and when *I* marry, I'll choose my own husband," she said, sounding equally firm. And it certainly wouldn't be a man her grandfather had chosen.

"I don't know if I like boys or not," thirteen-year-old Pam Hudson admitted over a cheeseburger and French fries. "They can be so dumb."

It'd been a week since Janine's dinner with Zach, and she was surprised that the teenager's assessment of the opposite sex should so closely match her own.

"I'm not even sure I like Charlie anymore," Pam said as she stirred her catsup with a French fry. Idly she smeared it around the edges of her plate in a haphazard pattern. "I used to be so crazy about him, remember?"

Janine smiled indulgently. "Every other word was Charlie this and Charlie that."

"He can be okay, though. Remember when he brought me that long-stemmed rose and left it on my porch?"

"I remember." Janine's mind flashed to the afternoon she'd met Zach. As they left the restaurant, he'd smiled at her. It wasn't much as smiles went, but for some reason, she couldn't seem to forget how he'd held her gaze, his dark eyes gentle, as he murmured polite nonsense. Funny how little things about this man tended to pop up in her mind at the strangest moments.

"But last week," Pam continued, "Charlie was playing basketball with the guys, and when I walked by, he pretended he didn't even know me."

"That hurt, didn't it?"

"Yeah, it did," Pam confessed. "And after I bought a T-shirt for him, too."

"Does he wear it?"

A gratified smile lit the girl's eyes. "All the time."

"By the way, I like how you're doing your hair."

Pam beamed. "I want it to look more like yours."

Actually, the style suited Pam far better than it did her, Janine thought. The sides were cut close to the head, but the long bangs flopped with a life of their own—at least on Janine they did. Lately she'd taken to pinning them back.

"How are things at home?" Janine asked, watching the girl carefully. Pam's father, Jerry Hudson, was divorced and had custody of his daughter. Pam's mother worked on the East Coast. With no family in the area, Jerry felt that his daughter needed a woman's influence. He'd contacted the Friendship Club about the same time Janine had applied to be a volunteer. Since Jerry worked odd hours as a short-order cook, she'd met him only once. He seemed a decent sort, working hard to make a good life for himself and his daughter.

Pam was a marvelous kid, Janine mused, and she possessed exceptional creative talent. Even before her father could afford to buy her a sewing machine, Pam had been designing and making clothes for her Barbie dolls. Janine's bandanna dress was one of the first projects she'd completed on her new machine. Pam had made several others since; they were popular with her friends, and she was ecstatic about the success of her ideas.

"I think I might forgive Charlie," she went on to say, her look contemplative. "I mean, he was with the guys and everything."

"It's not cool to let his friends know he's got a girlfriend, huh?"

"Yeah, I guess...."

Janine wasn't feeling nearly as forgiving toward Zach. He'd talked about their keeping in touch, but hadn't called her since. She didn't believe for an instant that Gramps had given up on his marriage campaign, but he'd apparently decided to let the matter rest. The pressure was off, yet Janine kept expecting some word from Zach. The least he could do was call, she grumbled to herself, although she made no attempt to analyze the reasons for her disappointment.

"Maybe Charlie isn't so bad, after all," Pam murmured, then added wisely, "This is an awkward age for boys, especially in their relationships with girls."

"Say," Janine teased, "who's supposed to be the adult here, anyway? That's my line."

"Oh, sorry."

Smiling, Janine stole a French fry from Pam's plate and popped it into her mouth.

"So when are you leaving for Scotland?" Pam wanted to know.

"Next week."

"How long are you going to be gone?"

"Ten days." The trip was an unexpected gift from her grandfather. One night shortly after she'd met Zach for dinner, Gramps had handed her a packet with airline tickets and hotel reservations. When she'd asked why, his reply had been vague, even cryptic—something about her needing to get away. Since she'd always dreamed of visiting Scotland, she'd leapt at the chance.

It wasn't until she'd driven Pam home that Janine thought she should let Zach know she was going to be out of the country. It probably wasn't important, but he'd made such a point of saying they should keep in touch....

Janine planned her visit to the office carefully, making sure Gramps would be occupied elsewhere. Since she'd been shopping for her trip, she was carrying several department and clothing store bags. She was doing this for a reason. She wanted her visit to appear unplanned, as if in the course of a busy day, she'd suddenly remembered their agreement. She felt that dropping in would seem more spontaneous than simply calling.

"Hello," she said to Zach's efficient secretary, smiling cheerfully. "Is Mr. Thomas available? I'll only need a moment of his time."

The older woman clearly disapproved of this intrusion, but although she pursed her lips, she didn't verbalize her objection. She pushed the intercom button and Janine felt a tingle of awareness at the sound of Zach's strong masculine voice.

"This is a pleasant surprise," he said, standing as Janine breezed into the room.

She set her bags on the floor and with an exaggerated sigh, eased herself into the chair opposite his desk and crossed her legs. "I'm sorry to drop in unannounced," she said casually, "but I have some news."

"No problem." His gaze fell to the bags heaped on the floor. "Looks like you had a busy afternoon."

"I was shopping."

"So I see. Any special reason?"

"It's my trousseau." Melodramatically, she pressed the back of her hand against her forehead. "I can't take the pressure anymore. I've come to tell you I told my grandfather to go ahead and arrange the wedding. Someday, somehow, we'll learn to love each other."

"This isn't amusing. Now what's so important that it can't—"

"Mr. Thomas," his secretary said crisply over the intercom, "Mr. Hartman is here to see you."

Janine's eyes widened in panic as her startled gaze flew to Zach, who looked equally alarmed. It would be the worst possible thing for Gramps to discover Janine alone with Zach in his office. She hated to think how he'd interpret that.

"Just a minute," Zach said, reading the hysteria in her eyes. She marveled at how composed he sounded. He pointed toward a closed door and ushered her into a small room—or a large closet—that was practically a home away from home. A bar, refrigerator, microwave, sink and other conveniences were neatly arranged inside. No sooner was the door slammed shut behind her than it was jerked open again and three large shopping bags were tossed in.

Janine felt utterly ridiculous. She kept as still as she could, afraid to turn on the light and almost afraid to breathe for fear of being discovered.

With her ear against the door, she tried to listen to the conversation, hoping to discover just how long Gramps intended to plant himself in Zach's office.

Unfortunately, she could barely hear a thing. She risked opening the door a crack; a quick glance revealed that both men were facing away from her. That explained why she couldn't understand their conversation.

It was then that Janine spotted her purse. Strangling a gasp, she eased the door shut and staggered away from it. She covered her mouth as she took deep breaths. When she found the courage to edge open the door and peek again, she saw that all her grandfather had to do was glance downward.

If he shuffled his feet, his shoe would catch on the strap and he'd drag it out of the office with him.

Zach turned away from the window, and for the first time Janine could hear and see him clearly.

"I'll take care of that right away," he said evenly. He was so calm, so composed, as though he often kept women hidden in his closet. He must have noticed Janine's purse because he frowned and his gaze flew accusingly toward her.

Well, for heaven's sake, she hadn't purposely left it there for Gramps to trip over! He wasn't even supposed to be in the building. That very morning, he'd told her he was lunching at the Athletic Club with his longtime friend, Burt Coleman. Whenever Gramps ate lunch with his cronies, he spent the afternoon playing pinochle. Apparently he'd changed his habits, just so her hair would turn prematurely gray.

Several tortured minutes passed before Zach escorted Gramps to the door. The instant it was shut, Janine stepped into the office, blinking against the brightness after her wait in the dark.

"My purse," she said in a strangled voice. "Do you think he saw it?"

"It would be a miracle if he didn't. Of all the stupid things to do!"

"I didn't purposely leave it out here!"

"I'm not talking about that," Zach growled. "I'm referring to your coming here in the first place. Are you crazy? You couldn't have called?"

"I...had something to tell you and I was in the neighborhood." So much for her suave, sophisticated facade. Zach was right, of course; she *could* have told him just as easily by phone.

He looked furious. "For the life of me I can't think of a solitary thing that's so important you'd do anything this foolish. If your grandfather saw the two of us together, he'd immediately jump to the wrong conclusion. Until this afternoon, everything's been peaceful. Anton hasn't mentioned your name once and, frankly, I appreciated that."

His words stung. "I... I won't make the mistake of coming again—ever," she vowed, trying to sound dignified and aloof. She gathered her purse and her bags as quickly as possible and hurried out of the office, not caring who saw her leave, including Gramps.

"Janine, you never did say why you came." Zach had followed her to the elevator.

Janine stared at the light above the elevator that indicated the floor number, as though it was a message of the utmost importance. Her hold on the bags was precarious and something was dragging against her feet, but she couldn't have cared less. "I'm sorry to have imposed on your valuable time. Now that I think about it, it wasn't even important."

"Janine," he coaxed, apparently regretting his earlier outburst. "I shouldn't have yelled."

"Yes, I know," she said smoothly. The elevator opened and with as little ceremony as possible, she slipped inside. It wasn't until she was over the threshold that she realized her purse strap was tangled around her feet.

So much for a dignified exit.

4

"The castle of Cawdor was built in the fifteenth century and to this day remains the seat of the earl of Cawdor," the guide intoned as Janine and several other sightseers toured the famous landmark. "In William Shakespeare's *Macbeth*, the castle plays an important role. Macbeth becomes the thane of Cawdor...."

For the first few days of Janine's visit to Scotland, she'd been content to explore on her own. The tours, however, helped fill in the bits and pieces of history she might otherwise have missed.

The castle of Cawdor was in northeastern Scotland. The next day, she planned to rent a car and take a meandering route toward Edinburgh, the political heart of Scotland. From what she'd read, Edinburgh Castle was an ancient fortress, built on a huge rock, that dominated the city's skyline. Gramps had booked reservations for her at an inn on the outskirts of town.

The Bonnie Inn, with its red-tiled roof and black-trimmed gables, had all the charm she'd expected, and more. Janine's room offered more character than comfort, but she felt its welcome as if she were visiting an old friend. A vase filled with fresh flowers and dainty jars of bath salts awaited her.

Eager to explore, she strolled outside to investigate the extensive garden. There was a chill in the April air and she tucked her hands in her pockets, watching with amusement as the partridges fed on the lush green lawn.

"Janine?"

At the sound of her name, she turned, and to her astonishment discovered Zach standing not more than ten feet away. "What are you doing here?" she demanded.

"Me? I was about to ask you the same question."

"I'm on vacation. Gramps gave me the trip as a gift."

"I'm here on business," Zach explained, and his brow furrowed in a suspicious frown.

Janine was doing her own share of frowning. "This is all rather convenient, don't you think?"

Zach took immediate offense. "You don't believe I planned this, do you?"

"No," she agreed reluctantly.

Zach continued to stand there, stiff and wary. "I had absolutely nothing to do with this," he said.

"If you hadn't been so rude to me the last time we met," she felt obliged to inform him, with a righteous tilt to her chin, "you'd have known well in advance that Gramps was sending me here, and we could have avoided this unpleasant shock."

"If you hadn't been in such an all-fired hurry to leave my office, you'd have discovered I was traveling here myself."

"Oh, that's perfect! Go ahead and blame me for everything," she shrieked. "As I recall, you were furious at my being anywhere near your precious office."

"All right, I'll admit I might have handled the situation poorly," Zach said, and the muscles in his jaw hardened. "But as you'll also recall, I did apologize."

"Sure you did," she said, "after you'd trampled all over my ego. I've never felt like more of a fool in my life."

"You?" Zach shouted. "It may surprise you to know that I don't make a habit of hiding women in my office."

"Do you think I enjoyed being stuffed in that...closet like a bag of dirty laundry?"

"What was I supposed to do? Hide you under my desk?"

"It might've been better than a pitch-black closet."

"If you're so keen on casting blame, let me remind you I wasn't the one who left my purse in full view of your grandfather," Zach said. "I did everything but perform card tricks to draw his attention away from it."

"You make it sound like I'm at fault," Janine snapped.

"I'm not the one who popped in unexpectedly. If you had a job like everyone else—"

"If I had a job," she broke in, outraged. "You mean all the volunteer work I do doesn't count? Apparently the thirty hours a week I put in mean nothing. Sure, I've got a degree. Sure, I could probably have my pick of a dozen different jobs, but why take employment away from someone who really needs it when so many worthwhile organizations are hurting for volunteers?" She was breathless by the time she finished, and so angry she could feel the heat radiating from her face.

She refused to tolerate Zach's offensive insinuations any longer. From the moment they'd met, Zach had clearly viewed her as spoiled and frivolous, without a brain in her head. And it seemed that nothing had altered his opinion.

"Listen, I didn't mean—"

"It's obvious to me," she said bluntly, "that you and I are never going to agree on anything." She was so furious she couldn't keep her anger in check. "The best thing for us to do is completely ignore each other. It's obvious that you don't want anything to do with me and, frankly, I feel the same way about you. So, good day, Mr. Thomas." With that she walked away, her head high and her pride intact.

For the very first time with this man, she'd been able to make a grand exit. It should have felt good. But it didn't.

An hour later, after Janine had taken the tourist bus into Edinburgh, she was still brooding over her latest encounter with Zachary Thomas. If there was any humor at all in this situation, it had to be the fact that her usually sage grandfather could possibly believe she and Zach were in any way suited.

Determined to put the man out of her mind, Janine wandered down Princes Street, which was packed with shoppers, troupes of actors giving impromptu performances and strolling musicians. Her mood couldn't help but be influenced by the festive flavor, and she soon found herself smiling despite the unpleasant confrontation with her grandfather's business partner.

Several of the men who passed her in the street were dressed in kilts, and Janine felt as if she'd stepped into another time, another world. The air swirled with bagpipe music. The city itself seemed gray and gloomy, a dull background for the colorful sights and sounds, the excitement of ages past.

It was as Janine walked out of a dress shop that she bumped into Zach a second time. He stopped, his eyes registering surprise and what looked to Janine like a hint of regret—as though confronting her twice in the same day was enough to try anyone's patience.

"I know what you're thinking," he said, pinning her with his dark intense gaze.

"And I'm equally confident that you don't." She held her packages close and edged against the shop window to avoid hindering other pedestrians on the crowded sidewalk.

"I came here to do some shopping," Zach said gruffly. "I wasn't following you."

"You can rest assured I wasn't following *you*."

"Fine," he said.

"Fine," she repeated.

But neither of them moved for several nerve-racking seconds. Janine assumed Zach was going to say something else. Perhaps she secretly hoped he would. If they couldn't be friends, Janine would've preferred they remain allies. They should be uniting their forces instead of battling each other. Without a word, Zach gestured abruptly and wheeled around to join the stream of people hurrying down the sidewalk.

A half hour later, with more packages added to her collection, Janine strolled into a fabric store, wanting to purchase a sizable length of wool as a gift for Pam. She ran her fingertips along several thick bolts of material, marveling at the bold colors. The wool felt soft, but when she lifted a corner with her palm, she was surprised by how heavy it was.

"Each clan has its own tartan," the white-haired lady in the shop explained. Janine enjoyed listening to her voice, with its enthusiastic warmth and distinct Scottish burr. "Some of the best-known tartans come in three patterns that are to be worn for different occasions—everyday, dress and battle."

Intrigued, Janine watched as the congenial woman walked around the table to remove a blue-and-green plaid. Janine had already seen that pattern several times. The shop owner said that tourists were often interested in this particular tartan, called Black Watch, because it was assigned to no particular clan. In choosing Black Watch, they weren't aligning themselves with any one clan, but showing total impartiality.

Pleased, Janine purchased several yards of the fabric.

Walking down the narrow street, she was shuffling her packages in her arms when she caught sight of Zach watching a troupe of musicians. She started to move away, then for no reason she could name, paused to study him. Her impression of him really hadn't changed since that first afternoon. She still thought Zach Thomas opinionated, unreasonable and…fine, she was willing to admit it, attractive. *Very* attractive, in a sort of rough-hewn way. He lacked the polish, the superficial sophistication of a man like Brian, but he had a vigor that seemed thoroughly masculine. He also had the uncanny ability to set her teeth on edge with a single look. No other man could irritate her so quickly.

The musicians began a lively song and Zach laughed unself-consciously. His rich husky tenor was smooth and relaxed as it drifted across the street toward her. Janine knew she should've left then, but she couldn't. Despite everything, she was intrigued.

Zach must have felt her scrutiny because he suddenly turned and their eyes locked before Janine could look away. The color rose to her cheeks and for a long moment, neither moved. Neither smiled.

It was in Janine's mind to cross the street, swallow her pride and put an end to this pointless antagonism. During the past several weeks her pride had become familiar fare; serving it up once more shouldn't be all that difficult.

She was entertaining that thought when a bus drove past her belching a thick cloud of black smoke, momentarily blocking her view of Zach. When the bus had passed, Janine noticed that he'd returned his attention to the musicians.

Disheartened, she headed in the opposite direction. She hadn't gone more than a block when she heard him call her name.

She stopped and waited for him to join her. With an inquiring lift of one eyebrow, he reached for some of her packages. She nodded, repressing a shiver of excitement as his hand brushed hers. Shifting his burden, he slowed his steps to match Janine's. Then he spoke. "We need to talk."

"I don't see how we can. Every time you open your mouth you say something insulting and offensive."

Only a few minutes earlier, Janine had been hoping to put an end to this foolish antagonism, yet here she was provoking an argument, acting just as unreasonable as she accused him of being. She stopped midstep, disgusted with herself. "I shouldn't have said that. I don't know what it is about us, but we seem to have a hard time being civil to each other."

"It might be the shock of finding each other here."

"Which brings up another subject," Janine added fervently. "If Gramps was going to arrange for us to meet, why send us halfway around the world to do it?"

"I used to think I knew your grandfather," Zach murmured. "But lately, I'm beginning to wonder. I haven't got a clue why he chose Scotland."

"He came to me with the tickets, reminding me it'd been almost a year since I'd traveled anywhere," Janine said. "He told me it was high time I took a vacation, that I needed to get away for a while. And I bought it hook, line and sinker."

"You?" Zach cried, shaking his head, clearly troubled. "Your grandfather sent me here on a wild-goose chase. Yes, there were contacts to make, but this was a trip any of our junior executives could've handled. It wasn't until I arrived at the inn and found you booked there that I realized what he was up to."

"If we hadn't been so distracted trying to figure out who was to blame for that fiasco at your office, we might've been able to prevent this. At least, we'd have guessed what Gramps was doing."

"Exactly," Zach said. "Forewarned is forearmed. Obviously, we have to put aside our differences and stay in communication. That's the key. Communication."

"Absolutely," Janine agreed, with a nod of her head.

"But letting him throw us together like this is only going to lead to trouble."

What kind of trouble, he didn't say, but Janine could guess all too easily. "I agree with you."

"The less time we spend together, the better." He paused when he noticed that she was standing in front of the bus stop.

"If we allow Gramps to throw us together, it'll just encourage him," she said. "We've got to be very firm about this, before things get completely out of hand."

"You're right." Without asking, he took the rest of the packages from her arms, adding them to the bags and parcels he already carried. "I rented a car. I don't suppose you'd accept a ride back to the inn?"

"Please." Janine was grateful for the offer. They'd started off badly, each blaming the other, but fortunately their relationship was beginning to improve. That relieved her. She'd much rather have Zachary for a friend than an enemy.

They spoke very little on the twenty-mile ride back to the Bonnie Inn. After an initial exchange of what sights they'd seen and what they'd purchased, there didn't seem to be much to say. They remained awkward and a little uneasy with each other. And Janine was all too aware of how intimate the confines of the small rented car were. Her shoulder and her thigh were within scant inches of brushing against Zach, something she was determined to ignore.

The one time Janine chanced a look in his direction, she saw how intent his features were, as if he was driving a dangerous, twisting course instead of a straight, well-maintained road with light traffic. His mouth was compressed, bracketed by deep grooves, and his dark eyes had narrowed. He glanced away from the road long enough for their eyes to meet. Janine smiled and quickly looked down, embarrassed that he'd caught her studying him so closely. She wished she could sort out her feelings, analyze all her contradictory emotions in a logical manner. She was attracted to Zach, but not in the same way she'd been attracted to Brian. Although Zach infuriated her, she admired him. Respected him. But he didn't send her senses whirling mindlessly, as Brian had. Then again, she didn't think of him as a brother, either. Her only conclusion was that her feelings for Zach were more confusing than ever.

After thanking him for the ride and collecting her parcels, she left Zach in the lobby and tiredly climbed the stairs to her room. She soaked in a hot scented bath, then changed into a blue-and-gold plaid kilt she'd bought that afternoon. With it, she wore a thin white sweater under her navy-blue blazer. She tied a navy scarf at her neck, pleased with the effect. A little blush, a dab of eye shadow and she was finished, by now more than ready for something to eat.

Zach was waiting to be seated in the dining room when she came downstairs. He wore a thick hand-knit sweater over black dress slacks and made such a virile sight she found it difficult not to stare.

The hostess greeted them with a warm smile. "Dinner for two?"

Janine reacted first, flustered and a little embarrassed. "We're not together," she said. "This gentleman was here before me." Anything else would negate the agreement they'd made earlier.

Zach frowned as he followed the hostess to a table set against the wall, close to the massive stone fireplace. The hostess returned and directed Janine to a table against the same wall, so close to Zach that she could practically read the menu over his shoulder. She was reading her own menu when Zach spoke. "Don't you think we're both being a little silly?"

"Yes," she admitted. "But earlier today we agreed that being thrown together like this could lead to trouble."

"I honestly don't think it would hurt either of us to have dinner together, do you?"

"No... I don't think it would." They'd spend the entire meal talking across the tables to each other, anyway.

He stood up, grinning. "May I join you?"

"Please." She couldn't help responding with a smile.

He pulled out the other chair, his gaze appreciative. "Those colors look good on you."

"Thanks." She had to admit he looked good—darkly vibrant and masculine—himself. She was about to return his compliment when it dawned on her how senselessly they were challenging fate.

"It's happening already," she whispered, leaning toward him in order to avoid being overheard.

"What?" Zach glanced around as though he expected ghostly clansmen to emerge from behind the drapes.

"You're telling me how good I look in blue and I was about to tell you how nice *you* look and we're smiling at each other and forming a mutual admiration society. Next thing you know, we'll be married."

"That's ridiculous!"

"Sure, you say that now, but I can see a real problem here."

"Does this mean you want me to go back to my table and eat alone?"

"Of course not. I just think it would be best if we limited the compliments. All right?"

"I'll never say anything nice about you again."

Janine smiled. "Thank you."

"You might want to watch that, as well," he warned with a roguish grin. "If we're too formal and polite with each other, that could lead us straight to the jewelers. Before we know what's happening, we'll be choosing wedding bands."

Janine's lips quivered with a barely restrained smile. "I hadn't thought about that." They glanced at each other and before either could hold it in, they were laughing, attracting the attention of everyone in the dining room. As abruptly as they'd started, they stopped, burying their faces in the menus.

After they'd ordered, Janine shared her theory with Zach, a theory that had come to her on their drive back to the inn. "I think I know why Gramps arranged for us to meet in Scotland."

"I'm dying to hear this."

"Actually, I'm afraid I'm the one responsible." She heaved a sigh of remorse. Every part of her seemed aware of Zach, which was exactly what she didn't want. She sighed again. "When Gramps first mentioned the idea of an arranged marriage, I tried to make him understand that love wasn't something one ordered like...like dinner from a menu. He genuinely didn't seem to grasp what I was saying and asked me what a woman needed to fall in love."

"And you told him a trip to Scotland?" Zach's eyes sparkled with the question.

"Of course not. I told him a woman needed romance."

Zach leaned forward. "I hate to appear dense, but I seem to have missed something."

Pretending to be annoyed with him, Janine explained, "Well, Gramps asked me to define romance..."

"I'd be interested in learning that myself." Zach wiped the edges of his mouth with his napkin. Janine suspected he did it to cover a growing need to smile.

"It isn't all that easy to explain, you know," Janine said. "And remember this was off the top of my head. I told Gramps romance was forbidden trysts on Scottish moors."

"With an enemy clan chieftain?"

"No, with the man I loved."

"What else did you tell him?"

"I don't remember exactly. I think I said something about a moonlight stroll on the beach, and...and desperate passion."

"I wonder how he'll arrange that?"

"I don't think I want to find out," Janine murmured. Considering how seriously Gramps had taken her impromptu definition, she almost dreaded the thought of what he might do next.

When they'd finished, their plates were removed by the attentive waiter and their coffee served. To complicate her feelings, she was actually a little sad their dinner was about to end.

They left the dining room, and Zach escorted her up the stairs. "Thank you for being willing to take a risk and share dinner with me," he said, his voice deadpan. "I enjoyed it, despite the, uh, danger."

"I did, too," Janine said softly. More than she cared to admit. Against her better judgment, her mind spun with possible ways to delay their parting, but she decided against each one, not wanting to tempt fate any more than she already had.

Zach walked her to her room, pausing outside her door. Janine found herself searching for the right words. She longed to tell him she'd enjoyed spending the evening with him, talking and laughing together, but she didn't know how to say it without sounding like a woman in love.

Zach appeared to be having the same problem. He raised one hand as though to touch her face, then apparently changed his mind, dropping his hand abruptly. She felt strangely disappointed.

"Good night," he said curtly, stepping back.

"Good night," she echoed, turning to walk into her room. She closed the door and leaned against it, feeling unsettled but at a loss to understand why.

After ten restless minutes she ventured out again. The country garden was well lit, and a paved pathway led to rocky cliffs that fell off sharply. Even from where she stood, Janine could hear the sea roaring below. She could smell its salty tang, mixed with the scent of heath. Thrusting her hands into her blazer pockets, Janine strolled along a narrow path into the garden. The night air was cool and she had no intention of walking far, not more than a few hundred feet. She'd return in the morning when she planned to walk as far as the cliffs with their buffeting winds.

The moon was full and so large it seemed to take up the entire sky, sending streaks of silvery light across the horizon. With her arms wrapped around her middle, she gazed up at it, certain she'd never felt more peaceful or serene. She closed her eyes, savoring the luxurious silence of the moment.

Suddenly it was broken. "So we meet again," Zach said from behind her.

"This is getting ridiculous." Janine turned to him and smiled, her heart beating fast. "Meeting on the moors..."

"It isn't exactly a tryst," Zach said.

"Not technically."

They stood side by side, looking into the night sky, both of them silent. During their meal they'd talked nonstop, but now Janine felt tongue-tied and ill at ease. If they'd been worried about having dinner together, they were placing themselves at even greater risk here in the moonlight.

Janine knew it. Zach knew it. But neither suggested leaving.

"It's a beautiful night," Zach said at last, linking his hands behind his back.

"It is, isn't it?" Janine replied brightly, as if he'd introduced the most stimulating topic of her entire vacation.

"I don't think we should put any stock in this," he surprised her by saying next.

"In what?"

"In meeting here, as if we'd arranged a tryst. Of course you're a beautiful woman and it would be only natural if a man...any red-blooded man were to find himself charmed. I'd blame it on the moonlight, wouldn't you?"

"Oh, I agree completely. I mean, we've been thrust together in a very romantic setting and it would be normal to...find ourselves momentarily...attracted to each other. It doesn't mean anything, though."

Zach moved behind her. "You're right, of course." He hesitated, then murmured, "You should've worn a heavier jacket." Before she could assure him that she was perfectly comfortable, he ran his hands slowly down the length of her arms, as though to warm her. Unable to restrain herself, Janine sighed and leaned against him, soaking up his warmth and his strength.

"This presents a problem, doesn't it?" he whispered, his voice husky and close to her ear. "Isn't moonlight supposed to do something strange to people?"

"I...think it only affects werewolves."

He chuckled and his breath shot a series of incredible light-as-air sensations along her neck. Janine felt she was about to crumple at his feet. Then his chin brushed the side of her face and she sighed again.

His hands on her shoulders, Zach urged her around so that she faced him, but not for anything would Janine allow her gaze to meet his.

He didn't say a word.

She didn't, either.

Janine experienced one worry after another, afraid to voice any of them. Zach apparently felt the same way, because he didn't seem any more eager to explain things than she did. Or to stop them…

After a moment, Zach pressed his hands over her cheekbones. Leisurely, his thumbs stroked the line of her jaw, her chin. His eyes were dark, his expression unreadable. Janine's heart was churning over and over, dragging her emotions with it. She swallowed, then moistened her lips.

He seemed to find her mouth mesmerizing. Somewhere deep inside, she discovered the strength to warn him that her grand-father's plan was working. She opened her mouth to speak, but before she could utter a single word, Zach's arms came around her and drew her close against him. She felt his comforting warmth seep through her, smelled the faint muskiness of his skin. The sensations were unlike anything she'd ever known. Then he lowered his mouth to hers.

The immediate shock of pleasure was almost frightening. She couldn't keep from trembling.

He drew back slightly. "You're cold. You should've said something."

"No, that's not it." Even her voice was quivering.

"Then what is?"

In response she kissed him back. She hadn't meant to, but before she could stop herself, she slipped her arms around his neck and slanted her mouth over his.

Zach's shoulders were heaving when at last she pulled her mouth away and hid her face against his chest.

"What are we doing?" he whispered. He broke hastily away from her.

Janine was too stunned to react. In an effort to hide his effect on her, she rubbed her face as though struggling to wake up from a deep sleep.

"That shouldn't have happened," Zach said stiffly.

"You're telling me," she returned raggedly. "It certainly wasn't the smartest move we could've made."

Zach jerked his fingers roughly through his hair and frowned. "I don't know what came over me. Over us. We both know better."

"It's probably because we're both tired," Janine said soothingly, offering a convenient excuse. "When you stop to think about it, the whole thing's perfectly understandable. Gramps arranged for us to meet, hoping something like this would happen. Clearly the power of suggestion is stronger than either of us realized."

"Clearly." But he continued to frown.

"Oh, gee," Janine said glancing at her watch, unable to read the numbers in the dark. Her voice was high and wavering. "Will you look at the time? I can't believe it's so late. I really should be getting back inside."

"Janine, listen. I think we should talk about this."

"Sure, but not now." All she wanted was to escape and gather some perspective on what had happened. It had all started so innocently, almost a game, but quickly turned into something far more serious.

"All right, we'll discuss it in the morning." Zach didn't sound pleased. He walked through the garden with her, muttering under his breath. "Damn it!" he said, again shoving his fingers through his hair. "I knew I should never have come here."

"There's no need to be so angry. Blame the moonlight. It

obviously disrupts the brain and interferes with wave patterns or something."

"Right," Zach said, his voice still gruff.

"Well, good night," Janine managed cheerfully when they reached the staircase.

"Good night." Zach's tone was equally nonchalant.

Once Janine was in her room, she threw herself on the bed and covered her eyes with one hand. *Oh, no,* she lamented silently. They'd crossed the line. Tempted fate. Spit in the eye of common sense.

They'd kissed.

Several minutes later, still shaking, Janine got up and undressed. She slid under the blankets and tried to find a relaxing position. But she didn't feel like sleeping. Tomorrow she'd have to make polite conversation with Zach and she didn't know if she could bear it. She was sure he'd feel just as uncomfortable with her. She'd seen how he could barely look at her when they entered the inn.

Tossing aside the blankets, Janine decided she had only one option. She'd leave Scotland, the sooner the better. Grabbing the phone, she called the airport, booked a seat on the earliest flight home and immediately set about packing her bags.

Not bothering to even try to sleep, she crept down the stairs a little before midnight and checked out.

"You're leaving sooner than you expected, aren't you, Miss Hartman?" the night manager asked after calling for a cab.

"Yes," she said.

"I hope everything was satisfactory?"

"It was wonderful." She pulled a folded piece of paper from her purse and placed it on the counter. "Would you see to it that Mr. Thomas receives this in the morning?"

"Of course." The young man tucked it in a small cubbyhole behind him.

Satisfied that Zach would know she was leaving and wouldn't

be concerned by her hurried return to Seattle, she sat in a chair in the small lobby to wait for her cab.

About fifteen minutes later, Janine watched silently as the cabdriver stowed her luggage in the trunk. She paused before climbing in the backseat of the car and glanced one last time at the muted moonlit landscape, disappointed that she wouldn't have an opportunity to visit the cliffs.

The ride to the airport seemed to take an eternity. She felt a burning sense of regret at leaving Scotland. She'd fallen in love with the country during her short visit and hoped someday to return. Although the memory of her evening stroll through the garden would always bring with it a certain chagrin, she couldn't completely regret that time with Zach. In fact, she'd always remember the fleeting sense of contentment she'd felt in his arms.

Janine arrived at the airport long before her flight was scheduled to leave. She spent an hour drinking coffee and leafing through fashion magazines, several of which she took with her to give to Pam later.

A cup of coffee in one hand, she approached the airline counter with her passport in the other. The bag she had draped over her shoulder accidentally collided with the man standing next to her. An automatic apology formed on her lips, but before she could voice it, that same man turned to face her.

"Zach," she cried, nearly dropping her coffee in shock. "What are you doing here?"

5

"You think this is intentional, don't you?" Zach demanded. "It's obvious *you're* the one running after me. You found the note I slipped under your door and—"

"I checked out just before midnight so I couldn't possibly have read your note," she said angrily. "And furthermore I left a message for you."

"I didn't get it."

"Then there's been a misunderstanding."

"To say the least," Zach muttered. "A misunderstanding..." His tone was doubtful, as if he suspected she'd purposely arranged to fly home with him. She launched into an indignant protest.

"Excuse me, please."

The interruption was from a uniformed airline employee who was leaning over the counter and waving in an effort to gain their attention.

"May I have your ticket and passport?" she asked Janine. "You're holding up the line."

"Of course. I'm sorry." The best thing to do, she decided, was to ignore Zach completely. Just because they were booked on the same flight didn't mean they had to have anything to do with each other. Evidently they'd both panicked after their encounter in the garden. He was as eager to escape as she was.

Okay, so she'd ignore him and he'd ignore her. She'd return to her life, and he'd return to his. From this point forward, they need never have contact with each other again. Then they'd both be satisfied.

The airline clerk punched something into her computer. "I can give you your seat assignment now," she remarked, concentrating on the screen.

Standing on tiptoe, Janine leaned toward the woman and lowered her voice to a whisper. "Could you make sure I'm as far from Mr. Thomas's seat as possible?"

"This flight is booked solid," the attendant said impatiently. "The only reason you and your...friend were able to get seats was because of a last-minute cancellation. I'll do the best I can, but I can't rearrange everyone's seat assignments just before the flight."

"I understand," Janine said, feeling foolish and petty. But the way her luck had been going, Zach would end up in the seat beside hers, believing she'd purposely arranged that, too.

They boarded the flight separately; in fact, Zach was one of the last passengers to step onto the plane.

By that time, Janine was settled in the second row of the first-class section, flipping through the in-flight magazine. Zach strolled past her, intent on the boarding pass clutched in his hand.

Pretending she hadn't seen him seemed the best tactic, and she turned to gaze out the window.

"It seems I'm sitting here," Zach announced brusquely, loading his carry-on luggage in the compartment above the seats.

Janine had to bite her tongue to keep from insisting she'd had nothing to do with that. She'd even tried to prevent it, but she doubted Zach would believe her.

"Before you claim otherwise, I want you to know I didn't arrange this," he said, sitting down beside her.

"I know that."

"You do?"

"Of course," Janine told him. "The fates are against us. I don't know how my grandfather arranged our meeting at the airport or the adjoining seats, any more than I know why I stumbled on you my first day at the Bonnie Inn. We might never have crossed paths. But somehow, some way, Gramps is responsible." That didn't sound entirely reasonable, but she thought it best not to mention their stroll in the moonlight.

"So you're not ready to unleash the full force of your anger on me?"

"I don't see how I can be upset with you—or the reverse. Neither of us asked for this."

"Exactly."

Janine yawned loudly and covered her mouth. "Excuse me. I didn't sleep last night and now it's catching up with me."

Her yawn was contagous and soon Zach's hand was warding off his own admission of drowsiness. The flight attendant came by with coffee, which both Zach and Janine declined.

"Frankly, I'd be more interested in a pillow," Janine said, yawning again. The attendant handed her one, as well as a blanket, then offered the same to Zach. He refused both, intending to work on some papers he'd withdrawn from his briefcase. The minute the plane was safely in the air, Janine laid her head back and closed her eyes. Almost immediately she felt herself drifting into a peaceful slumber.

She stirred twice in the long hours that followed, but both times a gentle voice soothed her back to sleep. Sighing, she snuggled into the warmth, feeling more comfortable than she had in weeks.

She began to dream and could see herself walking across

the moors, wearing traditional Scottish dress, while bagpipes wailed in the background.

Then, on the crest of a hill, Zach appeared, dressed in a Black Watch kilt and tam-o'-shanter; a set of bagpipes was draped over his shoulder. Their eyes met and the music ceased. Then, out of nowhere, her grandfather appeared, standing halfway between the two of them, looking distinctly pleased. He cupped his hands over his mouth and shouted to Janine, "Is this romance?"

"Yes," she shouted back.

"What else do you need?"

"Love."

"Love," Gramps repeated. He turned to Zach, apparently seeking some kind of assistance.

Zach started fiddling with his bagpipes, avoiding the question. He scowled as he concentrated on his task.

"Look at the pair of you," Gramps called. "You're perfect together. Zach, when are you going to wake up and realize what a wonderful girl my Janine is?"

"If I do get married, you can be sure I'll choose my own bride," Zach hollered.

"And I'd prefer to pick out my own husband!"

"You're falling in love with Zach!" Gramps declared, obviously elated.

"I—I—" Janine was so flustered she couldn't complete her thought, which only served to please her grandfather more.

"Look at her, boy." Gramps directed his attention to Zach again. "See how lovely she is. And think of what beautiful children you'll have."

"Gramps! Enough about babies! I'm not marrying Zach!"

"Janine." Zach's voice echoed in her ear.

"Keep out of this," she cried. He was the last person she wanted to hear from.

"You're having a dream."

Her eyes fluttered open and she saw Zach's face close to her own, her head nestled against his chest. "Oh…" she mumbled, bolting upright. "Oh, dear… I am sorry. I didn't realize I was leaning on you."

"I hated to wake you, but you seemed to be having a night-mare."

She blinked and tried to focus on him, but it was difficult, and to complicate matters her eyes started to water. She wiped her face with one sleeve. Then, straightening, she removed the pillow from behind her back and folded the blanket, trying to disguise how badly her hands were trembling.

"You're worried about what happened after dinner last night, aren't you?"

Janine released a pent-up breath and smiled brightly as she lied. "Nothing really happened."

"In the garden, when we kissed. Listen," Zach said in a low voice, glancing quickly around to ensure that no one could overhear their conversation, "I think it's time we talked about last night."

"I… You're right, of course." She didn't feel up to this, but she supposed it was best dealt with before she had to face her grandfather.

"Egos aside."

"By all means," Janine agreed. She braced herself, not know-ing what to expect. Zach had made his views on the idea of an arranged marriage plain from the first; so had she. In fact, even her feelings about a marriage based on love weren't all that pos-itive at the moment. Brian had taught her a valuable lesson, a painful lesson, one she wouldn't easily forget. She'd given him her heart and her trust, and he'd betrayed both. Falling in love had been the most shattering experience of her life, and she had no intention of repeating it anytime soon.

"I'd be a liar if I didn't admit how nice kissing you was," Zach said, "but I wish it had never happened. It created more problems than it solved."

Janine wasn't exactly flattered by his remark. Keeping egos out of this was harder than it sounded, she thought ruefully. Her expression must have revealed her thoughts because Zach elaborated. "Before I arrived in Scotland, we hardly knew each other. We met that first afternoon over lunch—with Anton—and talked a couple of times, but basically we were strangers."

"We had dinner one night," Janine reminded him, annoyed that he could so casually dismiss it.

"Right," he acknowledged. "Then we met at the Bonnie Inn and, bingo, we were having dinner together and walking in the moonlight, and before either of us knew how it happened, we were kissing."

Janine nodded, listening quietly.

"There are several factors we can take into account, but if we're going to place blame for that kiss, I'm the one at fault."

"You?"

"Me," he confirmed with a grimace. "Actually, I'm prepared to accept full responsibility. I doubt you were aware of what was going on. It didn't take me long to see how innocent you are, and—"

"Now just a minute," Janine snapped. Once again he was taking potshots at her dignity. "What do you mean by that?"

"It's obvious you haven't had a lot of sexual experience and—"

"In other words I'm so incredibly naive that I couldn't possibly be held accountable for a few kisses in the moonlight?"

"Something like that."

"Oh, brother," she muttered.

"There's no need to feel offended."

"I wasn't exactly raised in a convent, you know. And for your information, I've been kissed by more than one man."

"I'm sure you have. But we're getting sidetracked here—"

"I'm sorry you found me so inept. A man of your vast worldly experience must've been sorely disappointed by someone as unsophisticated as me, and—"

"Janine," he said firmly, stopping her. "You're putting words in my mouth. All I was saying is that we—I—let matters get out of hand and we can't blame your grandfather for what happened."

"I'm willing to accept my part in this. I can also see where this conversation is leading."

"Good," Zach said. It was clear that his composure was slipping. "Then you tell me."

"You think that because I enjoyed spending time with you and we shared this mildly romantic evening and—"

"*Mildly* romantic?"

"Yes, you did say egos aside, didn't you? I'm just being honest."

"Fine," he said, tight-lipped.

"You seem to think that because you have so much more experience than I do, there's a real danger I'll be *swooning* at your feet." She drew out the word, enjoying her silliness, and batted her eyelashes furiously.

"Janine, you're behaving like a child," he informed her coldly.

"Of course I am. That's exactly what you seem to expect of me."

Zach's fingers tightened on the armrest. "You're purposely misconstruing everything I said."

"Whatever you're trying to say isn't necessary. You figure we had a borderline interest in each other and now we've crossed that border. Right? Well, I'm telling you that you needn't worry." She sucked in a deep breath and glared at him. "I'm right, aren't I? That's what you think, isn't it?"

"Something like that, yes."

Janine nodded grimly. "And *now* you think that since you held me in your arms and you lost your control long enough to kiss me, I'm suddenly going to start entertaining thoughts of the M word."

"The... M word?"

"Marriage."

"That's ridiculous," Zach said, jamming the airline magazine back into the seat pocket in front of him.

"Well?"

"All I mean is that the temptation might be there and we should both beware of it."

"Oh, honestly, Zach," she said sarcastically, "you overestimate yourself."

"Listen, I wasn't the one mumbling about babies."

"I was having a dream! That has absolutely nothing to do with what we're talking about now."

"Could've fooled me." He reached for the same magazine he'd recently rejected and turned the pages hard enough to rip them in two. "I don't think this discussion is getting us anywhere."

Janine sighed. "You were right, though. We did need to clear the air."

Zach made a gruff indistinguishable reply.

"I'll try to keep out of your magnetic force field, but if I occasionally succumb to your overwhelming charm and forget myself, I can only beg your forgiveness."

"Enough, Janine."

He looked so annoyed with her that she couldn't help smiling. Zach Thomas was a man of such colossal ego it would serve him right if she pretended to faint every time he glanced in her direction. The image filled her mind with laughter.

Zach leaned his head back and closed his eyes, effectively concluding their conversation. Janine stared out the window at the first signs of sunrise, thinking about all kinds of things—except her chaotic feelings for the man beside her.

Some time later, the pilot announced that the plane was approaching Seattle-Tacoma International Airport. Home sounded good to Janine, although she fully intended to have a heart-to-heart talk with her grandfather about his matchmaking efforts.

Once they'd landed, she cleared customs quickly. She struggled with her two large pieces of luggage, pulling one by the handle and looping the long strap of her carry-on bag over her shoulder. Zach was still dealing with the customs agent when she maneuvered her way outside into the bright morning sunlight, joining the line of people waiting for cabs.

"Here," Zach said, from behind her, "I'll carry one of those for you." He'd managed to travel with only his briefcase and a garment bag, which was neatly folded and easily handled.

"Thank you," she said breathlessly.

"I thought we'd agreed to limit our expressions of gratitude toward each other," he grumbled, frowning as he lifted the suitcase.

"I apologize. It slipped my mind."

Zach continued to grumble. "What'd you pack in here, anyway? Bricks?"

"If you're going to complain, I'll carry it myself."

He muttered something she couldn't hear and shook his head. "Once we get a cab—"

"We?"

"We're going to confront your grandfather."

"Together? Now?" She was exhausted, mentally and physically. They both were.

"The sooner the better, don't you think?"

The problem was, Janine hadn't given much thought to what she was going to say. Yes, she intended to challenge Gramps but she'd planned to wait for the most opportune time. And she'd hoped to speak to him privately. "He might not even be home," she argued, "and if he is, I'm not sure now would really be best."

"I want this settled once and for all."

"So do I," she said vehemently. "But I think we should choose when and how we do this more carefully, don't you?"

"Perhaps…" His agreement seemed hesitant, even grudging. "All right, we'll do it your way."

"It isn't my way. It just makes sense to organize our thoughts first. Trust me, Zach, I want this cleared up as badly as you do."

His reply was little more than a grunt, but whether it was a comment on the weight of her suitcase or her tactics in dealing with Anton, she didn't know.

"And furthermore," she said, making a sweeping motion with her arm, "we've got to stop doubting each other. Nobody's following anyone and neither of us is in any danger of falling in love just because we were foolish enough to kiss."

"Fine," Zach murmured. He set her suitcase down as a cab arrived and the driver jumped out.

"How is it that we always seem to agree and yet we constantly find ourselves at odds?" she asked.

"I wish I knew," he said, looking weary in body and spirit. The cabdriver opened the trunk, storing her suitcases neatly inside. Zach threw his garment bag on top.

"We might as well still share this taxi," he said, holding the door for her.

"But isn't the Mt. Baker district out of your way?"

"I do need to talk to your grandfather. There're some estimates I need to give him."

"But can't it wait until tomorrow? Honestly, Zach, you're exhausted. One day isn't going to make any difference. And like I said, Gramps might not even be at the house."

Zach rubbed his eyes, then glanced irritably in her direction. "Honestly, Janine," he mocked, "you sound like a wife."

Biting her tongue to keep back her angry retort, Janine crossed her arms and glared out the side window. Indignation seeped through her with every breath she drew. Of its own accord, her foot started an impatient tapping. She could hardly wait to part company with this rude, unreasonable man.

Apparently Zach didn't know when to quit, because he added, "Now you even act like one."

She slowly turned to him and in a saccharine voice inquired, "And what's that supposed to mean?"

"Look at you, for heaven's sake. First you start nagging me and then—"

"Nagging you!" she exploded. "Let's get one thing straight, Zachary Thomas. I do *not* nag."

Zach rolled his eyes, then turned his head to gaze out the window on his side.

"Sir, sir," Janine said, sliding forward in the seat. She politely tapped the driver on the shoulder.

The middle-aged man glanced at her. "What is it, lady?"

"Sir," she said, offering him her warmest, most sincere smile. "Tell me, do I look like the kind of woman who'd nag?"

"Ah… Look, lady, all I do is drive a cab. You can ask me where a street is and I can tell you. If you want to go uptown, I can take you uptown. But when it comes to answering personal-type questions, I prefer to mind my own business."

"Are you satisfied?" Zach asked in a low voice.

"No, I'm not." She crossed her arms again and stared straight ahead.

The cabdriver's eyes met hers in the rearview mirror, and Janine tried to smile, but when she caught a glimpse of herself, she realized her effort looked more like a grimace.

"Me and the missus been married for near twenty years now," the driver said suddenly, stopping at a red light just off the James Street exit. "Me and the missus managed to stay married through the good times and the bad ones. Can't say that about a lot of folks."

"I don't suppose your wife is the type who nags, though, is she?" Zach made the question sound more like a statement, sending Janine a look that rankled.

"Betsy does her fair share. If you ask me, nagging's just part of a woman's nature."

"That's absurd," Janine countered stiffly. She should've

known better than to draw a complete stranger into the discussion, especially another male who was sure to take Zach's side.

"I'll tell you the real reason me and the missus stayed together all these years," the cabbie continued in a confiding tone. "We never go to bed mad. I know I look like an easygoing guy, but I've got a temper on me. Over the years, me and Betsy have had our share of fights, but we always kiss and make up."

Janine smiled and nodded, sorry she'd ever gotten involved in this conversation.

"Go on," the cabbie urged.

Janine's puzzled gaze briefly met Zach's.

"Go on and do what?" Zach wanted to know.

"Kiss and make up." The cabbie turned for a moment to smile at them and wink at Janine. "If my wife was as pretty as yours, mister, I wouldn't be hesitating."

Janine nearly swallowed her tongue. "We are *not* married."

"And have no intention whatsoever of marrying," Zach added quickly.

The driver chuckled. "That's what they all say. The harder they deny it, the more in love they are."

He turned off Broadway and a few minutes later pulled into the circular driveway that led to Janine's house. As the talkative cabbie leapt from the car and dashed for the trunk, Janine opened her door and climbed out.

Apparently, Zach had no intention of taking her advice, because he, too, got out of the cab. It was while they were tussling with the luggage that the front door opened and Mrs. McCormick hurried outside.

"Janine," she cried, her blue eyes lighting up with surprise. "What are you doing back so soon? We weren't expecting you for another two days."

"I missed your cooking so much, I couldn't bear to stay away any longer," Janine said, throwing her arms around the older woman in a warm hug. "Has Gramps been giving you any trouble?"

"Not a bit."

Zach paid the driver, who got back in his cab, but not before he'd winked at Janine again. "Remember what I told you," he yelled, speeding off.

"How much was the fare?" Janine asked, automatically opening her purse.

"I took care of it," Zach said, reaching for his garment bag and the heavier of Janine's two suitcases. He said it as though he expected an argument from her, but if that was the case, Janine didn't plan to give him one.

"Is Gramps home?" Janine curved her arm affectionately around the housekeeper's waist as she spoke.

"He went out early this morning, but he should be back soon."

"Good," Zach mumbled, following them into the house.

"I imagine you're both starved," Mrs. McCormick said, heading toward the kitchen. "Let me whip up something for you that'll make you both glad you're home."

Left alone with Zach, Janine wasn't sure what to say to him. They'd spent almost twenty-four hours in each other's company. They'd argued. They'd talked. They'd laughed. They'd kissed.

"Janine—"

"Zach—"

They spoke simultaneously, then exchanged nervous smiles.

"You first," Zach said, gesturing toward her.

"I… I just wanted to say thanks for everything. I'll be in touch," she said. "By phone," she assured him. "So you don't need to worry about me dropping by the office unannounced."

He grinned sheepishly. "Remember, communication is the key."

"I agree one hundred percent."

They stood facing each other in the foyer. "You wanted to say something?" she prompted after a moment.

"Yes." Zach exhaled sharply, then drew a hand along the side of his jaw. "What that cabbie said is true—even for us. I don't want us to part with any bad feelings. I shouldn't have said what I did back there, about nagging. You don't nag, and I had no right to say you did."

"I overreacted." The last thing she'd expected from Zach was an apology. His eyes, dark and tender, held hers, and without even realizing what she was doing, Janine took a step forward. Zach met her and she was about to slip into his arms when the sound of the front door opening drove them apart.

"Janine," Anton cried, delighted. "Zach. My, my, this is a pleasant surprise." He chuckled softly as he removed his coat. "Tell me, was your tryst on the moors as romantic as I hoped?"

6

"Our best bet is to present a united front," Janine said to Zach four days later. They'd met at her house early in the afternoon to outline their strategy. Gramps was gone for the day, but by the time he returned, Zach and Janine planned to be ready to talk him out of this marriage idea. The sooner Anton understood that his ploy wasn't working, the better. Then they could both get on with their lives and forget this unfortunate episode.

"It's important that we stand up to him together," Janine said when Zach didn't comment. From the moment he'd arrived, he'd given her the impression that he'd rather not be doing this. Well, she wasn't overjoyed about plotting against her grandfather, either, but in this instance it was necessary. "If we don't, I'm afraid Gramps will continue to play us against each other."

"I'm here, aren't I?" Zach grumbled. He certainly wasn't in one of his more charming moods.

"Listen, if you're going to act like this—"

"Like what?" he demanded, standing up. He walked over to the polished oak sideboard and poured himself a cup of coffee. When he'd finished, he ambled toward the fireplace and leaned against the mantel.

"Like you're doing me a big favor," Janine elaborated.

"You're the one who's left *me* dangling for three days. Do you realize what I've been forced to endure? Anton kept giving me these smug smiles, looking so pleased with himself and the way things worked out in Scotland. Yesterday he went so far as to mention the name of a good jeweler."

Before Janine could stop herself, she was on her feet, arms akimbo, glaring at Zach. "I thought you were going to call me! Weren't you the one who said communication is the key? Then it's as if you'd dropped off the face of the earth! And for your information, it hasn't exactly been a Sunday school picnic around here, either."

"It may surprise you to learn that I have other things on my mind besides dealing with you and your grandfather."

"Implying I don't have anything to do with *my* time?"

"No," he said slowly. "Damn it, Janine, we're arguing again."

She sighed regretfully. "I know. We've got to stop this squabbling. It's counterproductive."

Zach's nod was curt and she saw that he was frowning. "What bothers me most is the way your grandfather found us the other day. We were standing so close and you were staring up at me, practically begging me to kiss you."

"I most certainly was not," she denied, knowing Zach was right. Her cheeks grew pink. She *had* wanted him to kiss her, but she hated having to admit that she would've walked into his arms without a second's hesitation. She decided to blame that unexpected longing on the exhausting flight home.

Zach shook his head and set his coffee cup carefully on the mantel. He thrust both hands into his pockets, still slouching against the fireplace wall. "The problem is, I was ready to do it. If your grandfather hadn't walked in when he did, I would've kissed you."

"You would?" she asked softly, feeling almost light-headed at his words.

Zach straightened, and a nerve in his jaw pulsed, calling her attention to the strong chiseled lines of his face. "I'm only human," he said drly. "I'm as susceptible to a beautiful woman as the next man, especially when she all but asks me to take her in my arms."

That was too much. Janine pinched her lips together to keep from crying out in anger. Taking a moment to compose herself, she closed her eyes and drew in a deep breath. "Instead of blaming each other for something that *didn't* happen, could we please return to the subject at hand, which is my grandfather?"

"All right," Zach agreed. "I'm sorry. I shouldn't have said anything." He went to the leather wingback chair and sat down. Leaning forward, he rested his elbows on his knees. "What are you going to say to him?"

"Me? I thought… I'd hoped…you'd want to do the talking."

Zach shook his head. "Tact doesn't seem to be my strong point lately."

"Okay, okay, I'll do it, if that's what you really want." She gazed silently down at the richly patterned carpet, collecting her thoughts. "I think we should tell him how much we both love and respect him and that we realize his actions have been motivated by his concern for us both and his desire for our happiness. We might even go so far as to thank him—" She stopped abruptly when Zach gave a snort of laughter. "All right, if you think you can do better, you do the talking."

"If it was up to me, I'd just tell that meddling old fool to stay out of our lives."

"Your sensitivity is really heartwarming," she muttered. "At first, this whole thing was one big joke to you and you really enjoyed tormenting me."

"You're exaggerating."

"As I recall, you played that cow-and-ten-chickens business for all it was worth, but I notice you're singing a different tune now and frankly—"

The library door opened, interrupting her tirade. Her grandfather and his longtime friend, veterinarian Dr. Burt Coleman, walked into the room.

"Zach. Janine," Gramps said, grinning broadly.

"Gramps," Janine burst out, rushing to her feet. They weren't prepared for this, and Zach was being impossible, so she said the first thing that came to mind. Pointing at Zach, she cried, "I don't know how you could possibly expect me to marry that man. He's stubborn and rude and we're completely wrong for each other." She was trembling by the time she finished, and collapsed gracelessly into the nearest chair.

"In case you haven't figured it out yet, you're no angel yourself," Zach said, scowling at Janine.

"Children, please," Gramps implored, advancing into the library, hands held out in supplication. "What seems to be the problem?"

"I want this settled," Zach said forcefully. "I'm not about to be saddled with Janine for a wife."

"As if I want to be *your* wife? In your dreams, Zachary Thomas!"

"We realize you mean well," Zach added, his face looking pinched. He completely ignored Janine. "But neither of us appreciates your matchmaking efforts."

Gramps walked over to the leather chair recently occupied by Zach and sat down. He smiled weakly at each of them, his shoulders sagging. "I thought… I'd hoped you two would grow fond of each other."

"I'm sorry to disappoint you, Gramps, I really am," Janine said, feeling guilty. "But Zach and I don't even like each other. We can barely carry on a civil conversation. He's argumentative and unreasonable—"

"And she's illogical and stubborn."

"I don't think we need to trade insults to get our message

across," Janine said. Her face was so hot, she felt as if her cheeks were on fire.

"There's no hope?" Anton asked quietly.

"None whatsoever," Zach said. "Janine will make some man a wonderful wife one day, but unfortunately, he won't be me."

Her grandfather slumped against the back of his chair. "You're sure?"

"Positive," Zach said, loudly enough to convince Mrs. McCormick who was working in the kitchen.

"I love you, Gramps," said Janine, "and I'd do almost anything you wanted, but I can't and won't marry Zach. We know you have our best interests at heart, but neither of us is romantically interested in the other."

Burt Coleman, who stood by the library doors, looked as if he'd rather be anyplace else. His discomfort at witnessing this family scene was obvious. "I think it'd be best if I came back another time," he murmured as he turned to leave.

"No," Anton said, gesturing his friend back. "Come in. You've met Zachary Thomas, haven't you?"

The two men nodded at each other, but Janine noticed how rigidly Zach held himself. This meeting with Gramps hadn't gone the way she'd planned. She'd wanted everything to be calm and rational, a discussion uncluttered by messy emotions. Instead they'd ended up practically attacking each other, and worse, Janine had been the one to throw the first punch.

Without asking, she walked over to the sideboard and poured Gramps and his friend a cup of coffee. Burt sat across from her grandfather, clearly ill at ease.

"I should be going," Zach said starkly. "Good to see you again, Dr. Coleman."

"You, too," Gramps's friend said, glancing briefly at Zach. His puzzled gaze quickly returned to Anton.

"I'll walk you to the front door," Janine offered, eager to make her own escape. She closed the library door behind her.

Both she and Zach paused in the entryway. Janine tried to smile, but Zach was studying her intently, and her heart clenched like a fist inside her chest. They'd done what they had to do; she should be experiencing relief that the confrontation she'd dreaded for days was finally over. Instead she felt a strange sadness, one she couldn't fully understand or explain.

"Do you think we convinced him?"

"I don't know," Zach answered, keeping his tone low. "Your grandfather's a difficult man to read. Maybe he'll never bring up the subject of our marrying again and we're home free. I'd like to believe that's the case. It's just as likely, though, that he'll give us a few days' peace while he regroups. I don't expect him to back off quite so easily."

"No, I don't suppose he will."

Zach looked at his watch. "I should be going," he said again.

Janine was reluctant to see him leave, but there was no reason to detain him. Her hand was on the doorknob when she suddenly hesitated and turned around. "I didn't mean what I said in there," she blurted in a frenzy of regret.

"You mean you do want us to get married?"

"No," she cried, aghast. "I'm talking about when I said you were stubborn and rude. That isn't really true, but I had to come up with some reason for finding you objectionable. I don't really believe it, though."

"It was the same with me. I don't think you're so intolerable, either. I was trusting that you knew it was all an act for your grandfather's sake."

"I did," she assured him, but her pride *had* been dented, although that wasn't anything new.

"The last four days have been difficult," Zach went on. "Not only was Anton gloating about Scotland, but like I told you, he's been giving me these amused looks and odd little smiles. A couple of times I heard him saying something in his native tongue—I'm afraid to guess what."

"Well, I know what he was saying, because he's been doing the same thing to me. He's talking about babies."

"Babies?" Zach echoed, his eyes startled.

"Ours in particular."

One corner of Zach's mouth lifted, as if he found the thought of them as parents amusing. Or unlikely.

"That was my reaction, too. Every time I've seen Gramps in the last few days, he's started talking about…well, you know."

Zach nodded. "I do know. The situation hasn't been pleasant for either of us."

"Setting Gramps straight was for the best." But if that was the case, why did she feel this terrible letdown? "If he accepts us at our word—and he just might—then I guess this is goodbye."

"Yes, I suppose it is," Zach responded, but he made no effort to leave.

Janine was glad, because these few moments gave her the opportunity to memorize his features. She stored them for the future, when there'd be no reason for her to have anything but the most infrequent and perfunctory contact with Zach.

"Unless, of course, your grandfather continues to throw us together."

"Of course," Janine added quickly, hating the way her heart soared at the prospect. "Naturally, we'd have to confront him again. We can't allow ourselves to be his pawns."

Zach was about to say something else when the library door flew open and Burt Coleman hurried out, the urgency on his face unmistakable. "Janine, I think we should call a doctor for your grandfather."

"What's wrong?"

"I'm not sure. He's very pale and he seems to be having trouble breathing. It might be his heart."

With Zach following, Janine ran into the library, her own heart in jeopardy. Dr. Coleman was right—she'd never seen her grandfather look worse. His breath came noisily and his eyes were closed as he rested his head against the back of the chair. He looked old, far older than she could ever remember seeing him. She felt a sense of panic as she raced across the room to the desk where there was a phone.

"I'm fine," Gramps said hoarsely, opening his eyes and slowly straightening. He raised his hand in an effort to stop Janine. "There's no need for everyone to go into a tizzy just because an old man wants to rest his eyes for a few minutes." His smile was weak, his complexion still pale. "Now don't go calling any doctor. I was in last week for a checkup and I'm fit as a fiddle."

"You don't look so fit," Zach countered and Janine noticed that his face seemed almost as ashen as her grandfather's. Kneeling beside him, Zach grasped his wrist and began to check his pulse.

"I'm fine," Gramps insisted again.

"Are you in any pain?"

Gramps's gaze moved from Zach to Janine. "None," he answered, dismissing their concern with a shake of his head.

"Dr. Coleman?" Janine turned to her grandfather's longtime friend. "Should I phone his doctor?"

"What does Burt know about an old man and his heart?" Gramps objected. "Burt's expertise is with horses."

"Call the doctor. Having him checked over isn't going to hurt," Burt said after a moment.

"Fiddlesticks," Gramps roared. "I'm in perfect health."

"Good," Janine said brightly. "But I'll just let Dr. Madison reassure me." She punched out the phone number and had to speak loudly in order to be heard over her grandfather's protests. A couple of minutes later, she replaced the receiver and told Zach, "Dr. Madison says we can bring him in now."

"I'm not going to waste valuable time traipsing downtown. Burt and I were going to play a few hands of cribbage."

"We can play tomorrow," Dr. Coleman said gruffly. "You keep forgetting, Anton, we're both retiring."

"I've got things to do at the office."

"No, you don't," Zach said firmly. "You've got a doctor's appointment. Janine and I are going to escort you there and we're not going to listen to a single argument. Do you understand?"

Gramps's eyes narrowed as if he were preparing a loud rebuttal. But he apparently changed his mind, because he relaxed and nodded sluggishly, reluctantly. "All right, if it'll make you feel better. But I'm telling you right now, you're going to look like a fine pair of fools."

The next two hours felt like two years to Janine. While Dr. Madison examined Gramps, she and Zach paced the waiting room. Several patients came and went.

"What could be taking so long?" Janine asked, wringing her hands nervously. "Do you think we did the right thing bringing him here? I mean, should we have gone directly to the hospital emergency room instead?"

"I doubt he would have agreed to that," Zach said.

"Do you honestly believe I would've listened to him?" She sat on the edge of a chair, her hands clenched so tightly together her knuckles whitened. "It's ridiculous, but I've never thought of Gramps as old. He's always been so healthy, so alive. I've never once considered what would happen if he became ill."

"He's going to be fine, Janine."

"You saw him," she cried, struggling against the dread and horror that churned inside her.

Zach's hand clasped hers and the fears that had torn at her composure only seconds earlier seemed to abate with his touch. He lent her confidence and strength, and she was badly in need of both.

When the door leading to the doctor's office opened, they leapt to their feet. Zach's hand tightened around hers before he released it.

"Dr. Madison can talk to you now," the nurse told them briskly. She led them to a compact office and explained that the doctor would be with them in a few minutes. Janine sat in one of the cushioned chairs and studied the framed diplomas on the walls.

Dr. Madison came into the room moments later. He paused to shake hands with Janine and then with Zach. "So far, my tests don't show anything we need to be too concerned about," he said, shuffling through the papers on his desk.

"What happened? Why was he so pale? Why was he gasping like that?" Janine demanded.

Dr. Madison frowned and folded his hands. "I'm really not sure. He claims he hadn't been doing any strenuous exercise."

"No, he was drinking coffee and talking to a friend."

Dr. Madison nodded. "Did he recently receive any negative news regarding his business?"

"No," Janine replied, glancing at Zach. "If anything, the business is doing better than ever. Gramps is getting ready to retire. I hate the thought of anything happening to him now."

"I don't know what to tell you," Dr. Madison said thoughtfully. "He should take it easy for the next couple of days, but there's nothing to worry about that I can find."

Janine sighed and closed her eyes. "Thank God."

"Your grandfather's getting dressed now," Dr. Madison said. He stood, signaling the end of their interview. "He'll join you in a few minutes."

"Thank you, Doctor," Zach said fervently.

Relief washed through Janine like a tidal wave. She got up and smiled at Zach. It was a smile full of gratitude. A smile one might share with a good friend when something has gone unexpectedly right. The kind of smile a woman would share with her husband. The thought hit her full force and she quickly lowered her eyes to cover her reaction.

When Gramps joined them in the waiting room, he looked immeasurably better. His blue eyes were filled with indignation and his skin tone was a healthy pink. "I hope the two of you are satisfied," he said huskily, buttoning his coat. "Most of the afternoon was wasted with this nonsense."

"You were a hundred percent correct, Gramps," Janine said brightly. "You're as fit as a fiddle and we wasted valuable cribbage time dragging you down here."

"I should've been back at the office hours ago," Zach put in, sharing a smile with Janine.

"And whose fault is that?" Anton muttered. He brushed off his sleeves as though he'd been forced to pick himself up off the floor, thanks to them.

Once more Janine and Zach shared an intimate look. They both seemed to realize what they were doing at the same moment and abruptly glanced away.

Zach drove Gramps and Janine back to the house, Gramps protesting loudly all the while that they'd overreacted and ruined his afternoon. His first concern seemed to be rescheduling his cribbage game.

Afterward Janine walked Zach to his car. "Thanks for everything," she said, folding her arms to repress the sudden urge to hug him.

"If you're worried about anything, give me a call," Zach said as he opened the car door. He hesitated fractionally, then lifted his head and gazed directly into her eyes. "Goodbye, Janine."

She raised her hand in farewell as a sadness settled over her. "Goodbye, Zach," she said forcing a lightness into her voice. "Thanks again."

For the longest moment, he said nothing, although his eyes still held hers. Finally he repeated, "Call me if you need anything, all right?"

"I will."

But they both knew she wouldn't. It was best to end this now. Make a clean break.

Janine stood in the driveway until Zach's car was well out of sight. Only then did she return to the house.

★ ★ ★

"This is really good of you," Patty St. John whispered, handing the sleeping infant to Janine. "I don't know what I would've done if I'd had to drag Michael to the interview. I need this job so badly."

"I'm happy to help." Janine peered down at the sweet face of the sleeping six-month-old baby. "I apologize if it was inconvenient for you to bring Michael here, but I've been sticking close to the house for the past few days. My grandfather hasn't been feeling well."

"It wasn't any problem," Patty whispered, setting the diaper bag on the floor. She glanced around the house. "This place is really something. I didn't have any idea that you…well, you know, that you were so well off."

"This house belongs to my grandfather," Janine explained, gently rocking Michael in her arms. The warmth and tenderness she felt toward the baby was a revelation. She supposed it was understandable, though. Gramps had spent last week constantly telling her what remarkable babies she and Zach would have, and here she was with one in her arms. All the maternal instincts she didn't know she had came bubbling to the surface.

"I'll be back in about an hour," Patty said. She leaned over and kissed Michael's soft forehead. He didn't so much as stir.

Still carrying the baby, Janine walked to the door with her friend. "Good luck."

Patty gave a strained smile and crossed her fingers. "Thanks. Here's hoping."

No sooner had the door closed than Anton walked into the living room. He paused when he saw Janine rocking in the old chair that had once belonged to his wife. His face relaxed into a broad grin.

"Is that a baby you've got there?"

Janine smiled. "Nothing gets past you, does it, Gramps?"

He chuckled. "Who's he belong to?"

"Patty St. John. She's another volunteer at the Friendship Club. She quit her job when Michael was born, but now she'd like to find some part-time work."

"Are you volunteering to babysit for her?"

"Just for today," Janine explained. "Her regular sitter has the flu."

"I thought you were going out?" Gramps muttered with a slight frown. "You haven't left the house all week. Fact is, you're becoming a recluse."

"I've had other things to do," she returned, not raising her voice for fear of disturbing the baby.

"Right. The other things you had to do were keep an eye on your grandfather," he said. "You think I didn't notice? How long do you plan on being my shadow? You should be gadding about, doing the things you normally do, instead of worrying yourself sick over me. I'm fine, I tell you. When are you going to listen to me?"

"Dr. Madison said to watch you for a few days."

"It's been a week."

Janine was well aware of it. In fact, she was beginning to suffer from cabin fever. She'd hardly spoken to anyone all week. She hadn't heard from Zach, either. Not that she'd expected to. Perhaps Gramps had taken them at their word. Or else he was doing what Zach had suspected and simply regrouping for the next skirmish.

Michael stirred in her arms and she held him against her shoulder, rocking him back to sleep.

"I'm going to the office tomorrow," Gramps announced, eyeing her defiantly as though he anticipated a challenge.

"We'll see," she said, delaying the showdown.

Yawning, baby Michael raised his head and looked around. Gramps's weathered face broke into a tender smile. "All right," he agreed easily. "We'll see." He offered the little boy his finger and Michael gripped it firmly in his hand, then started to chew on it.

Janine laughed, enjoying her grandfather's reaction to the baby. After a couple of minutes, Michael grew tired of the game with Anton's finger and yawned again, arching his back. Janine decided it was time to check his diaper. She got up, reaching for the bag Patty had left.

"I'll be back in a minute," she told her grandfather.

She was halfway across the living room when Anton stopped her. "You look good with a baby in your arms. Natural."

Janine smiled. She didn't dare let him know it felt good, too.

While she was changing the baby, she heard the doorbell. Normally she would've answered it herself, but since she was busy, either Gramps or Mrs. McCormick would see to it.

Michael was happily investigating his toes and making cooing sounds as Janine pulled up his plastic pants. "You're going to have to be patient with me, kiddo," she told him, carefully untwisting the legs of his corduroy overalls and snapping them back in place. When she'd finished, she lifted him high above her head and laughed when Michael squealed delightedly. They were both smiling when she returned to the living room.

Gramps was sitting in the chair closest to the grand piano, and across from him sat Zach.

Janine's heart lurched as her eyes flew instantly to Zach's. "Hello, Zach," she said, striving to sound as nonchalant as possible, tucking Michael against her hip. She cast a suspicious glare at her grandfather, who smiled back, the picture of innocence.

"Zach brought some papers for me to sign," Gramps explained.

"I didn't mean to interrupt you," she apologized. Her eyes refused to leave Zach's. He smiled that slanted half-smile of his that wasn't really a smile at all. The one she'd always found so appealing. Something seemed to pass between them—a tenderness, a hunger.

"Janine's not interrupting anything, is she?" Gramps asked.

"No," Zach responded gruffly. He seemed to be taking in everything about her, from her worn jeans and oversize pink sweatshirt to the gurgling baby riding so casually on her hip.

Gramps cleared his throat. "If you'll excuse me a moment, I'll go get a pen," he said, leaving them alone together.

"How have you been?" Zach asked, his eyes riveted to her.

"Fine. Just fine."

"I see you haven't had any problems finding another admirer," he murmured, nodding at Michael.

Zach kept his tone light and teasing, and Janine followed his lead. "Michael St. John," she said, turning slightly to give Zach a better view of the baby, "meet Mr. Zachary Thomas."

"Hello," Zach said, holding up his palm. He seemed awkward around children. "I take it you're watching him for a friend."

"Yes, another volunteer. She's looking for a part-time job, but she's having a problem finding one with the right hours. She's at an interview."

"I see."

Janine sank down on the ottoman in front of Zach's chair and set Michael on her knee. She focused her attention on gently bouncing the baby. "Now that your life's back in order," she said playfully, glancing up at Zach, "have you discovered how much you miss me?"

He chuckled softly. "It's been how long since we last talked? Seven days? I'm telling you, Janine, I haven't had a single disagreement with anyone in all that time."

"That should make you happy."

"You're right. It should." He shook his head. "Unfortunately it doesn't. You know what, Janine? I was bored to death. So the answer is yes, I missed you."

7

Before Janine could respond, Gramps wandered back into the living room, pen in hand.

"So where are those papers you wanted me to sign?" he asked Zach.

With obvious reluctance, Zach tore his gaze from Janine's. He opened his briefcase and pulled out several papers. "Go ahead and read over these contracts."

"Do you need me to sign them or not?" her grandfather grumbled.

Once more Zach dragged his gaze away from Janine. "Please."

Muttering under his breath, Gramps took the documents to the small table, scanned them and quickly scrawled his name.

Janine knew she should leave; the two men probably had business to discuss. But she couldn't make herself stand up and walk away. Not when Zach had actually admitted that he'd missed her.

Gramps broke into her thoughts. "Janine, I—"

"I was just going," she said. She clambered to her feet, securing her hold on Michael.

But Gramps surprised her.

"I want you to stay," he declared. "I wanted to talk to you

and Zach. Fact is, I owe you both an apology. Burt and I had a good long talk the other day and I told him how I'd tried to arrange a marriage between the two of you. He laughed and called me an old fool, said it was time I stepped out of the Dark Ages."

"Gramps," Janine began anxiously, unwilling to discuss the subject that had brought such contention, "Zach and I have already settled that issue. We understand why you did it and... and we've laid it to rest, so there's no need to apologize."

"I'm afraid there is," Gramps insisted. "Don't worry, Burt pointed out the error of my ways. Haven't got any new tricks up my sleeve." He rose to bring Zach the signed papers, then sat wearily in the chair across from them. He'd never looked so fragile, so old and beaten.

"Janine's a wonderful woman," Zach said unexpectedly. "I want you to know I realize that."

"She's got her faults," Gramps responded, pulling a cigar from his pocket, "but she's pretty enough to compensate."

"Thank you very much," Janine whispered sarcastically and was rewarded with a grin from Zach. Gramps didn't seem to hear her; if he had, he was ignoring her comment.

"I only want the best for my granddaughter, but when I approached her about marrying you, she made a big fuss. Fact is, it would've been easier to pluck a live chicken. She said she needed *romance*." Gramps pronounced the word as if it evoked instant amusement.

"There isn't a woman alive who doesn't need romance," she wailed, defending herself.

"I'm from the old country," Gramps continued. "Romance wasn't something I knew about from personal experience, and when I asked Janine to explain, she had some trouble defining it herself. Said it was a tryst on the moors and a bunch of other hogwash. That's the reason I sent you both to Scotland."

"We figured that out soon enough," Zach said dryly.

"As you'll recall," Janine found herself saying, "that definition was off the top of my head. Romance isn't easy to explain,
especially to a man who scoffs at the entire idea."

Anton chuckled, moving the cigar to the side of his mouth.
"It's unfortunate the two of you caught on to me so soon. I
was looking forward to arranging the desperate passion part."

"Desperate passion?" Zach echoed.

"Yes. Janine said that was part of romance, too. I may be
over seventy, but I know about passion. Oh, yes, Anna and I
learned about that together." His blue eyes took on a faraway
look and his lips curved in the gentlest of smiles. He glanced
at Janine and his smile widened.

"I'm glad you find this so funny," Janine snapped.

Gramps dismissed her anger with a flick of his hand and
turned to Zach. "I suppose you've discovered she's got something of a temper?"

"From the start!" Zach declared.

"It may come as a surprise to you, Zachary Thomas," Janine
said, "but you're not exactly Mr. Perfect."

"No," Zach countered smoothly. "I suspect your grandfather
was thinking more along the lines of Mr. Right."

"Oh, brother!"

"Now, children, I don't see that arguing will do any good.
I've willingly accepted defeat. Trying to interest you in each
other was an old man's way of setting his world right before
he passes on."

The doorbell chimed and, grateful for an excuse to leave the
room, Janine hurried to answer it. Patty St. John stood there,
her face cheerless, her posture forlorn.

"I wasn't expecting you back so soon."

"They'd already hired someone," Patty said, walking into the
foyer and automatically taking her son from Janine. She held
the infant close, as if his small warm body might absorb her
disappointment. "I spent the whole day psyching myself up for

this interview and it was all for nothing. Ah, well, who wants to be a receptionist at a dental clinic, anyway?"

"I'm so sorry," Janine murmured.

"Was Michael any problem?"

"None at all," Janine told her, wishing she could think of something encouraging to say. "I'll get his things for you."

It took Janine only a minute to collect Michael's diaper bag, but when she returned to the entryway, she discovered Zach talking to Patty. Janine saw him hand her friend a business card and overheard him suggesting she report to the Human Resources department early the following week.

"Thanks again," Patty said enthusiastically. She lifted Michael's hand. "Say bye-bye," she coaxed the baby, then raised his arm and moved it for him.

Janine let her out, with Zach standing next to her. Gramps had gone into the library, and Zach glanced anxiously in that direction before lowering his voice to a whisper. "Can you meet me later?"

"When?"

"In an hour." He checked his watch, then mentioned the number of a pier along the waterfront. Janine had just managed to clarify the location when Gramps came back.

Zach left the house soon afterward and Janine was able to invent an excuse half an hour later. Gramps was reading and didn't bother to look up from his mystery novel, although Janine thought she saw the hint of a smile, as if he knew full well what she was doing. She didn't linger to investigate. The last time she'd agreed to a clandestine meeting with Zach had been the night they'd met at the Italian restaurant, when she'd all but blurted out the arrangements to her grandfather.

Zach was waiting for her, grim-faced. He stood against the pier railing, the wind whipping his raincoat against his legs.

"I hope there's a good reason for this, because I don't think Gramps was fooled," Janine said when she joined him. "He'll figure out that I'm meeting you if I'm not back soon." She buried her hands in her pockets, turning away from the wind. The afternoon sky was gray, threatening rain.

"Am I interrupting anything important?"

"Not really." Janine wouldn't have minded listing several pressing engagements, but she'd canceled everything for the next two weeks, wanting to stay close to home in case her grandfather needed her.

Zach clasped his hands behind his back and started strolling down the pier, the wind ruffling his neatly trimmed hair. Janine followed. "I'm worried about Anton," he said suddenly, stopping and facing Janine.

"Why?" Perhaps there was something she didn't know about his health, something Dr. Madison hadn't told her.

"He doesn't look good."

"What do you mean?" Although she asked, she already knew the answer. She'd felt the same thing during the past few days. Gramps was aging right before her eyes.

"I think you know."

"I do," she admitted reluctantly.

"Furthermore I'm worried about you."

"Me?" she asked, her voice rising. "Whatever for?"

"If, God forbid, anything should happen to Anton," Zach said, drawing in a ragged breath, "what will happen to you? You don't have any other family, do you?"

"No," she told him, her chest tightening at the thought. "But I'm not worried about it. There are several friends who are very close to the family, Burt Coleman for one, so I wouldn't be cast into the streets like an orphan. I'll have the house and more than enough money to live on. There's no need for you to be concerned. I'm not."

"I see." Zach frowned as he walked to the farthest end of the pier, seeming to fix his gaze on the snow-capped peaks of the Olympic mountains far in the distance.

Janine hurried to catch up with him. "Why do you ask?" she demanded.

"He's always said he was concerned about your not having any other family. But it wasn't until recently that I really understood his motivation in trying to arrange a marriage between us."

"Good, then you can explain it to me, because frankly, I'm at a loss. He admitted he was wrong, but I don't think he's given up on the idea. He'd do just about anything to see the two of us together."

"I *know* he hasn't given up on us."

"What did he do? Up the ante?"

Zach chuckled and his features relaxed into a smile as he met her eyes. "Nothing so explicit. He simply told me that he's getting on in years and hates the thought of you being left so alone when he dies."

"I'll adjust. I'm not a child," she said, although her heart filled with dread at the thought of life without her cantankerous, generous, good-hearted grandfather.

"I don't doubt you would." Zach hesitated, then resumed strolling, apparently taking it for granted that she'd continue to follow him.

"I have plenty of friends."

Zach nodded, although Janine wasn't certain he'd heard her. He stopped abruptly and turned to look at her. "What I'm about to say is going to shock you."

Janine stared up at him, not knowing what to expect.

"When you think about it, our getting married does make an odd kind of sense."

"What?" Janine couldn't believe he was saying this.

"From a practical point of view," he added quickly. "Since the business is in both our names, and we're both alone. I realize I'm not exactly Prince Charming…" Zach paused as if waiting for her to contradict him. When she didn't, he frowned but went on. "The problem has more to do with whether we can get along. I don't even know if we're capable of going an entire day without arguing."

"What are you suggesting?" Janine asked, wondering if she was reading more into this conversation than he intended.

"Nothing yet. I'm trying to be as open and as honest as I can." He gripped the railing with both hands and braced himself, as though expecting a fierce wind to uproot him.

"Are you saying that our getting married wouldn't be such a bad idea after all?" Janine ventured. Initially he'd made a joke of the whole thing. Then he'd seen it as an annoyance. Now he seemed to have changed his mind again.

"I...don't know yet. I'm mulling over my thoughts, which I'm willing to confess are hopelessly tangled at the moment."

"Mine aren't much better."

"Does this mean you'd consider the possibility?"

"I don't know, either." Janine had been so sure she was in love with Brian. She remembered how he'd done everything a romantic hero should do. He'd sent her flowers, said all the things a woman longs to hear—and then he'd casually broken her heart. When she thought about it now, she couldn't really imagine herself married to Brian. But Zach, who'd never made any romantic gestures, somehow seemed to fit almost naturally into her life. And yet...

As she pondered these contradictions, Zach started walking again. "I'm not the kind of husband you want," he was saying, "and not nearly as good as you deserve. I'd like to be the man of your dreams, but I'm not. Nor am I likely to change at this stage of my life." He paused, chancing a look in her direction. "What are you thinking?"

Janine sighed and concentrated as hard as she could, but her mind was filled with so many questions, so many doubts. "Would you mind kissing me?"

Shock widened his dark eyes. He glanced around, then scowled. "Now? Right here?"

"Yes."

"There are people everywhere. Is this really necessary?"

"Would I ask you to do it if it wasn't?"

As he searched her face, she moistened her lips and looked up at him, tilting her head slightly. Zach slipped one arm around her waist and drew her close. Her heart reacted immediately, leaping into a hard fast rhythm that made her feel breathless. He lifted her chin with his free hand and slowly lowered his mouth to hers.

The instant his lips grazed hers, Janine was flooded with a sensual languor. It was as if they'd returned to the moors of Scotland with the full moon overhead, pouring magic onto their small corner of earth. Everything around them faded. No longer did Janine hear the sound of water slapping against the wooden columns of the pier. The blustery day went calm.

She supported her hands on his chest, breathing erratically, when he stopped kissing her. Neither spoke. Janine wanted to, but none of her faculties seemed to be working. She parted her lips and Zach lowered his mouth to hers again. Only this time it was a full-fledged kiss, deep and probing. His hands slid up her back as his mouth abandoned hers to explore the sweep of her neck.

Several glorious moments passed before he shuddered, raised his head and drew back, although he continued to hold her. "Does that answer your question?"

"No," she answered, hating the way her voice trembled. "I'm afraid it only raised more."

"I know what you mean," Zach admitted, briefly closing his eyes. "This last week apart was an eye-opener for me. I thought I'd be glad to put this matter between your grandfather and us to rest. If you want the truth, I thought I'd be glad to be rid of you. I was convinced you felt the same way." He paused, waiting for a response.

"The days seemed so empty," she whispered.

His eyes burned into hers, and he nodded. "You were constantly on my mind, and I found myself wishing you were there to talk to." He groaned. "Heaven knows you deserve a different kind of husband than I could possibly be."

"What about you? I've heard you say a hundred times that when it comes to finding a wife, you'll choose your own."

He blinked, as though he didn't recognize his words. Then he shrugged. "Once I got to know you, I realized you're not so bad."

"Thanks." So much for wine and roses and sweet nothings whispered in her ear. But then again, she'd had those things and they hadn't brought her happiness.

"Like I said—and I hate to admit it—our getting married makes sense. We seem to like each other well enough, and there's a certain…attraction." Zach was frowning a little as he spoke. "It would be a smart move for both of us from a financial viewpoint, as well." He took her by the shoulders and gazed into her eyes. "The question is, Janine, can I make you happy?"

Her heart melted at the way he said it, at the simplicity and sincerity of his words. "What about you?" she asked. "Will you be content being married to me?"

The apprehension in his face eased. "I think so. We'll be good for each other. This isn't any grand passion. But I'm fond of you and you're fond of me."

"Fond?" Janine repeated, breaking away.

"What's wrong with that?"

"I hate that word," Janine said through gritted teeth. "*Fond* sounds so…watered down. So weak. I'm not looking for a grand passion, as you put it, but I want a whole lot more than *fond*." She gestured dramatically with her hands. "A man is fond of his dog or a favorite place to eat, not his wife." She spoke so vehemently that she was starting to attract attention from other walkers. "Would it be too much for you to come up with another word?"

"Stop looking at me as if it were a matter of life and death," he said.

"It's important," she insisted.

Zach looked distinctly uncomfortable. "I run a business. There are more than three hundred outlets in fifty states. I know the office-supply business inside out, but I'm not good with words. If you don't like the word *fond*, you choose another one."

"All right," she said thoughtfully, biting the corner of one lip. Her eyes brightened. "How about *cherish*?"

"Cherish." Zach repeated it as if he'd never heard the word before. "Okay, it's a deal. I'll cherish you."

"And I'll cherish you," she said emphatically, nodding with satisfaction.

They walked along the pier until they came to a seafood stand, where Zach bought them each a cup of steaming clam chowder. They found an unoccupied picnic table and sat down, side by side.

Occasionally they stopped eating to smile at each other. An oddly exciting sensation attacked Janine's stomach whenever that happened. Finally, finishing her soup, she licked the back of her white plastic spoon. She kept her eyes carefully lowered as she said, "I want to make sure I understand. Did we or did we not just agree to get married?"

Zach hesitated, his spoon halfway between his cup and his mouth as an odd look crossed his face. He swallowed once. "We decided to go through with it, both accepting that this isn't the traditional love match, but one based on practical and financial advantages."

Janine dropped her spoon in the plastic cup. "If that's the case, the wedding is off."

Zach threw back his head and stared into the sky. "*Now* what did I say that was so terrible?"

"Financial and practical advantages! You make it sound about as appealing as a dentist appointment. There's got to be more of a reason than that for us to get married."

Shrugging, Zach gestured helplessly with his hands. "I already told you I wasn't any good at this. Perhaps we'd do better if you explained why you're willing to marry me."

Before she could prevent it, a smile tugged at her mouth. "You won't like my reason any better than I like yours." She looked around to ensure that no one could overhear, then leaned toward him. "When we kissed a few minutes ago, the earth moved. I know it's a dreadful cliché—the worst—but that's exactly what I felt."

"The earth moved," Zach repeated deadpan. "Well, we are in an earthquake zone."

Janine rolled her eyes. "It happened when we were in Scotland, too. I don't know what's going on between us or even if we're doing the right thing, but there's definitely…something. Something special."

She wasn't surprised when Zach scowled. "You mean to say you're willing to marry me because I'm good at kissing?"

"It makes more sense to me than that stuff about financial advantages."

"You were absolutely correct," he said evenly. "I don't like your reason. Is there anything else that makes the prospect appealing?"

Janine giggled. "You know," she reflected, "Gramps was right. We're going to be good for each other."

A flash of light warmed his eyes and his hand reached for hers. He entwined their fingers as their eyes met. "Yes, we are."

The wedding was arranged so fast that Janine barely had time to reconsider their decision. They applied for a license that same afternoon. When they returned to the house, Gramps shouted for joy, slapped Zach on the back and repeatedly hugged Janine, whispering that she'd made an old man very happy.

Janine was so busy, the days and nights soon blended together and she lost all track of time. There were so many things to do—fittings and organizing caterers and inviting guests—that for the next five days she didn't talk to Zach even once.

The day before the ceremony, the garden was bustling with activity. Mrs. McCormick was supervising the men who were assembling the wedding canopy and setting up tables and chairs.

Exhausted, Janine wandered outside and glanced up at the bold blue sky, praying the sunshine would hold for at least another day. The lawn was lush and green, and freshly mowed. The roses were in bloom, perfuming the air with their rich fragrance.

"Janine."

She recognized his voice immediately. She turned to discover Zach striding purposefullly toward her, and her heart reacted of its own accord. Janine felt as though they'd been apart for a year instead of just a few days. She wore jeans and an old university sweatshirt and wished she'd chosen something less casual. In contrast, Zach was strikingly formal, dressed in a handsome pin-striped suit and dark tie. She was willing to admit she didn't know him as well as she should—as well as a woman who was about to become his wife. His habits, his likes and dislikes, were a mystery to her, yet those details seemed minor. It was the inner Zach she was coming to understand. Everything she'd learned assured her she'd made the right decision.

"Hello," she called, walking toward him. She saw that he looked as tired as she felt. Obviously he'd been busy, too, although the wedding preparations had been left to her.

They met halfway and stopped abruptly, gazing at each other. Zach didn't hug her or make any effort to touch her.

"How are you holding up?" he asked.

"Fine," she answered. "How about you?"

"I'll live." He glanced over at the activity near the rose garden and sighed. "Is there someplace we can talk privately?"

"Sure." Janine's heart leapt to her throat at his sober tone. "Is everything all right?"

He reassured her with a quick nod. "Of course."

"I don't think anyone's in the kitchen."

"Good." Hand at her elbow, he guided her toward the house. She pulled out a chair with trembling fingers and sat down at the oak table. As he lowered himself into a chair opposite her, she gripped the edge of the table. His eyes had never seemed darker. "Tomorrow's the day."

He said this as if he expected it to come as a shock to her. It didn't—but she understood what he was saying. Time was closing in on them, and if they wanted to back out, it would have to be now.

"Believe me, I know," she said, and her fingers tightened on the table. "Have you had a change of heart?"

"Have you?"

"No, but then again, I haven't had much time to think."

"I've done nothing *but* think about this wedding," Zach said, raking his hands through his hair.

"And?"

He shrugged. "We may both have been fools to agree to this."

"It all happened so fast," Janine said in a weak voice. "One minute we agreed on the word *cherish*, and the next thing I remember, we were deciding we'd be good for each other."

"Don't forget the kissing part," he added. "As I recall, that had quite a bit to do with this decision."

"If you're having second thoughts, I'd rather you said so now than after the ceremony."

His eyes narrowed fleetingly before he shook his head. "No."

"You're sure?"

He answered her by leaning forward, slipping his hand behind her neck and kissing her soundly. Tenderly. When they broke apart, they were silent. Not talking, not wanting to.

Janine stared into his dark warm eyes and suddenly she could hardly breathe.

"This is going to be a real marriage," he said forcefully.

She nodded. "I certainly hope so, Mr. Thomas." And her voice was strong and clear.

Less than twenty-four hours later, Janine stood at Zach's side, prepared to pledge her life to his. She'd never felt more uncertain—or, at the same time, more confident—of anything she'd ever done.

Zach seemed to grasp what she was feeling. His eyes held hers as she repeated the words that would bind them.

When she'd finished, Zach slid his arm around her waist and drew her close. The pastor smiled down on them, then looked to the fifty or so family friends who'd gathered on Anton's lawn and said, "I present to you Mr. and Mrs. Zachary Thomas."

A burst of applause followed his words.

Before Janine fully realized what was happening, they were mingling with their guests. One minute she was standing in front of the pastor, trembling but unafraid, and the next she was a wife.

"Janine, Janine!" Pam rushed to her side before anyone else could. "You look so gorgeous," she said softly, and bright tears shone in her eyes.

Janine hugged her young friend. "Thank you, sweetheart."

Pam gazed up at Zach and shook her head. "He sure is handsome."

"I think so, too."

Zach arched his brows, cocked his head toward her and murmured, "You never told me that."

"There's no need for you to be so smug."

"My children," Gramps said, rejoining them. He hugged Janine, and she saw that his eyes were as bright as Pam's. "You've never been more beautiful. I swear you look more like my Anna every year."

It was the highest compliment Gramps could have paid her. From the pictures Gramps kept of his wife, Janine knew her grandmother had been exceptionally beautiful.

"Thank you," she said, kissing his cheek.

"I have something for you." Pam thrust a neatly wrapped box into Janine's hands. "I made them myself," she announced proudly. "I think Zach will like them, too."

"Oh, Pam, you shouldn't have," Janine murmured. Sitting on a cushioned folding chair, she peeled away the paper and lifted the lid. The moment she did, her breath jammed in her throat. Inside were the sheerest white baby-doll pajamas Janine had ever seen. Her smile faltered as she glanced up to see half a dozen people staring at her.

Zach's hand, resting at the nape of Janine's neck, tightened as he spoke, though his voice was warm and amused. "You're right, Pam. I like them very much."

8

Janine sat next to Zach in the front seat of his car. Dressed in a pink suit and matching broad-brimmed hat, she clutched her small floral bouquet. Although the wedding had been arranged in seven short days, it had been a lovely affair.

Zach had taken care of planning the short honeymoon. All he could spare was three days, so instead of scheduling anything elaborate, he'd suggested they go to his summer place in Ocean Shores, a coastal town two and a half hours from Seattle by car. Janine had happily agreed.

"So you think I'm handsome?" Zach asked, keeping his eyes on the road. Neither of them had said much since they'd set off.

"I knew if I told you, it'd go straight to your head, and obviously I was right," she answered. Then, unable to hold back a wide yawn, she pressed one hand to her mouth.

"You're exhausted."

"Are you always this astute?"

"Testy, too."

"I don't mean to be," she apologized. She'd been up since before five that morning and in fact, hadn't slept well all week. This wasn't exactly the ideal way to start a marriage. There was an added stress, too, that had to do with the honeymoon.

Zach had made it understood that he intended their marriage to be real, but surely he didn't expect them to share a bed so soon. Or did he?

Every now and then as they drove, she glanced in his direction, wondering what, if anything, she should say. Even if she did decide to broach this delicate subject, she wasn't sure how.

"Go ahead and rest," Zach suggested. "I'll wake you when we arrive."

"It should be soon, shouldn't it?"

"Another fifteen minutes or so."

"Then I'll stay awake." Nervously, she twisted the small floral bouquet. Unwrapping Pam's gift had made her all the more apprehensive, but delaying the subject any longer was impossible.

"Zach…are we going to…you know…" she stammered, feeling like a naive schoolgirl.

"If you're referring to what I think you're referring to, the answer is no. So relax."

"No?" He didn't need to sound so casual about it, as if it hardly mattered one way or the other.

"Why do you ask, Janine? Are you having second thoughts about…that?"

"No. Just some reservations."

"Don't worry. When it happens, it happens. The last thing we need is that kind of pressure."

"You're right," she answered, relieved.

"We need some time to feel comfortable. There's no reason to rush into the physical aspect of our marriage, is there?"

"None whatsoever," she agreed quickly, perhaps too quickly, because when she looked at him again, Zach was frowning. Yet he seemed so willing to wait, as though their lovemaking was of minor importance. But as he'd said, this marriage wasn't one of grand passion. Well, *that* was certainly true.

Before another five minutes had passed, Zach left the highway and drove into the resort town of Ocean Shores. He didn't stop in the business district, but headed down a side street toward the beach. The sun was setting as he pulled into a driveway and turned off the engine.

Janine was too enthralled with the house to say a word.

The wind whipped at them ferociously when they climbed out of the car. Janine held on to her hair with one hand, still clutching the flowers, and to Zach with the other. The sun cast a pink and gold reflection over the rolling hills of sand.

"Home, sweet home," Zach said, nudging her toward the house.

The front door opened before they reached it and a trim middle-aged man stepped onto the porch to greet them. He was grinning broadly. "Hello, Zach. I trust you had a safe trip."

"We did."

"Everything's ready. The cupboards are stocked. The firewood's stacked by the side of the house, and dinner's prepared."

"Wonderful, Harry, thanks." Zach placed his hand on Janine's shoulder. "This is my wife, Janine," he said. "We were married this afternoon."

"Your wife?" Harry repeated, looking more than a little surprised. "Why, that's fantastic. Congratulations to you both."

"Thank you," Janine said politely.

"Harry Gleason looks after the place for me when I'm not around."

"Pleased to meet you, Harry."

"So Zach got himself a wife," Harry said, rubbing his jaw in apparent disbelief. "I couldn't be more—"

"Delighted," a frowning Zach supplied for him, ushering Janine toward the front door.

"Right," Harry said. "I couldn't be more delighted."

Janine tilted back her head to survey the sprawling single-story house.

"Go on inside," Zach said. "I'll get the luggage."

Janine started to protest, suddenly wanting him to follow the traditional wedding custom of carrying her over the threshold. She paused, and Zach gave her a puzzled look. "Is something wrong?"

"No." She had no real grounds for complaint. She wasn't even sure why it mattered. Swallowing her disappointment, she made her way into the house. She stopped just inside the front door and gazed with wide-eyed wonder at the immense living room with its three long sofas and several upholstered chairs. A brick fireplace took up an entire wall; another was dominated by a floor-to-ceiling window that looked over the ocean. Drawn to it, Janine watched powerful waves crash against the shore.

Zach followed her inside, carrying their luggage, barely taking time to appreciate the scene before him. "Harry's putting the car away," he said.

"This place is incredible," Janine breathed, gesturing around her. She placed the flowers on the coffee table, then trailed after Zach into a hallway, off which were four bedrooms and an equal number of baths. At the back of the house, she found an exercise room, an office and an ultramodern kitchen where a pot of coq au vin was simmering.

In the formal dining room, the polished mahogany table was set for two. On the deck, designed to take advantage of the ocean view, she discovered a steaming hot tub, along with a bottle of French champagne on ice.

Zach returned as she wandered back into the kitchen and a strained silence fell between them. He was the first to speak. "I put your suitcases in the master bedroom," he said brusquely. "I'm in the one across the hall."

She nodded, not taking time to question her growing sense of disappointment. They'd agreed to delay their wedding night, hadn't they?

"Are you hungry?" he asked, walking to the stove and lifting the pot's lid, as she'd done earlier.

"Only a little. I was thinking about slipping into the hot tub, unless you want to eat first."

"Sure. The hot tub's fine. Whatever you want."

Janine unpacked and located her swimsuit, then changed into it quickly. The warm water sounded appealing. And maybe it would help her relax. Draping a beach towel over her arm, she hurried into the kitchen, but Zach was nowhere to be seen. Not waiting for him, she walked out to the deck and stepped gingerly into the hot tub. The water felt like a soothing liquid blanket and she slid down, letting it lap just under her breasts.

Zach sauntered onto the deck a minute later, still in his suit. He stopped short when he saw her. "I…didn't realize you'd be out so soon," he said, staring at her with undisguised appreciation. He inhaled sharply and occupied himself by uncorking the bottle of champagne, then pouring a liberal glass. When he'd gulped it down, he reached for a second one and filled it for Janine.

"You're coming in, aren't you?" she asked, when he handed her the crystal flute.

"No," he said abruptly. "I won't join you, after all. There were several things I wasn't able to finish at the office this week, and I thought I'd look over some papers. You go ahead and enjoy yourself."

He was going to *work* on their wedding night! But she didn't feel she had any right to comment or complain. She was determined to conceal her bitter disappointment.

"The water's wonderful," she said, as cheerfully as she could manage, hoping her words would convince him to join her.

Zach nodded, but his eyes now avoided Janine. "It looks… great." He strode to the end of the deck, ran his fingers through his hair, then twisted around to face her. He seemed about to say something, but evidently changed his mind.

Baffled by his odd behavior, Janine set aside her glass of champagne and stood up so abruptly that water sloshed over the edge of the tub. "You don't need to say it," she muttered, climbing out and grabbing her towel.

"Say what?"

"You warned me before the wedding, so I walked into this with my eyes wide open. Well, you needn't worry. I got the message the minute we arrived at the house."

"What message is that?"

"Never mind." Vigorously, she rubbed her arms with the towel.

"No," he said. "I want you to tell me."

Against her better judgment, she pointed a quaking finger at the front door. "You went out of your way to tell me how *fond* of me you were and how there wasn't going to be any grand passion. Great. Perfect. I agreed to those terms. That's all fine with me, but—"

"But what?"

Mutely, she shook her head.

He sighed. "Oh, great, we're fighting. I suppose you're going to ask for a divorce and make this the shortest marriage in Washington state history."

Janine paled. Divorce was such an ugly word, and it struck her as viciously as a slap. Despite her efforts, scalding tears spilled down her cheeks. With as much dignity as she could muster, which admittedly wasn't a lot, Janine went back inside the house, leaving a wet trail in her wake.

"Janine!" Zach shouted, following her into the kitchen. "Listen, Janine, I didn't intend to argue with you."

She turned abruptly. "This marriage doesn't mean anything to you, does it? You won't even interrupt your work long enough to...to act like a man who just got married."

With her head held high, she stared past him to a painting of yellow flowers on the dining room wall. When her tears blurred the flowers beyond recognition, she defiantly rubbed her eyes.

"I'm sorry," he whispered, reaching for her as if he needed to hold her. But then his arms fell to his sides. "I should've real-ized wedding traditions would be important to you. Like that carrying-you-over-the-threshold business. I'm sorry," he said again. "I completely forgot."

"It's not just that, it's everything. How many men bring a briefcase with them on their honeymoon? I feel like...like ex-cess baggage in your life—and we haven't even been married for twenty-four hours."

Zach looked perplexed. "What does catching up on my read-ing have to do with any of this?"

His question only irritated her more. "You don't have the foggiest notion of how impossible you are, do you?"

He didn't answer right away, but seemed to be studying her, weighing his answer before he spoke. "I just thought I might have a chance to read over some papers," he said slowly. "Ap-parently that bothers you."

Janine placed her hands on her hips. "Yes, it bothers me."

Zach frowned. "Since we've agreed to delay the honeymoon part, what would you suggest we do for the next three days?"

"Couldn't we spend the time having fun? Becoming better acquainted?"

"I guess I do seem like a stranger to you," he said. "No won-der you're so nervous."

"I am *not* nervous. Just tired and trying hard not to say or do anything that'll make you think of me as a...a nag."

"A nag?" Zach repeated incredulously. "I don't think of you as anything but lovely. The truth is, I'm having one heck of a time keeping my eyes off you."

"You are?" The towel she was holding slipped unnoticed to the floor. "I thought you said you didn't know how to say anything romantic."

"That was romantic?"

"And very sweet. I was beginning to think you didn't find me...attractive."

Astonished, Zach stared at her. "You've got to be kidding!"

"I'm not."

"I can see that the next few days are going to be difficult," he said. "You'll just need to be patient with me, all right?"

"All right." She nodded, already feeling worlds better.

"How about if I dish up dinner while you're changing?"

"Thanks," she said, smiling.

By the time she got back to the kitchen, wearing gray slacks and a sweater that was the color of fresh cream, Zach had served their meal and poured the wine. He stood behind her chair, waiting politely.

"Before we sit down, there's something I need to do."

The last thing Janine expected was to be lifted in his strong arms. A gasp of surprise lodged in her throat as her startled gaze met his.

"What are you doing?"

"It's tradition to carry the bride over the threshold, isn't it?"

"Yes, but you're doing it all wrong! You're supposed to carry me from the outside in—not the other way around."

Zach shrugged, unconcerned. "There's nothing traditional about this marriage. Why start now?" He made a show of pretending his knees were buckling under her weight as he staggered through the living room.

"This is supposed to be serious," she chastised him, but no matter how hard she tried, she couldn't keep the laughter out of her voice.

With a great deal of feigned effort, he managed to open the front door and then ceremoniously step onto the porch. Slowly he released her, letting her feet drop first, holding her upper body close against his chest for a long moment. The humor left his eyes. "There," he said tenderly. "Am I forgetting anything?"

It wouldn't hurt to kiss me, Janine told him in her heart, but the words didn't make it to her lips. When Zach kissed her again, she wanted it to be *his* idea.

"Janine?"

"Everything's perfect. Thank you."

"Not quite," he muttered. He turned her to face him, then covered her mouth with his own. Janine trembled, slipping her arms around his neck and giving herself completely to the kiss. She quivered at the heat that began to warm her from the inside out. This kiss was better than any they'd ever shared, something she hadn't thought possible. And what that meant, she had no idea.

Zach pulled his mouth abruptly from hers, but his eyes remained closed. Almost visibly he composed himself, and when he broke away he seemed in control of his emotions once again. Janine sighed inwardly, unsure of what she'd expected.

The next two days flew past. They took long walks on the shore, collecting shells. They rented mopeds and raced along the beach. They launched kites into the sky and delighted in their colorful dipping and soaring. The day before they were scheduled to return to Seattle, Zach declared that he intended to cook dinner. With that announcement, he informed her he had to go into town to buy the necessary groceries. After the first night, he'd given Harry a week off, and Janine had been fixing simple meals for them.

"What are you serving?" she wanted to know when he pulled into the parking lot of the town's only grocery store. "Tell me so I can buy an appropriate wine."

"Wine," he muttered under his breath. "I don't normally serve wine with this dish."

She followed him in, but when he discovered her trailing down the aisle after him, he gripped her by the shoulders and directed her back outside. "I am an artist, and I insist upon working alone."

Janine had a difficult time not laughing outright.

"In order to make this dinner as perfect as possible, I must concentrate completely on the selection of ingredients. You, my dear wife," he said, pressing his index finger to the tip of her nose, "are too much of a distraction. A lovely one, but nevertheless a distraction."

Janine smiled, her heart singing. Zach wasn't free with his compliments, and she found herself prizing each one.

While Zach was busy in the grocery store, Janine wandered around town. She bought a lifelike ceramic sea gull, which she promptly named Chester, and a bag of saltwater taffy. Then on impulse, she purchased a bottle of sun lotion in case they decided to lie outside, tempting a tan.

When she returned to the car, Zach was already there, waiting for her. She was licking a double-decker chocolate ice-cream cone and feeling incredibly happy.

"Did the master chef find everything he needed?" she asked. Two brown paper bags were sitting on the floor and she restrained herself from peeking inside.

"Our meal tonight will be one you'll long remember, I promise you."

"I'm glad to hear it." Holding out her ice-cream cone, she asked, "Do you want a taste?"

"Please." He rejected the offer of the cone itself and instead bent forward and lowered his mouth to hers. As she gazed into his dark heavy-lidded eyes her heartbeat accelerated and she was filled with a sudden intense longing. Janine wasn't sure what was happening between them, but it felt, quite simply, right.

Although the kiss was fleeting, a shiver of awareness twisted its way through her. Neither of them spoke or moved. He'd meant the kiss to be gentle and teasing, but it had quickly assumed another purpose. For a breathless second, the smile faded from his eyes. He continued to hold her, his breathing rapid.

After nearly two full days alone together, Janine found it amusing that when he finally chose to kiss her, he'd do it in a crowded parking lot.

"I don't remember chocolate being quite that rich," he murmured. He strove for a casual tone, but Janine wasn't fooled. He was as affected by their kiss as she was, and struggling just as hard to disguise it.

They were uncharacteristically quiet on the short drive back to the house. Until the kiss, they'd spent companionable days together, enjoying each other's company. Then, in the space of no more than a few seconds, all that had changed.

"Am I banished from the kitchen?" Janine asked once they were inside the house, forcing an airy note into her voice.

"Not entirely," Zach surprised her by saying. "I'll need you later to wash the dishes."

Janine laughed and pulled her suntan lotion out of her bag. While Zach puttered around inside, she put on her swimsuit, then dragged the lounge chair into the sun to soak up the last of the afternoon's rays.

Zach soon joined her, carrying a tall glass of iced tea. "You look like you could use this."

"Thanks. If I'd known how handy you were in the kitchen, I'd have let you take over long before now."

He set the glass down beside her and headed back to the kitchen. "You'd be amazed by the list of my talents," he threw over his shoulder.

Kissing was certainly one of them, she thought. The sample he'd given her earlier had created a sharp need for more. If she was a sophisticated, experienced kind of woman, she wouldn't have any problem finding her way back into his arms. It would all appear so effortless and casual. He'd kiss her, and she'd kiss him, and then… They'd truly be husband and wife.

Lying on her back with her eyes closed, Janine imagined how wonderful it would be if Zach were to take her in his arms and make love to her.…

She awoke from her doze with a start. She hurried inside to change, and as soon as she was ready, Zach announced that dinner was about to be served. He'd set the patio table so they could eat on the deck.

"Do you need any help?" she asked, trying to peek inside the kitchen.

"None. Sit down before everything cools." He pointed to the chair and waited until she was comfortable.

"I only have a spoon," she said, after unfolding the napkin on her lap. He must have made a mistake.

"A spoon is all you need," he shouted to her from the kitchen.

Playfully she asked, "You went to all this trouble for soup?"

"Wait and see. I'll be there in a minute."

He sounded so serious, Janine had to smile. She was running through a list of words to praise his efforts—"deliciously unique," "refreshingly different"—when Zach walked onto the deck, carrying a tin can with a pair of tongs.

"Good grief, what's that?" she asked in dismay.

"Dinner," he said. "The only real cooking I ever did was while I belonged to the Boy Scouts."

As though he was presenting lobster bisque, he set the steaming can in front of her. Janine leaned forward, almost afraid to examine its contents.

"Barbecued beans. With sliced hot dogs," he said proudly.

"And to think I doubted you."

Her reservations vanished, however, the moment she tasted his specialty. The beans were actually quite appetizing. He surprised her, too, by bringing out dessert, a concoction consisting of graham crackers covered with melted chocolate and marshmallows. He'd warmed them in the oven and served them on a cookie sheet.

Janine ate four of what Zach called "s'mores." He explained that once they'd been tasted, everyone asked for "some more."

"I don't know how you've managed to stay single all these years," she teased, forgetting for the moment that they were married. "If the news about your talent in the kitchen got out, women would be knocking at your door."

Zach chuckled, looking extraordinarily pleased with himself.

An unexpected thought entered Janine's mind, filling her with curiosity. She was astonished that she'd never asked Zach about other women in his life. It would be naive to assume there hadn't been any. She'd had her relationship with Brian; surely there were women in Zach's past.

She waited until later that night when they were sipping wine and listening to classical music in front of the fireplace. Zach seemed relaxed, sitting with one knee raised and the other leg stretched out. Janine lay on her stomach, staring into the fire.

"Have you ever been in love?" She was trying for a casual tone.

Zach didn't answer her right away. "Would you be jealous if I said I had?"

"No." She sounded more confident than she felt.

"I didn't think so. What about you?"

She took her time answering, too. She'd thought she was in love with Brian. It wasn't until later, after the pain of Brian's rejection had eased, that she realized she'd been in love with the *idea* of being in love.

"No," she said, completely honest in her response. What she felt for Zach, whom she was only beginning to know, was already a thousand times stronger than what she'd ever felt for any other man. She didn't know how to explain it, so she avoided the issue by reminding him, "I asked you first."

"I'm a married man. Naturally I'm in love."

"You're fond of me, remember?"

"I thought you detested that word."

"I do. Now stop tiptoeing around the subject. Have you ever *really* been in love—I mean head over heels in love? You don't need to go into any details—a simple yes or no will suffice."

"A desperate-passion kind of love?"

"Yes," she told him impatiently. "Don't make fun of me and please don't give me a list of all the women you've been *fond* of."

He grew so quiet and so intense that her smile began to fade. She pulled herself into a sitting position and looped her arms around her bent knees.

Zach stared at her. As she watched the harsh pain move into his eyes, Janine felt her chest tighten.

"Yes," he answered in a hoarse whisper. "I've been in love."

9

"Her name was Marie."

"Marie," Janine repeated the name as though she'd never heard it before.

"We met in Europe when I was on assignment with the armed forces. She spoke five languages fluently and helped me learn my way around two of them in the time we worked together."

"She was in the military with you?"

"I was army, she worked for the secret service. We were thrown together for a top-secret project that was only supposed to last a few days and instead dragged on for weeks."

"This was when you fell in love with her?" The ache inside her chest wouldn't go away. Her heart felt weighed down with the pain.

"We both were aware that the assignment was a dangerous one, and our working closely together was essential." He paused, sighing deeply. "To make a long story short, I fell in love with her. But she didn't love me."

"Then what?"

"I wanted her to leave the secret service and marry me. She wasn't interested. If you insist on knowing the details, I'll give them to you."

"No."

Zach took a sip of his wine. "I left the army soon after that. I didn't have the heart for it anymore. Unlike Marie—her work, with all its risks, was her whole life. She was the bravest and most dedicated woman I've ever known. Although it was painful at the time, she was right to turn down my proposal. Marriage and a family would have bored her within a year. It *was* painful, don't misunderstand me. I loved her more than I thought possible."

They both were silent for a moment, then Janine asked, "What did you do once you left the army?"

"Over the years, I'd managed to put aside some money, make a few investments. Once I was on my own, I decided to go into business for myself. I read everything I could get my hands on about the business-supply field and modeled the way I dealt with my clients and accounts after your grandfather's enterprise. Within five years, I was his major competitor. We met at a conference last year, and decided that instead of competing with each other, we'd join forces. And as they say, the rest is history."

"Was she pretty?" Even as she asked the question, Janine knew it was ridiculous. What difference would it make if his Marie was a former Miss America or had a face like a gorilla? None. Zach had loved Marie. Loved her as he'd probably never love again. Loved her more than he'd thought possible. By comparison, what he felt for her, Janine, was indeed only fondness.

"She was blond and, yes, she was beautiful."

Janine made a feeble attempt at a smile. "Somehow I knew that."

Zach shook himself lightly as if dragging himself back to the present and away from the powerful lure of the past. "You don't need to worry. It was a long time ago."

"I wasn't worried," Janine muttered. She got to her feet and collected their wineglasses. "I'm a little tired. If you don't mind, I'll go to bed now."

Zach was still staring into the fire and Janine doubted he'd even heard her. She didn't need a crystal ball to know he was thinking of the beautiful Marie.

No more than ten minutes after she'd turned off her bedroom light, Janine heard Zach move down the hallway to his room. For a moment she thought he'd hesitated in front of her door, but Janine convinced herself that was just wishful thinking.

From the second Zach had told her about the one great love of his life, Janine had felt as if a lump were building inside her. A huge lump of disillusionment that seemed to be located somewhere between her heart and her stomach. With every breath she took, it grew larger. But why should she care about Marie? Zach had never confessed to any deep feeling for *her*. He hadn't cheated Janine out of anything that was her right.

An hour later, she lay on her side, wide awake, her hands pressed to her stomach. She didn't mind that Zach had loved another woman so deeply, but what did hurt was that he could never love her with the same intensity. Marrying her, he'd claimed, made practical and financial sense. He was *fond* of her.

Like a romantic idiot, Janine had been frolicking through their short marriage, confident that they'd soon be in love with each other and live happily ever after with their two-point-five children in their perfect little home with the white picket fence.

Zach had loved Marie, who'd dedicated herself to her country.

The most patriotic thing Janine had ever done was cast her vote at election time. She didn't think she should include the two occasions she'd made coffee at Red Cross meetings.

Marie was a linguist. After two years of high-school French, Janine wasn't bad at conjugating verbs, but got hopelessly lost in real conversations.

"I had to ask," she groaned to herself. She was almost certain that Zach would never have mentioned Marie if she hadn't forced the subject. How blissful her ignorance had been. How comfortable.

She could never be the great love of his life and would always remain in the background. Far in the background…

When Janine heard Zach moving around the house a few hours later, she rolled over and glanced at the clock, assuming it was the middle of the night. Then she noticed it was mid-morning; they'd planned to be on the road before now. Tossing aside the blankets, she stumbled out of bed and reached blindly for her robe. But she wasn't paying attention. She collided with the wall and gave a shout of pain. She cupped her hand over her nose and closed her eyes. Tears rolled slowly down her cheeks.

"Janine." Zach pounded on the door. "Are you all right?"

"No," she cried, still holding her nose. She looked in the mirror and lowered her hand. Just as she'd suspected, her nose was bleeding.

"Can I come in?" Zach asked next.

"No…go away." She hurried to the adjoining bathroom, tilting back her head and clamping both hands over her nose.

"You sound funny. I'm coming in."

"No," she hollered again. "Go away." She groped for a washcloth. The tears rained down now, more from humiliation than pain.

"I'm coming in," Zach shouted, his voice distinctly irritated.

Before Janine could protest, the bedroom door flew open and Zach stalked inside. He stopped in the bathroom doorway. "What happened?"

Pressing the cold cloth over the lower half of her face with one hand, Janine gestured violently with the other, demanding that he leave.

"Let me look at that," he said, obviously determined to deal with her bloody nose, as well as her anger. He pushed gently against her shoulders, lowering her onto the edge of the tub, and carefully removed the cloth.

"What did you do? Meet up with a prizefighter?"

"Don't you dare make fun of me!" The tears ran down her cheeks again and plummeted on her silk collar.

It took only a minute or so to control the bleeding. Zach seemed to know exactly what to do. Janine no longer had any desire to fight, and she allowed him to do what he wanted.

Zach wiped the tears from her cheeks. "Do you want me to kiss it and make it better?"

Without waiting for an answer, Zach brought his mouth to hers. Janine felt herself go completely and utterly still. Her heart started to explode and before she realized what she was doing, she'd linked her arms around his neck and was clinging to him helplessly. Zach kissed her forehead and her eyes. His thumbs brushed the remaining tears from her cheeks. Then he nuzzled her neck. Trembling, she immersed herself in his tenderness. No matter what had happened in the past, Zach was hers for this minute, this day.

He lifted Janine to her feet and seemed to be leading her toward the bed. She might have been tempted to let him if she hadn't learned about his love for Marie. Knowing she'd always place a remote second in his affections was a crippling blow to her pride—and her heart. It would take time and effort to accept that she could never be the woman who evoked an all-consuming passion in him.

With that thought in mind, she pushed him away, needing to put some distance between them before it was too late.

Accepting Janine's decision, Zach dropped his arms and moved to lean against the doorjamb, as if he needed its support to remain upright.

Janine couldn't look at him, couldn't speak. She began fumbling with her clothes.

"I'll give you a few minutes to dress while I begin loading the car," Zach said a moment later, sounding oddly unlike himself.

Janine nodded miserably. There was nothing she could say.

Nothing she could do. He'd wanted to make love to her, and she'd turned him away.

While he packed the car, Janine dressed. She met him fifteen minutes later, her suitcase in hand. She was determined to act cool toward him. But not too cool. Friendly, she decided, but not excessively so.

"I'm ready," she announced, with her most cheerful smile.

Zach locked the house, and they were on their way. Pretending there was nothing out of the ordinary, Janine chatted amicably during the drive home. If Zach noticed anything amiss, he didn't comment. For his part, he seemed as hesitant as she was to talk about what had happened. They seemed to be of one mind about the morning's incident. The whole thing was best forgotten.

Only once did Zach refer to it. He asked her if her nose was causing her any pain, but she quickly assured him she was fine. She flashed a smile bright enough to blind him and immediately changed the subject.

The Seattle sky was gray and drizzling rain when they pulled into the parking garage at the downtown condominium owned by Zach. Silently, she helped him unload the car. They were both unusually quiet as they rode the elevator to the tenth floor.

Zach paused outside his door and eyed her skeptically. "Am I obliged to haul you over the threshold again, or is once enough?"

"Once is enough."

"Good." He grinned and unlocked the door, then pushed it open for her to precede him. Curious, she quickened her pace as she walked inside. The living room was a warm mixture of leather and wood, and its wide window offered a breathtaking view of the Seattle skyline.

"It's lovely."

He nodded, seeming pleased at her reaction. "If you prefer, we can move. I suppose now that we're married, we should think about purchasing a house."

"Why?" she inquired innocently.

"I'm hoping we'll have children someday. Whenever you're ready, that is. There's no pressure, Janine."

"I...know that." She looked past him at the panoramic view, and wrapped her arms around herself, her heart speeding up at his words.

Walking to his desk, Zach listened to his voice mail messages; apparently there were a lot.

While he did that, Janine wandered from room to room, eager to see her new home. In the hallway, she noted that Zach had diplomatically left her luggage on the carpet between the two bedrooms. His was in the master. In his own way, he was telling her that where she slept would be her decision. If she wished to become his wife in the fullest sense, all she had to do was place her suitcase in the master bedroom. Nothing more needed to be said.

It didn't take Janine long to decide. She pulled her suitcase toward the guest room. When she looked up, Zach was standing in the hall, studying her, his expression aggrieved.

"Unless you need me for anything, I'm going to the office," he said gruffly.

"See you tonight."

His gaze moved past her and rested briefly on the bed in the guest room. He cocked one eyebrow questioningly, as though to give her the opportunity to reconsider. "Are you sure you'd rather sleep in here?" he asked.

"I'm sure."

Zach raked his fingers through his hair. "I was afraid of that."

A minute later, he was gone.

Zach didn't come home for dinner that night. Janine had been in the bathroom when the phone rang; Zach had left her a message saying he'd be late. So she ate by herself in front of the television, feeling abandoned and unloved. She was just putting the dishes in the dishwasher when he came home.

"Sorry I'm late."

"That's okay," she lied, never having felt more alone.

Zach glanced through the mail on his desk, although Janine was sure he'd looked at it earlier. "You got the message I wouldn't be home for dinner?"

"Yes. Did you want anything to eat? I could fix you something."

"I ate earlier. Thanks, anyway."

They watched an hour's worth of television and then decided to go to bed.

Janine changed into her pajamas—the same no-nonsense type she'd been wearing all week, since she couldn't bring herself to wear the baby-dolls Pam had given her—and had just finished washing her face. She was coming out of the bathroom, her toothbrush between her teeth, when she nearly collided with Zach in the hallway. She'd forgotten her slippers and was going to her bedroom to retrieve them. They'd already said their good-nights, and Janine hadn't expected to see him again until morning. She wasn't prepared for this encounter, and the air between them crackled with tension.

She had to force herself not to throw her toothbrush aside. Not to tell him that she longed for him to love her with the same passion he'd felt for Marie.

His hands reached out to steady her, and when she didn't immediately move away, he ran the tips of his fingers down her thick brown hair, edging her bangs to the side of her face so he could gaze into her eyes.

Janine lowered her head. "Esh-coo me," she managed, but it was difficult to speak with a toothbrush poking out of her mouth.

"Pardon?"

Janine hurried back to the bathroom and rinsed out her mouth. Turning, she braced her hands on the sink. "I said excuse me for bumping into you."

"Will you be comfortable in the guest room?"

"Yes, I'll be fine."

He held a blanket in his arms. "I thought you might need this."

"Thanks," she said as smoothly as possible, coming out of the bathroom to take the blanket from him. She wanted to be swept off her feet. She wanted love. She wanted passion.

He was offering a warm blanket.

"I...phoned Gramps," she said, looking for a way to delay their parting and cursing herself for her weakness.

"I intended to call him myself, but got sidetracked."

"He sounded good. Dr. Coleman and a couple of his other friends were at the house and the four of them were playing pinochle."

"I'm glad to hear he's enjoying his semi-retirement."

"I am, too."

A short silence followed.

"Good night, Janine," Zach said after a moment. He glanced, frowning, into the guest room.

"Good night," she said awkwardly.

Janine was sure neither of them slept a wink that night. They were across the hall from each other, but might as well have been on opposite sides of the state, so great was the emotional distance between them.

In the morning, Zach's alarm rang at seven, but Janine was already awake. She threw back her covers, dressed and had coffee waiting when he entered the kitchen.

Zach seemed surprised to see her. "Thanks," he murmured as she handed him a cup. "That's a very...wifely thing to do."

"What? Make coffee?"

"Get up to see your husband off to work."

"I happened to be awake and figured I should get out of bed and do something useful."

He opened the refrigerator, took out the orange juice and poured himself a glass. "I see." He replaced the carton and leaned against the counter. "You did agree that our marriage would be a real one."

"Yes, I did," she said somewhat defensively. But that agreement had been before she'd learned about the one great love of his life. Zach had warned her their marriage would be advantageous for a variety of reasons, the least of which was love. At the time, Janine had agreed, convinced their relationship would find a storybook ending nonetheless—convinced that one day they'd realize they were in love. Now she understood that would never happen. And she didn't know if she could stand it.

"Janine," Zach said, distracting her, "what's wrong?"

"What could possibly be wrong?"

"Obviously something's bothering you. You look like you've lost your best friend."

"You should've told me," she burst out, running from the kitchen.

"Told you what?" Zach shouted, following her down the hall.

Furious, she hurried into her room and sat on the end of the bed, her hands in tight fists at her sides.

"What are you talking about?" he demanded, blocking the doorway.

"About…this woman you loved."

"Marie? What about her? What's she got to do with you and me?"

"You loved her more than…more than you thought possible. She was brave and wonderful, and I'm none of those things. I don't deal with pain very well and… I'd like to be patriotic but all I do is vote and all I know in French are verbs."

"What's any of that got to do with you and me?" Zach repeated hoarsely, then threw his hands in the air. "What's it got to do with *anything*?"

Knowing she'd never be able to explain, Janine shook her head, sending her bangs fanning out in several directions. "All you are is *fond* of me."

"Correction," Zach said as he stepped into the bedroom. "I *cherish* you."

"It isn't enough," she said, feeling miserable and wretched and unworthy.

"What do you mean, it isn't enough? According to you the only reason you married me was that I was a good kisser, so you can't fault me for *my* reasons."

"I don't, it's just that you…you never told me about loving someone else. Not only that, you *admired* her—she was a hero. All you feel for me is fondness. Well, I don't want your fondness, Zachary Thomas!" She leapt to her feet, trying to collect her scattered thoughts. "If you cared for me, you would've told me about Marie before. Not mentioning her was a form of dishonesty. You were completely…unfair."

"And you weren't?" Zach's expression darkened and he buried his hands in his pockets. "You didn't say one word to me about Brian."

Janine was so shocked she sank back onto the bed. Zach still glared at her, challenging her to contradict him. Slowly gathering her composure, she stood, her eyes narrowing as she studied her husband. "Who told you about Brian?"

"Your grandfather."

"How did he know? I never said a word to him about Brian. Not one solitary word."

"But obviously he knew."

"Obviously." Janine had never felt more like weeping. "I suppose he told you Brian lied to me and claimed to love me when all the while he was seeing someone else." Another, more troubling thought entered her mind. "I...bet Gramps told you that to make you feel sorry for me, sorry enough to marry me."

"Janine, no."

She hid her face in both hands, humiliation burning her cheeks. It was all so much worse than she'd imagined. "You felt sorry for me, didn't you?"

Zach paced the length of the bedroom. "I'm not going to lie to you, although I suspect it would be better if I did. Your grandfather didn't mention that you'd fallen in love with Brian until after the day we took him to the doctor."

"He waited until we got to know each other a little," Janine whispered, staggered by the realization that her grandfather had known about Brian all along.

"By then I'd discovered I liked you."

"The word *like* is possibly even worse than *fond*," she muttered.

"Just hear me out, would you?"

"All right," she sighed, fearing that nothing he said now mattered, anyway. Her pride had suffered another major blow. The one love of his life had been this marvelous patriot, while Janine had fallen for a weak-willed womanizer.

"It isn't as bad as it seems," Zach tried to assure her.

"I can just imagine what Gramps told you."

"All he said was that he was afraid you'd never learn to trust your own judgment again. For quite a while now, he's watched you avoid any hint of a relationship. It was as though you'd retreated from men and were content just to lick your wounds."

"That's not true! I was seeing Peter Donahue on a regular basis."

"Safe dates with safe men. There was never any likelihood that you'd fall in love with Peter, and you knew it. It was the only reason you went out with him."

"Is...is what happened with Brian why Gramps decided to play matchmaker?"

"I suspect that was part of it. Also his concern for your future. But I don't fully understand his intentions even now. I don't think it matters, though. He wanted you to be happy and secure. Anton knew I'd never purposely hurt you. And in his eyes, the two of us were perfect for each other." Zach sat down next to her and reached for her hand, lacing her fingers with his own. "*Does* it matter? We're married now."

She looked away from him and swallowed hard. "I…may not be blond and gorgeous or brave, but I deserve a husband who'll love me. You and Gramps both failed to take that into account. I don't want your pity, Zach."

"Good, because I don't pity you. You're my wife, and frankly, I'm happy about it. We can have a good life if you'll put this nonsense behind you."

"You'd never have chosen me on your own. I knew what you thought of me from the moment we met. You assumed I was a rich spoiled woman who'd never had anything real to worry about. I bet you thought I'd consider a broken nail a major disaster."

"All right, I'll admit I had the wrong impression, but that was before," Zach insisted.

"Before what?"

"Before I got to know you."

Janine's shoulders heaved with barely suppressed emotion. "As I recall, the reason you were willing to marry me was because I wasn't so bad. And let's not forget the financial benefits," she added sarcastically.

Zach's sigh was filled with frustration. "I told you I wasn't ever going to say the stuff you women like to hear. I don't know a thing about romance. But I care about you, Janine, I honestly care. Isn't that enough?"

"I need more than that," she said miserably. It was the promise of their future, the promise of learning about love together, that had intrigued her.

Zach frowned. "You told me even before we were married that you didn't need romantic words. You were content before I mentioned Marie. Why should my telling you change anything?"

She saw that Zach was losing his patience with her. She stared down at the thick carpet. "I really wish I could explain, but it does make a difference. I'm sorry, Zach, I really am."

A lifetime seemed to pass before he spoke again. "So am I," he whispered before turning away. A moment later the front door opened and almost immediately closed again. Zach had left.

"What did you expect?" she wailed, covering her face with both hands. "Did you think he was going to fall at your knees and declare his undying love?" The picture of the proud and mighty Zach Thomas playing the role of besotted husband was actually comical. If he'd done that for any woman, it would've been the brave and beautiful Marie. Not Janine.

After that disastrous morning, their relationship grew more strained than ever. Zach went to work early every day and returned late, usually past dinnertime. Janine never questioned where he was or who he was with, although she had to bite her tongue to keep from asking.

Zach proved to be a model housemate, if not a husband—cordial, courteous and remote. For her part, she threw herself into her volunteer work at the Friendship Club, spending hours each week with the children. She did her best to hide her unhappiness from her grandfather, although that was difficult.

"You look pale," he told her when she joined him for lunch one afternoon, several days after her return from Ocean Shores. "Are you losing weight?"

"I wish," she said, attempting to make a joke of it. They sat in the dining room, with Mrs. McCormick wandering in and out, casting Janine concerned glances. Janine resisted the urge to leap up and do aerobic exercises to demonstrate that she was in perfect health.

"You can't afford to get much thinner," Gramps said, eyeing her solemnly. He placed a dinner roll on the side of her plate and plunked the butter dish down in front of her.

"I'm not losing weight," she told him, spreading butter on the roll in order to please him.

"I took that sea gull you gave me into the office," Gramps said as he continued to study her. "Zach asked me where I got it. When I told him, he didn't say anything, but I could tell he wasn't pleased. Do you want it back?"

"No, of course not." Janine dropped her gaze. She'd never intended for Gramps to take Chester into the office. On impulse, she'd given him the ceramic bird, reluctant to have it around the condominium to remind her of those first glorious days with Zach.

"I wish I knew what was wrong with you two," Gramps blurted out in an uncharacteristic display of frustration. He tossed his napkin onto his dinner plate. "You should be happy! Instead, the pair of you look like you're recovering from a bad bout of flu. Zach's working so many hours it's a wonder he doesn't fall over from sheer exhaustion."

Janine carefully tore her roll into pieces. She toyed with the idea of bringing up the subject of Brian, but in the end, she didn't.

"So you say you're fine, and there's nothing wrong between you and Zach," Gramps said sarcastically. "Funny, that's exactly what he said when I asked him. Except he also told me to mind my own business—not quite in those words, but I got the message. The thing is, he looks as pathetic as you do. I can't understand it—you're perfect for each other!"

Gramps reached into his pocket for a cigar. "I'll be seeing Zach this afternoon and I intend to give that boy a piece of my mind. By all rights, you should be a happy bride." He tapped one end of the cigar against the table.

"We'll be fine, Gramps. Please stay out of it."

For a long moment, he said nothing; he only stared at the cigar between his fingers. "You're sure you don't want me to talk some sense into the boy?" he finally asked.

The mental picture of him trying to do so brought a quivering smile to her lips. "I'm sure," she said, then glanced at her watch. Pam would be waiting for her. "But since you're seeing Zach, would you please let him know I'll probably be late for dinner? He...should go ahead and eat without me."

"Do you do this often?" His question was an accusation.

"No," she replied, shaking her head. "This is the first time. Pam needs my help with a school project and I don't know when we'll be finished."

Gramps glowered as he lit his cigar, puffing mightily before he spoke. "I'll tell him."

As it turned out, Janine spent longer with Pam than she'd expected. The homework assignment wasn't difficult, but Pam begged Janine to stay with her. Pam's father was working late and the girl seemed to need Janine more than ever. They made dinner together, then ate in the kitchen while Pam chatted about her friends and life in general.

It was almost nine by the time Janine pulled into the parking garage. The first thing she noticed was Zach's car. The atmosphere had been so falsely courteous between them that she dreaded each encounter, however brief. Since that first morning, Zach hadn't made any effort to talk about her role in his life. Janine wasn't looking for a long flowery declaration of love. Just a word or two more profound than *fond* or *like* to let her know she was important to him.

Drawing a deep breath, she headed for the condominium. She'd just unlocked the door when Zach stormed into the room like a Minnesota blizzard. "Where the hell have you been?" he demanded.

Janine was so shocked by his fierce anger that she said nothing.

"I demand to know exactly where you were!"

She removed her sweater, hanging it carefully in the entry closet, along with her purse. Zach scowled at her silence, fists clenched at his sides. "Do you have any idea of the time? Did it even cross your mind that I might've been concerned about you? Your cell phone was off and you didn't return any calls."

"I'm sorry." Janine turned to face him. "But you knew where I was," she said calmly.

"All Anton said was that you'd be late. Not where you were going or who you were with. So naturally I was worried."

"I'm sorry. Next time I'll tell you myself." Janine yawned; the day had been exhausting. "If you don't mind, I think I'll go to bed now. Unless there's anything else you'd like to know?"

He glared at her, then shook his head. Wheeling around abruptly, he walked away.

Hours later, Janine was awakened by a gruff sobbing sound coming from the other room. It took her a moment to realize it was Zach. Was he having a nightmare?

Folding back the covers, she got out of bed and hurried into his room. The cries of anguish grew louder. In the light from the hallway, she could see him thrashing about, the bedding in disarray.

"Zach," she cried, rushing to his side. She sat on the edge of the bed and placed her hands gently on his shoulders. "Wake up. You're having a dream. Just a dream. It's okay…."

Zach's eyes slowly opened. "Janine." He ground out her name as though in torment and reached for her, hauling her into his arms with such force that he left her breathless. "Janine," he said, his voice so husky she could barely understand him. "I thought I'd lost you."

10

"Zach, I'm fine," Janine whispered. Emotion clogged her throat at the hungry way his eyes roamed her face. He seemed to have difficulty believing, even now, that she was unhurt.

"It was so real," he continued, his chest heaving. He hid his face as if to block out the vivid images the dream had induced. Making room in the large bed, he pulled her down beside him. His hands stroked her hair as he released several jagged breaths. "We were at the ocean," he told her, "and although I'd warned you against it, you decided to swim. A huge wave knocked you off your feet and you were drowning. Heaven help me, I tried, but I couldn't get to you fast enough." He shut his eyes briefly. "You kept calling out to me and I couldn't find you. I just couldn't get to you fast enough."

"Zach," she whispered, her mouth so close to his that their breath mingled, "I'm right here. It was only a dream. It wasn't real."

He nodded, but his eyes still seemed troubled, refusing to leave her face. Then ever so slowly, as though he expected her to object, he moved his mouth even closer to hers. "I couldn't bear to lose you. I'd rather die myself."

Helpless to deny him anything, Janine turned her face to receive his kiss.

His hands tangled in her thick dark hair, effectively holding her captive, while his mouth seized hers in a kiss that sent her senses swirling. Nothing mattered except his touch. Overcome for a moment by the fierce tenderness she felt in him, Janine eagerly fed his need.

"Janine, oh, my dear sweet Janine. I couldn't bear to lose you."

"I'm here… I'm here." Melting against him, she molded her body to the unyielding contours of his, offering her lips and her heart to his loving possession. Again and again, he kissed her. Janine slid her hands up his chest and twined them around his neck. This was what she'd longed for from the first, the knowledge that he needed her, and she gloried in the sensation.

With a groan, he reluctantly pulled his mouth from hers. He held her firmly to his chest, his breathing harsh and rapid. Peace combined with a delirious sense of happiness, and Janine released a deep sigh. Pressing her ear to his chest, she listened, content, to the heavy pounding of his heart.

"Did I frighten you?" he asked after a minute.

"No," she whispered.

He resumed stroking her hair as she nestled more securely in his arms. Zach had made her feel wondrous, exciting things every time he kissed her, but the way he held and touched her now went far beyond those kisses. She'd experienced a bonding with Zach, a true joining of spirits that had been missing until now. He had told her he'd cherish her, but she hadn't believed it until this moment. Tears clouded her eyes and she struggled to restrain them.

For a long while neither of them spoke. But Janine didn't need words. Her eyes were closed as she savored this precious time.

When Zach did speak, his voice was little more than a hoarse whisper. "I had a sister who drowned. Her name was Beth

Ann. I'd promised I'd always be there for her—but I failed her. I couldn't bear to lose you, too."

Janine tightened her hold, knowing how difficult it must be for him to speak of his sister.

"I never forgave myself." His body tensed and his fingers dug roughly into her shoulder. "Losing Beth Ann still haunts me. She wouldn't have drowned if I'd been with her. She—"

Lifting her head slightly, Janine's misty gaze met his. "It wasn't your fault. How could it have been?"

"But I was responsible for her," he returned harshly.

Janine suspected that Zach had rarely, if ever, shared his sorrow or his guilt over his sister's death with anyone. A low groan worked its way through him and he squeezed his eyes tightly shut. "For years, I've drummed out the memories of Beth Ann's death. The nightmare was so real, only this time it wasn't her—it was you."

"But I'm safe and sound. See?" She pressed her hands to both sides of his face, smiling down on him.

He sighed and smiled back, a little uncertainly. "I'm all right now. I shouldn't have burdened you with this."

"It wasn't a burden."

His arms tightened around her, and he inhaled deeply as if absorbing her scent. "Stay with me?"

She nodded, grateful that he needed her.

Within minutes, Janine felt herself drifting into drowsiness. From Zach's relaxed, even breathing, she knew he was already asleep.

When Janine next stirred, she was lying on her side, and Zach was cuddling her spoon fashion, his arm about her waist. At some point during the night, she'd slipped under the covers, but she had no recollection of doing so. A small satisfied smile touched the edges of her mouth. She rolled carefully onto her back so as not to disturb Zach, and wondered what she should do. When Zach woke and found her in bed with him, she was afraid he might regret what had happened, regret asking her to stay. He might feel embarrassed that he'd told her about his sister's death and the guilt he still felt.

Closing her eyes, Janine debated with herself. If she left his bed and returned to her own room, he might think she was rejecting him, shocked by his heart-wrenching account of Beth Ann's death.

"Janine?" He whispered her name, his voice husky with sleep.

Her eyes flew open. "I...we fell asleep. What time is it?"

"Early. The alarm won't go off for another couple of hours."

She nodded, hoping to disguise any hint of disappointment in her voice. He didn't want her with him, she was sure of it. He was embarrassed to find her still in his bed. "I'll leave now if you want."

"No."

The single word was filled with such longing that Janine thought she'd misunderstood him. She tipped her head back to meet his gaze. The light from the hall allowed her to see the passion smoldering in his dark eyes. Turning onto her side, Janine lovingly traced the lines of his face.

"I'm sorry about the way I behaved over... Marie," she whispered. "I was jealous and I knew I was being ridiculous, but I couldn't help myself."

The corners of his eyes crinkled with his smile. "I'll forgive you if you're willing to overlook the way I behaved when you got home last night."

She answered him with a light kiss, and he hugged her to him. Janine surrendered to the sheer pleasure of being in Zach's arms, savoring the rush of warm sensations that sprang to life inside her.

"I don't know how to say all the words you deserve to hear, but I know one thing, Janine. I love you. It happened without my even being aware of it. One day I woke up and realized how important you'd become to me. It wasn't the grand passion you wanted, and I'm sorry for that. The love I feel for you is the quiet steady kind. It's buried deep in my heart, but trust me, it's there. You're the most important person in my life."

"Oh, Zach, I love you so much."

"You love me?"

"I have for weeks, even before we were married. That's what bothered me so much when I learned about Marie. I wanted you to love *me* with the same intensity that you felt for her... that I feel for you."

"It isn't like that. It never was. Marie was as brave as she was beautiful, but what we shared was never meant to last. And she was smart enough to understand that. I fell in love with her, but she was too much of a professional to involve her heart. She was the kind of person who thrives on excitement and danger. It wasn't until you and I met that I realized if I were ever to marry, it would be to someone like you."

"Someone like me?"

He kissed her briefly. "A woman who's warm and gentle and caring. Someone unselfish and—" he hesitated "—desirable."

Her throat tightened with emotion, and it was all she could do to meet his gaze. Zach found her desirable. He wanted to make love to her. He didn't need to say it; the message was there for her to read in his eyes. It wasn't the desperate passion she'd once craved, but his love, his need to have her in his life, was far more potent than any action he could have taken, any words he could have said.

"Love me, Zach," she whispered simply.

Zach's mouth touched hers with a sweet desperate ardor. If she had any lingering doubts they vanished like mist in the sun as his lips took hers, twisting her into tight knots of desire.

His arms locked around her and he rolled onto his back, pulling her with him. His hands outlined her face as though he half expected her to stop him.

"Make me your wife," she said, bending forward to brush her moist mouth over his.

Zach groaned, and then he did the strangest, most wonderful thing. He laughed. The robust sound echoed across the room and was so infectious that it made Janine laugh, too.

"My sweet Janine," he said. "You've changed my life." And then he kissed her again, leaving her with no doubts at all.

For a long time afterward, their happiness could be heard in their sighs and gasps and whispered words of love....

The buzzing sound refused to go away. Janine moaned softly and flung out her hand, hoping to find the source of the distraction. But before she could locate it, the noise ceased abruptly.

"Good morning, wife," Zach whispered.

Her eyes remained closed as she smiled leisurely. "Good morning, husband." Rolling onto her back, she held her arms open to him. "I had the most marvelous dream last night."

Zach chuckled softly. "That wasn't any dream."

"But it must've been," she said, slipping her arms around his neck and smiling lazily. "Nothing could be that incredible in real life."

"I didn't think so, either, but you proved me wrong." He kissed her tenderly, and then so thoroughly that by the time he lifted his head, Janine was breathless.

Slowly, almost against her will, her eyes drifted open. His were dark with desire. "You'll be late for work," she warned him.

His smile was sensuous. "Who cares?"

"Not me," she murmured. And with a small cry of pleasure, she willingly gave herself to her husband.

Zach was already an hour late for the office when he dragged himself out of bed and headed for the shower. Wearing her husband's pajama top, Janine wandered into the kitchen and prepared a pot of coffee. She leaned against the counter and smiled into space, hardly aware of the passage of time.

A few minutes later—or perhaps it was longer—Zach stepped behind her and slid his arms around her waist, nuzzling her neck.

"Zach," she protested, but not too strenuously. She closed her eyes and cradled her arms over his, leaning back against his solid strength. "You're already late."

"I know," he murmured. "If I didn't have an important meeting this morning, I'd skip work altogether."

Turning in his arms, Janine tilted back her head to gaze into his eyes. "You'll be home for dinner?"

"Keep looking at me like that and I'll be home for lunch."

Janine smiled. "It's almost that time now."

"I know," he growled, reluctantly pulling away from her. "We'll go out to dinner tonight," he said, kissing her again. His mouth was hot on her own, feverish with demand and passion and need. He raised his head, but his eyes remained shut. "Then we'll come home and celebrate."

Janine sighed. Married life was beginning to agree with her.

At precisely five, Zach was back. He stood by the door, loosening his tie, when Janine appeared. A smile traveled to his mouth as their eyes met. Neither moved. They stared at each other as if they'd spent years apart instead of a few short hours.

Janine was feeling distinctly light-headed. "Hi," she managed to say, shocked that her voice sounded more like a hoarse whisper than the cheery greeting she'd intended. "How'd the meeting go?"

"Bad."

"Bad?"

He nodded slowly and stepped forward, placing his briefcase on the desk. "I was supposed to be listening to an important financial report, but unfortunately all I could do was wonder how much longer the thing would take so I could get home to my wife."

"Oh." That wasn't the most intelligent bit of conversation

she'd ever delivered, but just looking at Zach was enough to wipe out all her normal thought processes.

"It got to be almost embarrassing." His look was intimate and loving as he advanced two more steps toward her. "In the middle of it, I started smiling, and then I embarrassed myself further by laughing outright."

"Laughing? Something was funny?"

"I was thinking about your definition of romance. The tryst on the moors was supplied by your grandfather. The walk along the beach, hand in hand, was supplied by me after the wedding. But the desperate passion, my dear sweet wife, was something we found together."

Her eyes filled with tears.

"I love you."

They moved toward each other then, but stopped abruptly when the doorbell chimed. Zach's questioning eyes met hers. Janine shrugged, not knowing who it could possibly be.

The second Zach answered the door, Anton flew into the room, looking more determined than Janine had ever seen him.

"All right, you two, sit down," he ordered, waving them in the direction of the sofa.

"Gramps?"

"Anton?"

Janine glanced at Zach, but he looked as mystified as she did. So she just shrugged and complied with her grandfather's demand. Zach sat down next to her.

Gramps paced the carpet directly in front of them. "Janine and I had lunch the other day," he said, speaking to Zach. "Two things became clear to me then. First and foremost, she's crazy in love with you, but I doubt she's told you that."

"Gramps—" Janine began, but her grandfather silenced her with a single look.

"The next thing I realized is that she's unhappy. Terribly unhappy. Being in love is difficult enough but—"

"Anton," Zach broke in, "if you'd—"

Gramps cut him off with the same laser-eyed look he'd sent Janine.

"Don't interrupt me, boy. I'm on a roll and I'm not about to stop now. If I noticed Janine was a little melancholy at lunch, it was nothing compared to what I've been noticing about you." Suddenly he ceased his pacing and planted himself squarely in front of Zach. "All week I've been hearing complaints and rumors about you. Folks in the office claim you're there all hours of the day and night, working until you're ready to drop." He paused. "I know you, Zach, probably better than anyone else does. You're in love with my granddaughter, and it's got you all tangled up inside."

"Gramps—"

"Shh." He dismissed Janine with a shake of his head. "Now, I may be an old man, but I'm not stupid. Maybe the way I went about bringing the two of you together wasn't the smartest, or the most conventional, but by golly it worked." He hesitated long enough to smile proudly. "In the beginning I had my doubts. Janine put up a bit of a fuss."

"I believe you said something about how it's easier to pluck a live chicken," Zach inserted, slanting a secret smile at Janine.

"True enough. I never knew that girl had so much spunk. But the fact is, Zachary, as you'll recall, you weren't all that keen on the idea yourself. You both think because I'm an old man, I don't see things. But I do. You were two lonely people, filling up your lives with unimportant relationships, avoiding love, avoiding life. I care about you. Too much to sit back and do nothing."

"It worked out," Janine said, wanting to reassure him.

"At first I thought it had. I arranged the trip to Scotland and it looked like everything was falling neatly into place, like in one of those old movies. I couldn't have been more pleased when you announced that you were going to get married. It was sooner than I'd expected, but I assumed that meant things were progressing nicely. Apparently I was wrong. Now I'm worried."

"You don't need to be."

"That's not the way I see it," Gramps said with a fierce glare. "Tell him you love him, Janine. Look Zach in the eye and put aside that silly pride of yours. He needs to know it. He needs to hear it. I told you from the first that he wasn't going to be an easy man to know, and that you'd have to be patient with him. What I didn't count on was that damnable pride of yours."

"You want me to tell Zach I love him? Here? Now?"

"Yes!"

Janine turned to her husband and, feeling a little self-conscious, lowered her eyes.

"Tell him," Gramps barked.

"I love you, Zach," she said softly. "I really do."

Gramps gave a loud satisfied sigh. "Good, good. Okay, Zach, it's your turn."

"My turn?"

"Tell Janine what you feel and don't go all arrogant on me."

Zach reached for Janine's hand. He lifted her palm to his mouth and brushed his lips against it. "I love you," he whispered.

"Add something else," Gramps instructed, gesturing toward him. "Something like...you'd be a lost and lonely soul without her. Women are impressed by that sort of thing. Damn foolishness, I know, but necessary."

"I'd be a lost and lonely soul without you," Zach repeated, then looked back at Janine's grandfather. "How'd I do?"

"Better than most. Is there anything else you'd like him to say, Janine?"

She gave an expressive sigh. "I don't think so."

"Good. Now I want the two of you to kiss."

"Here? In front of you?"

"Yes," Gramps insisted.

Janine slipped into Zach's arms. The smile he shared with

her was so devastating that she felt her heart race with anticipation. Her eyes fluttered closed as his mouth settled on hers, thrilling her with promises for all the years to come.

Gently, provocatively, Zach moved his mouth over hers, ending his kiss far too soon to suit Janine. From the shudder that coursed through him, Janine knew it was too soon for him, too. Reluctantly they drew apart. Zach gazed into her eyes, and Janine responded with a soft smile.

"Excellent, excellent."

Janine had all but forgotten her grandfather's presence. When she turned away from Zach, she discovered Gramps sitting across from them, his hands on the arms of the leather chair. He looked exceedingly proud of himself. "Are you two going to be all right now?"

"Yes, sir," Zach answered for them both, his eyes hazy with desire as he smiled at Janine. She could feel herself blushing, and knew her eyes were foggy with the same longing.

"Good!" Gramps declared, nodding once for emphasis. A slow grin overtook his mouth. "I knew all the two of you needed was a little assistance from me." He inhaled deeply. "Since you're getting along so well, maybe now would be the time to bring up the subject of children."

"Anton," Zach said, rising to his feet. He strode across the room and opened the door. "If you don't mind, I'll take care of that myself."

"Soon?" Gramps wanted to know.

Zach's eyes met Janine's. "Soon," he promised.

★ ★ ★ ★ ★